Signs of Life

Signs of Life

Valerie Banfield

ISBN: 978-1542768313

Cover photograph used under license from Shutterstock.com.

To those whose light led me to truth and
directed my path toward the hope of life everlasting.
May you continue to illuminate the darkness.

I love the Lord, because he has heard
my voice and my pleas for mercy.
Because he inclined his ear to me,
therefore I will call on him as long as I live.

Psalm 116: 1, 2

One

A shiver rippled across Juanita Hoyt's shoulders, an involuntary spasm induced by the cold metal encircling her wrists. The officer must have hung his handcuffs from his side-view mirror while he roamed the streets looking for offenders. Before she could grab her coat from her SUV, he shoved her into the back seat of his patrol car. She didn't hear Zach's protests, but watched as the officer who arrived in the second cruiser forced him to his knees. The last she'd seen of her husband was his hands, raised behind his head, his fingers knitted together. That was hours ago.

Juanita lifted her manacled hands to her face and brushed the tender bruise on her cheek. The damage to her skin most likely complimented her soiled dress and her broken spirit. If the officers' treatment of her was rough, what might they have done to Zach? Her hero, her defender. What might he have done to protest their unrestrained behavior? Juanita knew two things: her incessant shivering was a product of trauma; Zach's situation, regardless of where he was at this instant in time, was a thousand times worse.

The dusky sky on the other side of the window conveyed the passage of time, and the lengthening interlude between her arrival at the station and the present left Juanita stymied.

Instead of the expected fingerprints, crude photograph, and escort to some sort of holding cell, those in charge seemed not to know what to do with her. She sat in a chair in what looked like one of those interrogation rooms the police in the television shows always used to confront the accused.

The woman of the pair of officers who upended Juanita's evening took pity on her charge and replaced the handcuffs so that Juanita's hands were in her lap instead of behind her back. Why they wouldn't remove them altogether was beyond her imagination, just like everything that had transpired since the flashing lights in her rearview mirror directed her to pull the SUV to the side of the road.

She rocked her torso back and forth, a motion that did little to calm her agitated state. Her head and her shoulders ached. Her body craved food. Her heart, wrenched inside out, begged to know the condition of her spouse. And what of Conner and Izzy? How long would it take them to worry over their parents' absence?

Juanita stiffened her spine and shrank back against her chair as both arresting officers came into view. When they stopped in the hallway, the gruff male placed his feet apart, much as a wrestler preparing to take down his opponent. In those brief moments when he didn't curl his hands into fists, his fingers twitched.

The female officer waved her arms at her partner while her face went from pink to fiery red. Whatever she spewed at him . . . A little more. Come on. She needed to turn just a little more. Yes. Like that. Juanita narrowed her eyes and studied the woman's mouth.

"Yes you are," the woman said.

The man, who had his back toward Juanita, pushed his pointy finger into the woman's arm. His partner reacted in kind and shoved the base of her palm against his chest.

"I won't cover for you. Not again. You were out of line, Benton. You come to work in a foul mood and then you take your nasty temper out on the first person who crosses your path. This time—" She snapped her mouth shut as her eyes met Juanita's inspection.

Juanita winced and dropped her gaze. She pressed her lips together and took tiny sips of air. They didn't know. She refused to give herself away, but instead of fortitude, her intake of oxygen produced another shiver.

Too late. She didn't have to look up to know one—no, both—of the arresting officers were standing inches from her chair. The female cop's sweet perfume and his acrid breath gave them away; that, and Juanita's keen ability to sense the presence of another living soul. She had only four senses left, but they worked overtime to compensate for the missing piece. Should she continue to hang her head? Could she pretend she didn't know they were there?

The woman's index finger appeared below Juanita's chin. As the officer crooked her finger and lifted it, Juanita raised her face until her dark brown eyes met the unflinching hazel orbs of one very angry policewoman—the one whose partner liked taking charge.

The cop called Benton stooped, bringing his face in line with Juanita's eyes. Except for the rough patch of hours-old beard, his skin, the color of charcoal, was smooth and even-toned. Although his eyes bore the same rich hue, their angry sheen rendered an image of briquettes doused with lighter fluid—volatile and primed to ignite. His mouth moved slowly and stiffly, as if he were speaking to a dimwitted drunkard. "Before we talk, you probably want to know about your husband."

Juanita clenched her teeth and shivered. She stared at her mocker. No way would she play into his hand. When the standoff lingered, the woman shoved Benton sideways. Benton teetered, righted himself, and stood.

Juanita crinkled her forehead and watched as the woman said, "See? She doesn't know anything. Does it look like she reads lips to you?"

Juanita let her eyes dart between the two officers, but managed to catch Benton's reply. "Looks pretty ignorant to me. How'd she get a driver's license?"

"You don't know anything. You're such a jerk."

"Am not. I expect you to back me up. Understand?"

When Benton edged his chin up and eyed his partner, Juanita lowered her gaze to her hands. She didn't want to know how the woman might reply.

~

How did a burned-out taillight lead to an accusation of resisting arrest? Zach seethed at the absurdity. They pulled his wife over for failing to signal her intention to turn? The accompanying offense for using a license plate frame that obscured a portion of the plate's lettering—trivial lettering that displayed the state's website for Pete's sake—infuriated him, but nothing compared to the rage invoked by the officers' mistreatment of his wife.

He'd do nothing differently if the event unfolded again. Nothing. No one had the right to manhandle Juanita, and her minor transgression offered nothing in the way of a defense to the overzealous officers. If someone didn't rectify this situation soon, the number of Zach's own trumped-up charges might grow into an extensive list.

When his clamped jaw protested with a sharp tremor, he forced his mouth open and worked his rigid muscles back and forth. He redirected his attention to a different pain source while he massaged his tender kneecaps and examined his ruined trousers. The thin fabric did little to protect the flesh underneath when the officer "helped" him kneel on the grimy salt-encrusted roadway. Zach's military training prepared him for threats and physical confrontations, but he didn't expect this kind of treatment. Not here. Not on his home turf.

Once the cop who drove Zach to the station finally shut his yap long enough to hear Zach's explanation, the man's haughty tone changed. He got quiet. When they arrived at headquarters, Zach's overseer took him to a stark room filled with two chairs and a small table, and handed Zach's phone back to him.

The officer looked over his shoulder. "Suggest you call an attorney. Hurry up."

Thirty seconds into the call, as several voices carried from the hallway to the holding room, the cop grabbed the phone back and ended the call, walked out, and shut the door.

Zach sucked in stale air and wrinkled his nose at the scent of bleach, mildew, and sweat. His impatience grew at the same tempo as the second hand that spun around the face of the clock . . . over and over again. When someone jostled the door handle, a pair of feet blocked some of the light that filtered into the room from the gap at the bottom of the door. Two distinct voices—one low; the other agitated—traded unintelligible words for several long minutes. The agitated voice had better belong to his lawyer.

The door's tired hinges tendered a jarring screech as the policeman opened the door and stepped aside to let Zach's visitor enter. The hardware complained just as loudly when the cop stepped back into the hallway and pulled the door shut again.

"You don't look so good." Craig Morrison dropped his coat over the back of a chair and ran his hand through his fashionable mini-afro, the style Craig claimed as reminiscent of his 1980's pretty-boy cut. In spite of the man's unexpected summons to the police station, Craig's impeccable attire and carriage suggested he'd just walked out of a dinner party rather than a casual gathering held in the basement of his church.

Zach grabbed the offered hand and shook it as he said, "What a nightmare. Thanks for coming. I'm sorry I interrupted your meeting."

"No need to apologize. I have a capable wife who loves taking charge, but you might extend some apologies to the students next time you see them. Yolanda can be too exuberant at times." Craig's momentary levity evaporated as his eyes narrowed and solemnity overtook his manner. "First things first. After the meeting ends, Yolanda will head over to your house, explain what happened, and stay with Conner and Izzy until you get home—whether your teenagers want her to or not."

Zach squeezed his eyes shut. How had he forgotten about his own children? He needed to pull himself together.

"Next," Craig said, "Juanita will join us in a few minutes."

For the first time since the police pulled them over, Zach managed to expand his chest and fill his lungs to capacity. He wiped his mouth with the side of his hand. "Thank you."

"We'll chat here for a minute, and then the three of us have an unscheduled audience with some uppity-up. Don't know if it's an internal affairs guy, the precinct captain, or the mayor. Whomever they select will get an earful. This is ridiculous."

"Would you like the details?" Zach asked.

"I know you. I don't need any."

"Will you wear your attorney hat or your pastoral vestment?"

"Haven't decided. Maybe the folks here need a lesson from both perspectives," Craig replied.

"Whatever it takes. Just get Juanita out of this place. I'm so angry I could spit."

"I see that. Before we present ourselves to their designated mediator, you need to calm down."

"Calm down? You're kidding."

"I'm not. If you display this kind of agitation, you look like an aggressor who had to be subdued, instead of the victim that you are."

"Just settle down? Flip a switch?" Zach asked. As if he could make that happen.

"Maybe you ought to say a quick prayer," Craig said.

"Don't you think I've done that already?"

Craig splayed his fingers and said, "Hey, I'm here, aren't I?"

Before Zach could reply, the screeching door opened and Juanita stepped into the room. His pulse quickened as another bout of fury pierced his core. Instead of highlighting her delicate features, the long wisps of coffee-colored hair that framed her face accentuated her ashen complexion and drawn expression. She reached for Zach as he wrapped his arms around her. After he hugged her, he pulled back and examined her.

"Are you all right? Did they hurt you?" He already knew about the bruise on her cheek, the one inflicted by the cop who pushed her into the back seat of the police car at the same time she hesitated to follow his directive to sit. The vision notched up Zach's irritation. It's not as if Juanita heard the command.

He brushed his fingertip along the narrow blue and purple blemish, an ugly backdrop for the sprinkling of freckles that ran across her cheekbones and nose. Craig wanted him to calm down? How?

Juanita hung onto Zach, but pressed her free hand against Craig's arm. "Thank you," she mouthed.

Craig pointed to one of the two chairs, and said, "Please sit." He looked at Zach as he pointed to the other chair. Once they sat, Craig kept his face toward Juanita while he talked.

"I understand neither of you was officially arrested. No fingerprinting, no mug shot. Is that correct?"

"Yes," Zach said.

With her hands, Juanita signed, "Correct."

Zach relayed her response to Craig.

Craig scowled when he directed his next comment to Zach. "They didn't process either of you, but they didn't take the handcuffs off of her until I protested."

Zach yanked his head toward Juanita and asked, "You had handcuffs on all this time?"

She nodded, but drew back against her seat as Zach's irritation multiplied. He didn't need to make matters worse, but while he held his tongue, he imagined his rising blood pressure had the capacity to erupt.

A knock preceded the whining hinges and the appearance of a weary face in the doorway.

"Would you follow me, please?" The officer cast his glance downward in what appeared to be embarrassment.

After they turned down a corridor, their escort knocked on a door that bore the name of Captain Emily Snodgrass.

A voice from inside the room hollered, "Enter."

Zach held Juanita's hand as he followed Craig into the small office where a harsh ceiling fixture glared over piles of paperwork, coffee cups, and files, all strewn across a massive desktop. Without a doubt, the place was a pigsty. Equally obvious was that the smirking official standing behind the mess was not one Captain Emily Snodgrass.

"Zachary Hoyt. Mr. Hustler, himself. My, my." The man's sardonic tone hadn't changed in—what? Twenty-five years? Twenty-six? "Heard you were back in town." The pronouncement ended with a snivel, which earned a grin from the cop who stood near the corner of the room—the male officer who yanked Juanita out of the SUV. His partner, the female cop, grimaced and looked away.

As Zach's empty hand clenched, Craig Morrison gripped Zach's elbow and nudged him forward.

Two

Officer Stan Benton's nightmare vaporized at the same time the disdain he held for the acting captain morphed into the realm of friend-not-foe. He leaned into his partner and whispered, "See? No problemo."

In response, a still-peeved Holly Norris stepped aside and folded her arms over her ample chest. When Stan's arched eyebrows earned Holly's indignation, he didn't bother to bury his crude amusement.

If Stan had to have a female partner, at least this one was easy on the eye. Nice figure, although she was on the short side; long auburn hair that fell into soft curls when she tugged her ponytail clip off at the end of her shift; and a pretty face that reminded him of one of those collector dolls his six-year-old daughter kept hounding him to buy for her. Stan scoffed at the recollection. Between his lackluster salary and child support payments, Lauren had to get in line behind her brother Tyler to collect all the stuff on her wish list. At the front of the "gimme" line was his ex-wife.

Stan flashed another glance at Norris who, in all other respects, was a pain. The woman was too self-righteous and by the book. Not only did Norris expect him to follow every rule, regulation, and suggestion delivered from the top brass down to their paltry ranks, she pushed him to get over himself and put his life together. Holly Norris didn't have a clue.

In response to the captain's inference, as well as the derogatory tone he directed toward Zach Hoyt, the man in the suit inched up his shoulders and cleared his throat. He looked like trouble to Stan. The man jutted his chin and narrowed his eyes when he offered his hand to the captain. His voice was smooth and confident when he said, "I'm Craig Morrison, the Hoyts' attorney. And you are . . ."

When the captain dismissed the gesture by stepping back and taking a seat behind his desk, Stan shuffled his feet. The captain could be glib all he wanted, especially if it worked in Stan's favor, but the attorney's demeanor demanded more than a brush-off. Even a nobody like Patrolman Stan Benton could see that. For her part, Norris didn't flinch.

"I am Acting Captain Hollister." He pointed to the chairs in front of his desk. "Have a seat."

"Has Captain Snodgrass had her baby yet?" Morrison asked.

Stan held his breath while Hollister leaned back in his seat and studied his three guests.

"You know the good captain?"

"I do. We've corroborated on some of the mayor's neighborhood task force initiatives."

Stan covered a cough with his hand as the lining of his throat turned to sandpaper.

Hollister swallowed with some effort and pasted a cheerful, and blatantly insincere, expression on his face. "No news yet. But I believe it's due any day now."

"While we're bantering about personal things," Morrison said, "tell me about Zach's 'Hustler' nickname. Did you two go to college together? Play ball? What?"

When amusement played across Hollister's face, Stan took that as a positive move and lowered his guard. Maybe his career wasn't over yet.

"We played high school football together, but if he's honest, he'll tell you he earned the nickname off the field."

Stan's lungs collapsed again.

"What about you?" Morrison asked Hollister. "You have a nickname back then?"

"Sumo."

Captain wrenched his head toward Zach Hoyt, the source of the response. The guy's incensed demeanor dared the captain to utter a rejoinder. The animosity between the two men was as clear as the trouble staring Stan in the face. The revelation initiated an unwelcome wave of perspiration and a dose of nausea.

"Sumo?" Morrison asked. "I like that. Did you foot-wrestle your opponents off the field?" The attorney's imitation of a sumo wrestler accompanied his chuckle, and while none of the others seated around the desk reacted, Stan watched the edges of Norris' lips curl upward.

Captain Hollister brushed off the remark and said, "Let's focus on business, shall we? I believe your clients' presence at this station is a result of nothing more than a series of misunderstandings. Your clients did not respond to the directives of these two officers, dedicated civil servants who were unaware of Mrs. Hoyt's inability to hear them."

"Are you tendering an apology?" Morrison asked.

"An apology? No. I asked to meet with you to explain why we won't press charges against either of your clients. In my opinion, that's a gift."

Stan leaned back as he watched Juanita Hoyt's hands. Her

fingers moved with the same ferocity as her facial expression. If she couldn't hear, what sparked her outrage?

Hollister rolled his eyes and said, "What—"

The attorney cut off Hollister's words with a flick of his wrist. "Hold on a minute."

By the time the wife's hands stopped jerking through the air, the rigid muscles in her husband's jaw flinched. He looked at Hollister when he said, "It appears this isn't the first instance in which one of these dedicated civil servants has been accused of overreacting and employing overreaching methods."

Stan swatted at the beads of sweat collecting on his upper lip. He couldn't do anything to hide the expanding damp mark on the cloth beneath his armpits. Norris was wrong. This woman could read lips. She read Hollister's comments, and she read Norris' hallway diatribe. Stan's own partner incriminated him. How he hated women. Every one of them.

Hollister tapped a finger on the file folder resting front and center on the disarray that was his desk. The color-coded personnel file. Stan didn't need to see the name on the tab to know it was his record. His future was toast. Nasty, stinky, burnt-to-a-crisp toast.

Hollister's dramatic sigh washed over the room's occupants. "I find your innuendo rather offensive. I'm offering free get-out-of-jail cards. While you consider my cautionary suggestion that you simply take your clients home, I might mention that most defamation of character charges tend to draw a mess of publicity."

"The issue here isn't publicity," Morrison said. "It's called fair play. Your officers, one in particular, didn't play fairly. My client thinks a lesson is as important as an apology. We can go public, which will initiate an internal investigation on the part of your department, or we can negotiate something that is fair to all parties."

"You're bluffing. What evidence do you have that one of these officers has a history of overreach? Hmm?"

Morrison pulled his lips into a tight line. "Those are the things we attorneys share after we file suit. You, however, are privy to the details of that personnel file." The attorney steered his attention toward the folder on the desk. "The contents should weigh on your decision to consider our recommendation—or not."

Stan hid his growing agitation by shoving his hands into his back pockets. He relished a lesson just a notch less than he feared unemployment. Internal Affairs would have a heyday if they saw another accusation alongside his name. Regardless of the outcome, Hollister would have his head on a platter.

Hollister pouted when he said, "What kind of lesson did you have in mind?"

"Mrs. Hoyt suggests that Officer Benton attend sign language classes."

Stan pulled his hands out of his pockets, but when he didn't know what to make of the request, he shoved them back in again. Sign language classes? He couldn't care less whether he could converse with a deaf person. After today, he'd make it a point to avoid them. He'd have to figure out how to do that, exactly, but he'd find a way. In the meantime, watching people wave their hands for an hour sounded more palatable than an investigation. Or worse.

"Why would he do that?" Hollister asked.

"I'd go with him," Norris said as she stepped forward. "I would. We need to know how to communicate with everyone in this community."

Hollister lowered his head and coughed. "Fine. We'll have Officer Norris attend sign language classes."

Mrs. Hoyt's hands started flapping again. Great. Just great.

Zach Hoyt looked at Hollister and said, "No. Officer Norris is more than welcome to attend the class, but the arrangement requires Officer Benton's attendance. Otherwise, we don't have a deal."

The flash of indignation and resentment that flitted between Hollister and Hoyt carried as much baggage as one or the other might acquire over a lifetime. Whatever happened between the two hadn't diminished during Hoyt's absence from Shelburg.

"When's the class?" Hollister asked.

"The next session begins in two weeks," Hoyt said. "Monday nights at seven, in the lower level of New Life Chapel, over on Third Street. It's an eight week class, but with the holidays, it will carry over into the new year."

"Eight weeks!" Stan didn't mean to open his mouth, much less screech with indignation.

Norris reached over, wrapped her hand around his bicep, and pinched a layer of skin between her thumb and index finger. "We'll be there."

When Stan gathered the nerve to look Hollister in the eye, the acting captain asked, "Are we in agreement?"

Stan pulled his hands out of his pocket, unlatched Norris' fingernails from his arm, and said. "Yeah. Sure."

"And the apologies?"

Stan stared at the attorney. Of course he wanted an apology. Stan just wanted to end his shift, go home, and suck on a bottle of beer. Maybe two or three.

"I'm sorry I didn't read the situation properly. I should

have been more patient," Stan said. There. His ex-wife's marriage counselor would be proud of him. If he'd learned nothing else, he'd picked up the proper format and posture for groveling, not that it did anything to save his marriage. Maybe that particular failure had something to do with the insincerity that attended the kowtowing.

Norris picked up during the lull. "I'd like to apologize as well. I'm sorry things got out of hand. We—I—need to be more sensitive to events as they unfold. I'm sorry for all of this."

"Great," Hollister said. "I think we're done here. You're free to go. These two officers will follow through with the sign language classes."

Morrison turned to Stan and said, "I'm sure I'll see you at New Life. It's kind of my second home."

As the warning etched its mark on Stan's brain, he watched the attorney pause at the doorway. Morrison turned back toward Hollister and said, "If you see the mayor before our pickup game next weekend, please give him my regards." With that menacing mouthful spewed, Morrison escorted his clients out of the captain's office.

Stan released his ragged inhale with the slow, uncontrollable discharge of a leaky balloon. The worst part of his night sat behind the desk. He turned and faced his greatest obstacle.

Hollister pointed to Norris. "You. Leave." He glared at Stan and said, "You. Sit."

Three

"No kidding? They cuffed you and everything?" Seventeen-year-old Conner appeared to be more impressed by his mother's episode with the Shelburg Police Department than offended. "Hey, too bad you didn't have on that sweatshirt. You know, the one that says something about women who don't make waves never find their names in the history books."

Juanita summoned a perturbed expression and leveled it at Zach. "I knew I shouldn't have let you buy that for me," she signed with her hands.

Zach, in turn, mouthed a sheepish, "Sorry."

Conner shoved his chair away from the table as he grabbed his empty plate and the empty pizza box. "Wait 'til the guys on the swim team hear about—"

"Stop." Zach raised his hand as if he were directing a line of traffic to an abrupt standstill. "Any talk about this incident is limited to the four of us. We cut a deal with the police captain that we would not initiate a complaint if the officer involved showed up at the sign language classes. If word gets out that we're bad-mouthing the cops, Hollister will renege. Do you both understand?"

As Conner's hopes of a moment in the spotlight dimmed,

Juanita regarded her son. He didn't need a spotlight. His easy manner, charm, and sense of humor brought him plenty of attention and earned him a broad array of friends.

Izzy, who hadn't said much about the incident, carried her opinion in the guise of deep lines across her forehead and lips pulled into a thin frown. The move to Shelburg hit Izzy hard. Between leaving her best friend behind and trying to cope with her body's awkward transition from childhood to adolescence, Izzy suffered. Juanita tapped her fourteen-year-old on the shoulder.

"Are you all right?"

"I don't see why Conner thinks this is funny. Look what they did to you. How do you plan to explain the bruise on your cheek? That stupid cop ought to be in jail. It's not right." After Izzy stuffed her plate into the dishwasher, she folded her arms across her chest and contorted her face when she said, "I hate this place. I want to go home."

As Izzy spun on her heels and ran down the hallway, Conner's short-lived levity faded.

"What's with her?" he asked.

"Give her a break," Zach said. "You know where you're headed. Six months from now you'll graduate, move back out west, maybe, and start college. Izzy is lost here, and her future doesn't look any more promising than the misery she feels today."

"What about you?" Conner asked. "If you can't turn the business around, will you go back to Arizona?"

Juanita blinked a couple of times as a pair of teardrops threatened to give her away. It wasn't anyone's first choice to move to Shelburg. They'd moved to Ohio when the worst of the hot, humid summer air sucked the life out of them. Their new home, the one Zach lived in all through junior and senior high, exhibited a decade of neglect. During the three long months it took for them to set aside the funds they needed to replace the ductwork and heating and air conditioning units, stifling, sleepless nights followed wretched sticky-hot days.

Would they move back to Arizona if the company went under? Back to dry air, blue skies, and all things familiar? How could they? Where would they find the money for another cross-country move?

And what of Zach? If he failed to revive his father's thirty-year-old business, would he take it as a personal failure? The company's financial history suggested the introduction of a new manager accompanied the steep decline. By the time Zach learned of his father's diminished mental state, the damage was done.

Now? Zach's father was dead. The manager was gone. What remained was a long list of unhappy creditors and a slim staff of honorable people who remained loyal to Zach's father throughout the turmoil. The company's heartbeat was frail and intermittent; its lung capacity was too shallow to leave a trace of breath on a mirror.

Juanita swiped at her eyes and forced a brave face. Stewing over the unknown robbed the present. Tomorrow she'd deal with tomorrow's worries. Which reminded her . . . "We need the car tomorrow. Can you get a ride to school?" she signed.

Her son's shoulders fell, and his incredulous, "Why?" made her wince.

"We have to pick up the SUV."

"Where is it? How did you get home?"

"Pastor Morrison gave us a ride. The SUV is in the impound lot," Zach answered.

"Well, let's go get it now," Conner said.

"The lot's not open until morning," Zach said.

"Terrific. Fine" Conner grabbed his cell phone. "I'll call Derrick."

"It could be worse," Zach said.

"Not much worse than being without wheels," Conner quipped.

"You could be entertaining the folks from Children Services while they placed you in a temporary foster home. Losing the car for one day doesn't sound like a bad alternative."

"Not funny," Juanita signed. Conner's grin, however, was warmer than the sunshine.

"Gotcha," Conner replied. "I gotta get my homework done. Stay out of trouble, will you?"

"We'll try," Zach said. When Conner was out of earshot, Zach said, "I'm sorry. If I hadn't taken the phone call, I would have been driving when those two yahoos pulled the SUV over."

"That is beside the point."

"It's not. I may have protested the ticket for the taillight, and they would have heard an earful about the obscured lettering on the license plate. We'd have come home, paid the fines, and been done with it."

Juanita lowered her gaze and studied her hands, the appendages that substituted for her voice. Her inability to hear carried an unfathomable cost: misunderstandings, isolation, ridicule, humiliation, and more. It was tough to bear the burden herself, but when it heaped hurt and shame upon her family, self-deprecation smothered her.

Why did God let her lose her hearing? What life-lesson was she supposed to grasp? Whatever it was, it didn't soothe her soul. Not in the least. As her heart and her spirit tripped into that wretched abyss of self-pity, a pair of tender hands wrapped around her, and gentle lips caressed her neck. Zach wiped the tear from her cheek and picked her up out of her chair. He carried her to their room and lowered her to their bed.

"I'll go talk to Izzy. It's okay, Juanita. We're okay. All of us."

It wasn't until Zach left the room and closed their door that Juanita punched her pillow and pressed it to her face to collect her tears.

~

Stan sat with his back ramrod straight while Hollister paced. On what had to be his tenth lap, he stopped in front of the window and put his hands on his hips. His head wagged back and forth at the same time a "pfft" escaped into the room.

As Hollister took a seat, he gestured toward the window. "Go figure. Hustler Hoyt shows up in my office with an Hispanic wife and an African American attorney. Or maybe she's American Indian. What do you think?"

Stan felt his eyes bulge at the question. Did Hollister, whose chalky white skin was more than a few shades lighter than Stan's, want an answer or was he just talking out loud?

"Hmm?"

"Uh, I don't know, sir."

Hollister flicked his hand at Stan. "Not that I care. I pictured Hoyt with Miss Perfect, not some defective wife. Interesting how things turn out. Right, Benton?"

Another question Stan didn't feel up to answering. "Sir?"

"Well, what did he expect? You marry someone who

can't hear, you have to expect things won't always work out like they would with normal people. Know what I mean?"

Stan's eyes darted from one side of the room to the other. Was a recording device picking up this conversation? Was this a trap? A joke? Or was Hollister for real? Which?

"Look," Hollister said as he pointed his finger at Stan, "your file says you have a temper and that you don't treat women with respect. I get that. You have to learn to control yourself around the people you are called to protect. You know that, don't you?"

"Yes, sir."

"I don't care about your personal opinion. I don't care about your personal problems. But when you end up in this office, you force me to act. Understand?"

"Yes, sir."

Hollister narrowed his eyes when he said, "I demand the same level of respect that you give to Captain Snodgrass. Just so we are on the same page, I'll let you in on a secret. Seems Snodgrass tried to have a baby for years. This pregnancy came as a surprise. Rumor has it that she'll return to duty just as long as required to justify her maternity leave and arrange for an early retirement. If that occurs, I intend to take her place on a permanent basis. Your future depends on the way you play out this arrangement with the Hoyts."

"I understand." So Stan said, but a sliver of doubt the size of a giant sequoia suggested otherwise.

"Do you?" Hollister asked as he strode around his desk and hovered over Stan like a bird of prey eyeing his next meal.

"I intend to cooperate. I'll attend every class. I give you my word."

"I may call on you to do a little more than that."

Stan cleared his throat and craned his neck to keep eye contact with Hollister. "Sir?"

"If Craig Morrison expects to see you at that church, and since he's a friend of the mayor, you might be in a position to sweeten my chance to fill the captain's spot."

"Sir?" Stan gave himself a mental kick in the butt. Why did he take his foul mood out on Juanita Hoyt? Why did he let his ex-wife needle him in the first place? After all, she's the one who fueled his fury. No more. Somehow, he'd learn how to ignore her relentless and callous barbs. Obviously, he had to.

The long-ago speech of the marriage counselor smacked Stan in the face. "Mr. Benton, you attempt to dominate a situation by bullying and by using controlling methods. Instead, you lose control of the situation." Her conclusions were true back then. He tried to manipulate his wife. In the end, she took control, took the kids, and left him.

The counselor's words rang true today. The only person in control was the maniac who towered over Stan: one Frederick Sumo Hollister. Could things get any worse?

Four

Zach grabbed a fistful of hair but stopped short of yanking it out at the roots. Juanita already put up with the extra ten pounds he amassed since he retired from the Air Force. She probably wouldn't be thrilled if he showed up at the house with a patch of bare skull.

Numbers were not his friend. Yeah, Zach could toss them around and manipulate them on a computer spreadsheet or a calculator, but no matter how he figured and refigured, the measurements glaring at him from the reports were inflexible. Regardless of the angle, the debits exceeded the credits, and had done so for a very long time.

His initial tour of the shop was as comforting as the indigestion it delivered. Some of the shelves held either inordinate amounts of one product or too many empty spaces. Worse than the absence of product was the vast amount of inventory that was so old that it was worthless. Once Zach wrote off the wasted materials, the company's balance sheet might declare that the negative net worth was beyond repair.

He and Juanita had college money tucked away for Conner, but if they had to divert every dime they earned to this business, they would have to borrow a fortune to provide for Izzy's higher education. Zach understood that challenge. Took him ten years to pay off his student loans, and that was before the cost of college skyrocketed.

When Zach replayed the scene at the police station, Sumo Hollister's condescending tone made its way to the present. Zach didn't have to prove anything to Hollister, but he wanted to rub success in the man's face. Zach scoffed as he lifted the stack of papers, shuffled them together, and evened the edges with a slap against the desktop. This little enterprise was not capable of impressing Hollister. Not even.

"Zach?" Nancy Ringold knocked on the doorframe as she peeked into the office. Her short crop of gray hair accentuated the two faint circles of blush that rested on her cheekbones, and her smile lifted the skin around her eyes into fine crinkles.

"Come on in. What's up?"

Nancy dusted her hands on her faded cranberry-colored apron, and lowered herself onto one of the two chairs that sat in his cubbyhole called an office.

"Would you consider closing the shop for three days? Sometimes other suppliers do that when they take their wares to a show or a weaving retreat."

"If you need a few days off, I think we can let you go without closing our doors. Can't you switch hours with Mae?"

"Um, well, we both wanted to sign up for classes at the weaving retreat in Kentucky. We wanted to go together. We can share a hotel and cut costs. I can't afford three days otherwise. You know?"

"Why would the two of you drive all the way to Kentucky and pay for three nights at a hotel in order to weave baskets? I know I've been on the fringes as far as Dad's business was concerned, but I can't believe you'd invest that much time and money to weave somewhere else, especially since you already know how to weave everything."

"It's not like that," Nancy said. "And, just so you understand the depth of the commitment, you need to know that we also have to pay stiff fees to the instructors for the classes and the materials. This is not a cheap event. I don't dare ask my husband to let me go very often. But the baskets offered in Kentucky this year are gorgeous." With a voice that reminded Zach of his teenage daughter's pleading, she upped her hand. "We really want to go. Really bad. What do you think?"

Zach scratched the top of his head as he asked, "Are all the participants as eager as you?"

"Eager isn't the right word. Passionate might be a better description."

Passionate? Zach never heard his father describe his clientele that way. Or had he, and Zach's feigned interest in the business just didn't absorb the communication? "I'm digesting your information. A bunch of weavers gather in one place and weave a basket."

"Three baskets. We'll each weave three. One each day."

"Okay. Three. And shops like ours close down, haul their inventory to the retreat, and sell a trailer-full of product while they have a captive audience." Zach knitted his brow. "Right?"

"Pretty much."

"How many people sign up?"

"For the Kentucky retreat? They max out at 300."

Once he dislodged the catch in his throat, Zach almost spit. "You're joking."

"You wouldn't believe the line-up of instructors. They're

from all over the place. Once I took a class from a woman who lived in Alaska. Can you believe that?"

"I want to believe that. Why do you have to go all the way to Kentucky? Doesn't anyone sponsor a retreat in Ohio?"

"No. Well, not a big one anyway." Nancy's eyes expanded at the same time Zach sat up straight in his seat. "Are you thinking what I'm thinking?" she asked.

"Why couldn't we? You and Mae know the weavers in the area, the guilds, the instructors. Why couldn't we? Cover your ears with our hands," Zach said.

Nancy didn't hide her displeasure at the command, but when she obeyed, Zach hollered, "Hey, Mae, we need you in here."

Mae's flip-flops, a wardrobe staple, slapped on the flooring and announced her arrival. She stuck a pencil over her ear before she rested her empty hands against her hips. In her typical gruff voice she asked, "What?"

"We're talking about the weaving retreat in Kentucky," Nancy said.

"And? You need me to come in here and pout until he says yes?" Mae asked Nancy.

Zach waved his hand at her when he said, "No. You can go. Both of you."

"Then let me get back to work," Mae said as she turned toward the door.

"Wait a sec. Nancy and I have an idea."

Mae rolled her eyes at Zach and glowered at Nancy. "What?"

Zach loved Mae Baxter. The stubborn old woman had a heart that was as vast as the Atlantic Ocean. Why she had to play belligerent was beyond him, but in all the years she worked for his father, this was the way Mae chose to present herself.

Zach must have been about twelve the first time he met Mae. She scared him half to death. Her fondness for baking snickerdoodle cookies and her willingness to share them eventually breached the chasm of terror that separated the two of them. Zach licked his lips at the reminder. Maybe he could negotiate a plateful before Mae and Nancy snuck out of work and went to Kentucky.

"Why don't we organize a retreat here? In Shelburg?" Zach asked.

"I might know a lot about weaving and retreats, but what makes you think I want to work that hard, Zachary Hoyt?" This, from Mae. Her face took on a sullen expression, but those blue eyes sparkled with mischief.

"I believe you'd do anything to keep my daddy's business going. In return, I can continue to pay you some stingy wages, which you can use to attend more basket weaving retreats."

Nancy turned to Mae and winked. "I told you. *The Basket Works* isn't folding shop. No, sir. And you and I are going to Kentucky. Hot Diggity-Dog."

Nancy started for the door and guided Mae into the hallway. Nancy glanced back and yelled, "Thanks, boss," at the same time Mae muttered something about working overtime.

Zach leaned back in his seat for about a nanosecond, but then he grabbed his computer mouse. He entered an internet search for basket weaving retreats and watched in awe as websites flashed on the screen. They were everywhere: Tennessee, Indiana, Vermont, California, Florida, North Carolina, and more. Why didn't he know this before?

Duh, because he had no reason to care before. Dad's basket weaving supply business was just something his father ran in order to make a living and pay the bills. Or was it? Did he share any of the enthusiasm Nancy and Mae had for the art? His mom sure didn't.

Mom didn't have a creative bone in her fingers. Her artistic bent was cerebral, and her quick wit and imagination filled the pages between the covers of more than thirty children's books. Zach did not inherit his mother's talent, but he devoured literature on a more regular basis than he ate . . . or exercised.

He glanced at the wall clock and powered off his computer. Juanita expected him home in less than an hour and he had to stop at the automotive supply store and pick up a taillight bulb. He set the security system and then followed Nancy and Mae out the front door.

As he climbed into the SUV, he looked at the old sign above the building's entryway. What did he know about *The Basket Works?* Nothing. After dinner and some time with his family, he'd stick his nose back into the internet sites. It was time to learn a new trade.

~

When Izzy plopped down in the seat opposite Juanita's workspace, Juanita's unaware body leaped into action. She flinched so badly she almost toppled out of her chair.

"Did I scare you?" Izzy's face reflected Juanita's temporary alarm. "You always know when I come home. Is something wrong?"

Juanita shook her head while she gasped for air. She signed, "I'm fine. I was . . ." She pointed to the stack of paper sitting on the table. "I was engrossed in this mess of a manuscript."

She wasn't fine, but Izzy didn't need to know that. The fiasco with the SUV and police cost her a good night's sleep, and when she eyed her discolored cheekbone after her morning shower, the new yellow hue reminded her of the mess that was her life.

Just like every other day since they arrived in Shelburg, Juanita donned a pleasant face in the hope that her masquerade might protect her family from the sniveling whiner that she'd become. She loved her family. More than life. She loved the Lord. Why couldn't she shake off the gloom that beckoned her out of bed each day?

"What's wrong with the manuscript?" Izzy asked as she thumbed through the first few pages. "Yuck. Non-fiction. Boring."

"Non-fiction has its place. Like history books," Juanita signed.

"And what value does this one impart?" Izzy's face conveyed the sarcasm that Juanita could not hear.

In addition to being skilled at sign language, all of them—Izzy, Conner, Zach, and Juanita—owned a set of facial expressions and body language that conveyed much more than the average person might notice. Their special traits helped communicate, but they sure didn't replace the sound of a human voice. Would she ever get over it? Sometimes she thought it might have been kinder to have been born deaf than to have lost her hearing.

Juanita shoved her discouragement away, although it never fully withdrew. Instead, like an unread chapter, it sat on the shelf of self-pity, ready to fall open and into her lap at some future time. "This book? He must have an audience or he would not have earned a contract with a publisher."

"If it's that bad, why did you agree to edit it?"

Truth? They needed the money. "I knew it was a monster when I picked it up, and I negotiated a better fee. I guess that helps."

"I'll bet you negotiated low."

Izzy had her on that one. "I may have a headache while I red-ink this one, but just think of all I'll learn in the process."

"I'm not buying your enthusiasm," Izzy said. "When are you going to write your own stuff? You talk about it. Why don't you do it?"

"I don't think I have the same kind of talent your grandmother had. That skill came from your dad's side of the family. Not mine."

"Not true. You tell good stories."

When Juanita frowned and looked away, Izzy smacked her hand on the table. The vibration caught Juanita's attention, as did Izzy's agitated expression.

"I remember. When we were too little to sign, you'd sit on the edge of the bed and wave your hands around. I thought it was like magic, Mom. The movement was fast but elegant. I didn't understand, but I knew that Dad had to wait for your hands to quit moving so that he could tell us the next part. They were good stories. They were."

"You thought my signing was elegant?" Juanita scoffed at the suggestion.

"Mom," Izzy answered in what had to be a two-syllable rendition of the title, "haven't you ever watched choir members who signed the words to a song while they sang? It's beautiful. You know that. Right?"

The flood of tears caught Juanita unprepared. She wiped both cheeks and squeezed her eyes. The tender fingers of her daughter reached across the table and tugged at her hand. When she looked at Izzy, Juanita's determined façade fell away. She put her free hand over her mouth.

"Mom?"

Juanita lowered her hand and mouthed, "I'm sorry." She reached toward Izzy's face and curled a wisp of dark brown hair around her finger. Since the move to Shelburg, Izzy's image often reflected more than the physical traits she inherited from her mother. Right now, the same unsettled countenance that challenged Juanita's best intentions accompanied the soulful brown eyes peering from beneath Izzy' dark lashes. After Juanita released the long silky tendril, she signed, "I'm just tired. The past two days took a toll on me."

An unexpected shimmer of good humor played across Izzy's face when she said, "We're broke as far as Christmas gifts are concerned. Right?"

"Why does that make you smile?" Juanita signed. "It's more pathetic than funny."

"Will you do a project with me? Something you and I can give to Dad and Conner?" Izzy scratched her chin before she added, "Although Conner will probably think it's a cheesy idea. Too bad."

"What do you have in mind?" Juanita signed.

"You write down your favorite children's story. I'll illustrate it."

"Clever idea, but I don't think we'll find anyone who might be willing to publish it for us. I suppose you—not we—could do a spiral-bound rendition to hold letter-size paper together."

"We can publish it ourselves. We'll use that website Mrs. Kirby talked about. Come on. How difficult can it be?"

Juanita studied the sparkle in her daughter's eyes. Izzy's face wore a measure of hope that exceeded Juanita's ability to honor. If she weren't already overwhelmed . . . but she was.

"Honey, I don't have time right now. Christmas isn't far away."

"Then I'll do it. I'll write the story the way I remember it. I'll start painting pictures and when you need a break from that awful manuscript, you can edit the text. I love it." Izzy bounded around the table, wrapped Juanita in a bear hug, and skipped down the hallway.

Izzy knew her mother couldn't call after her to protest the proposition. No fair. She also knew that her little caper tugged at her mother's heartstrings. It also buried Juanita's anxiety in a wave of gratitude, much as Jesus' grace washed a multitude of sins. A reality check. Juanita needed an attitude check.

Juanita lifted her hands and examined the palms. She turned them over and paused at the sight of her wedding ring as the ceiling light reflected against the diamond's facets. Izzy thought her hand-speak was elegant? Could Juanita ever—in this lifetime—consider her silent existence in the same light? Could she?

Five

"Hang a right at the next light," Stan said.

"Why? It's outside our watch," Norris answered.

When Norris failed to move into the right-turn lane, Stan raised his voice. "Hang a right."

"That's not in our watch."

"It's on the fringes. Just do it, will ya?"

"Fine," Norris said as she signaled and maneuvered into the right lane. "Did I give sufficient notice with my turn signal, Benton? Wanna get out and inspect the lights?"

When Stan glowered at her, she took the turn slower than a granny ambling behind a two-wheeled walker.

"Would you knock it off? I already apologized fifteen times for pulling over the Hoyts. Give it a rest," Stan said.

"Right. As if it's over and done with. Sumo Hollister is going to ride both of us until Captain comes back from maternity leave. That's—like—months from now."

"Might be worse than that."

"How?" Norris pulled her foot off the accelerator again. Stan could push the cruiser faster than she drove.

"Hollister thinks she won't stay on the job. He plans to take her place."

"Permanently?" Norris asked.

When Norris turned on the right-turn signal again, Stan sat up in his seat. "What are you doing?"

Norris pulled the squad car to the curb and put it in park. "I need you to tell me you're kidding."

"Why do you think he asked me to stick around his office after the Hoyts left? After he made you leave."

Norris shifted in her seat, but it was her shifty eyes that burned a flame into Stan. "Spill it."

"It's confidential."

"You already compromised confidentiality with your rumor. Might as well share the rest of it."

Stan studied the perturbed look Norris blasted in his direction. He looked past her frosty hazel eyes and focused on the old red brick building on the far side of the intersection.

After a driver in a blue sedan stopped for the red light, he turned right and followed the last visible car heading south. The empty roadway exposed a sign resting in front of the building, near the sidewalk. The sign held removable letters that someone painstakingly updated for the benefit of the passersby.

Stan chugged a mouthful of water and wiped his mouth with the back of his hand as he read.

Teen B'ball Thursday night
6:00 Guys cheer the Gals
7:00 Gals cheer the Guys
8:00 all cheer the pizza man

The permanent part of the sign, the space reserved below the weekly advertisement, read:

New Life Chapel, Pastor Craig Morrison.

Stan gagged on the trace of water that lined his throat.

"What's your problem?" Norris asked. While Stan fought for air, she followed his pointy finger. When she turned back to face him, the flared nostrils and smoke emitted from Norris' ears suggested she'd like to wrap her hands around his neck and choke him. Maybe it was a good thing the water was doing it for her.

"I thought Craig Morrison was an attorney."

Stan waved his hand back and forth, still working to fetch some air. "Me too," he rasped.

"He's a pastor?" Norris massaged the back of her neck before she glared at Stan. She shoved the transmission into drive and pulled away from the curb.

"You know," Norris said in a smooth, controlled voice, "I would not have volunteered to take a sign language class if I'd known it was held at a church. Any church. But *Morrison's* church? Benton, I can't ditch you as a partner soon enough. You know that. Right?"

"This is not the first time you've made that abundantly clear. What can I say?"

"It's in your best interest to say nothing. Not. One. Thing."

~

Zach rubbed his knees before he stood and stretched. A draft of wind picked up some yellow and orange leaves, shuffled them mid-air, and deposited them in the growing pile that littered the grass along the driveway. He'd mulch them into the yard next time he mowed, a chore the changing season would soon bring to a halt.

The warmth of the fickle autumn sun rested on the landscape while a nearby fireplace released the relaxing scent of burning wood. As Zach closed the back of the SUV, he watched Conner put the last tool into the toolbox and carry it to its place in the garage.

"When did life get so complicated?" Zach asked. "Used to be you'd pull off the lens cover, pull out the dead lamp, shove in a new one, and reverse the process. Now? You have to be Houdini to climb into the fender from the inside of the SUV to reach the lamp. I feel like a surgeon who just performed microsurgery without benefit of the high tech instruments."

"Let's just be grateful you didn't break anything in the process," Conner replied.

"You implying your dad is not mechanically inclined? Hmm?"

Conner shuffled his feet and looked down, but failed to neutralize the effervescent humor that surfaced. "I didn't say that. Maybe you lack training in that department?"

Zach grabbed a basketball from the corner of the garage and tossed it to Conner. "Back in the day, we boys had to take industrial arts classes. We must have changed the oil in the teacher's car once a month. He owned an ancient two-door sedan, big as a boat. Don't know how he kept the thing running. I know my class participation didn't earn the rattletrap any new miles."

Conner bounced the ball a few times before he slipped it over the hoop and into the net. Easy. The boy made everything look easy. His blue eyes—darker than Zach's, and far more intense—glimmered with satisfaction as gravity propelled the swooshing mass downward.

Zach caught the ball before it bounced. He dribbled and then lofted it toward the hoop. It hit the backboard, caught the edge of the ring, and dropped into Conner's open arms. Conner spun the ball before he lobbed it back to Zach.

"Let me know when you're done warming up," Conner said.

Zach's second shot was worse than the first. He hefted his shoulders, one at a time, and hesitated when a knot grabbed at his muscles. Was he getting old? Except for a few extra pounds, he still looked as lean and lanky as his son, didn't he? In truth, maybe the only thing they had in common any more was their nondescript shade of brown hair.

"Maybe you need to pretend I'm your high school adversary. That Sumo guy."

This time, Zach's toss slid past the hoop and into the net with nary a whisper against the metal frame.

"Whoa. Looks like I found a sore spot," Conner said as he swept the ball from under the net, dribbled, and laid another one into the hoop.

Zach yanked the ball back after it bounced on the pavement. He jumped and then tipped the ball into the air. The bounce against the backboard stole the shot again.

"Yep, a sore spot. You want to talk about it?" Conner chuckled as he let the ball flit off the tip of his fingers. The kid was good.

Zach couldn't talk about Hollister. Not now. He'd worked up a sweat and couldn't fill his lungs with a sufficient amount of oxygen to keep up the banter with his son. He needed to get back to the gym. Zach's athletic performance was pathetic, and Conner tendered zero mercy.

After Zach missed three shots in a row, he wrapped his arm around the basketball, leaned forward, and rested his free hand against his thigh. "I'm done," he wheezed. "So done."

Conner grabbed the ball, twisted his torso toward the net, and dropped in a clean shot. "Tell me about Hollister. Why was he on your case the other night?"

Zach wiped the sweat off his brow and took inventory of his son. Conner liked to win, but he wasn't crazy competitive like Zach had been.

"Already told you. Went to high school together. We weren't pals."

"That's obvious. What's the story?" Conner quit bouncing the basketball and stood, one hand on a hip, waiting for something more.

"I didn't live here until middle school, but Hollister probably earned the nickname Fatty on the first day he went to kindergarten. By the time I showed up in town, he was still big, but he pushed his bulk around the football field and earned himself a hefty reputation. Pun intended.

"Hollister turned his fat into legend and managed to change his nickname to Sumo. He must have slimmed down after high school, because he wasn't big as a house when we ran into him, but I suspect that in most people's minds, his reputation is first and foremost linked to obesity."

"What's that got to do with you? Your rivalry sounds kind of personal."

"That's a story for another day. Maybe."

Conner waited, but when Zach failed to provide details, he asked, "You called him Sumo when he was dressing down you and Mom?"

"He started it."

"He called you a name?" Conner peered into Zach's eyes. "He did, didn't he? What was *your* nickname? Hmm?"

"Doesn't matter. It was a long time ago."

"I can go to the library and dig through old yearbooks, or you can tell me yourself." The smirk his son wore didn't make the confession any easier. Bantering was good. Delving into Zach's past wasn't necessarily a safe topic of conversation to have with his child.

"Hustler. They called me The Hustler."

Conner pulled his mouth into a tight circle. He worked his jaw back and forth, as if he were trying to process the implications. He scratched his chin and asked, "You want to explain?"

"Not especially."

"So, did you, like, hustle on the football field?"

"I wasn't too bad on the field."

"What did you do off the field? Hustle people for money? Huh?" Conner's smug stance vanished when he saw Zach's sober expression.

"Dad made what he needed at *The Basket Works* to squeak by. The business paid the bills, for the most part."

"What about the other part?" Conner asked.

"Mom didn't earn a lot of royalties from her children's books, so she did some babysitting. When she watched someone else's children at our house, I hated coming home. I found other things to do. Found a way to make an easy buck."

"You gonna tell me, or what?" Conner asked. He bounced the ball a couple of times before he grappled it with his long fingers.

"I started taking bets on the side."

"You mean like a bookie?" While Conner's expression still reflected an element of surprise, the grin he wore moments earlier flashed into history, right along with Zach's parental reputation.

"It started with baseball. I didn't play the game. Didn't see any conflict of interest. I made more money after one game than my dad had leftover in a month. Suddenly, I could dress the part of a popular jock. I had money to go on a date. I earned a name for myself. I liked it." Zach looked away.

"The Hustler is not the man I know. What happened?"

Relief washed over Zach at Conner's statement. From the outside looking in, Conner led a charmed life. He hadn't. Zach's boy just learned to overcome the hurdles, and he did it in a manner that made Zach proud. So unlike the grief he hurled at his own parents.

"When I couldn't explain my financial good fortune to my folks, my dad did some investigating. It didn't take but five minutes to see where I'd not bothered to hide all of my racketeering activities."

"What did he do?" Conner asked.

"What did he do?" Zach repeated. "He could have ended my misdeeds with a lecture. If he had, I would have stopped. He thought my misfortune of having been caught lacked genuine remorse, so he decided he'd help me be sorry."

"Is this where you and your folks went separate ways in the family arena?" Conner asked.

"I can't say my dad was wrong in what he did. He wanted to make a point. At the time, I believed his method was rather cruel."

"And now?"

"Now? I still can't be objective. When Dad escorted me to school and made me relinquish my position on the basketball and football teams, he wanted to teach me lesson in honesty. He knew, however, that his decision tossed my college education into the trash heap. No sports scholarship for a boy who placed bets. Dad didn't just steal the present from me, he cost me my future."

"Ouch. No wonder we never spent more than a rushed holiday with your parents. I always wondered." Conner pulled the edges of lips down further when he said, "But you did go to college."

"I did, but it wasn't easy. Worked fulltime. Studied fulltime. Earned a degree along with a ton of debt. I did what I needed to do, but it was a whole lot more painful than it would have been with a scholarship."

"And, here we are," Conner said.

"Not sure what to make of that comment, Son." Zach didn't have a clue what this conversation might do to their relationship. He could only hope Conner might learn from his telling the story rather than repeating Zach's missteps.

"So you're back in Shelburg, trying to save the very business that didn't do so well when your dad ran it. That's kind of weird."

"Can't argue with that. I'm not sure why we decided to come."

"Maybe you're searching for some kind of redemption." Conner ended his statement in the form of a question. One Zach didn't think he was equipped to answer. The thought never occurred to him. Now that Conner had him staring the possibility in the face, what might Zach do about it?

"Some good did come out of my foolishness," Zach said. "The football coach got the idea that I needed to experience real poverty and hardship. With Dad's blessing, of course, he sent me to a church on the edge of town where I could help serve meals to the homeless and help organize basketball games for the down-and-out kids in the neighborhood."

"You did that?"

"For months. Six months, I think. Had to walk, too. Long

way from my white Anglo-Saxon roots. That's where I met Craig Morrison. That man, more than my father, turned my head around. I am a far better person today than the obstinate whiner Pastor Morrison met all those years ago."

"No kidding. Just for the record," Conner asked, "would you have spilled this to me if you hadn't been locked up by Sumo Hollister?"

Zach walked over to Conner, tapped the basketball out of his hands, and dribbled it down the driveway. "Probably not." His final attempt to prove his basketball prowess ended with a smack against the backboard, a tap against the right side of the rim, a jostle to the left, and a wavering slide through the net.

"We done with this?" Zach asked.

Conner grabbed the ball. "The confession? Yeah, we're done. Closed the book on it. The b'ball? Not even. Ready for a little Twenty-one?"

Six

It figured. For the first time in forever, Tina called and demanded Stan pick up Lauren and Tyler while she met with her study group at the library. No, she couldn't reschedule. Yes, she had to attend. The professor required the students to submit their semester work as a team. The only day they could meet this week was Monday.

The dutiful father rolled his eyes while he waited for someone to pick up his transferred call. He hoped they'd sympathize with his plight and tell him to stay home tonight. Start next week. Then again, if he didn't show up for the first sign language class, Hollister might decide to put him back on night shift.

Stan hated night shift. How anyone slept during the day was inexplicable. He couldn't, no matter how many methods he tried: darkening the windows with black plastic; filtering static into the room; turning on an endless recording of waves rolling in and out with the tide. Glass of whiskey made him drowsy, but it didn't help him stay asleep.

Finally, a voice proclaimed the answer to his question.

"You do? You sure? Well, yeah, okay. Yeah. Thanks."

Stan regarded his son and daughter, both of whom were thrilled by his invitation to hop into the car and go to his apartment. It wasn't the sight of their dad that lit up their faces. It was the pair of little white bags filled with dinner delight: chicken chunks, French fries, and a toy. The sodas probably weren't the most brilliant selection he could have made, but he'd return the two to his ex-wife before their bedtime, and she could sort out the inconvenience.

"Are you almost finished? We gotta roll," Stan said.

"Where?" Lauren asked.

"I have a class tonight. You get to come along."

"Are you in college like Mom?" Tyler asked. "Are you tired of being a policeman?"

"I like being a cop just fine. This class is to make me a better one. It's not college, but it's important."

"Mom says school is more important than anything. Is it, Dad?" Tyler asked.

"It's important. You like school, don't you?"

"I do," Lauren said.

"That's 'cause you don't have homework yet," Tyler said.

"Do you have a pedigree?" Lauren asked.

"A pedigree?" Stan asked.

"What you get in college," Lauren said.

"It's not a pedigree, like a dog," Tyler said. "It's a degree. *De*-gree."

"Yeah. That. Do you have one of those?" Lauren asked.

"Nope. I have a badge instead." Stan gathered empty wrappers, shoved them into the take-out bags, and balanced them on the top of the overflowing trashcan that he kept under the kitchen sink. "Grab a book or a puzzle. Something. You need to entertain yourself for about an hour. Come on. Hup, hup."

After he secured his children in the back seat, Stan climbed into his tired vehicle and pulled out of the massive apartment complex. The high-density units helped keep the rent down, but had a tendency to invite tenants of ill repute to sign short-term leases. Stan's badge encouraged most of the residents to behave, at least while they were in his line of vision, but if he had custody of Tyler and Lauren, he'd have to move to another neighborhood. Then again, tonight's destination location was pretty seedy too. If Tina knew where he meant to take their children, she'd annihilate him.

"Daddy," Lauren said from her low-perch, "how come Mommy says we hafta go to college after high school? I want to be a movie star. I don't want to go to college."

"You can't be a movie star," Tyler said. "Everybody wants to be a movie star or an All Star football player, but nobody gets to be."

"Hold on, you two. No fighting. Lauren, it's as hard to become a famous movie star as it is to be a famous football player, but a few people get the chance. College will give you more choices. That's what your mom wants for you."

"Why didn't she go to college before she got old?" Tyler asked.

Stan swallowed the terse response he'd let loose too many times over the past nine years. Yes, indeed, why didn't Tina go to college, something she swore was more important to her than anything or anyone?

"I don't think she'd appreciate you calling her old," Stan said with amusement. "She didn't go to college because she decided she wanted to be a mommy instead."

When silence greeted Stan's comment, he stretched his neck and regarded his children from the rearview mirror. Lauren looked as if she were still ruminating over the dismal prospects of becoming a movie star, but Tyler's face reflected bewilderment.

"So now she wants to go to college instead of being our mom?" Tyler asked.

Stan's lungs deflated. Leave it to Tina to make him explain the selfish choices she made.

"Not instead," Stan replied. "Also. She'll always want to be your mom. She wants an education too. When she graduates, she'll be your mom *and* a teacher."

"Like Amy's mommy," Lauren said. "She's a teacher and a mommy."

"Exactly," Stan said. Another glance in the mirror measured a miniscule weakening of Tyler's scowl.

"So why do we have to go to college first?" Tyler asked.

"It's easier to do things in that order, bud. That's all. She might say school is the most important thing, but I know better. You two are always her number one."

"How can we be number one if there's two of us?" Tyler asked.

Stan lifted his eyes toward the red light, waiting for a chance to move forward. If only he knew how to maneuver through life as easily as he followed driving rules. The pit of his stomach roiled as he considered his thoughts. If only he knew how to follow police protocol. No, he knew his job. It was his attitude he needed to check. Hopefully the little sessions at Morrison's church would fly by without flattening the rest of his ego. Fat chance, though, with Holly Norris enrolled.

Stan pulled into the well-lit parking lot at New Life Chapel. Before he could cut the engine, Norris pulled into the space next to his. Her little two-seater coupe, despite the recent weather, looked freshly washed and waxed. Must be nice to be young and single. Stan wouldn't know. He never got the chance to fill that role.

Norris stepped over to Stan's car, tapped her finger on the side window, and waved to Tyler and Lauren. Her easy manner matched her comfortable lifestyle. Stan yanked the keys out of the switch and opened the door abruptly. When Norris jumped sideways, Stan bit his tongue. Norris didn't get Stan. She didn't have a clue about his life. Not one.

~

Juanita stood at the front of the spacious room, facing the blackboard and writing the names of the two instructors, while Suzanne Kirby sorted handouts into neat stacks on the nearby table. Izzy, a perennial American Sign Language class assistant who often worked with students during the practical application part of the sessions, added a pile of nametags and two pens to the tabletop array.

"Everything's ready," Izzy signed. "I'll be back there." She pointed to the far corner of the room before she gathered her drawing paper and her treasured set of pastels. "Holler if you need me." She pushed her hair away from her face and pressed earbuds into each ear.

Juanita turned toward Suzanne and signed, "How many?"

Suzanne's fingers delivered her response.

"Twelve?" Juanita signed.

Suzanne handed a clipboard to Juanita as a middle-aged man entered the room, wandered to the table, and followed Suzanne's instructions as she pointed to the nametags and paperwork.

A young woman arrived next, followed by a trio of women and one man. The ages of the students, thus far, ranged from mid-twenties to somewhere in the sixties, or maybe the seventies. Their attire was as varied as the colors of their skin and the expressions on their faces.

Juanita scanned the roster. Officer Holly Norris volunteered, so she was a welcome participant. It seemed natural to identify her by her first name. Juanita still saw Officer Benton, on the other hand, as just Benton. Brusque, just like the man.

Four teenagers, yet to arrive, might be as big a headache as Benton. Juanita pressed her fingers to her lips to hide her discouragement. Students forced to take the ASL classes tended to steal the other attendees' enthusiasm.

Juanita looked at Suzanne and signed, "Diversion program?"

Suzanne nodded.

"Do you think it works? Do teens really stay out of trouble if they finish that program?"

"Hard to say," Suzanne signed.

"Why this class? Did they choose this or did the courts do it for them?"

"The courts decided this time. Two got in trouble for social media bullying, two for fighting," Suzanne signed.

Suzanne tossed the comment about fighting into the air as if it were a harmless and insignificant behavior, but as Juanita eyed Izzy, a cloud of apprehension descended.

"We're here to teach them to be sensitive," Suzanne said. A smile wove its way across her face as she rebuffed the worry. How the woman dismissed the obvious, that the teens' bad actions warranted police and courtroom intervention, was beyond Juanita. For her part, Juanita would stand on high alert.

Her tension eased as Holly Norris entered the room. The presence of a cop or two, Officer Benton's demeanor notwithstanding, lightened Juanita's angst. On Holly's heels were two children, followed by a sober-faced Benton. The children's skin tone, unlike Stan's sable hue, was warm caramel. Their brown eyes were lighter too, but the resemblance was unmistakable.

Juanita never pictured Benton as a parent. With his bulked-up frame and his haughty attitude, she imagined him too selfish to have a family. She wouldn't argue his good looks, from his strong physique to his deep-set brown eyes, but the distaste and disdain he displayed the night he stopped her SUV outweighed any pleasant attributes. With two children in tow, Benton carried himself in a different manner than he did at the station.

Juanita bit her lip. Who was she to judge? Two bad habits clung to her no matter how many times she thought she'd overcome them. Those two—judgment and criticism—just wouldn't release their hold.

Benton's gaze flashed between Juanita and Suzanne, as if he didn't know where to direct his question.

"Um, I called. They said I could bring my kids."

Juanita waved to her daughter, and exchanged a short conversation via sign language as Izzy made her way to the front of the room.

"Hey. I'm Izzy." She stuck a hand out to the boy.

The child exchanged a wary expression with his father before he let Izzy shake his hand. "Tyler," he said.

When the little girl clasped her hands behind her back, Izzy did likewise and asked, "What's your name?"

The child delivered her answer with a pout and a step towards Benton. "Lauren."

"Can I get you two to help me with an art project? I'm stuck and need some ideas." Izzy pointed to the back table.

"We brought stuff," Tyler said as he lifted a coloring

book and a box of crayons.

"Nice," Izzy said. "Ever use pastels?"

"What are those?" Lauren asked.

"Ooh," Izzy said as she rubbed her palms together. "Come see." She turned to Benton and asked, "Uh, is it okay if they get a little, uh, dirty? Chalk gets messy sometimes."

"Chalk?" Lauren asked as she lifted her face to her father. "Can we? Please? I'll be careful. I won't get dirty."

The expectation of collecting grubby children at the end of the class sure didn't seem to sit well with Benton, but he relented with, "Uh, yeah. Sure. Thanks."

Izzy tilted her head toward her big worktable and gestured for the two children to follow her. Relief, along with a hint of embarrassment, washed over Benton's face.

Suzanne pointed to her watch, which read seven o'clock, and took charge of the classroom. As she always did for these classes, she signed as she spoke. After welcoming the group and introducing herself, she directed everyone's attention to Juanita.

As they turned to stare at her, Juanita projected what she could only hope was an unexpressive face. She didn't watch Suzanne's hands while the students learned that one of their instructors was deaf but could read lips. After encouraging everyone to look at Juanita when they spoke, Suzanne asked each person to share their name and their reason for taking the class.

Several minutes into the introductions, a sober-faced Craig Morrison stood in the doorway. He stepped aside and waved several latecomers into the room. Once each of the teens found a chair, instead of heading back to his office, Pastor Craig took a seat near the door, crossed one leg over the other, and folded his arms across his chest.

Juanita exchanged a worried look with Suzanne. These teens looked hardened and cold, and evoked an air of cruelty. They were younger than Conner but carried themselves as if they'd experienced decades of harsh living. Ugly living. A tremor careened down Juanita's back.

The boys, one Asian and the other white, wore saggy pants, expensive tennis shoes, and earlobe expanders. Both girls wore black, from the collar-like leather encircling their necks to their heavy black boots. One wore foundation on her face so white that she looked ghoulish. The girl had silver rings in her ears, her nose, and her lips, and when she tossed her Goth-black hair away from her face, she revealed clusters of tattoos on her fingers and wrist. The second girl, who was African-American, didn't have visible piercings, but her makeup accentuated angry eyes, and the scar on her cheek suggested she'd found herself in at least one nasty altercation.

The teenagers' blatant assessment of the adults in the room caused a couple of the women to shuffle in their seats, but it was the interaction among the four that elicited the knot in Juanita's stomach. The intent glares the teens exchanged with one another suggested that each had already identified the others as adversaries.

Juanita raised her maternal defenses as she surveyed the juveniles, even as the rush to judge them gnawed at her. It wasn't their clothing, piercings, or tattoos that unnerved her, it was their collective sinister mien. It was dark and heavy—something that sucked the oxygen from the air.

At the back corner of the room sat three innocents: two young children and Juanita's beloved daughter. In the space between the juveniles and the cheerful artists sat a grim-faced lawman, his back rigid against his chair, and his fingers twitching, just as they had when he and Holly had their disagreement in the police station hallway.

Juanita tried to swallow, but her throat was dry. Would the cops' presence garner respect from the teens, or at least put fear in them, or would it stoke explosive dispositions?

Seven

Stan thought his biggest challenge of the night lay in the possibility that chalk-covered clothes would set off one of Tina's tirades. If Tyler and Lauren described these teenage classmates to Tina, she'd make his miserable life unbearable. For now, Tyler and Lauren were engrossed in their artwork. Maybe they hadn't noticed the little darlings that the pastor escorted to the room. What had the foursome already done to warrant Morrison's stern behavior?

Teenagers. Most of the ones Stan interacted with were punks. Disrespectful troublemakers with mouths as nasty and loud as the worst characters the idiot networks glorified on their horrible sitcoms. Didn't the writers know their tawdry and rude actors incited similar actions on the part of their viewers? These kids? They ate it up. They wanted to be street smart, noticed, respected. Instead, they were stupid and reckless. As far as Stan could tell, exceptions to the rule were rare.

He turned around and watched Izzy rub the side of her hand over her paper. She glanced at Stan as she inspected the purple smudge on her skin. She shrugged, as if to say, "Gee, I'm sorry. A little dirty? I may have understated that part."

Izzy might be one of the few good kids, but she might

mutate into a wholly different individual if her mother left the room. Kids were good actors. Slick. The prospect of being responsible for two teenagers in just a few years was about as welcome to Stan as another showdown with his captain.

Right now, Tyler was busy with his project and oblivious to the activity on the other side of the room, which was good. And Lauren, who didn't take easily to strangers, especially white ones, seemed in awe of Izzy and her art supplies. Somehow, he'd end this night on a good note, unlike most of the others.

After Suzanne ended a brief—thank you very much—history of ASL, she switched into rapid-fire mode, first demonstrating the signs for vowels, then the first eight consonants. Did she really expect the class to learn half of the alphabet in one session?

"I know this seems like a lot of information," Suzanne said, "but if you practice just half an hour a day, when you return next Monday you'll be amazed at the conversations you can have with each other."

That clarification, and the implication that Stan wanted to invest personal time in this class beyond the mandatory classroom sessions, provoked his irritation.

Suzanne lifted another piece of paper and said, "If you want to study ahead, the rest of the alphabet is on a separate sheet."

Holly leaned into Stan and whispered, "I love this. Next time the captain rips into you, I can stand across the room and sign my agreement. No one will be the wiser except you." She covered her mouth to stifle a giggle. Stan wanted to seal her mouth with duct tape.

"Now, we'll split into groups of two," Suzanne said. "Using the signs for the thirteen letters I just reviewed, I want you and your partner to come up with some three-letter or four-letter words. You'll feel clumsy, and this little exercise might seem slow, but you'll be amazed at how fast the last fifteen minutes of class time will fly."

Suzanne put her fingertip to her mouth and scanned the group before she continued. As she paired the participants, she pointed them to different areas of the room, whether to prevent distractions or to frustrate the students' attempts to incite a protest, was Stan's guess.

"Holly, please sit with Zoe."

Stan stretched forward and cracked his knuckles while he pushed his pleasure aside. Holly and the African American girl with the scar on her face? His partner wouldn't have any trouble with race relations, not after spending nine months on the beat with Stan. It was the teenager's attitude that would test Holly's civility, for Officer Holly Norris had zero patience for anything Goth and any association with darkness. The high schooler might not dabble in witchcraft, but she sure wasn't a shining light of goodness.

"Wellington?" Suzanne said the name as if it were a question.

Stan looked around the room. Nobody owned up to that name before. Not that he could blame them. Who'd name their kid Wellington? He started to scoff, but the intensity of the narrowed eyes and defiant visage of the teenager who sat across from him sobered Stan's momentary levity. Ah, yes, the kid who, during their introductions, claimed his name was Snake. This particular kid, this Wellington, reeked of trouble. Not that that was a problem. Stan made sure he landed on top any time he wrestled with trouble. *Wellington* was just a little twerp.

Stan waited until Wellington took his new seat before he

turned around so that he could sit backwards and rest his arms over the back of the chair. He liked officer intimidation.

Suzanne walked over and said, "I don't think you can sign very well with your hands in the air like that." She didn't wait for a reply.

Repositioned in his seat, Stan looked up to see a derisive sneer on Wellington's face, probably a defensive measure intended to draw the viewer's attention away from the blotchy patches of acne that dotted his pallid skin. The kid's intense almond-shaped eyes gleamed with satisfaction. Stan didn't know whether to describe them as brown or black, but the grayish flecks dotting the edges of Wellington's irises were reminiscent of liquid mercury—a toxic element, just like the kid.

Stan started to clench his hands, but a more amusing form of wrestling came to mind. He studied his handouts, the ones with the thirteen letters they reviewed tonight, along with drawings of the hand movements.

He could manage three letters. A smile tugged at his lips as he signed, "G-O-O-F-O-F-F."

Stan's ASL partner didn't flinch. Wellington preserved his poker face, glanced at his paperwork, and responded, "D-I-E."

Heat and agitation crawled up Stan's neck and face. His reaction earned a close-mouthed grin from the teenager.

"D-O-G," Stan signed.

Wellington snuck another two-second peek at his notes before he signed, "O-I," followed by a letter Stan didn't recognize.

When Wellington repeated his gestures, Stan scanned the page that depicted the signs for the second half of the alphabet. After a long minute, he found it. Yep. Wellington wanted to play.

"O-I-N-K?" Stan signed.

Wellington pulled in the sides of his mouth until his lips parted with a noisy pop.

Just to prove he could employ the same technique as the arrogant teenager—the finger spelling, not the facial contortions—Stan signed, "P-U-N-K," and underscored his choice of words by tipping up his chin.

A scoff and an eyeball roll accompanied Wellington's reply, "J-A-C-K-A—"

Juanita—where did she come from?—reached out and slapped Wellington's hand as he started to form another letter. Her face was angry, her mouth drawn into a tight line. Same look Stan encountered from her when they held their little counseling session in Acting Captain Hollister's office. It was nice not to be on the receiving end this time.

Juanita spun around and stuck her index finger an inch away from Stan's face, which motivated Morrison to stride over in quick time. Although the pastor loomed over Wellington, dimples framed the teenager's smug, I-don't-care leer at Stan.

"Something wrong, Juanita?" Morrison motioned to Suzanne to join them.

"What's up?" Suzanne asked.

As Juanita's hands flew, Suzanne's pleasant expression evaporated, and with obvious reluctance she translated for the man of the cloth. "It looks like these bright students have learned to communicate quite effectively."

Morrison ran his tongue along his upper lip. "And?"

Suzanne hesitated. Before she answered, she directed her attention to the back of the room where Stan's children sat with Izzy. "Let's just say that their vocabulary leaves a lot to be desired. They need to up their game to a civil level."

Suzanne gave Stan a break. Because of his kids. Why hadn't he given them a thought? The little punk got the best of him tonight, no question about it. Stan wouldn't let that happen again.

"You're right," Stan said. "I apologize."

Morrison looked at Wellington. "What about you?"

Wellington looked at his watch before he folded his arms and said, "Not a chance." He checked the time again, stood, and stretched his arms over his head.

"Where do you think you're going?" Morrison asked.

"My ride's here."

"Class isn't over. Sit down."

Wellington curled up one side of his mouth as he said, "Uh, yeah, it is."

A high-pitched whine preceded a flash of light so intense that it lit up the interior of the building as much as it did the night sky. Screams erupted throughout the classroom. Beyond the window, a plume of white-hot sparks lifted into the air, and a resounding boom rattled the glass. Chairs toppled over as people ran toward the door.

"Daddy," Lauren shrieked as she ran across the room, Tyler right behind her.

"Stay calm," Norris shouted. "Don't panic. Into the hallway. Hurry."

Trembling, Lauren and Tyler, leaped into their father's arms. Stan held them fast as he turned to Morrison and said, "Keep everyone inside and away from the windows. Call 911. Kids, stay here." Stan released his grip, torn between his professional and paternal duties. It was Juanita who swept his children into her arms. Stan motioned to Norris and yelled, "Let's go."

Stan scanned the faces of the people cowering in the hallway. The last thing that registered before he ran out of the building was that Wellington, aka The Snake, was long gone.

Eight

Zach righted a chair and pushed it in line with the other ten chairs he and Craig had already picked up from the floor and put back in place. The incandescent ceiling lights glared against the glossy tile floor, a stark contrast to the dark shadows that skimmed between the faint glows of the distant parking lot lights.

Although silence hung heavy in the air, the malicious incident levied a greater weight to Zach's spirit. How much more so for the man who gathered pieces of papers strewn across the floor?

"You ever think of leaving this neighborhood?" Zach asked.

"Why? Do you?"

"Hadn't. Not until I got Izzy's frantic call. When Juanita and I decided to move into my folks' old place, we knew things were different—a lot different—from when I grew up here. We decided to be vigilant while we tried to do our part to make this a safer place again."

"And now?" Craig asked.

Zach stood over the table next to the window, the one nearest the dumpster, and picked up one of Izzy's drawings. Colorful bands of chalk faded into each other with startling effect. His girl had talent. He eyed the window again. Tonight Izzy had been in harm's way. Juanita too.

"Now? I'm angry, although not nearly as much as Juanita is. She's spitting mad and more determined than ever to dig in her heels. We're not going anywhere, I promise you."

"Good."

Zach inched up his shoulders and puffed out his chest. "Her bodyguard will accompany her for the duration of this ASL class."

Craig lifted the left side of his sports coat and patted the area under his arm. "Me and Miss Mabel? We've got your backs."

Mabel. The agreed-upon code word to alert a few chosen church members that someone in the proximity had a gun. Zach had mixed feelings about his spiritual leader arming himself. The congregation was not privy to that particular detail, but more than a handful had to suspect their cautious leader intended to protect his congregation in whatever manner he found necessary.

"Will you let Izzy come back? Benton's two kids bonded with her like pastrami takes to rye. Like whipped cream belongs on sweet potato pie."

"You hungry?" Zach asked.

Craig patted his belly. "Guesso. Didn't have time to eat, but Yolanda promised to keep my dinner warm." He looked at the wall clock and tsk'd. "That pastrami is probably dried up worse than beef jerky." His eyes shimmered when he said, "Pie's probably still good, though. I ought to get on home."

Zach tucked Izzy's artwork under his arm and gripped her box of pastels with one hand while he turned out the light. He followed Craig down the hallway, watched as he set the alarm, and followed the man into the crisp night air. The stink of burned trash hovered over the landscape. Remnants of the fire department's call to action formed a slick puddle around the charred metal container.

"Hard to believe that a cherry bomb could do so much damage," Zach said as they crossed the parking lot.

"Bad timing," Craig replied. "Yolanda said it was time to update all the props and decorations they use for the children's plays. Couple of days ago we tossed out a mountain of stuff. Apparently, it was highly flammable stuff."

"You think one of the teens had something to do with this?"

"I don't like to jump to conclusions, but I suspect the perpetrator's accomplice looked me in the face at the same time his friend lit the fuse."

When he reached his car, which sat a few spaces away from the pastor's van, Zach unlocked the door, but stopped before he climbed inside. "I can't believe having two cops in the class didn't serve as a deterrent."

"All the more reason for the thugs to brag about their caper. This particular student doesn't seem to care about consequences. The scariest kids are the ones who have no qualms about throwing someone's life away because they don't place any value on their own." Craig ducked his head and slid into his van.

Zach climbed into his car, turned the key, and stared into the darkness while the engine warmed. He watched Craig back up and drive across the empty parking lot. Zach put his car in gear and followed the same path.

Before he pulled into the roadway, he looked in his rearview mirror. Spotlights illuminated the face and sides of the building. A brighter light over the front door, along with the overtly displayed security camera, served as a warning for would-be thieves.

Zach checked the street for oncoming traffic before he lifted his foot from the brake pedal, and then ran his eyes over the church property one last time. What didn't fit the scene was the bobbing light that bounced off the windows at the side of the building.

With his heart picking up its tempo and his eyes glued to the intermittent flashes of light, he grabbed his cell phone. The useless phone went dead earlier when Juanita called to confirm that she and Izzy were safely back at their house. Zach scowled at the blank screen and dropped the phone onto the passenger seat. No way would he permit another incident to damage or disrupt this house of worship.

He shifted the car into park, slipped out the door, and shut it with what he hoped was a muffled shove. He couldn't have made too much noise. The prowler's flashlight still swung back and forth in the same area next to the building where he first saw it.

Zach pulled his coat collar up and hunched his shoulders, as much to protect himself from the wind as to hide his pale face. He tiptoed to the front of the building and inched along a line of bushes that wrapped around the corner. If he survived his unwise impulse to protect property instead of his person, he'd tell Craig to get rid of the greenery. The shrubs made a good hiding place.

When he crouched down and peeked around the corner, the person with the flashlight was in the same place. Still. Did the hoodlum want to break in or did he hope to execute some form of exterior vandalism? Regardless of intent, it was time for Zach to take action. He pulled the flashlight that he kept in the car for emergencies out of his pocket. The little LEDs might be bright, but the device was anything but fearsome. Surprise and good acting might be in Zach's favor.

He raced around the corner, turned the flashlight's beam on the interloper, and yelled, "Freeze."

The person, stooped over and facing away from Zach, did just that. Froze. Slowly, two hands reached upward.

"Show yourself." Zach used the tone of voice the detectives on TV used when they barked orders to the accused. Or so it sounded to him. Except for the slight quaver, anyway.

"I'm not armed."

Zach tripped over his next command as the prowler's voice reached his ears. "T-t-turn around."

As the trespasser obeyed, Zach directed his flashlight to the person's face. In response, she closed her eyes and turned her head. Zach's heart thudded in his chest. Now what? More good acting? "Officer Norris?" he asked, his voice suddenly sheepish instead of loaded with bravado.

"Who wants to know?"

"Uh, it's me." He lowered the light until the beam settled on her shoes. When he gathered the courage he needed to raise his eyes, her expression confused him. The animated laughter that followed confounded him more.

"Zach Hoyt," Holly said. Her expression changed from amused to sober over the course of about five seconds. "What are you doing?" Her new tone of voice was far too familiar. Peeved. Impatient.

"Huh?"

"What are you doing?"

"Running off a troublemaker. You?"

"Me?" Holly let out a windy, "Pfft. When I got home, I discovered I'd lost an earring. I came back here to see if I could find it."

The look on Holly's face forced Zach to choke back his guffaw. The effort to curtail the action brought tears to his eyes. She was serious. Okay then. He spun around and scanned the parking lot. "Where's you car?"

"Parked on the side street. It's closer to this side of the building."

Zach didn't get it. Why not wait until daylight? "You're looking for an earring in the dark. In a not-so-nice neighborhood."

"Hey, I'm a cop. I'm fearless."

"No you're not."

"I'm too tired to argue, Hoyt. I'm fearless. End of discussion."

"Why don't you look for the earring tomorrow when it's daylight? And warmer."

"The earrings belonged to my mom. Passed down several generations before she inherited them. The set was one of the few things the family didn't leave behind when they ran from the Nazis during the war." Her sigh stole some of Zach's insensitive posture.

"What's it look like? I'll help."

She waved him off. "I'm sure it's gone. Too many people trampled over this property after the cherry bomb went off. Come on. Both of us need to go home."

"In a minute. Do you have a cell phone?" Zach asked.

"Yeah."

Zach pointed to Holly's left ear. "Is that the other half of the missing pair?"

She reached up and fingered the gold earring. "Yeah."

"Give me your phone and let me take a picture of it."

"What? No."

When Zach held out his hand, she relented and passed

her phone to him. When he finished taking a picture, he lowered the phone so she could watch as he selected her messaging icon, entered his phone number, and sent the picture to his dead cell phone.

He handed the phone back and said, "I'll forward a copy to Pastor Morrison in the morning and ask him if he can have someone scour the grounds for you."

"You don't need to do that."

"Sure I do. It's your job to protect and defend. Part of my personal mission is uncovering things."

"What do you mean?"

"You know. Exposing the devil's lies, sharing the truth of the scriptures, finding family heirlooms. Stuff."

Puzzlement settled over Holly's features, but she seemed to shake it off when she answered with a simple, "Thanks."

"For what?" Zach asked.

"For choosing not to shoot me with your flashlight. For offering to help. Thanks."

"You knew I wasn't armed?"

"Your 'freeze' carried more vibrato than a string bass."

"Hey now."

"Before I go, you might want to thank me," Holly said.

"Hmm. For what?"

"For letting you return to your family with your body intact."

"Huh?"

"I lied. About not being armed." As the wind lifted Holly's snicker, it resounded into the darkened skies.

Nine

"But, Daddy, I don't want to go to Miss Opal's house. She's mean and her house smells 'cause she's got six cats."

"And four rabbits," mumbled Tyler as he crinkled his nose.

Stan helped Lauren into the back seat and waited while she and Tyler secured their seatbelts. This Monday evening was as messed up as the last one. A late call from Tina included an unexpected need for transportation for the children and a venom-laced warning about his need to follow directions.

"Sorry, Sunshine, but I don't have a choice," Stan replied.

When he took the kids home from the first class, Stan had to tell Tina about the incident at New Life Chapel. She seemed more upset about his taking them to church than about the fire in the dumpster. How was he to know she loathed religion? They never talked about it. Neither of them had the need nor the desire to enter that territory.

Still, all these years later, Tina remained an enigma. Or, maybe it was women in general who baffled him. All Stan knew was that whenever he crossed paths with his ex-wife, he was in over his head. He couldn't win. No way. No how.

"Your mom has another group study session tonight and

she doesn't want you to go back to the church."

"But I liked it. Maybe Izzy will bring her chalk again." Lauren's high-pitched whine added to Stan's prickly mood.

"Yeah, Dad," Tyler said. "Can't you take us to the church? We won't tell."

"Guys, your mom plans to pick you up at Miss Opal's place. You can't trick her, and it's dishonest to try. If you pulled something like that on me, I'd be disappointed. You hear?"

"But I want to go to the church," Lauren crossed her arms and shoved her back against her seat.

Before Stan closed the car door, he leaned in and said, "Maybe we can buy you some chalk. Okay?" What a dumb thing for him to say. It wasn't as if he had the cash to do anything frivolous. He was broke, and had been since he met Tina and let her lead him away from his future. His empty pockets and late payment fees seemed like an eternal punishment for his adolescent blunder.

Lauren wore her pout while they travelled to the babysitter's house. Tyler didn't look mad, just resigned. Stan pulled up to the curb, but the darkened interior of the house and the empty driveway didn't bode well. He checked his watch. No, he wasn't early, and if he didn't get moving, he'd be late to the ASL class.

"Stay here."

No one answered when he rang the doorbell. When he knocked on the door, the only movement inside came in the form of a yellow cat that scooted onto the windowsill. Stan's irritation notched upward every time the feline licked its paws.

"You lookin' for Opal?"

Stan turned to see an elderly woman standing on the

front porch of the house next door.

"Yeah. Seen her?"

"She's playing Bingo. When she gets on a roll, sometimes she stays until they close down."

"What time do they close?" Stan asked.

"Midnight. Can I help you with something?" The skin around the woman's eyes wrinkled as she studied Stan's face.

"Uh. No. Thanks."

Stan dropped into the driver's seat and slammed his hand against the steering wheel.

"What's the matter?" Tyler asked.

"Looks like Miss Opal forgot about watching you."

Stan twisted around and looked at his children. Now what? Tina would pulverize him with a forty-minute tirade if he took them to New Life Chapel, but if he lost his job, she'd have his hide for that failure too. He couldn't win no matter what choice he made, but he needed a job a whole lot more than he needed his ego.

He pulled into traffic and headed toward the church. Tina would have to get over it. Didn't she know she could trust him to protect his own children? He was a cop, for Pete's sake.

When he drove into the parking lot, Lauren's face lit up like he'd just given her a new puppy.

"Come on. Class starts in three minutes."

Both children popped out of the car and started racing toward the door.

"Hold on. Get back here," Stan called. Once he lassoed his charges' enthusiasm, they walked to the entryway together. Zach Hoyt and a lanky teenage boy intercepted them on the sidewalk.

"Officer Benton. Nice to see you again."

Stan chewed on the words a second, but couldn't detect any insincerity. Maybe after last week's cherry bomb fiasco, Hoyt didn't want to thrash Stan quite as much as he did after their first encounter.

"Hoyt." Stan nodded.

Hoyt jostled the teen's shoulder. "This is my son Conner."

"Nice to meet you," Stan said. "This is Lauren and this is Tyler."

"I heard about you two," Conner said.

Tyler frowned. "Like what?"

Stan winced. His son's posture and attitude resembled his dad's—to a *T*.

"Izzy told me about your artwork."

Conner, who must have sensed Lauren's confusion, said, "She's my sister." He narrowed his eyes and looked at Tyler when he said, "*Baby* sister. Know what I mean?"

Tyler dropped his tough guy stance and giggled.

"You joining the class tonight?" Stan asked Hoyt.

"Naw. We have security detail."

Ah, yes, that pesky little necessity, the one that induced Tina to forbid Stan to do exactly what he was doing right now. "Well, we need to get inside. Nice to meet you, Conner"

Lauren danced on tiptoes after they descended the stairs to the lower level. When they reached the classroom, she didn't give her old dad a second glance. Although Tyler looked as anxious to draw as his sister did, he donned his "I'm cool" manner and strutted across the room with as much style as any eight-year-old could muster.

"Welcome back, everyone," Suzanne said. "Juanita and I hope you all had a chance to talk with your hands this week. How did you do? Anyone?"

Dan, the realtor, raised his hand. Instead of a verbal answer, he stood up and signed "G-O-O-D" before he took an exaggerated bow.

Several people clapped, including the enthusiastic teachers, and a couple voiced their approval with a "Woohoo," but Dan's actions drew ridicule from the teenagers. The only practice Stan had during the week was when neither he nor Norris was driving the squad car. In those moments, his obnoxious partner insisted they practice forming letters. Even now, as she stared at him from her seat across the room, he wanted to slug her.

"Anyone else?" Suzanne asked. "Zoe? How about you?"

Miss Attitude stopped filing her nails, a short-lived acknowledgment that she'd heard someone speak her name.

"How did your practicing go?"

"Great," Zoe answered. Her voice was flat and mechanical as she added. "Taught my pit bull the sign for 'food.' "

Except for Wellington's snort, silence fell over the room.

"I have a question." Dottie dressed and acted the part of one of those pleasant granny types who used to fill the screen of an old black and white TV. Stan could picture her toiling in a kitchen, wearing a frilly apron over a crisp cotton dress and a dusting of white flour on her cheekbones. Judging from her build, she liked to cook.

"Yes?" Suzanne asked.

"I signed up for this class because the courts awarded me custody of my granddaughter Paige, who is deaf. Up until now, I never had a chance to get to know her, but that's another story for another day. Paige is struggling with her relocation, and for now, we have to write notes to each other in order to communicate. She doesn't have friends here yet."

When Juanita flicked her hands faster than Stan could follow them, Suzanne said, "Juanita wants to know how we can help."

Dottie turned to Juanita. "Paige is thirteen, almost as old as Izzy. Izzy knows how to sign. Would you let me bring Paige to class with me so that she could spend some time with your daughter?"

When Juanita's eyes teared, the pain in her face buried Stan in discomfort. He cast his eyes downward. Norris was right. Wise Guy Stan didn't know anything.

Suzanne, who seemed close to losing her composure too, translated Juanita's answer. "I don't have to ask Izzy. I know how she'd reply. We'd love to have her. Please bring her next week."

As class kicked into gear, Stan strained to keep up. The second half of the alphabet was as foreign to him as was the first half, and Suzanne and Juanita planned to introduce phrases beginning next week. Suzanne promised that learning phrases, what she called shortcuts to everyday communication, would be easy. She said the same thing about the alphabet. Maybe he needed to pay more attention to Norris' plea to practice.

Wellington proved to be his congenial self during the practice-with-your-assigned-partner time. Access to the entire alphabet delighted the little snake, although he seemed fixated on four-letter words. Each time Stan wanted to answer in kind, he pictured his children sitting across the room. He didn't intend to earn Juanita's wrath again, nor did he need to embarrass Lauren and Tyler.

The Snake seemed to have trouble understanding Stan's greater-than-fourth-grade-level vocabulary, which Stan found rather amusing. For his next word, Stan began signing, "D-I-

S-C-I-P-L-I-N—"

Someone threw the door open with such force that papers blew off the top of the table and scattered across the floor. Stan leaned forward to catch a glimpse of the visitor. In return, he encountered an extreme case of venom and hatred. He swallowed hard and inhaled through his nostrils. He'd hoped for a more private scene, but this showy entrance might top all of Tina's former performances. He braced himself.

Tina pointed to the back of the room. "Lauren. Tyler. Get in the car. Now."

Stan closed his eyes. Better to let them escape than to witness the unraveling of his ex-wife. Tyler held Lauren's hand as he led her toward the door. When he paused in front of his daddy, Stan brushed the boy's arm with his hand and patted the top of Lauren's head.

"Go on," he whispered. "I'll get her to calm down. It's okay."

Tyler looked at his dad with disbelief, but tugged on Lauren's hand and said, "Come on." He led her into the hallway.

Intermittent murmuring from the others in the classroom implied that they pretended not to have noticed the simmering spectacle. Aside from a cough, a nervous titter, and a few chairs scraping the floor, the rest of the world moved along as if normal.

Morrison, who'd not said a word all evening, stayed in his corner near the door. He looked disappointed. Weary.

Tina strode over to Stan and towered over him. Her handbag, the size and heft of which could knock him senseless, swayed at her hip—and at his eye level.

She leaned forward and put her finger in his face. A burst

of saliva accompanied her first words. "I warned you."

"Opal wasn't home. I had to bring them. I didn't have a choice."

Tina glared at him. So far, he'd put up with the tirade pretty well, but with every button she pushed, Stan's blood pressure climbed. He felt the veins on his neck respond. Walk away. He had to walk away. How? Push past her? Past the pastor? The longer Tina stared, the more acute was his rage.

Finally, she straightened up and with a tone of utter disdain she said, "You'll hear from my lawyer, you jerk." She spun on her heels and started for the door.

Stan arose from his chair and followed her. He was furious, but Tina needed to diffuse her anger before she drove home. A private conversation with the woman might provoke her more, but he told Tyler he'd fix things. Stan had about two seconds to come up with something.

Tina stomped to the door, but jerked to a stop when she encountered Morrison, who blocked her exit. He stood in the middle of the doorway, and although he still had his arms folded over his chest, instead of looking tired, his face displayed a deep sorrow. Tina started tapping her foot while she waited for him to get out of her way. He didn't budge.

"Tina?" The pastor's voice was soft, like a soothing brush of the wind. "Tina Hastings?"

Stan balked. Morrison knew Tina? Since when?

Tina narrowed her eyes. She didn't answer.

"Been a while."

A muscle in Tina's cheek twitched.

"How long?"

Stan could almost hear Tina's teeth grinding. He'd never seen her turn on anyone else before. Not like this. She reserved this treatment for Stan Benton.

Stan had to lean forward to hear her response. Tina set her wrath on the pastor's eyes and locked in on her target when she said, "I haven't stepped foot in this place since I got knocked up and you and your self-righteous congregation turned their backs on me."

Morrison's eyes widened. He looked past Tina and studied Stan. "Is this . . ."

"My mistake?" Tina said. "The biggest one I ever made." As she stepped forward, Morrison stepped back. Tina slipped through the narrow opening and stormed out of the room.

"I'm sorry," Stan said. He lifted his hands and splayed his fingers.

"Come walk with me for a while."

The rest of the building was quiet except for two pairs of shoes tapping against the linoleum floor. Stan followed the pastor upstairs and into the back of the sanctuary. The security lights from outside the building glinted through the windows.

They took a seat at the back of the room and sat in silence for a while. Stan's heartbeat, which hammered an agitated rhythm in his ear, slowed. Neither of the men moved when voices crept into the nearby hallway, lingered momentarily, and then faded away.

"Tina Hastings. Girl broke my heart. Tore up my flock." Morrison exposed his empathy when he turned toward Stan and said, "Looks like she messed you up pretty good too."

"That's an understatement."

"I heard she got married, had a son, then a daughter. Beautiful children, by the way."

"Thanks. I miss them."

"I suppose you do. Divorce exacts a toll on everyone." Morrison paused for a moment before he said, "It looks as if you could use some help."

"With Tina? Help? I need a miracle."

"Then it looks like you've come to the right place. Funny how God works things out. You thought you needed to come to an ASL class." Morrison pointed heavenward and said, "Looks like He might have something else in mind entirely. Uh huh."

Stan didn't have the energy to argue, to explain why that little revelation didn't apply to him. Instead of answering with the disrespectful "whatever" that lay in wait at the tip of his tongue, he murmured, "Hmm."

"My door's always open."

"Good to know. Thanks." Stan's gratitude might be more genuine if he could just go home and bury this miserable night in a bottle of beer.

The men left the sanctuary and walked toward the double doors at the front of the church. The hallway lights to the lower level were off. Exit signs over the doors emitted a faint red glow.

"Looks like you're the last one. Before I set the alarm, I need to do my circuit through the building."

"Want me to stay until you're through?" Stan asked.

"No. I do this every night. But thanks for offering. You go on home and mull over the miracle request. You hear?"

"I hear you. Good night."

Stan walked out into the dank night air. A fickle wind wrapped around his neck, only to disappear without a trace. His warm breath left a foggy trail as he walked to his car. He plopped into his seat and started to turn his key. Something, though, was out of kilter. Impatient fists wrapped around the steering wheel while he assessed the unfamiliar sensation.

When a car turned at the nearby intersection, its

headlights glanced off Stan's windshield. He might have blamed the damage on his deranged ex-wife, but she wouldn't have known how he would respond to the four-letter word smudged on his windshield.

Stan didn't bother to examine the tire; he knew it was beyond repair. He popped the trunk open, dragged out his tire iron, and lugged the little donut-sized spare to the passenger side of the car. A good cop knows how to change a tire in a matter of minutes. It would take more than a minute and probably three or four beers before he could bury his anger.

He slammed the trunk shut, fired up the engine, and glared at the message on the windshield as he pulled out of the parking lot: H-I-S-S.

Ten

Juanita scrunched her face as a brisk wind attempted to numb the tip of her tingling nose. After she caught up with Zach, she lowered her bicycle's kickstand and wiggled her frozen fingers in an attempt to regain some movement of their joints. She managed to grab a tissue from her pocket to press against her frozen skin. Sniffles caught up with her as she dabbed her watery eyes.

When the two left the house, the late-in-the-season outing sounded exhilarating, but as the easy breeze gained strength and the sun slipped behind a small mass of clouds, the ride to the park became more challenging than pleasurable.

By the time Juanita joined Zach at the picnic table, he'd poured a cup of tea. He held it out to her as the hot liquid released swirls of steam into the atmosphere. She signed, "Thanks," before she put greedy fingers around the vessel. The warmth to her hands was as welcome as the ginger and lemon tea was to her throat.

Zach poured a second cup for himself and took a sip before he unwrapped a pair of honey wheat bagels from their paper coverings. Juanita opened a plastic container and used a flimsy plastic knife to apply a generous layer of cream cheese.

She bit into the chewy roll and released a long sigh when the indecisive sun chose to drench the land with its welcome rays once again.

After consuming half of the bagel, Juanita flexed her defrosted fingers and signed, "We talked so long about Stan Benton's wife showing up at class that I forgot to ask you what you were doing last night."

"What do you mean?" Zach asked.

"You and Conner paced outside the window in front of the classroom a hundred times. You looked like toy soldiers, not security men." Juanita took her index and middle fingers and thrummed them on the park bench, mimicking stiff legs walking.

"We weren't searching for lawbreakers. We were treasure hunting."

"You were pirates instead of soldiers?"

"Yes, ma'am. Looking for gold."

"Find any?" Juanita signed.

"Matter of fact . . ." Zach lowered the zipper on his jacket and reached into an interior pocket, and when he withdrew his hand, he hovered his closed fist over Juanita's cup. "Wanna see?"

She opened her hand, and her mouth too, when Zach dropped a heavy gold earring into her palm.

"You found this? Looks expensive," Juanita signed.

"Might be," Zach said. "Definitely has sentimental value."

How would he know that?

"It belongs to Holly Norris."

When Juanita responded with a perplexed expression, Zach said, "She lost it last week when they went after the cherry bomb bomber."

Cherry bomb bomber. Juanita couldn't hear Zach's

rendition of his terminology, but she saw hesitation in his lips as he formed the words *bomb bomber.* His playful eyes told her that he thought himself rather cute. And that, he was.

"I didn't think we'd find it, but Conner and I didn't have anything else to do while we defended the church and all its occupants."

When Juanita started to return the earring, Zach didn't open his hand. "I didn't catch her before she left last night. I know you'll see her in class next week. Will you give it to her for me?"

"Yes," Juanita signed. She flinched when, out of the corner of her eye, she saw something move. She searched the treetops until she found the culprit, and followed the bird as it hoisted itself from the limb of an ancient oak tree. When she grabbed Zach's arm to get his attention, his gaze followed her pointed finger.

In a mighty display of power, the avian wonder climbed skyward in search of unsuspecting prey. After the majestic neighborhood stalker stretched its huge wings, it dipped and circled back. The early morning sun glanced off the tip of its feathers, producing a flash of color as brilliant as the earring's spun gold.

Juanita couldn't hear the rush of wind that held the golden eagle aloft, but as the bird soared above her and made its journey across the landscape, a ground-level breeze brushed her hair away from her face. Then, just as unexpectedly as he had appeared, the eagle disappeared from view.

"I've thought a lot about Nancy and Mae and the basket weaving retreat they plan to attend."

Zach's jovial demeanor transitioned into serious territory. The thin lines etched around his mouth deepened, a trait that often exposed his anxiety. Where others might gain that insight by the tone or pitch of a voice, Juanita discovered Zach's moods—his glee, his joy, his misgivings, his anger—with subtle visual variations. She imagined she was aware of the nuances, while he was not.

"I spent a lot of time the past couple of weeks researching these retreats. Nancy's right. People pay a pretty penny to attend them, and to hear Nancy and Mae talk, most of the participants spend a ton of money buying supplies while they're hyped up by the classes and the other weavers."

Zach's words picked up speed as he shared his information, but if he was excited about something, why did he wear worry across his forehead?

"If we could find a venue, a place with a big open room, good lighting, plenty of parking, and in close proximity to affordable hotels, we could have one here."

"We? You want *The Basket Works* to sponsor a workshop?"

"We need to do something. The business is limping along but each step seems to lag behind the last. Supply costs went up, but Dad didn't raise prices to his customers. When that lame manager he hired started scrimping on new purchases, the weavers found other suppliers. Now we have to write off a bunch of old inventory."

The creases in Zach's face deepened. When he caught Juanita studying him, he turned away and pretended to fumble with the thermos lid.

She tapped his arm and signed, "Are we in trouble? Do I need to take more editing work?"

"You already have more to do than you can handle. We're not in trouble-trouble, but we're hurting."

Trouble-trouble? That clever term lacked the whimsical

delivery of Zach's bomb bomber.

"Listen," he said.

Juanita cupped her ears with her hands and mouthed, "What? I can't hear you." Her attempt at humor earned an insincere shake of Zach's head.

"Yeah, you're cute. But let me be serious. Hosting a retreat might help us earn back our customers. Dad never made a lot of money with *The Basket Works*, but he did okay, and with the right marketing strategy, we can too."

"If this is such a good idea, why do you seem upset?" Juanita signed.

"I'm not upset, but we have an obstacle or two."

"What?"

"In order to pull this off, we'll have to front the money for deposits on the venue, and we'll need to invest in a sizable inventory purchase."

"How much money do we need?"

"More than we have."

"I'll get more editing contracts."

"You'd have to edit around the clock to fill the gap," Zach said. When his mouth pulled into an apologetic grimace, Juanita's cautious optimism deflated before she could plug the leak. "I have an idea, but you won't like it. Will you hear me out?" Zach's countenance failed to convey any degree of confidence.

Juanita wanted to cup her hands over her ears again, and close her eyes too.

"We could borrow against Conner's college funds."

"No," Juanita signed.

"Just for a couple of months. We'd put it back by late spring. It'll be there for fall."

"No." Juanita sat up straighter and made the gesture

larger than the first time she shared it.

"We have to make a go of this business. I need you to think about it. Let's pray about it. Together." Zach reached over and grasped Juanita's hand.

Pray about it? Yes, she'd pray that Zach would come to his senses and pretend he never brought the question to the surface. Juanita could not let Zach divert Conner's future. It was too precious. Just as quickly as they rerouted the funds to the business, no matter how temporary the intention, the promise of college, like the golden eagle, had the potential to disappear.

Juanita signed, "I'll pray about it," and she would. She had no qualms about her petition because the only possible answer to Zach's request and her prayer would be no. No. No!

~

Zach stared at the assortment of products sitting in front of him, but it was Mae's delighted smirk that tickled his wariness. If not for the plate of snickerdoodle cookies resting in the center of the table, he might beg off the class time.

"Ready, boss?" Mae asked.

He was absolutely not ready, nor was he particularly willing. "Let's get started," he replied.

Mae pointed to a neat stack of cut material and said, "This wide reed will make up the base and sides of the basket. We call these spokes. Some folks, particularly some of those persnickety Nantucket Lightship Basket weavers, call them staves."

She redirected her aim to several hanks of reed, some flat, some round, and some with the trademark curve of flat oval reed. Zach knew the lingo; he needed to understand basic basketry construction—and his customers' love of the art, even more so.

"The reed that goes around the sides and makes up the wall of the basket is called a weaver."

For more than two hours, Zach followed Mae's instructions. This weaving process, in some respects, was easier than he imagined, but a few steps challenged his patience. His hands fumbled as he followed her directives to cut and tuck the ends of the spokes, actions that didn't turn out to be the last of the procedures, as he had hoped. By the time Mae taught him how to lash the rim, she probably wanted to throttle him.

"You mumble more than any student I ever taught," Mae said.

"I'm almost finished. Be kind to me," Zach said as he missed his target and stabbed a tool against his fingertip. He pulled his hand back, licked his wound, and tried again. Eventually, he snipped off some excess reed, held up his prize, and declared, "Voilà."

"Not bad for your first one," Mae said. "I was beginning to wonder if I had to run back home and bake another batch of cookies just to get you through this." She looked at the ceiling as she basked in what Zach perceived as unrestrained gloating.

He examined his work, turning it around and inspecting it top to bottom. "So what's the draw? Where does the passion to weave, as you and Nancy call it, enter into this?"

"Most of us have a hefty sense of satisfaction in completing a piece of art in just a few hours."

Piece of art? This? It wasn't bad, but Zach didn't think he'd win any State Fair prizes for his efforts. Mae seemed to gauge his less-than-enthusiastic response.

"Don't you do anything creative?"

Zach's nanosecond self-inventory ended with, "Uh."

"Do you paint? Draw?"

He raised his brows and batted his eyes.

"Build things? Work with wood?"

"My dad had a wood shop. Didn't interest me. I was kind of into sports. Still am."

"My daughter doesn't make anything either. Drives me crazy because she doesn't understand the satisfaction that comes from producing something with her hands." Mae ended her opinion with a mumbled, "Doesn't appreciate the effort either."

"Sorry." Had he done that? Failed to recognize someone's talents and accomplishments? Images of a younger Izzy materialized, her face beaming while she showed her dad a new drawing displayed on the refrigerator. Had he added to her delight or passed it by as inconsequential?

He heard the echo of his own, "Good job," pat-on-the-back he bestowed on Conner with each grade card he brought home. Zach expected high marks from his son, but he neglected to celebrate them with the sincerity they deserved. And what of Juanita? Zach banished the mental snapshots, fearful of the list his slights to Juanita might generate. He suppressed the uncomfortable pang of regret and turned his attention back to his instructor.

Mae picked up a small catalogue from a nearby desk, opened it, and spread it on the table in front of Zach. "When you got online and looked at weaving retreats, did you bother to look at their course selections?" As she said the word *bother*, her question held a dash of accusation.

Zach grabbed a cookie and took a bite. He brushed

crumbs off the table and settled his gaze on the open pages. He skirted the question with, "Those look a little more difficult than the one I just made."

His comment earned a snort. "Your project was for a beginner, and there's nothing wrong with that, but look at this basket, or that one." Mae pointed to two pictures. "These require a level of expertise that would earn them a spot on a museum shelf. And look at this one," Mae said as she turned the page. "It's beautiful. Intricate. This little number has the power to baffle the most serious weavers."

"Why would anyone pay good money to do something exasperating?"

When Mae's arms crossed and wrapped around her middle, Zach leaned away from her.

"Let's try an analogy," Mae said as she lowered her hands to her hips. "You went to sports camps when other kids had the summer off. They played around the pool, slept late, ate whatever they wanted."

"Yeah." Sports and basket weaving held little in common. No, they had nothing in common. What was the woman's point?

"You and your teammates got up early, sweated and practiced through the heat and humidity of a Midwest summer. You had a curfew. You didn't dare pig out on junk food because you knew it would affect your performance."

"Pretty accurate."

"Why did you do those things?"

"I wanted to make the team. I wanted to win."

"Did you finish the camps and the summers with more skill than when you started?"

"Uh, yes."

Mae reached across the table and helped herself to a

cookie. After she swallowed a small bite she asked, "How did that make you feel?"

Who cared about then? Right now, with his face and neck turning a deep shade of humble-pie-red, Zach felt like a ten-year-old. "Okay. I get it. I'm not passionate or attached to the basket weaving process, but I understand determination and wanting to be a better player."

Mae finished eating her cookie before she added, "You don't have to share the enthusiasm, but you need to capture it and reward it with a product that is worthy of a weaver's time and money."

"Agreed. With my passion for all things customer related, I want to proceed with putting a workshop together."

"Good." Mae reached into a pocket on her apron and pulled out a piece of paper. As she unfolded it and smoothed the creases, she said, "Nancy and I made a list of people who might be willing to teach a class on short notice."

"We're talking about four or five months from now," Zach replied.

Mae lowered her chin and looked at Zach over the tops of her glasses. "That is short notice."

"Oh."

"If you need her to teach, Nancy said she'd consider half-day classes with easy projects for beginners."

"Great. What about you?" Zach asked.

"You think I have what it takes to put up with a group of students?" Mae snorted again.

Zach started to comment, but clamped his jaw shut. Point taken.

"We made a list of inventory you might want to get back in stock between now and then."

Although Mae handed Zach a single piece of paper,

handwriting filled two columns. He scanned the sheet, but his determination floundered when he turned the paper over and discovered a second set of columns on the other side. "All of this?"

When Mae tilted her head and pressed her lips together, Zach cringed. How would he pull off an order this size?

Mae reached into her apron pocket again. "Here's a list of some places we might rent for the retreat, along with the dates they have open." She pulled her lips into a pucker and said, "You may want to read that after you've had a chance to digest the inventory sheet."

"Thanks for doing my homework for me." Zach scratched the back of his head and sighed. When he glanced at the clock he said, "Time for you to call it a day. Thanks for the lesson, too. The snickerdoodles were the best part, you know."

"I stashed another dozen at the house. I'll bring you one or two tomorrow if you promise you'll take one more weaving lesson. You don't know everything yet."

"For your cookies? You bet."

Zach followed Mae to the door and watched as she climbed into her car and drove away. When he returned to the worktable, he dropped into his chair and stuck his elbows on the table. While he rested his chin in his hands, his gaze ran past the inventory list and landed on the folded piece of paper. He sat up straight, leaned back, and braced himself for the second set of figures. As his mind absorbed the cost to rent a suitable space, he choked.

This brilliant save-the-business endeavor wouldn't require a small loan from Conner's college funds. Not at all. Instead, it demanded something in the neighborhood of every single dime they'd set aside for his freshmen and sophomore years.

How could Zach ask Juanita for her blessing? She'd never be able to read his lips because he couldn't say the sum aloud.

Eleven

"You can't fool them. They'll know." Norris pulled the patrol car up to the stoplight and braked. She released the steering wheel and methodically signed the letters, T-H-E-Y-W-I-L-L-K-N-O-W.

"They all look alike," Stan replied. When Norris started to express herself with her hands again, he pointed to the traffic light. "Just drive."

"It's not right to deceive your own children."

"It doesn't count if I do it to protect them."

"When they catch you lying—and they will—they'll think they can pick and choose when they tell the truth."

"They won't know. Give it a rest," Stan said.

Norris gave him a dirty look before she crossed the intersection and headed back toward the precinct. "I have zero tolerance for lying. You know that."

"I'm not lying to you."

"You don't get it. Tell me something. Did they name the fish?"

"Miss Fulgermuffin."

"That's creative. Fulgermuffin. It implies your deceased goldfish was on the overweight side. Probably a pleasant, let-me-blow-kisses-at-you-while-I-swim-around-the-tank kind of pet."

"What are you talking about?" Stan asked. His morning started way before Norris made it to the station. He found an auto service center that opened hours earlier than the general population arose from bed, and drove his wobbly car into the place on its miniature tire. If not for the good news that The Snake didn't slice, dice, or stab the tire, Stan would have written the day off before the sun lit up the cityscape.

Who would have thought that Wellington had a heart big enough to deflate, rather than to destroy? The slithery reptile was more of a garden-variety nuisance than a deadly cobra, which was not to say that the little twerp didn't achieve his anger-inducing objective. That, he did with aplomb.

As their shift ended and the two parted ways in the employee parking lot, Norris insisted on one more lecture when she said, "Don't do it, Benton."

"Tell you what." Stan took off his hat and ran his fingers across his shaved head. A fine stubble of regrowth, in all places except the naturally balding and expanding spot, reminded him he needed an appointment with his barber. "Tomorrow morning when you ask me how much my children enjoyed their evening with their dad, I intend to use the same sanctimonious voice that you've thrown at me all day." He donned his hat and gave her the "get lost" pained expression he used to use on his sister.

Pain was an understatement. First he had to drive to the pet store, which was a half-mile from his apartment, then he had to retrace his steps to the opposite side of town to retrieve Tyler and Lauren. At each stoplight he eyed the downward direction of the orange indicator on the gas gauge.

Priorities. The goldfish was a no-brainer, and although a replacement was cheap, the ride and the fresh batch of fish food emptied his pockets of a few dollars and some coins. The gas tank? He wouldn't be able to ignore it after tomorrow, for sure. Stan glided his fingertips over his head again. Last time he had to run the razor over his sensitive skin himself, he whimpered like a baby. With luck, and unwelcome practice, maybe he'd suffer fewer nicks this time.

Having finished his errands, including the introduction of the surrogate Miss Fulgermuffin to the fish tank, he made his way to Tina's place. He pulled around the corner, started to pull into the first driveway, and slammed the brakes. Tina's old four-door sedan sat in its usual place alongside the white clapboard house she and the children had rented since Stan and Tina's marriage fizzled.

Stan backed up his car, grateful he hadn't hit the blue SUV parked behind Tina's car, and pulled up to the curb. Fizzled? No, that wasn't an apt description. He inspected the outside of the SUV as he got out of his car, and as he walked along the driveway he scanned the contents and the condition of the interior.

His union with Tina heated up long and hot, and eventually burst in spontaneous combustion. Somehow, they survived the explosion, although the wounded pair bore only a vague resemblance to the couple who married in the first place. Their having survived the eruption was incomprehensible, given its ferocity.

"You planning to take pictures?"

So engrossed was Stan with the unfamiliar SUV that he hadn't noticed the sour-faced man leaning against the front porch railing. The guy was slight in build, wore large-framed wire-rimmed glasses, and dressed like a prissy college professor. His skin was the shade of unfinished mahogany, but its translucent texture made him look rather sickly. He stood with his feet set apart and his arms folded across his scrawny chest. This introduction suggested the guy's mouth forced him to take his defensive stance as a matter of habit.

"Where's Tina?" Stan started to climb the steps to the porch, but the stranger stood in his way.

"What do you want?" For a skinny dude he had a deep voice, and although the decibels were few his curt tone spoke volumes.

The screen door opened and smacked the front siding on the house. "Daddy!" Lauren pushed past the human barrier and leaped into Stan's arms.

When Tyler stepped outside, the man blocked his path and said, "Back inside. Your momma said you weren't allowed to leave."

Tyler twisted sideways, ducked out of the man's reach, and scampered down the steps. Stan pulled him to his side and moved to put a greater distance between the man and his children.

"Both of you. Back inside. Now."

Stan's temper flared as fast as that of a protective grizzly, his posture and claws ready to rip the loudmouth apart. No one ordered his kids around. "Who are you? Where's Tina?"

"Name's DeWayne. DeWayne Davis. Tina's out."

"Well, Dwayne—"

"It's DeWayne. Not Dwayne."

Tyler cupped his hand over his mouth and looked up at Stan when he said, "He doesn't like it when you say his name wrong."

"Good to know," Stan said before turning his attention back to the dweeb on the steps. "Listen, Dwayne, these are my children, and they have plans to spend the evening with me. Tell Tina I'll have them back at nine."

"You can't take them. Tina said they had to stay here. She specifically said you were not to take them."

"Come on, guys. We're leaving."

"I'll call the cops."

Stan chortled. "You do that." He pressed Tyler's shoulder in the direction of the car, and the three started down the driveway.

"I'm calling. You hear?"

When Stan cast a glance backward, he saw the jerk stabbing his fingers across the screen of his cell phone.

"Daddy, you'll get in trouble," Tyler said.

"How? You're my kids and it's my night to take you to my place. Just hop in and fasten your seat belts."

Lauren jumped into her seat. "She's gonna be mad." In spite of the warning, Lauren looked as if she were enjoying the theatrics.

"Who's the dude?" Stan asked as he adjusted her seatbelt.

"He's in Mommy's study group," Lauren replied.

"I don't think he's very smart," Tyler said.

"Why?" Stan watched *De*Wayne gesture with his free hand while he talked on the phone.

"He never finishes his homework when the group meets. He keeps coming here to get Mom's help," Tyler answered.

"Are they dating?"

"You mean like a boyfriend?" Lauren asked. "Ew."

"You don't like him?" Stan asked.

"He's okay," Tyler said. "Mom acts weird around him though. She laughs a lot when he comes over, but it sounds fake."

Stan put the car in drive and looked over his shoulder before he started to pull away.

"Daddy, look out," Tyler screamed.

What in the—? Stan shoved the car back into park, threw open his car door, and glowered at Tina, who stood just inches from the hood of the car.

"What are you doing? You trying to get run over?" Stan yelled.

Tina's hands were wagging in his face by the time DeWayne joined her at the curb.

"Where do you think you're taking my kids? You have no right."

"Since when? It's my night and these are my children. What's wrong with you?" The fury started in Stan's belly, worked its way to his neck, and settled in every muscle in his face.

"I got a restraining order. You can't take them."

"A restraining order? For what?"

"To keep you from taking them places where they're going to get hurt. You're not a fit parent. You always put yourself first, Stanley Benton, and I won't let you do it at the expense of my kids."

"Get out of the way," Stan said as he climbed back into his seat. The distant wail of a siren increased with every second Tina held her position in front of the car. He couldn't put the car in reverse for fear of someone turning the corner and ramming the rear end. Stupid bushes blocked every inch of the view of the intersection.

"Daddy?" Lauren whispered. "Is Mommy gonna send you to jail?"

"Of course not."

When the black and white pulled in front of Stan's car, and a pair of his fellow defenders of the peace alit from their cruiser, he stayed seated and gripped the top of the steering wheel with both hands. Neither officer looked familiar.

"Out of the car," one of the officers ordered as he inventoried the occupants and interior of Stan's car. Before Stan replied, the officer looked in the back seat and said, "You kids doing okay back there?"

Tyler's squeaky, "Yes," didn't appear to ease the cop's concern.

"How about you? Where are you headed tonight?"

Laruen, bless her innocent heart, said, "We're going to Daddy's house. If we don't hurry, the pizza man won't leave us any dinner. Can we go now?"

"We'll see," the officer said.

Stan tilted his head toward the passenger seat where he'd tossed the hat to his uniform. "Stan Benton, eleventh precinct."

"You can show your badge after you get out of the car."

While Tina and her interfering study partner described her gripe to the other officer, Stan produced his credentials and traded a sarcastic snicker with the on-duty officer, nametag Newlander, who joked about the trouble Stan would have when his boss caught wind of this call.

The spectacle, which was now the source of the neighborhood's evening entertainment, drew people to nearby windows and their front stoops. At least the media hadn't arrived yet. Not that it mattered. More than one person held a cell phone aloft, taking a video of the affair. Such was the world of the police force. This time, however, Stan was on the wrong side of the picture.

The other officer said, "She says she has a restraining order and he can't take the kids."

Newlander flicked his finger in Stan's direction and said, "Perkins, this is Stan Benton, eleventh precinct. He says he doesn't know anything about a restraining order."

"If she produces one that's been through the courts and signed by the judge, I'll leave," Stan said as he glared at Tina.

Perkins turned toward Tina and asked, "You got a copy in the house?"

Tina's eyes darted to DeWayne, who continued to act as if he belonged several social tiers above the miscreant named Stan Benton. DeWayne's right eye twitched; otherwise, he remained stone-faced.

"I . . . I don't have it yet," Tina said.

"Is that because you don't have any grounds to file one?" Stan asked.

Newlander threw him a warning glance.

"Oh, it's in the works. You better believe it," Tina said. "You'll see one soon. I promise."

"Look," Perkins said. "If you don't have any paperwork prohibiting him from exercising his parental rights, and you refuse to let them go, then he has a right to take you back to court. Can't you two act like adults for the sake of the kids? Hmm?"

Stan glowered at Tina. Perkins wasn't talking about him. She contracted her eyes, probably the only action that could hold back the smoke. Her nostrils flared. Perkins hit her where it hurt. Pride.

Tina's fire didn't diminish, but Newlander said in an offhand sort of way, "You might consider that you engaged the police department over a false accusation, not that either of us intends to charge you with anything."

Stan bit the inside of his cheek so that the neighborhood videographer couldn't capture his victory celebration. He loved his fellow officers.

"Still," Newlander continued, "I don't suppose that situation would look good in a courtroom setting. Not for you anyway."

"What's it going to be?" Perkins asked.

Tina looked past both lawmen and said, "You have my babies back here by nine. Understand?"

Stan nodded to Perkins and Newlander and said, "You two have a pleasant evening."

As Stan and his children drove away, a sour stomach trounced his self-righteous triumph. What would Sumo Hollister do if he heard about this? Stan choked on the inevitable. It wasn't a matter of if; it was when.

Twelve

Juanita entwined her fingers and stretched her arms above her head. Finishing an editing assignment usually brought a sense of satisfaction, and in some instances her reward included consuming a good story or non-fiction work as she made her way from the first page to the last. Completing this particular piece, for which she earned a pittance, given the author's poor grammar skills and unusual writing style, brought nothing more than relief. She ought to celebrate before she picked up the next manuscript in her work queue.

How could she celebrate, though, knowing all of her efforts came up short? Since moving back to Shelburg, God answered their family's financial needs with enough: enough funds for food, clothing, housing, utilities. She would not complain about "enough." The condition of *The Basket Works* was another story, and Zach's plot to host a basket weaving retreat sounded like a brilliant idea until he tallied the upfront expenses.

Juanita pressed her thumb against her temple and flinched as little threads of pain pulsed beneath her skin. She pushed her chair away from her desk and walked into the kitchen. While she brewed a cup of coffee she took inventory of the home's heart. The pantry shelves were full and a vast amount of perishable food filled the refrigerator. Yes, they had enough. In contrast, during her last visit to *The Basket Work's* warehouse, she encountered empty shelf space. Lots of it.

She listened to Zach's plan, held her tongue during his plea to use Conner's college funds, and managed to end the prior evening's conversation with a promise to pray about it. The thought of devouring Conner's monies pricked at Juanita long after she and Zach climbed into bed. It needled her throughout the morning, and now in this late afternoon hour, the potential for disaster grabbed hold and strummed across her temples with increasing intensity.

She poured the coffee, closed her eyes, and looked heavenward. *What now, Lord?*

The warmth of the coffee mug against her cold fingers soothed some of the turmoil, and as Juanita sipped the hot beverage, the caffeine staved off a simmering migraine.

She stood in front of the large picture window and watched as the steam from her coffee fogged the cold glass. In just seconds, the cold overwhelmed the condensation, leaving not a trace. A misstep with Conner's college funds could turn his dreams into vapor just as quickly. *Please show me.*

Juanita watched the familiar black car pull up to the curb. From his position behind the wheel, Derrick lowered the passenger window and called after Conner and Izzy. Whatever the swim team friend said drew a snigger from both of her children.

Despite Juanita's misgivings about Zach's business plans, as she watched her teenagers approach the house, the scene brought gratitude to the forefront of her mind. Enough? She had much more than that. If she lost all of the trimmings and securities that surrounded her, she'd still be a wealthy woman.

"Hey, Mom," Conner said as he headed down the hallway and into the kitchen.

"How was your science test?" Juanita signed to Izzy.

"Good." Izzy's face lacked her I-hate-it-here gloom, but failed to reveal any hint of happiness.

"Did you ask your friend if she wanted to spend the night this weekend?"

"Courtney?" Izzy pouted and said. "She's too busy. Somebody else is having a party."

"Another time?" Juanita signed.

"Yeah. Sure."

Juanita followed Izzy to the kitchen where Conner sat with the plate of snickerdoodle cookies Zach brought home the night before. Conner pointed at the leftovers and said, "Mrs. Baxter makes the best cookies." When he saw Juanita's silent reproach, he asked. "Have you tried them?"

How could she scold him for devouring half the sweets? She'd helped herself to more than a handful while she worked at her computer today. "I have, but I think we both ate too many." Juanita turned to her daughter and signed, "Izzy?"

Izzy stopped chewing her cookie and said, "What?"

"Dottie's granddaughter will be at the ASL class tomorrow night. Do you think you can help Paige feel a little more comfortable in her new surroundings? You know how hard it is to start over."

Juanita didn't expect Izzy's eyes to tear. Was her question too blunt? "I didn't mean to make you feel bad," Juanita signed.

"It's okay. It'll be fine." Izzy pushed the cookie plate back towards Conner and said, "I have homework."

While Juanita watched her lonely daughter walk down the

hallway, Conner tapped her on the arm. "She'll be fine. She just needs one friend. One good friend."

"Can you find one for her?" Juanita signed.

"Maybe you already have," Conner said.

"Who?"

"Paige. Maybe Izzy needs Paige as much as Paige needs Izzy."

"I hope you're right," Juanita signed.

Conner's casual manner changed when he signed, "I saw you talking with Dad last night."

"We had something important to discuss."

"That's not what I meant." Conner lifted his hands and reverted to signing. "I *saw* you talking."

Juanita, who held her cup to her lips, stopped before she took a sip. He saw?

"You eavesdropped?" Juanita signed. She could almost hear the blood vessels in her neck and head react to the comment. Her pulse hammered across her temples again, more persistent and demanding than before.

"I didn't mean to," Conner said. "I saw you signing my name. I stopped and watched for a minute—maybe more than a minute."

As Juanita read his lips, she acknowledged his apologetic expression and signed, "It's nothing for you to worry about."

"Dad's business isn't worth worrying about?"

"That's not what I meant."

"If *The Basket Works* closes, we're all in trouble."

"Your dad will find something else if that happens."

"In this town? What? This place hasn't boomed since the auto industry went bust. Shelburg's been on life support for more than a decade."

"The company isn't going to close." Juanita's own words

mocked her. How could she say that?

"Listen," Conner said.

"No. This conversation is not for you."

"Yes it is. I can't run off to college if the rest of my family can't make ends meet. If you need to borrow the college money, you have to do it."

"No."

"Yes."

"No." Juanita stomped her foot on the floor. Conner was more exasperating than Zach was. It was not Conner's place to tell his mother what to do.

"It's just a loan. It's okay."

"What if it doesn't get repaid? What then? Your dad and I scrimped and sacrificed to put the money away for you. We're not touching it."

"If it doesn't get repaid, I'll do what every other penny-poor student does. I'll get a job, go to school, study my rear end off, and graduate."

"We're not taking the money."

"If this money is earmarked for me, don't you think I should have a say in its use?"

"No."

"No?" Conner rubbed his chin and said, "If you think I'm ready for college, don't you think I'm ready to participate in a family discussion that involves my future?"

"It's not as if we're arranging a marriage for you." Juanita recognized the lame analogy, but couldn't construe a better one. Not with her brain making warfare with her throbbing head.

"If you think it's inappropriate or unnecessary for you to arrange a marriage for me, why is the decision to finance my education any more critical?"

Not only was hers a poor comparison, Conner used it to steal her objection. Juanita studied her handsome son's earnest face. His blue eyes, a gift from his father's side of the family, bore into hers. Conner's resolve and his genial personality held more to Zach's lineage than her own. Sometimes Juanita wished she carried the same traits, but skepticism and caution were at the forefront of her disposition.

"Can we talk to Dad about it?" Conner asked.

Juanita lowered her gaze to her hands, and when she looked up, Zach stood in the doorway. He wore a million-dollar smile when he said, "Talk about what?"

The strumming across her head increased ten-fold as Juanita conceded her circumstances. While she saw only two others in the room, she was markedly out-numbered.

~

Less than five seconds after running into the apartment, Lauren peered into the fish tank, turned around, and blubbered, "That's not Miss Fulgermuffin. Where's my fish?" Tears brimmed and spilled over her cheeks.

"Honey, she got sick."

"You mean she's dead?" Lauren's voice quavered as she pulled in a ragged breath.

"I'm sorry," Stan replied. Geesh, Lauren didn't even give him an opportunity to pass off the new fish as the deceased one. Norris would be relieved to hear he hadn't lied about the replacement pet.

"Where is she? We have to have a funeral."

So certain was he that he could dupe his children, Stan hadn't thought to prepare a statement regarding the victim.

He stammered when he said, "I already buried her." Now Norris had reason to lecture him.

"Where? In the backyard?" Lauren asked.

"Uh, no. I buried her at sea."

"What sea?" asked Tyler.

Norris had a point about lying. Now what? "Uh, you know. The big pond outside my apartment building."

The muscles that etched lines in Lauren's face rearranged her expression from distraught to bewildered. When she started to cry, Tyler said, "It's okay. Miss Fulgermuffin wouldn't mind." The look Tyler reserved for his father was all knowing and saturated with accusation.

"Goldfish just don't live very long," Stan said.

"Yes they do," Tyler said. "If they have a good place to live, they can live at least five years. My teacher said one goldfish lived more than forty years."

"Do my fish die because we don't have a good fish tank? Do they need more food? Daddy?" Lauren's pout tugged at Stan's heart. Childhood was supposed to be joyful.

"I don't know what happened, kiddo. It could be a lot of things. The water was too hot or too cold, or maybe the fish had an allergy to the food I picked. Maybe she was old before we brought her home." The possible explanations sounded lousy, even as Stan expressed them, but the last suggestion seemed to glean a minute level of acceptance from Lauren.

"Yeah, she must have been old," Tyler said. Why was Tyler standing up for him?

"You know what, Tyler?"

"What?"

"For a third grader, you're pretty smart."

Tyler's eyes brightened at the compliment. "That's what Mrs. Jenkins says."

"Who?"

"Mrs. Jenkins. My teacher."

"Well, she's right." Stan's ignorance where his children, their schoolwork, and their friends were concerned wrapped around his conscience with the same discomfort as his willingness to lie. Did this stuff make him a bad person? A rotten parent?

"Does this fish have a name?" Lauren asked.

"The man at the pet store didn't have her birth certificate, so I guess you and Tyler get to choose."

"That's silly. Fish don't have birth certificates." Lauren looked at Tyler and asked, "Do they?"

"I dunno," Tyler said.

"Is it a boy or a girl?" Lauren asked.

Stan's jaw dropped a notch. The little scaly wonder swimming around the tank was more trouble than it was worth. If he'd known the outcome of his intent to deceive, he'd have been wiser to have emptied the tank and tossed it into the dumpster.

"Look," Tyler said. "Its mouth makes lots of bubbles."

"Must be a girl fish," Stan said. When Tyler squinted at his comment, Stan mumbled, "Never mind."

"Bubbles. I want to call it Bubbles. That's a girl name or a boy name," Lauren said.

"Tyler?" Stan asked.

"I like Bubbles okay."

When the doorbell sounded, Lauren raced to the door. "Pizza's here," she yelled.

As Stan and Tyler followed her, Tyler looked up at his dad. "You flushed her, didn't you?"

"Let's talk about your school Christmas program instead of worrying about the fish."

"Thought so," Tyler said.

Stan leaned into Tyler and tapped him on the top of his head. "Forgive me?"

"Yeah."

"Can we keep the details between us men?"

Tyler's eyes, so much like Stan's own, were dark and somber when he answered, "Yeah." They lit up as soon as Stan paid the deliveryman and placed the pizza box in Tyler's outstretched arms.

At the end of their once-a-week evening at his place, Stan helped secure his children into his car and drove across town again. Lauren closed her eyes and started bobbing her weary head before they stopped at the first traffic light.

"Dad?" Tyler's voice was subdued. He leaned forward to keep from waking his sister.

"Hmm?"

"What if Mom likes DeWayne. You know . . . really likes him?"

The unexpected question hit Stan with the same effect as a brick hurled at his midsection. It wasn't as if he wanted the woman back—he didn't exactly miss her—but he never pictured her with someone else. Naw, Tyler had to have it wrong. Who'd put up with Tina? *De*Wayne? Hardly.

"She's gone on dates before."

"Yeah, but they never come back after the first one."

Stan could only hope the streetlamps didn't light up the interior of the car so much that Tyler could see his dad's dimples. No way could Stan erase such intense satisfaction from his face. Not even.

"DeWayne's been around a lot?"

"All the time."

"Does he ever do things with you and Lauren?" Stan tried

to catch a glimpse of Tyler's expression in the rearview mirror, but his son hung his head as he talked.

"Once. We went to the zoo."

"Was he nice to you?"

"Guess so."

"Tyler."

He lifted his head. "Huh?"

"You know I'll always be your daddy. Always."

"I know." Tyler's voice betrayed his disappointment.

"I miss you too," Stan said. "Maybe your mom will let me have more visitation days. I'll ask."

"What if she gets the 'straining order. Like she said?"

"She didn't mean it. She's just mad about what happened at the church. She'll get over it."

"What if she doesn't? I don't want DeWayne to be my dad."

"That'll never happen. I promise." Now fully aware of Tyler's burden, a flicker of resentment took hold. Although Tyler grew quiet, Stan's annoyance stoked the irritant and by the time he pulled around the corner and saw the second vehicle still parked in Tina's driveway, he was livid—something he could ill afford.

Tyler stepped out of the car and waited on the sidewalk while Stan unfastened Lauren's seatbelt and hefted her into his arms.

"Come on, buddy. Time for you to get some sleep," he said to Tyler.

"Will you come on Saturday?"

"It's not my weekend. I'll see you next Wednesday, and after that we'll have the whole weekend."

Stan followed Tyler into the entryway and stood, still holding Lauren, while Tina descended the stairs. Her face was flush with either embarrassment or defiance, or maybe a little of both.

"Give her to me," Tina said.

"She's too heavy. I'll take her up." Stan sidestepped Tina and took the stairs. He lowered Lauren to her bed, pulled off her shoes, and snugged her favorite stuffed animal under her arm. When he kissed her soft cheek, she mumbled, "Love you, Daddy."

"Love you too. G'night, kiddo."

Stan pulled the door shut and turned toward the stairs, where he collided with one arrogant DeWayne Davis. The hormones that pumped through Stan's system baffled him. If he didn't care for Tina any longer, why did he have an irascible desire to lock horns with the puny stranger? Stan stepped back, pointed to the stairs, and said, "After you."

When they reached the threshold, Stan leaned down, hugged Tyler, and said, "Get some sleep, little man. I'll be back before you know it." Stan's gaze followed his son's form as he ascended the stairs. After Tyler closed his bedroom door, Stan directed a warning to DeWayne and Tina. "I'll be back soon. Don't hurt my kids. Either of you."

Before he lost what little control he maintained, Stan strode to the car, pulled away from the curb, and headed back to his apartment. That blue SUV better be gone by morning.

Thirteen

Zach had ten minutes until his meeting with Pastor Morrison. As they prepared the budget for the coming year, he and four other men who served on the church finance team planned to relay the needs of the committees they represented. Zach's own assignment, that of building and grounds maintenance, entailed a list almost as long and formidable as the one Nancy and Mae calculated for *The Basket Works'* weaving retreat. No doubt, his next audience would be as tough as Juanita proved herself to be. For now, the jury was still out on Zach's borrowing scheme.

He sat near the door to the ASL classroom and watched Izzy interact with the teenager who came to the session with Dottie. Although she was a year younger than Izzy, Paige was half a foot taller and at least twenty pounds heavier. In that respect, the girl took after her grandmother.

The similarities between grandmother and granddaughter ended there. Dottie was fair-skinned and green-eyed, and wore her short gray hair in tight curls, whereas Paige possessed long and straight, dark brown hair that reached her waist. Her dark eyes rivaled Izzy's rich chocolate hue, and her complexion was a light shade of toffee.

During their introduction before class began, Paige kept

her distance from the others by hovering behind Dottie, but when he, along with Izzy, Juanita, and Suzanne, started communicating with their hands, Paige lowered her guard. Now, as she and Izzy bantered silently in the corner of the room, the teens exchanged cheerful facial expressions that spoke more clearly than their hands.

When was the last time Zach saw Izzy share a pleasant moment with a friend? Too long. His push to relocate to Shelburg came with a heavy dose of guilt. Coming here was more painful and costly than he anticipated. Meeting Paige was a positive step for Izzy, but what about everything else, especially *The Basket Works?* His stomach churned as another round of misgivings about using the college funds assailed him.

Zach needed to push the sense of foreboding away. Where had he misplaced his self-confidence? It sure hadn't followed him to Shelburg. He turned his attention to Suzanne, who stood at the front of the class.

"Are any of you tired of finger spelling?" Murmurs accompanied a mass of raised hands. "It looks like it's time to move on to conversation." She held up a paperback book and said, "For those of you who expect to use ASL as a second language, you might want to purchase a copy of this phrase book. It's one of the best. For class purposes, we'll pass out copies of some of the most basic phrases and expressions that fill our everyday dialogue."

"What about sentence structure and grammar? Is this as complicated as learning French?" Holly Norris asked. She toyed with her lost-but-found gold earring while she waited for a response.

"It's not remotely similar," Suzanne said. "You can throw out all of those rules. Instead, you'll learn the names for various signs. And, just as tone and volume add meaning to a spoken sentence, so do facial expressions and body language come into play while signing."

Zach remembered his own confusion when he tried to teach himself ASL. The ordeal left him almost as perplexed as did his first encounter with one Juanita Perez. When his eyes wandered to his wife, she angled her head to the side and pulled her lips into a smile. She still amazed him all these years later. How he managed to worm his way into her silent world, and then her heart, was nothing short of a miracle.

The queasy wave meandering across his midsection made note of all he had to lose. Zach dared not jeopardize Juanita's love or her trust. Was his business endeavor a wise tactical move or a potential disaster? He slouched in his seat. Would he reach a point where he quit second-guessing his position?

"You might think of signs as doing the opposite of a thesaurus," Suzanne said. "Instead of giving more options to find similar words, signs condense words with comparable meanings into one."

"I have an example," Juanita signed using finger spelling.

"Did everyone understand Juanita's comment?" Suzanne asked.

"She has an example," Dottie said, followed by, "I think."

Juanita nodded and then faced Suzanne, who translated Juanita's hand movements while she demonstrated her example.

"The sign for compete looks like this," Suzanne said as she repeated Juanita's gesture. "We use it for race, competition, and contest."

Zach watched more than one student grimace. It sounded more complicated than it was, but they just needed to stick with it. All those years ago, he had proper motivation in that he needed the language in order to pursue Juanita. Pangs of yearning and tenderness accompanied Zach as he patted himself on the back. That quest, he had accomplished with excellence. He'd do well not to ruin their lives now.

"Let's look at another example," Suzanne said. "Let's take the word 'fly' and use it in a few sentences. Dan? How about you?"

"I fly an airplane," Dan said.

"Zoe?" Suzanne said.

"Huh?" The teen lifted her head from the top of the table and didn't bother to cover her mouth when she yawned.

"Use the word 'fly' in a sentence, please."

"Uh, I swatted the fly."

"Good. Anyone else?"

"The outfielder caught a fly ball." This, from another one of the sullen-faced teenagers.

"Good. You see how one sign won't work for all the ways we use the word. In Dan's sentence, we would use the sign for airplane, which looks like this."

"I thought that was the sign for 'I love you,' " Zoe said.

"It is, but it also looks like an airplane in flight."

"If you say so," Zoe said.

"Notice that I flattened my palm a little, but it's the forward and backward motion that implies the word 'airplane.' "

Officer Benton leaned back in his seat and wiped his brow. "This is supposed to be easy?"

Suzanne said, "In some respects it is. Let's keep going. I think you'll catch on. For Zoe's flying insect, you can spell out the three letters F-L-Y or you can form your fingers to show how an insect flies, then smash your hands together, like this, to demonstrate swatting.

"For Brad's, 'The outfielder caught a fly ball,' we'd simplify the sentence by using the gestures for catch and baseball." Suzanne raised the index finger of her left hand at the same time she raised her right hand and grabbed the index finger. "This is catch." Then she held her hands in fists, one above the other, as if she were holding a baseball bat. While holding the pose, she flexed her arms up and down twice. "Baseball uses a double movement."

Zach looked at his watch, and as he stood to leave for his meeting, he heard Benton mutter, "Aye-yi-yi."

When Zach reached Craig's office, a piece of paper taped to the door redirected the meeting attendees to the sanctuary. Zach intercepted Bernard Ames in the hallway.

"Hey Bernard, how you doing?"

"Got no complaints. You?"

"I'm good. I didn't expect to see you this evening."

"That makes two of us."

"Pastor got a look at my proposed budget and called you in to help toss me out of the building?"

"Don't think I'm here about finances."

"Did my meeting get cancelled?" Zach asked as he lifted his cell phone out of his pocket. No new messages.

"Pastor called everybody who holds a leadership position to an emergency meeting. Since you were already scheduled to be here, he probably didn't bother to call you with an update."

"Do you know what's up?" Zach asked.

"Don't know a thing."

Zach held open the heavy door to the sanctuary and followed Bernard inside. A dozen others sat at the front of the room, sharing small talk and conversations among themselves. Zach slid into a bench and greeted Erlene Starr, who headed up the children's programs.

"Folks, I apologize for the lack of notice, and I want to thank each of you for dropping everything you planned to do tonight so you could be here. Let's start with prayer." Craig bowed his head and beseeched the Father for wisdom and discernment. It was the plea for protection that echoed in Zach's ears after the pastor said, "amen."

"I don't want to steal your entire evening, so I'll get to the point." Craig held up one of the flyers the church printed and distributed to area businesses and residents. The flyers announced the church's intention to keep the neighborhood safe, and asked others to be on watch and to report suspicious behavior.

He waved the marked up paper too quickly for Zach to focus on words scrawled across the message. "This came in the mail today. It reads, 'You ain't taking back nothing. We own this turf.' "

Craig paced in front of the pews, his hands clasped behind his back. He acted as if he wasn't sure whether he wanted to burden his crew with what had to be the point of the meeting.

"When we started the campaign to take back our neighborhood, we knew we would stir up opposition. It's no secret we have a couple of gangs operating here. Up until now, they've directed their hatred toward their rivals. I fear we've earned the notice of at least one of the gangs."

"Something more than that letter is troubling you," Bernard said.

"Yesterday's mail included a copy of last week's bulletin. On the back page where we congratulated members who celebrated anniversaries and birthdays, someone circled one of the names in heavy red ink. Didn't know what to make of it at the time.

"Y'all know Harriett Gardner celebrated her eightieth birthday on Tuesday. Mother Gardner called me this morning. Said she found an envelope stuck inside her screen door. It was a birthday card, just like she thought, but it came with a warning, 'If you want to see another birthday, tell Morrison and the other neighborhood watch do-gooders to back off.' "

Zach choked at the implication. Someone was close enough to grab a copy of the bulletin, savvy enough to track down Harriett Gardner's address, and bold enough to threaten an old lady.

"Although I already reported this incident to the police—I had a personal meeting with Captain Hollister—I want all of you to be aware of it. We all need to be cautious, watchful, and prayerful."

The hair on the back of Zach's neck rose at the mention of Hollister. His uniform and title notwithstanding, Sumo always let his personal ambitions direct his course. What might he gain by publicizing his involvement in keeping law and order in the vicinity?

"You plan to tell the church?" one of the deacons asked.

"Without providing details, I'll tell everyone we received letters from those who are opposed to our work."

"What about security?" Bernard asked.

"That's one of the reasons I wanted the finance team to attend this meeting. After we're done here, I want you number crunchers to find a way to pay for some police presence. My wish list includes coverage for our Sabbath service and any evening activities.

"I don't know how we'll move funds from one account to another, but I hope we can manage without taking a special collection. Most folks in this church struggle to put food on the table. I don't want to burden them if we can avoid it."

Zach traded how-are-we-going-to-pull-that-off glances with another member of the finance team. Money was tight everywhere, and they ran on a lean budget. Most years, the budget collection fell short of goal, but the church managed to pay its bills. How much longer could they defer maintenance on the building? Apparently, until the church met this newest demand head-on; otherwise, the Hoyt family would spend their Sabbaths on their home turf—which is exactly what the letter-sender hoped to achieve.

Fourteen

"What's eating you? You still mad about the goldfish I-told-you-so?" When Stan didn't answer, Norris turned her face away from him, but the second Stan hit the brakes with more force than was necessary, she lit into him again. "The City doesn't pay me to suffer whiplash. Pull over."

"I'm driving."

"You're not driving. You're using the cruiser as a hissy fit device. Knock it off."

The man driving the sedan in front of the patrol car slowed. He turned on his flashers, but didn't bother to pull his car to the curb before his slow-motion passenger tried to extricate herself from her seat.

As traffic blocked him in, Stan's neck and shoulder muscles went from tight to rigid. Norris was only partially correct in her assessment of her partner. Stan's built up steam rivaled Old Faithful's supply. Unlike the national park geyser, however, no one in the immediate vicinity had an inkling that Stan was about to blow.

While the heavy-set woman rested with her arm on the side of the car, the driver got out, circled the vehicle, and dragged a walker out of the back seat.

"I can't take any more," Stan said between clenched teeth.

He shoved the car into park, walked up to the other driver, and took the walker out of his hand.

"Here, let me help you with that." Stan fumbled with the malfunctioning button until he managed to free the metal and unfold the mechanism.

"Mighty nice of you, young man," the driver said. He was either unaware or unconcerned about the traffic piling up behind him.

Once the passenger took a hundred baby steps to the sidewalk, Stan helped her negotiate the curb. He turned to the driver and said, "We'd better get moving."

Instead of following the man to the driver's side of their vehicles, Stan tapped on Norris' window and gestured for her to get out.

"Drive," he said.

Once Norris joined the mass of rush hour traffic, she asked, "You wanna talk about it?"

Hardly, although even Norris seemed more sympathetic to Stan's plight since she and the others in the ASL class witnessed Tina's tantrum. Maybe he ought to quit driving by Tina's place. He'd only meant to do it once. Had to drive by just to be certain that the blue SUV was gone. So far, he'd been wrong every single morning. Had DeWayne the jerk moved in with her, and with the children, or was he just a sleepover pal?

"Did she do it?" Norris asked. "Did your ex file a restraining order?"

"She can't. Doesn't have grounds." Did Stan? "Your parents divorced when you were still in elementary school, right?"

"I was ten."

"Your mother ever . . . you know . . . have men stay

over?"

Norris's snort initiated a coughing fit. She grabbed her bottle of water and took a slug before she said, "We moved in with my grandmother after my dad left. Don't think my mom dared consider something like that." Norris turned and scrutinized Stan. "You think Tina's entertaining while your kids are there?"

"Either that or her study partner rents half of her driveway."

"You meet the guy?" Norris asked.

"During our ten-second face-off, I warned him not to hurt Tyler or Lauren."

"How did he react?"

"He was ticked. Thinks he's better than me."

"What do you know about him?"

"Couldn't find any public records on him, but that doesn't mean he's got a clean past. Don't know where he grew up. Nothing."

"Too bad you can't use the database at the station."

"Thought about it," Stan said. With his luck, someone would catch him in the act. Unemployed police officer was not something to which Stan aspired.

"You try to talk to Tina?"

"As if she'd hear me," Stan said.

"You need to warn her."

"About what?"

"Statistics," Norris said.

"What statistics?"

"The ones that say it's always the boyfriend who hurts the kids. You know . . ."

"What are you getting at?" Stan asked.

"When someone hurts or abuses the children, it's often

the mom's boyfriend."

Although Stan scoffed, a series of warning bells pinged in his conscience. "He's too busy drooling over Tina to notice the kids."

"That's what all the victims' moms say." Norris cringed at Stan's reaction. "Just saying. Maybe you need to spring for some private company to do a background check."

"Can't afford to."

"You can't afford not to."

~

At the end of the day, Stan stood in front of his locker and stared at last year's school pictures of Lauren and Tyler. The photographer who memorialized the unnatural expressions in their not-inexpensive value pack was as pathetic a shutterbug as the ones who captured Stan's year-to-year childhood.

Lauren's two front teeth went missing weeks before the photo shoot, and the permanent replacements barely poked through the surface of her pink gums. Bright lights washed away the warm butterscotch hue of her skin and turned her gold-flecked brown eyes into an eerie shade of yellow.

Tyler's pictures didn't fare any better than Lauren's did. Stan could almost see the reflection of the ceiling lights that stole the warmth of his son's expressive eyes. Had anyone bothered to tell him about it, Tyler might have licked off the white toothpaste residue that lined his upper lip. Instead, he had to endure his classmates' teasing.

Sure would be nice to sit for a decent photograph, just the three of them. If Stan took a vote, though, Tyler and Lauren would rather have a pizza than a stuffy memory. Stan wanted both. More than anything, he wanted them happy.

And safe.

"Benton? You still here?" The voice originated from the locker room doorway.

"Back here," Stan replied as he slid his sweatshirt over his head.

One of the newest officers poked his head around the line of lockers and said, "Captain's looking for you."

"His office?" Stan asked.

"Yeah."

"Mood?"

The officer looked at Stan as if he'd just asked the most ludicrous question he'd ever heard. Obviously, the newcomer hadn't been around long; otherwise, he'd understand Stan's need to know.

"I'm on my way," Stan said as he leaned over to tie his shoe.

Stan's civilian clothes stripped him of the innate power of his uniform. He slinked down the hallway as if he were naked. If he'd seen the summons coming, he wouldn't have changed clothes, but he'd let down his guard. It had been days since DeWayne called the cops to Tina's place, and Stan thought himself invisible as far as his superiors were concerned.

The administrative assistant who guarded Acting Captain Sumo Hollister's office door didn't hide her annoyance when she had to interrupt her cell phone call.

"Name?"

"Benton."

"Go on in," she said as she stuck her phone back to her ear.

Hollister stood with his back to the door and his face to the window, just as he did the last time he and Stan had a little chat. Hollister looked as if he were measuring his kingdom again, probably for nothing better than to remind Stan of their little agreement: whatever Hollister's whim, Stan would comply.

"I thought we had an understanding," Hollister said as he turned around.

"Sir?"

"When I hear about a disturbance involving one of my own, it angers me."

Stan didn't look for trouble. He didn't. He didn't hate Tina, even when he failed to understand her nasty temperament and her self-centeredness. He didn't particularly like the woman, couldn't understand what drew him to her in the first place. Seemed like that attraction happened in another century, or maybe another dimension. Still, Stan conceded his faults and his less than admirable opinion of his ex-wife. At this particular moment, DeWayne Davis now held the same level of scorn that Stan reserved for Tina.

"It was a bad call," Stan said. "Nothing happened."

"You can't erase the incident just because it doesn't pass your definition of a credible emergency."

"I know that, sir."

"You know about the trouble at the church?" Hollister asked.

"It was a prank. Some kids set off a cherry bomb in the dumpster."

"Not that trouble."

"Haven't heard of anything else."

Hollister pointed to a chair. Stan sat. If he'd worn his uniform, his agitated hands could have found some comfort in fidgeting with his hat.

After Hollister apprised Stan of the church's campaign to

keep a watchful eye on the happenings of their neighborhood, and the incident with the birthday card, he pointed a finger at Stan.

"You look like you need some overtime."

Stan always needed overtime. Trouble was, one shift was all it took to deplete his energy. If he wasn't bored with quiet and calm, calamity and frenzy ruled. Either way, forty hours a week was already plenty.

"Overtime?"

"Morrison asked for security detail during their weekly service and for every event held in the evening. You already attend the sign language class, so you can cover them on that night. Morrison will like the fact that we won't have to bill them for your security presence. Convenient for them."

"Are you asking me to provide security instead of attending class?"

"No. You'll do both. You just need to babysit everyone until the last person leaves the parking lot. No big deal."

And no overtime.

"I'm inviting you to apply for the weekly service stint. You'll get three hours O.T."

Right in the middle of his weekend visitation with Lauren and Tyler. "What about my kids?"

"Take 'em with you. Be good for them."

Take Lauren and Tyler back to New Life Chapel? Tina would string Stan up. Or file that restraining order.

"Far as I can tell, you'd do yourself a favor to get in Morrison's good graces. Maybe he'll give you some free legal advice where your ex is concerned."

"Hadn't thought about that," Stan said. Morrison knew Tina before Stan married her, and he seemed sympathetic to Stan's situation. Not a bad idea.

"I'll be upfront with you, Benton," Hollister said. "Morrison has some clout. If my officers keep his congregation safe, his gratitude is bound to reach the ears of the mayor and other influential people. I want my name to be on the top of the list when it's time to find Captain Snodgrass' replacement."

"How does my working security help?"

"You're my eyes and ears. I want you to be a fly on the wall. If anyone hints of trouble, you bring it to me."

"Morrison won't confide in me. Unless something happens on my watch, this fly won't hear a thing."

"He'll talk openly with you if you confide in him about your ex-wife and her threats to keep your children from you."

A flutter of misgiving settled over the fleeting glimmer of free legal advice.

"Instead of bringing me trouble, I expect you to make me look good. I expect you to tell me everything you hear over there. And I expect you to be on the lookout for any subversive activities in the neighborhood. Understand?"

"Yes, sir."

"Good. You start this weekend." Sumo started to pivot toward the window but paused. "One more thing. Grab a copy of the church bulletin for me. I want to monitor all their activities. Have it in my mail slot first thing every Monday morning."

"Yes, sir."

By the time Stan walked out of the building, scraped ice from his windshield, and waited for the film on the glass to clear, his nose was as numb as his brain. He flexed his hands, finger-spelled F-L-Y, and smashed his palms together. If he was such a brilliant student, why did his future always look so grim?

Fifteen

Juanita closed her eyes to the soundless movement made by the members of the congregation who gathered in the sanctuary. She picked up the beat as vibrations from the bass drum pulsated against her chest. When she opened her eyes, she scanned the large screen located at the front of the room, and then turned her attention to the song leader's lips. Once she managed to track the singer's lip movements to the printed words, Juanita used the steady beat of the drum to keep her place in the music as she signed the lyrics.

Music. If she'd known her hearing would disappear in the wink of a fever, she might have made an effort to sear every frequency, every rhythm, every harmony, and every beloved voice into her memory. Instead, as fast as the illness descended, her hearing vanished. Gone were her mommy's, "I love you," her daddy's, "Princess, I'm home," and every trace of laughter and song. Her seven-year-old world fell silent.

Juanita acquiesced to her parents' persistent demands to speak her side of a conversation, even though she couldn't hear her own voice. The more adept she, her family, and a few friends became with ASL, the more Juanita hid behind the language. By the time she turned nine, the perplexed expressions her voice garnered from those who were within her decibel range, betrayed her inability to enunciate, to control her tone and her volume. No amount of cajoling changed her decision to quiet her voice. She succeeded in eradicating the ridicule, but her world narrowed to a degree that isolated her.

While friends gathered in groups to play outside or share make-believe dreams with their dolls, Juanita found her own source of wonder and pleasure resting on the shelves of the local library. When she burrowed her heart and mind into the unimaginable realms of fiction, she unearthed innumerable companions as she flipped through pages.

When the worship song ended and everyone sat down, a young man took to the pulpit and began reciting the announcements. Juanita looked at the printed bulletin in her lap, something to distract her until the mustached-speaker finished. She couldn't read lips if she couldn't see them.

Christmas was on the horizon, and bold letters on an insert to the bulletin highlighted the need for helping hands. Juanita remembered Christmas carols. In the weeks to come, when the projector displayed the lyrics across the screen, her memory would sing along, although the urge to give way to melancholy wrestled with the bittersweet remembrance.

"You okay?" Zach signed.

Juanita nodded.

"Something on your mind?"

"Music."

Zach reacted with surprise. "Music?"

"Christmas music." When his puzzled expression lingered, she signed, "I remember. I can hear it."

He reached over, wrapped his hand around hers, and squeezed. While he couldn't fathom her reality, Zach tried to relate. He pulled his hand away, and as he pretended to listen to the speaker, he kept his fingers down toward his lap and signed, "Why are you grinning?"

"Remembering you."

He puffed out his chest.

"Wrapping your gifts," she signed.

"How many?"

Juanita raised six fingers.

Zach pointed to himself and spelled, "Persistent."

Izzy leaned forward and put a fingertip to her lips. The child reprimanding the parent. The parents.

It was Becca Finley who took credit for the Zach and Juanita pairing. The college roommate talked Juanita into joining a dozen other volunteers in wrapping Christmas gifts at the mall. It was for a good cause. The youth group at church would use the proceeds to purchase new clothing for needy children who lived in the community.

The task seemed simple. All Juanita had to do was take a seat in the way-way back of the wrapping area where she didn't have to interact with any frenzied shoppers. One of the volunteers would bring a gift to her, along with a paper that included the customer's order number and wrapping paper selection. She'd wrap the gift, locate the bearer of the corresponding number in the waiting area, and hand the finished product back to the shopper.

Over the course of four chaotic hours, during which Becca delivered orders to the various volunteers, Zach waited with outstretched hands as Juanita placed a wrapped gift in his arms—six times. Six gifts. Six wrapping paper selections. Six goofy grins, one tendered each time she delivered his festive goods. In every instance he tried to drum up a conversation, but she put her hand to her ear, as if she couldn't hear him—which she couldn't—and fled to her appointed seat.

At the end of the wrapping flurry, Becca and Juanita joined the throng of shoppers who sidestepped one another as they jockeyed for open paths to their destinations. All Juanita wanted was a ride to their apartment. A nap sounded good.

"Who was that guy? Why me?" Juanita signed.

"He asked for you," Becca said.

"Six times?"

Becca nudged Juanita's arm and with overt facial and hand expressions, implied that the guy was good looking. "Agreed?"

"Yes. So?" Juanita signed. She collided with a woman who darted in front of her, and raised her hand as an act of apology. The woman donned a dense veil of irritation before she pushed her way through the crowd. When Juanita looked up, her most attentive gift-wrapping customer stood across the walkway. In his arms he juggled six gaily-wrapped boxes.

Becca, who didn't see him at first, lifted her hand and formed the ASL sign for pretty. The stranger's eager countenance faded as his gaze darted from Juanita's face, to her hands, and back to her face. When he looked away in embarrassment, Juanita grabbed Becca by the elbow and steered her out of the mall.

"I'm sorry," Becca signed.

"Why? He's just like everyone else."

"I didn't think he was when I gave him our phone number."

With the same force that an aircraft carrier's deck cable snags an incoming fighter jet, Juanita halted. She stretched her thumb and little finger and raised them to her face, as if she, the deaf friend, were talking on the phone. She pointed to herself and batted her eyelashes. Becca covered her gaping mouth with her hand and after several failed attempts to stop laughing, she managed to say, "I didn't think about that."

Dear, dear Becca. Who knew? Juanita looked at her hand, intertwined with that of her pretty husband. As Pastor Morrison took his place behind the lectern, Juanita tightened her grip. As it turned out, Zach Hoyt wasn't everyone else.

~

Was this brilliant or just plain senseless? Stan squirmed while he sat in the uncomfortable wood seat. Antsy didn't begin to describe his mood, physical and mental. Instead of the anticipated increase in pre-holiday incidents requiring police presence, today was one of the longest and most tedious of Stan's career. Downright boring, in spite of Norris' efforts to practice ASL.

He needed a full-body workout. His first choice in sweat building exercises was a prolonged squabble with a punching bag. It wasn't as if he had any gym equipment in his apartment, but the image of his pounding his irritation into oblivion won a level of satisfaction.

Stan accepted the offered cup of coffee, but declined the sugar and creamer. "Thanks." He sipped the coffee and asked, "You sure this is decaf?"

"Better be. I need my beauty sleep," Pastor Morrison said. He stirred in a packet of artificial sweetener before placing his cup on the corner of his desk. "What'd you think of the service?"

"Huh?"

"Unless you wore earplugs, you couldn't have missed my

dissertation, even out in the foyer."

"Uh, no. I listened. I did." Kind of. During most of the service, while Morrison's congregation sang and prayed, and then listened to a really long message, Stan's mind wandered to Norris' comments about a mom's boyfriend always being the bad guy. That conversation, more than Hollister's directive, led Stan to request a meeting with Morrison. Since he was here, he ought to give the man his full attention. First, a question.

"Are you sure you don't mind if I bring Tyler and Lauren with me next week? I mean, I'm supposed to be on duty, and all."

"You can be on duty while they search out God's call on their lives. You bring them here and we'll take good care of them."

Morrison's religious lingo was as foreign to Stan as ASL. He'd heard others use the term "God's call" before, but it meant nothing to him. Since it was the Tina problem that brought him here, and not God calling, Stan chose to let the comment ride.

"Thanks. They'll behave. They like it here."

"Good to know. No better place to be than in His house." Morrison leaned forward and placed his clasped hands on the top of his desk. "Now, how might I help you?"

"Truth is, I could use some legal advice."

Morrison sat back while he mulled over Stan's comment. "Your spiritual condition is my first concern, but since the laws of the land often mirror the Lord's laws—they used to, anyway—we might delve into a bit of both."

What? Stan didn't want to venture into that maelstrom either, so he kept his mouth shut. During the silence that accompanied Morrison's prolonged assessment, Stan's skin prickled in discomfort. He filed this request for a meeting with Morrison on his endless list of regrets. What was he thinking?

"Let me tell you a little about myself. How I arrived here," Morrison said as he gestured to their surroundings. "My momma made sure I knew my future included a college education. No one else in my family ever went past high school; lots of my kin didn't get past eighth grade.

"A sports scholarship got me through college, then I borrowed money to go to law school. I thought I needed to give back, as they say, so I was a public defender for a time. Then one day I heard God tell me to move to Shelburg. He had a church He wanted me to lead. Not what I expected, but what God planned all along."

Morrison drank some of his coffee before he said, "I still defend the public, members of my flock, and some of the folks in the neighborhood. Folks like the Hoyts."

Benton's eye twitched. He didn't need Morrison to remind him of their first meeting in Hollister's office.

"Folks like you," Morrison continued. He pointed to Stan when he said, "I suspect your life didn't roll out the way you expected either."

"You're referring to Tina?"

"I prayed for that girl long before she got herself pregnant. Tina wanted someone to love her. Instead of looking for the Lord and His perfect love, she went looking for the cheap kind."

When Stan winced, Morrison held up a hand and said, "I'm not passing judgment on you, son."

"It's not as if I wasn't a guilty party."

"Oh, I know you played your part, but if you hadn't fallen for her, she'd have found someone else. Now, I don't mean to belittle your relationship. I don't. I just remember Tina Hastings as she was in high school."

"Are you saying she wanted to get pregnant?" Stan asked. "That doesn't make sense. More than anything, Tina wanted to go to college. She had her first semester's coursework all planned out."

"Is that what she told you?"

"Yes. That and the fact that I didn't need to worry about birth control because she had taken care of that part."

"Hmm. Sounds like Tina."

Stan sat up straight as a fire ignited somewhere in his belly. "You're saying she lied about the birth control?"

"I didn't ask Tina to leave the congregation because she made a mistake. We're all sinners. I asked her to leave because she planned it all."

Tina planned it? She lied? About college? About the pregnancy being an accident? All of it? Stan fought to keep his composure as Morrison's words whirled in his brain.

"I got wind of a pact she and two other girls made. One of them was only fifteen. I managed to talk some sense into the other two, but when I warned Tina of the consequences she faced, she didn't care. When she had her way—with you, apparently—and found herself pregnant, she was elated when she needed to be repentant."

"She used me?" Stan's voice sounded like an eight-year-old blubbering over a dead goldfish. "Why would she do that? She threw her future away too." The air in the room resembled a generously stoked furnace. He wiped a trickle of sweat from his forehead.

"Officer Benton—Stan—she may have thrown your life in a direction you couldn't have anticipated, but you have two beautiful children. Regardless of the circumstances surrounding their births, those precious little ones are a blessing. Don't ever forget that."

Stan clenched his hands, released them long enough to stretch his fingers, and curled them tight again. "Why'd she want to have a baby? We were just kids. I don't get it."

"You might know that Tina had an ugly home life."

No, Stan didn't know about her home life. Her kin tossed her on the sidewalk the day her pregnancy test turned up positive. She got ugly every time he mentioned her family, so he quit asking about it.

"A hurtful situation," Morrison said, "that left her empty. Sometimes teenagers choose to have a baby because they want to love someone, and so they think the baby will return their love and fill their own emptiness. Trouble is, that kind of thinking always comes up short."

Comes up short? That trouble hijacked Stan's life. He loved Tyler and Lauren, no doubt, but he wasn't ready to be a dad. Not when he was eighteen. Tina's recklessness—no, her scheme—made every single thing that came afterwards a hundred times harder than it should have been.

"Do you know the Lord, Stan?"

What? Not now. Not while fury and loathing found a foothold deep in his core. The sensations multiplied until they filled each cell to capacity. Tina annoyed Stan. Frustrated him. Irritated him. Baited him. Morrison wanted to know if he knew the Lord? How could he? The only thing Stan didn't question at this moment was the level of hatred that occupied his soul.

"Hmm?" Morrison prodded.

Stan worked to control his respirations. In. Out. In. Out. He had a good poker face, and he donned it as his eyes locked with Morrison's penetrating gaze.

"I don't mean to sound disrespectful, but I don't understand how people can have faith in a God who doesn't step in when people need him. He let Tina ruin my life. Besides that, I've seen bad things on my watch. I don't have much need for a God who doesn't punish evil."

"I hear you. Now I know how to put my prayers for you in order."

Stan fumbled to retrieve his cell phone from his pants pocket. He picked it up, pretended urgency as he stared at the blank screen, and stood. "I'm sorry. I have to go."

"We didn't get to your legal woes."

"I have to leave. Thanks for your time."

"Same time next week?" Morrison asked.

"Dunno. I have to go."

Stan closed the office door behind him and took broad strides down the hallway and to the front door. When he stepped outside and closed the door behind him, he leaned against the heavy wood and gasped as bitter, wintry air filled his lungs. He closed his eyes and lifted his face to the heavens.

God? Up there? Maybe. He sure wasn't down here doing anything good for Stan Benton. Stan wiped the weariness and frustration out of his eyes. It wasn't until he opened them again that he saw the camera. Great. Good to know he provided Morrison with his evening entertainment.

Sixteen

Zach didn't know if he should panic or celebrate. Nancy and Mae returned to work after their Kentucky basket weaving retreat, both bouncing off the walls with a degree of enthusiasm generally relegated to girls in middle school. They gushed over their instructors like they might have talked about the cutest boy in homeroom, and tee-heed about the money they spent while they were under the influence of all things weave-able. The two swooned over the number and complexity of the basket kits they brought home.

Zach still didn't get it—the weaving thing—but if he could entice more than a hundred like-minded and deep-pocketed fanatics to come to his playground, he'd do his best to satisfy their every whim.

When Nancy presented a list of potential instructors fourteen names long, Zach figured he might be able to talk four or five of them into committing to their proposition. Instead, in his hands he held the eighth signed contract. It's not that the others on the list turned him down; they had yet to respond.

They had teachers lined up and the dates of the retreat confirmed. Zach raised his pen for the umpteenth time and hovered the nib over the signature line, only to put it down again. How hard could it be? Sign the contract for the venue and send a hefty deposit check. Set up an account at the bank to collect registration fees. Submit the inventory order. Stock the shelves. Never mind that the order represented half of what the business sold in all of the prior year. Have faith. Do it.

When his morning coffee came around a second time in the form of heartburn, he repeated his personalized version of an old movie tag line, "If we invite them, they will come." He sucked in a mouthful of courage and picked up the pen.

"What are you mumbling about?" Mae asked as she dropped a pile of paperwork on Zach's desk.

"If we invite them, they will come."

"Huh?"

"To the retreat. If we invite them, they will come. Right?"

"What are you worried about? Nancy and I chatted up *The Basket Works'* inaugural weaving retreat to every single person who walked into the Kentucky workshops."

"Your selling skills will insure we break even?" Zach asked. Cranky Mae? A sales person? The retreat was sunk, for sure.

"Break even? Ha. You'll see. The retreat will pay for itself and you'll drum up some new business. Repeat business."

Zach pointed to the stack of instructor contracts. "Are any of these people customers?"

"A few."

"How do we get their business? They have to buy supplies to make kits for their students. I want to be their supplier."

"Offer them a discount," Mae said. Her voice grew animated when she said, "Wait a minute. I have an idea." She walked out of the office and hollered, "Nancy. Come here."

Several minutes passed before Mae returned, a bedraggled Nancy huffing alongside her. Nancy wore a heavy apron covered with splotches of various hues. Zach bit his lower lip as he spied a streak of navy blue running across Nancy's cheek. Those dyes were supposed to be permanent, weren't they?

"Dyeing reed?" Zach asked.

"Trying to. What'd ya want?"

"Mae fetched you. You'll have to ask her."

Nancy glared at Mae, but pulled her face back as Mae peered at her cheek. "What?"

"Hmm? Nothing."

"Why am I here?" Nancy asked.

"Question. I have a question," Mae said.

"Couldn't you have waited until I finished the batch?"

Mae dipped her head toward Zach and said, "Naw, he needs to know now."

"Know what?" Zach asked.

"Here's the deal," Mae said. "You can offer the instructors a discount when they order the supplies to make up their class kits. Our competitors offer discounts, though, so that's not my brainchild."

"And?" Nancy asked.

"Every weaver wants the luxury of a ready-to-weave kit as opposed to preparing one. Every teacher dreams of a way to teach a class without preparing all of the kits."

"Why? What's the big deal?" asked Zach.

"If the basket has any color, first you have to dye the reed," Nancy said as she waved both hands over the front of her stained apron.

"No, first you have to drag out all the different sizes of reed," Mae said.

Nancy tapped her toe when she said, “You wanted my input. Let me speak.”

Mae curled her mouth into a pout and swung her head back and forth like a five-year-old conceding to a tattletale.

“A basket might use a dozen different sizes or types of reed. You have to grab each size, pull out however much reed you need to dye, dye the reed, set the dye, rinse the reed, and hang it up to dry. You have to measure and cut the spokes, sand the wood bases and handles, pick the right rim filler. All that stuff. It’s a lot of work.”

Zach turned to Mae. “I get it. What’s your point?”

“What if we offered to put their kits together for them? Instead of offering a discount, we’d add a surcharge.”

Nancy stepped aside and eyed Mae from her feet to the top of her head.

“What?” Mae asked.

No matter how he viewed this gathering, Zach could not eradicate the grammar and middle school images the two women conveyed.

“It’s brilliant,” Nancy said.

Mae, who stood ready to defend herself, if fists and a puffed out lower lip were any indication, paused at the comment. “It is?”

Zach sat up taller. Nancy thought Mae brilliant? It was his duty to take notes.

“I don’t know if any of them will take us up on the offer, but time is money.”

“What about our manpower?” Zach asked.

“Boss. Honey,” Mae said, “until we get these instructors as recurring customers, we have plenty of time to put a few kits together. In fact, I think we should look through your daddy’s pattern collection and put some of our own kits together to sell along with the rest of our supplies."

Nancy's pointed finger wagged in time with her head. "Another good idea. If we pick the right basket patterns, make up kits, and price 'em right, we'll sell out."

The weight of the pen in Zach's hand went from two-ton to feather-light. Better, the rollers in his stomach went from high tide to smooth as glass.

"I need two things," Zach said. "A formula to determine a weaving kit set-up surcharge, and a selection of patterns for our own kits."

"Better let Nancy help with the formula," Mae said.

"Why's that?" Nancy asked.

"My skills are with marketing. I'll pick basket patterns that sell."

Zach was out of his element and at the mercy of two senior citizens who both claimed super powers. If not for the fact that this event put everything at stake, Zach might find the ladies' self-proclaimed business expertise exemplary. Instead, Nancy and Mae scared him half to death.

As the women left Zach to his role of decision-maker, they bantered and giggled about dyed reed and weaving patterns. He raised his pen, scribbled his name on the rental hall contract and the check that covered one-half of the fee.

As he stuffed the papers into an envelope, his eye caught the family photograph sitting on the corner of his desk. His gaze rested on Conner. It was just a loan. A short-term loan. Zach slid his tongue over the nasty-tasting adhesive on the flap and flinched when the edge of the paper sliced his tongue.

"Good thing we don't believe in omens, right son?" Zach asked the image in the photograph. His hollow chuckle echoed from one side of the room to the other. He stuck a stamp on the envelope. If we invite them, they will come. How risky could it be?

~

Juanita eyed the stack of envelopes Zach dumped on the kitchen table. His expression was both comical and frazzled. Although she still disagreed with Zach and Conner's decision to override her vote against borrowing from the college funds, the initial response stunned her. It was as if Zach unlocked the secret to the success of operating a basket weaving supply business.

"How many today?" she signed.

"Thirty-two."

Juanita made the sign for number and raised her eyebrows.

"All together?" Zach's eyes glinted as a liberal supply of satisfaction meandered across his face. "One thirty. This is insane. Can you believe it? A hundred and thirty participants. Already."

"Why did you bring these home?" Juanita pointed to the envelopes.

"I have to create a spreadsheet."

"You? A spreadsheet?" Juanita made a mental note to stay away from the computer. Far away.

"Maybe Conner will help."

"Maybe Conner will help with what?" Conner asked as he dropped into a chair. "Something smells good."

"Lasagna."

Conner's fingers drummed the top of the table when he said, "How can I go away to school when you feed me lasagna? Maybe I should apply at the local community college for the first two years."

"If we don't earn your money back, you might have to," Zach said.

Juanita flicked her tongue against the back of her teeth, but her "tsk" was either inaudible or disregarded. In his elation over the number of people who had already registered for the retreat, Zach had no idea that Juanita found his quip to be anything but funny.

"I'm not worried about it," Conner said.

Juanita was.

"Why do you need my help?" Conner asked Zach.

"I have to create a spreadsheet in order to assign the students to the classes."

This was news to Juanita. "Don't they pick what they want to weave before they register?"

"What if everyone wanted the same class? Each class has a maximum number of students."

"How do you choose?" she signed.

"They have to give first, second, and third choices for each weaving day. We'll try to honor their preferences, but we won't be able to please everyone."

"What if they don't like the assignments?"

"They're not supposed to sign up for anything they are not willing to make. In reality, I guess some of them might be disappointed and drop out."

The answer thudded against Juanita's protective instincts—the ones that voted against borrowing Conner's money. People could back out. Demand their money back.

While Izzy set the table and Juanita prepared a salad, Zach and Conner sat on stools at the kitchen counter and scribbled on several sheets of notebook paper. They looked cute with their heads bumped together. Juanita's heart took another misstep. She'd miss her son. When did he grow up? Where had the years gone? The emotion caught her off guard. She wiped a tear from her eye, pulled the lasagna out of the oven, and invited her family to join her for dinner.

After they ate and she and Izzy cleaned up the kitchen, Juanita went upstairs and pulled her box of Christmas cards from a closet shelf. As she descended the stairs, the lingering scent of garlic met her before she was halfway down. She sneaked into the den where Zach and Conner worked at the computer, slipped her address book from a shelf, and retreated to the dining room table.

She knew he was there, standing in the doorway, watching. Waiting. When his warm lips tickled her neck, she pretended to ignore him. She failed, utterly, to ignore the bear hug that lifted her out of her seat and spun her around. His kiss was warm, hungry. When he pulled back to look at her face, his eyes wore mischief.

"Are you and Conner finished?" she signed.

"I am."

"Conner?"

"He has work to do. He's smarter than I am." Zach looked at the stack of envelopes. "Sending Christmas cards or inviting more people to weave?"

"The weaving event is yours. All yours," she signed.

Conner stood in the doorway and waved to get her attention. "The weaving event is a family affair. Didn't Dad tell you about our next assignment?"

Juanita turned toward Zach. "What?"

Zach wagged his finger and said, "It's nothing." He sent a perturbed scowl in Conner's direction when he asked, "You finish that spreadsheet?"

"I did."

"How?"

"I know people."

"What are you talking about?"

Juanita watched the banter between her son and husband. She'd miss that too.

"Your spreadsheet is attached to an email message. Go look in your inbox." Conner said.

Zach tapped a finger to his lip and feigned annoyance.

"Okay, okay. Here's the deal. If someone else already invented the wheel, why start over?"

Izzy sidestepped Conner and took a seat next to Juanita. "What are we talking about?" she asked.

"Wheels," Zach answered.

"You brought home brochures from the retreat in Kentucky. Remember?" Conner asked.

"Yeah."

"I emailed the contact person. I told her what we were doing and asked how they assigned classes."

"Why would she share that with you?" Zach asked.

"The workshop was sponsored by a weaving guild. They're not competing with you. In fact, she said she'd be happy to answer any questions. She figures that if we keep people enthused with weaving, they'll show up next year at their retreat."

"So . . . basket weavers are just one big happy family?" Izzy asked.

"You're asking me?" Zach replied. "I guess so. What about the class assignments?"

"Dad, if you open your email, you will find the template for assigning classes, and for keeping tabs on instructors, class size, class times, and table assignments." Conner pointed to the den. "Go. Observe the work of genius."

"No kidding?" Zach asked.

"I'll even help you start to fill in the blanks."

"You know what this means?" Zach's eyes danced in the light of the ceiling lamp.

Izzy inched backward, as if she needed to brace herself against the chair. Juanita exchanged glances with her daughter and did likewise. Yeah, something was coming.

"Now that Conner has a handle on the assignments, we can get started on the weaving kits. Who's in?" Zach rubbed his hands together and said, "I can pay my beloved family members exactly nothing in return for dyeing reed, measuring and cutting, sorting, stuffing, and whatever else it is that Mae and Nancy tell us we need to do. Y'all ready?"

Juanita attempted to mimic Izzy again as she slithered from her seat and made a dash for the door. Izzy reached her hand behind her, grabbed her mother's wrist, and ran down the hallway. Juanita couldn't hear the laughter, but her heart lit up, just the same.

Seventeen

Zach scanned the parking lot for vans with satellite dishes on their roofs. At the least, he expected a cameraman and a local news anchor to have set up an on-site interview, not with Pastor Morrison, but with guest speaker Sumo Hollister. Either Zach missed the media moment, or Hollister failed to win another glimmer in the limelight. Had the grandstander lost his touch?

Zach tugged the heavy door open and stepped into the empty vestibule. He followed the low murmur of voices and took a seat toward the front of the sanctuary. The leaders of the various church committees, deacons, and program coordinators conversed with one another while they waited for the meeting to begin. Déjà vu—except for the presence of Hollister.

Craig stood in front of the group, in the aisle between the first pew and the raised platform reserved for the pastor, guest speakers, and the choir. He opened the meeting with prayer, and then gestured toward Hollister.

"The heat is on, my friends, because New Life Chapel is making headway in this neighborhood. While progress is a soothing balm to the residents and the members of this congregation, our success has angered the evil forces that want to thwart our good work. In light of recent incidents meant to undermine our efforts, I asked Acting Captain Frederick Hollister to address our leadership.

"Before I turn the pulpit over to the captain, let me remind you of a few appropriate scriptures. Jesus said, 'In the world you will have tribulation. But take heart; I have overcome the world.' Let me remind you that God gave believers a head-to-toe defense system. We shall fasten the belt of truth, put on the breastplate of righteousness, and take up the shield of faith, the helmet of salvation, and the sword of the Spirit."

Craig took time to exchange eye contact with everyone. He shook his finger and said, "Write out the 'Armor of God' verses found in Ephesians and plaster the paper to your bathroom mirror. Read the passage as soon as your eyes blink past the glare of the lightbulbs that try to scrub the sleep out of your eyes."

Deacon Bernard Ames, who sat in front of Zach, said, "Amen, brother. Amen."

"Captain, now that the troops are sufficiently aware of their callings, their duties, and their weaponry, I'll turn the time over to you."

Hollister took his place behind the small dais that someone had positioned in front of the pews. He ran his index finger behind his stiff white shirt collar, and tugged at his navy blue tie, as if he needed more room for his Adam's apple to bob while he swallowed a mouthful of discomfort.

Were the surroundings unfamiliar because the parishioners were a variety of colors and ages, or was the pompous civil servant ill at ease because he had positioned his adult life in the same worldly places as he did his youthful self?

A pang as small but effective as a needle's prick collided with Zach's conscience. Would Hollister turning his life around appease Zach's distaste for the man? Since that didn't appear to be the case, the righteous anger Zach held for Hollister seemed acceptable. The stinging sensation vanished as soon as Hollister rested his scorn on Zach, cleared his throat, and began his speech.

"Thank you for having me here," Hollister said. "I'd prefer to meet you under different circumstances, like one of your barbeques." He closed his eyes, inhaled, and said, "Uh huh, fried chicken . . . sweet potato pie."

Zach clenched his jaw as he saw several people sit taller in their seats. If Hollister were so dumb as to add watermelon to his menu, Zach would climb over the three people sitting between him and the aisle, and put his fist down Hollister's throat on behalf of everyone present.

Instead, when Hollister opened his eyes and encountered what had to be a room full of people all too familiar with prejudice and its cost, he coughed, found his place, and fumbled forward. He'd do everyone a favor if he stuck to the written material. "But that's a topic for another time. Right now, I want to assure you that my officers are on your side."

Zach hung his head. If Hollister had to define sides, he was ill prepared to serve as an acting police captain. No one in the room said a word, but rustling papers and Erlene Starr rocking her body back and forth weren't positive responses. The air bore the weight of a humid summer evening—one that held the power to produce a wicked thunderstorm.

"We appreciate your organizing watch groups and designating safe houses on almost every block," Hollister continued. "I'm here tonight because we need to talk about those safe houses."

"How are kids supposed to feel safe if the place they're supposed to go has a boarded up window?" someone asked. "Ain't no secret some hoodlum hurled a brick through it."

"And what about the swastika someone spray-painted on Brother Thomas' window? It may have washed off that time, but what happens when they paint one on the side of the house? Or the church?" another asked.

"I'm having second thoughts about being a safe house," one of the women said. "I can't afford to repair vandalism. None of us folks can."

The more people questioned, the larger Hollister's eyeballs grew. He wasn't prepared for emotional outbursts? What did he expect?

"Let me assure you that we've stepped up patrols in the area," Hollister said as he raised his hands.

"Where are they?" Bernard asked. "I sure don't see them."

"Trouble usually comes at night. It's my night crew," Hollister replied. "I had my officers report on streetlights that need repair, and sent a request to the city's utility division to put them on a priority list."

"What do you suggest *we* do?" Craig asked. "You know, as a former athlete, that a mighty defense is a formidable thing. How might we prepare?"

Hollister's chest expanded at the mention of his high school sports reputation. Zach's teeth ground.

"Stay vigilant. If you see cars that don't belong, note the make, model, color, and license plate. If you see suspicious activity, call."

"Your 911 operators are willing to dispatch someone just because we think a group of kids is up to no good?" Erlene asked.

"Make it clear you don't have an emergency, but that you request an officer drive by the area. If we do nothing more than alert troublemakers to our ready presence, they'll think twice about doing harm. Prevention, like defense, is key."

"What if we put signs in our yard like 'Premises guarded by Smith and Wesson'?" one of the deacons asked.

"Sounds like an invitation for a robbery. You don't need to alert anyone that you have something worth the risk of breaking and entering. I suspect you all know the law about owning and carrying weapons. That's a personal decision. Just follow the law. And don't advertise."

"Anything else?" Craig asked.

"Keep your front and back porch lights on—all night long. If you can afford to install security cameras above your doors, do it. They're affordable, but the monthly monitoring fee can be a deterrent."

That little tidbit set off a room full of grumbling, Zach included. He still had the security company's signs in front of the door and loading dock at *The Basket Works*, but if anyone broke into the building, no one would be the wiser. Until the company started generating a profit, the cameras were nothing but a charade.

As the meeting ended and people spilled out of the building, Craig sidled up to Zach.

"Got a minute?"

"Sure."

"What's your beef with Hollister?"

"Beside the fact that his subordinates hauled Juanita and me to the precinct?" After forty minutes in the same room with Sumo, Zach wasn't in the mood for chitchat. Neither was the pastor.

"I'm not talking about that."

"It was a lifetime ago. Doesn't matter," Zach said. He had about four seconds to come up with a reason to end this conversation. Its destination was a place he didn't want to go.

"Something eating you. If you were a porcupine, you'd be quill-less and Hollister would have nine-thousand poison-tipped spikes sticking out of his body."

Zach paused at the remark. "I know you want to be serious, but you have to admit that image is classic. Classic what, I don't know."

"It's true, though."

"Yeah. Bad feelings go deep."

"Not right for you to harbor them all these years."

"Is this where you remind me to forgive my enemies?"

"I don't need to tell you that. You already know. What you need is to get it out so you can get on with it."

Pastor—the title Zach used when his conversation with Craig ran beyond the realm of friendship—had a point, but could Zach lug the mess out from under decades of silence? If he aired his grievance, which would expose the depth of his own anger, could he put a lid back on it again? An unlikely outcome.

On the other hand, until the real police captain returned to duty, the turmoil that accompanied every mention of Hollister's name would continue to eat at Zach. And what of unexpected encounters with the man? Zach did not like the person he became when he was in Hollister's presence.

"Fine."

"Fine?" Pastor asked.

"Since I don't know how long it takes a porcupine to grow a new set of quills, I worry that I won't have sufficient weaponry for the next confrontation."

Pastor clapped Zach on the shoulder and said, "Let's go

to my office. Take a load off. Have a cup of tea."

The sun peeked through intermittent cloud cover and danced across the top of the desk while the wind tugged at a few stubborn leaves clinging to the scraggly limbs of the old oak tree that stood just beyond the office window.

"Gonna be a cold night," Pastor said. "Good thing we had the furnace serviced. Thing will run all night."

"If we're lucky," Zach said.

"Don't believe in luck."

"Neither do I."

"I do believe in dealing with sin."

"Like holding a grudge?" Zach's entire body sagged. The past was a heavy weight.

Pastor's eyes bore into Zach's face.

"I don't know why you quit practicing law," Zach said. "You'd intimidate a confession out of the accused without opening your mouth."

"I served as a defender, not a prosecutor," Pastor said. A wry smile filled his face. "I was good, though."

"Good enough to prompt my confession. I don't harbor a grudge. The more correct description is hate. I hate Frederick Hollister." There. Zach said it. Out loud. The statement released more heat into the room than the furnace transported hot air from the basement, but if the declaration instigated such a reaction, the explanation might incite an inferno.

"Most truthful thing I've heard all day. Uh huh. Go on."

"Hollister and I nurtured a general dislike of each other all through middle school and high school. His parents had money, coddled him, and taught him to defend himself against the fatty jokes by putting everybody in their place. His mouth was as effective a repellent as DDT, and like the insecticide, its stench and sting lingered long after it was applied."

"That's almost as good as my porcupine analogy."

"When my foray into taking bets for high school sports ended with my dismissal from the basketball and football teams, Hollister's delight in antagonizing me increased tenfold. Trouble was, he had substance behind his words after that."

Zach waited for the pastor's assessment of him to reflect disappointment. Judgment was sure to follow. In the quiet, Pastor tapped his fingers against his lips.

"Not what I expected, but that doesn't explain the hatred. No, sir. Hatred comes when somebody does something ugly to us that we don't deserve."

The burst of heat that assaulted Zach's body was just one of the discernable signs of his mounting discomfort. Before he started foaming at the mouth, he swallowed bitterness and continued his tale. "The weekend after graduation, a lot of the seniors held parties at their homes. Groups went from one place to another, eating, drinking."

"Alcohol?"

"Yeah. Plenty of that."

"Where were the parents?"

"Most places, they were home. I remember one house where the parents waited at the front door and poured cups of spiked punch before we could get inside. It was crazy."

"Foolish."

"I know that now. Back then, we thought we were invincible."

"So what happened with Hollister?"

"The guys who offered to drive decided to go to Hollister's house. Rumor had it that his parents put out quite a spread. We were hungry, so we hit their house. I remember it as if it were yesterday. Bunch of us stood around the table, scarfing food and enjoying our share of beverages. The best part was that Sumo wasn't around."

Visions of platters filled with roast beef sandwiches, tiers of glass plates holding cookies, brownies, and fudge, and bowls brimming with nuts and mints turned Zach's stomach into an acidic cauldron. He could still smell the sickly sweet punch and the sour breath of his companions.

"You're looking a little pasty. Need some water?"

Zach waved the offer away. "When it came time for us to go, we couldn't find one of the girls. We split up and searched all the obvious places: family room, basement, patio. Nobody holed up in the bathrooms. Couldn't find her. The guys got mad and left."

"Why'd you stick around?"

"I was responsible for her."

"Why you?"

How long could Zack sidestep direct questions? "I snuck upstairs and started checking the bedrooms." The image the memory revived was already bad. How could he put this into words?

"Zach?"

"I heard her whimpering, ran down the hallway, and rammed the door open. He had his hands all over her. Her crying meant nothing to him. Neither did my appearance. He turned around, still holding her wrists, and laughed." Zach raised his hand and put his thumb and index finger together. "Frederick Hollister was this short of committing rape—and he laughed."

Zach's eye twitched and his heart raced at the same speed as it had the day he knocked Sumo off his feet.

"I remember how the bridge of his nose gave way to my fist. He didn't go down with my first swing, so I clocked him on the chin. Hollister may have had eighty pounds on me, but he was drunk and I was angry. If she hadn't pulled me off, I don't know if I would have let him see another day."

Pastor Morrison sat quietly while Zach let the seconds and minutes dull his overwrought emotions. He'd never told anyone. Only three people knew what happened. Now, four.

"She didn't go to the police?"

Zach lifted his eyes toward the ceiling, squinted, and grappled for the nerve he needed to tell the whole story. "We talked about it on the way home. Our ride left us, remember?" Zach didn't want a reply. He kept going. "I wanted her to report him. She wouldn't let me."

"I understand, but that's why so many get away with the crime."

"She was afraid of the publicity. He said. She said. You know about that."

"That, I do."

"She didn't want to shame her family. Any good defense attorney would try to show her at fault. You know that too."

"Like I said, I understand. Something still troubles me, though."

What more did he want? Zach had no more to tell. "Hollister went to college, I enrolled at the community college, and the girl went on with her life. End of story."

"I can see that the incident would give you a reason to treat Hollister with disdain, but you hold something personal against him." Pastor looked up, locked his knowing brown eyes on Zach, and waited.

Zach's stomach churned. He labored to bring the words to his lips. "It was personal. The girl was only fifteen. She tagged along because I told our parents I'd take care of her. Which I didn't."

"Our parents?" Pastor asked.

"Yeah. Mandi, my baby sister, was fifteen when Hollister tried to assault her."

Eighteen

Stan rehearsed his story on the way to Tina's house. He did not request the overtime assignment. That's why they call it an assignment. No, better to leave the sarcasm out of it. He didn't call ahead because he didn't want to interfere with her plans. As if she'd buy that one. Stan doing Tina a favor?

Tyler and Lauren would be safe in the basement of the church where they held the children's program. Safe, because he, the dutiful peacekeeper, would be standing guard at the front door to the building. Uniformed. Armed. Tina hated guns. Heck, Tina hated Stan. He couldn't win.

It wasn't until his conversation with Pastor Morrison, though, that Stan realized how cruel Tina was in her gamesmanship. He was so angry he couldn't get his head around the news. Tina Hastings deliberately manipulated Stan and annihilated his plans. She'd treated the man who stood at her front door, posed to knock, like a chess piece. Tina, the queen, used up people and spit 'em out. Knocked them off the board and thwarted their plans. She did it then, and she sure hadn't changed.

Pawn number two opened the door. DeWayne narrowed his eyes at the uniform and pulled his lips back as if they just sucked on sour lemon.

"You working or are you here to pick up the kids?"

"Where's Tina?"

"I'm asking the question. You picking them up or not?"

Stan could cuff the dweeb, easy, but it wasn't DeWayne's wiry frame that irritated him. Stan stuck his thumbs under the edge of his belt, the one that held his portable law enforcement arsenal. Too bad his official police-sanctioned accessories lacked a tool that could shut DeWayne's mouth.

Tina poked her head around DeWayne's arm. "You're working today?"

"I'm here to pick up the kids."

"You just get off night shift?"

"No. I'm taking them to church, then we're going to my place."

"Church? You? You always show up at church in your uni—. Uh, no way. You think you're taking my kids to New Life Chapel, don't you? You think your putting on a uniform will make me believe you can protect them from the scum that lives over there?"

Now was not the time to point out to Tina that she grew up in that neighborhood, and that her family, if you could call them that, still lived there.

"Captain asked me to do O.T. detail at the church. Wasn't my choice, but Tyler and Lauren like it there."

"Did you not hear me when I said I would file a restraining order?"

"The world heard you, Tina. Just like your neighbors are hearing you now." Stan veered his attention toward DeWayne's SUV. "Courts might have something to say about a woman who entertains men over night. You want to play that game?"

Tina's eyes bulged when she reached past the open door

and lashed at Stan's face. He took a fast step backwards. Tina's fingernails were lethal.

DeWayne put his hand around Tina's arm and tugged her back into the house. He didn't say a word, but the look he exchanged with Tina said something to the effect of, "If you let them go to church, you and I will have some privacy. Know what I mean? Uh huh?"

Stan wanted to thump him, a recurring urge. A bigger part of him wanted to tell Tina what a wretched person she was, but Stan still grappled with the conversation he had with Pastor Morrison. If Stan ventured into that territory, he might not find a way out. What he wanted right now was a day with his children.

Tina turned her back to Stan and called to the children. "Tyler. Lauren. Hurry up. Your dad's here." After DeWayne mumbled something into her ear, Tina said, "If you want, you can keep the kids overnight. Bring them back in the morning." Tina folded her arms and dared Stan to comment.

"Tell 'em to pack their pajamas."

DeWayne did an about-face and walked toward the kitchen. Although the light in the hallway was dim, Stan watched him sway his hips as he sauntered away. A muzzle was insufficient for what Stan wanted to do to the sleazebag.

Lauren and Tyler giggled and teased each other as they climbed into the car. Somehow, in spite of the mountains of upheaval that surrounded them, they tossed aside the shadows and brightened the morning with their innocent delight. Pastor Morrison's words came to mind. *Those precious little ones are a blessing. Don't ever forget that.*

~

"How come we get to stay over?" Lauren asked. "Does Mommy have study group? A late one?"

"She's too little to know better," Tyler said.

Where did that come from? With a glance to his rearview mirror, Stan looked at Tyler. Tyler responded with an expression that said he knew far too much for an eight-year-old child. Then again, how can a boyfriend sleepover be anything but indiscreet?

How was Stan supposed to react? Tina and DeWayne weren't acting like decent role models, but who was Stan to judge? One of these days, Tyler would know that he was well on the way before his parents got married. Stan glimpsed the reflection in the mirror again. More than likely, the boy had already done the math. Any words out of Stan's mouth would be those of a hypocrite.

Instead of changing the subject, Stan, the guilty and powerless pawn, ignored Lauren's question and sidestepped with, "What's DeWayne do? He got a job?"

"He works in the electric department," Lauren replied.

"Electric department? You mean he works for the city?"

"Yeah," Tyler said. "He thinks he's real smart."

"Then why's he taking college courses?"

"His boss won't let him be a manager until he gets his degree," Tyler said.

"He doesn't look like he works outdoors. What's he do there?"

"He has a big office," Lauren said. "And he tells people what to do."

Hence, the man's mouth. City employee? Nice benefits. Job security. Same as Stan, although if DeWayne's SUV and taste in clothing were a gauge, they might find a sizeable gap between their wages. The revelation didn't mean anything. All

Stan wanted was some assurance that DeWayne Davis and Tina wouldn't do anything to hurt Lauren and Tyler.

When they arrived at New Life Chapel, Stan grabbed both children by the hand as they plowed out of the car and tried to run to the building.

"Whoa. Slow down."

Lauren didn't seem to mind, but Tyler wrenched his hand free and mumbled a two syllable, "Da-ad," and said, "Let go. Somebody'll see." Yep, Tyler was a teenager inhabiting a little boy's body.

Just like the previous week, while Stan kept watch near the front door, the building's PA system delivered Pastor Morrison's sermon to every nook and cranny. Unlike the last message, this one seemed to needle more than a few people. As his discourse on forgiveness filled an hour of the morning's service, the congregation seemed pretty antsy. Some coughed or squirmed in their seats, and four people slithered down the aisle and left the building.

When the pastor called people to forgive their offenders, he also invited them to the front of the sanctuary for prayer—as if anyone would admit to holding a grudge. Out of curiosity, Stan crossed the vestibule and peeked into the chapel.

It was no surprise when half a dozen people slipped past him and high-tailed it to the parking lot. Pastor Morrison presented compelling reasons why people should forgive and repent for holding on to their anger, but expecting them to make a public admission by asking for prayer? Never happen. People had too much pride. Besides, folks like Tina didn't deserve forgiveness. Nothing she could ever do would make up for what she'd done.

Twenty people, maybe more, stood at the front of the

room, heads bowed. People wandered down the aisle, some stepping into the line for prayer, others laying a hand on the shoulder of the person in front of them. The figure at the far end of the first row looked familiar. Zach Hoyt? Asking for prayer? No way. What was that all about?

Stan backed away from the doorway as his skin prickled. Heat climbed up his spine with an intensity sufficient to dispense a layer of sweat across his bare skull. Stan took off his hat and wiped the sheen away. The effort did little to dissuade the discomfort. Was Hoyt praying because he needed to forgive Stan for taking his wife to the station? Stan balked. He couldn't undo or fix that episode any more than Tina could reverse her actions.

By the time the last of the congregation left the building and Stan mouthed a gratuitous, "Fine sermon," to Morrison, he was one spent guard dog. With two happy children escorting him back to their car, he expected his consternation to go away. Instead, it hung to his ankles like a ball and chain pinned to leg irons.

Stan oversaw the seatbelt buckling and started to get into the car. Hollister would hang him out to dry if he forgot. He dashed back to the building, begged a copy of the bulletin from Morrison, and tipped his hat as he backed away from the building and bolted to his getaway vehicle. He turned the key, put the car into gear, and looked in his rearview mirror. Go, go, go!

Nineteen

Zach was right. This was insane. Juanita lowered the basket shears to the table and flexed her fingers. They protested while she massaged away the curled-around-the-handle shape that they'd held for the last hour.

Two jumbled piles of flat reed sat in front of her. If she counted right, she was finished cutting the spokes. Next on her list was gathering seven spokes from the pile of long pieces and fastening them with a twist tie. Then she would bunch and tie eleven of the shorter spokes. After that, she had to repeat the process eleven more times. What a chore—and just the tip of the proverbial iceberg. How would they ever finish?

The tap on Juanita's shoulder startled her. She looked up to see impish grins on the faces of Izzy and Paige. Splotches of dark green, black, pumpkin, and red covered their aprons. Juanita's inspection of the mess ended at their feet. She looked up at the girls, horrified.

"It's okay, Mom," Izzy said. "After the first drips, we decided to add a little color here, a little color there." Izzy's ponytail bounced as she talked. A deep pink hue colored her cheeks, a side effect of wrestling with a vat filled with hot water, reed, and basket dye.

"Will your grandmother be angry?" Juanita signed.

Paige pointed to Izzy and finger-spelled, "Her shoes."

"Old shoes," Izzy signed. "Lunch is here. Come on."

Juanita took another look at two pairs of canvas shoes. They were colorful. Good move on Izzy's part to lend a pair of her sneakers to Paige. Work clothes, too. When Paige spent the night at their house, none of them expected her to volunteer to help with the basket kits. Her helping hands were welcome, but the friendship the girls nurtured was priceless.

As the group gathered around an empty table, Conner unfolded a spreadsheet and asked, "Who wants the latest statistics?"

Zach, who chewed on a big bite of turkey on rye, raised a hand. Conner didn't wait for the others to respond.

"So far, four of the basket-weaving instructors who signed up to teach at the retreat decided to have us make their student kits."

"That's a lot," Juanita signed.

Mae pooh-poohed the comment and said, "They just want to enjoy the holidays and have a calm and peaceful New Year."

Nancy pointed a finger at Zach and said, "I told you. Your offer was like a salve to their chapped and Rit-dyed hands. They cut a little off their profit for the sake of mental and physical relief."

"You won't hear me complain," Zach replied. "Still, they have to stick out their necks on a retreat, just like we do."

"How?" Juanita asked.

"They have to pay for the supplies before they get paid."

"I thought you collected class payments from the students after they accepted the assignments," Juanita signed.

"I did, but we don't cash those checks. The student makes the check out to the instructor and post-dates it. We don't hand them over to the instructor until after the retreat."

"The good news," Conner said, "is that the supplies we use to assemble these kits are already counted as sales to *The Basket Works.* We get our net profit from the supplies now, and the fee to assemble the kits is pure profit."

"Only because you're not paying any of us for our slave labor," Izzy said. Her facial expression satisfied Juanita that Izzy wasn't just okay with her work, but was thrilled to spend time goofing around with Paige. A look at their shoes and their mischievous eyes wiped away any worry about her comment.

The reed-dyeing part of the process was arduous, the other assignments repetitive and messy. So far, Juanita managed to hide when Zach designated members of his haphazard team of volunteers to the reed-dyeing task, or maybe Zach knew better than to ask her.

"You want to trade assignments with your mom after lunch?" Zach asked.

Juanita could feel the whites of her eyes expand as she paused somewhere between lifting her sandwich from her plate and drawing it to her gaping mouth. She lowered her sandwich and pointed to herself. She finger-spelled, "Dye reed?"

"No, we're good." Izzy to the rescue.

"I'm kidding," Zach said. "The reed looks fantastic. The girls are doing a great job." Zach's playfulness trekked across the table and landed somewhere in that special place in Juanita's heart that she kept just for him.

"Back to the numbers," Conner said. "We have eleven instructors coming from around the area. Each of them committed to one class on each of the three days, so a total of thirty-three classes."

"Does that include my four-hour classes?" Nancy asked.

"No. You bring the number of classes to thirty-six," Conner said. "With twelve classes a day, and a maximum of twelve students per class, we can accommodate up to 144 weavers."

"How many?" Juanita asked. Had she erred when she voiced her objection to this risky venture?

"We sent class assignments to 144; 131 have accepted them and submitted payment," Conner said. "We have a waiting list if we don't hear from the other 13 by the end of the week.

"Better than I imagined," Zach said.

Mae said, "I told you." Although Mae leveled her retort at Zach, the jab landed squarely on Juanita's skepticism. Conner ignored the wisecrack as he continued. "We'll make kits for the 4 instructors. Three classes each, times 12 students, makes 144 kits."

"Their classes are full?" Juanita asked.

"Every one of them," Zach said.

Nancy put an elbow on the table and tapped a finger to her lips. Zach was first to interpret the body language. "We also have to assemble the kits for Nancy's classes, so 36 more, for a total of 180."

"A hundred and eighty?" Izzy asked. "Wow."

Yes, wow. Juanita leaned sideways and reviewed Conner's spreadsheet. In the left-most column was a small photo of each class project. They were colorful, no doubt.

"Do all of the kits we have to assemble include dyed reed?" Juanita signed.

Conner left a tiny pencil mark beside some of the photos,

and when he reached the last page, he chuckled. "Every one of them. Well, no, that's not true. This kit has smoked reed; nothing dyed."

"That's the one I'm working on right now." Juanita held up her fingers, which looked as if they had some serious tobacco stains. She held her hand under Izzy's nose.

"Ew. It smells smoky, all right. I don't want to know what they used for fuel." Izzy pushed Juanita's hand away and stuck out her tongue.

"It's pretty. Look at the photo," Juanita signed.

"I'd rather dye the reed brown than use that stuff," Izzy replied.

"That wouldn't be authentic," Mae said. "Smoked reed has its place. Smell or no smell, we like it. Right, Nancy?"

"Yeah, we do. We like it a lot."

Zach leaned his head toward Izzy and Paige and sniffed. "You two smell like . . . what?"

"Vinegar," Izzy said.

"Way to attract the guys," Conner quipped as he curled his nose.

Paige rolled her eyes at him, but Izzy, always on her toes and ready to defend her little sisterhood, said, "Hey, wise guy, it helps set the dyes."

Juanita started to gather the paper plates, napkins, and the deli's white paper bags while Zach grabbed the paper cups and emptied leftover ice into the nearby sink.

Conner drummed the tabletop with his knuckles and said, "Don't forget the other basket kit list."

What other list? Juanita watched the contentment wash out of Zach's face. It was the did-you-have-to-bring-it-up-now look that drew the memory to the forefront. In addition to 180 kits to assemble for the instructors, *The Basket Works'* plan entailed the preparation of a dozen kits for each of the patterns Nancy and Mae selected from the store's archives.

"How many?" Juanita signed, although she didn't want to know the answer.

It was Mae who lowered her gaze and pretended not to hear Izzy's translation of Juanita's question.

"Uh," Conner started, "I have a list of eight patterns. If we go with the plan, eight times twelve is—"

"Ninety-six?" Juanita signed. Her hands hurt. They threatened to cramp all night long, just as they had after her first shift at the reed-cutting table four days earlier. Ninety-six? What about her real job, her editing gig?

Insane was not the appropriate term, but she was at a loss to find a more severe adjective for Zach's brilliant save-the-business plan.

~

Zach wasn't dancing yet, but some of the angst vanished as another wave of signed instructor contracts and weaver registrations landed in the business mailbox. He patted himself on the back, just a little, when the weaving kit tasks brought his family closer together. If only it were in his power to freeze this blink in time.

Who knew where Conner might end up after he graduated? Scholarships might direct his path as much, or more, than his personal choice. He wanted to go to the local university, which would eliminate the need to fund room and board, but the private tuition all but put that choice beyond his reach. The chance to earn a full scholarship was about as likely as Zach weaving a Nantucket Lightship Basket. Zero.

After everyone left for the day, Zach turned on the

security cameras and set the alarm. While the attempts to thwart thieves lacked a monitoring service that might alert the authorities to a break-in, the sound of the alarm might encourage a trespasser to abandon his plot to rob the place.

It's not that the warehouse held anything that might be of value on the black market. Zach hadn't heard of any covert trading in basket supplies, but if some of the weavers were as intense as Mae and Nancy, who knew? As much as he wanted to summon the image, Zach couldn't fathom a room full of more than 150 weaving enthusiasts.

When he pulled into the driveway, a streak of stubborn orange sat low on the horizon while stars began to glimmer against an indigo sky. Although the house was dark, it came as no surprise that Juanita wasn't home yet. She had to drop Paige back at her Grandma Dottie's house.

Zach climbed out of the car and filled his lungs with a hefty provision of sharp, icy air. This would be one of the coldest nights yet. He opened the screen door and fumbled with his key. He shoved and coaxed, but when the key refused to slide into the lock, he pulled it back, held it up to the waning light, and squinted. Right key. Wrong house?

It hadn't rained, so the lock couldn't have frozen, but no amount of cajoling earned a space for the key to enter the locking mechanism. Stupid door. Old lock.

He made his way to the back door and tried the key. This didn't make any sense. Juanita had the garage door opener, the only other method for gaining access to the house short of breaking a window. Zach retraced his steps to the front of the house.

As he made his way back to his car, where he'd find some protection from the cold, a piece of paper taped to the mailbox rustled in the wind. What was that? A note from the locksmith Zach didn't remember hiring to re-key his doors? He grabbed the note, climbed into his car, and ripped open the envelope.

The sudden flash of heat inside the car could have melted a polar icecap. His hands quaked as indignation won over fear. The text reminded Zach of a bad crime scene in a B-rated movie. Dozens of mismatched letters, glued in haphazard lines, filled the page:

> *YOUR KIND DON'T BELONG HERE NO MORE. THIS BE YOUR INVITATION TO GO AWAY. NEXT TIME YOU WON'T HAVE NUTHING LEFT TO LOCK UP. PS AIN'T SUPER GLUE SUPER? Y'ALL HAVE A REAL NICE NIGHT, BUT PACK YOUR BAGS TOMORROW.*

Twenty

"You bringing Tyler and Lauren to the ASL class tonight?" Norris rolled down her window and picked off pieces of ice that clung to the edge of the side-view mirror. Sub-zero air swept the interior of the cruiser, sucking out the heater's efforts as fast as a shop vac swallows sawdust.

Stan didn't care if Norris left the window open. The change in temperature might chill his skin, but it sure didn't have the ability to cool the source of his hot temper. Every time he revisited last night's episode with Tina, after another unplanned gift of spending time with his children so that she and DeWayne had some privacy, anger broiled.

"Yeah, they're coming with me."

"I know you don't like *De*Wayne, but you get to see your kids more since he showed up."

"Yep."

Norris flicked a sliver of ice at Stan's face. "I don't get it. I thought that's what you wanted."

Stan kept his eyes on the road while he took a hand off the steering wheel and wiped his cheek. "I want to spend time with them for the right reason, not so Tina and her stud can mess up their home life. It's not right."

"I don't approve of what they're doing, but most of the

world doesn't think it's wrong."

"I didn't care before, but Tyler understands what's going on. I don't want him to think that sex is cheap and easy. Even when someone gives it away, it costs a bundle. Tyler and Lauren have already paid too much for the farce Tina and I called a marriage, and divorce doesn't fix anything. It just reassembles the mess into a different package."

"Tell them what's right and what's wrong."

"Then it sounds as if I'm bad-mouthing their mom."

"Lead by example."

"How can I be an example when I don't have anyone in my life?"

"Let them see how you treat women in general," Norris said.

Stan's guffaw reverberated throughout the vehicle and glanced against the windows before the upholstery absorbed the racket. The action stole more air from his lungs than he'd deposited, forcing him to wheeze.

"What?" Norris asked.

"Did you hear what you just said? To me?"

"Let them see how you treat women in gen—" Norris pressed her hand against her chest, leaned forward, and discharged a belly laugh that grew in volume and intensity.

"Maybe I can get Juanita Hoyt to testify on my behalf," Stan said. The thought sobered him as deftly as a slap to the face. The sickly stomach that hit him when Pastor Morrison preached about forgiveness threatened an encore.

"Now what? What's with you today? You're all over the place," Norris said.

"Astute of you to notice," Stan said. He didn't intend to direct his sour tone toward Norris; it just came along with the nausea.

"I mean it. One second you're angry, then serious. Then you just lose it. What gives?"

"What's with the inquisition?" Stan asked. "You working on your detective badge?" The sarcasm, he relayed with premeditation.

"I don't get it. That's all. This thing between Tina and DeWayne has been going on for a while. Why the fuss now?"

"Ask me that question again in about three or four weeks."

"Benton, I'm tired. You're irritable and about as much fun as a case of the flu. Would you just pull the car to the curb and let me out? I'll walk back to the station. You can clock me out." When Norris caught Stan rolling his eyes, she folded her arms across her chest and harrumphed.

If he said it, he'd never be able to retrieve the notion, but if he kept it to himself, he'd explode. Better pull over first.

"I wasn't serious about walking, Benton. What's the matter with you?"

"It's not the flu. I'll put money on it." Stan spoke the words aloud, trying them on for size.

Norris slapped the palms of her hands against the sides of her head. "You drive me crazy. Why is it impossible to have an adult conversation with you? Huh?"

Stan spoke slowly, quietly, and with as much restraint as he could muster. "Ask me again in three weeks. If she's still green around the gills every time I pick up and drop off my kids, it's not the flu."

Norris' jaw fell open, a disquieting complement to her bulging eyes. "No." A second, prolonged assessment of Stan's comment induced a stronger reply. "No!"

"I may be wrong. I want to be wrong, but it looks to me like Tina's done it again."

~

"I can't believe you," Norris said. "Don't you have an indicator on your dash to tell you when you have to quit driving on fumes and put some petrol in the tank?"

"Yeah, I'm pathetic, but could you give me a lift to the gas station so I can buy a gallon or two?"

"You keep an empty gas can in your trunk? Huh? I sure don't."

"They'll have one at the gas station."

"With a price tag that cost you more than if you'd bothered to fill up before you ran out of vapor."

Stan blew into his bare hands. Without a hat, his head and his ears hovered around ten degrees below zero. At least Tina changed plans and kept Tyler and Lauren home tonight. They grumbled about missing a coloring session with Izzy while he fried his brain with ASL information, but having to deal with the side trip to the gas station wasn't on their top-ten list of favorite dad-time activities.

"Get in," Norris said.

After she turned into the gas station and convenience store parking lot, she pulled into an empty space near the entrance. The only other vehicle in the lot was a tired gray van with an inch of road salt clinging to its paint job. Exhaust swirled into the air, but not before its metallic odor seeped into Norris' car.

"Hurry up."

Stan slid out of his seat and leaned into the car when he said, "If I take my time in the warm store, maybe your jalopy will be warm by the time I come out."

"Or maybe the van will asphyxiate me before that. It's a

long walk back to the church, partner."

She won that round. Stan pushed open the heavy glass door and headed toward the cashier. Other than a man looking through some magazines, the place was empty.

"You sell gas cans?" Stan asked.

The short stocky man, probably of Indian descent, widened his eyes and flicked them toward the man in the dark jacket. His mouth quivered when he said, "Sold out. Sorry. Try the station around the corner."

Stan followed the clerk's eye movement. The hand in the jacket pocket, the raised collar, and the tapping feet sent a ripple of adrenaline throughout Stan's nervous system. He shrugged at the cashier while he took count: one in the store, maybe more hiding in the aisles, and at least one in the van.

"You sure?" Stan asked.

"Sold the last one yesterday."

"If I have to get my ride to take me somewhere else, I better get her a bag of chips and a six-pack of beer." Stan's casual banter, notably lacking the strident tone of someone in a dangerous situation, surprised him. He sounded cool, which he was not.

Stan walked past one aisle. Empty. Then another. Empty. When he reached the last aisle, the one with the coolers and freezers lining the wall, his count remained the same: one victim, one bad guy, one cop. As he retraced his steps toward the cashier, Norris' slamming car door changed everything.

The would-be thief pulled his nasty semi-automatic out of his pocket and fastened his aim on the cashier. Norris wouldn't see him until she was in harm's way.

She looked madder than a hornet as she strode to the door. As soon as it swung open, Stan yelled, "Don't hurt her. She can't hear." He turned toward her and put his finger up to his mouth before she could make a sound. His fingers fumbled when he spelled G-U-N.

Norris stopped and squinted her eyes while she spelled R-O-B-B-E-R-Y. Stan tipped his chin just enough to give an answer.

"What are you doing?" The robber, who still couldn't see Norris from his position in the aisle, tugged his hood forward before he turned around and looked Stan square in the face. Kid wasn't more than sixteen, seventeen. His heavy coat hung on his scrawny form. The tattoo that wrapped around his neck and throat identified him as a member of one of the newest gangs to set up shop in town.

"She's deaf. She speaks with her hands." Stan's gaze bounced from Norris, to the teenager, and back again.

The gun wavered up and down while the teenager absorbed the comment. "What's she saying?"

"She wants to know what's taking so long."

"Tell her you're done shopping here and get out. Now."

Stan glanced at the cashier, whose face was ashen, his eyes filled with panic. When his eyes darted toward the cash register, another boost of adrenaline coursed through Stan's veins. The last thing they needed was an armed employee playing hero.

Stan moved his lips slightly and mouthed, "No." He turned to Norris and signed, "Go, water, behind."

She responded with a question, "You armed?"

He nodded and then pointed at her. "You?"

"What's she saying?" the kid asked.

"She wants a bottle of water." Norris was already on her way to the coolers.

"No. Tell her to leave."

"She's out of view." Stan waved a hand back and forth.

"If she can't see me, she can't hear me. You know? Just put that away, let her pay, and we'll leave."

When the kid dug in his heels, Stan said, "Come on, you don't want to hurt anyone." Stan held a lungful of air until the thief slid his weapon back into his pocket.

"Police! Freeze!" Norris stood at the far end of the aisle, three yards from the robber, feet planted, arms raised, her firearm aimed at his chest.

When the gang member tried to brandish his gun again, Stan tackled him. He pressed his knee into the teenager's back while Norris held her gun on him.

The sound of the van pealing away from the sidewalk removed the second of Stan's fears. He breathed easy for the first time in three minutes. It felt like he'd deprived his body of air for three hours.

"You got any cuffs?" Stan asked.

"No. You?"

Stan looked at the cashier. "You have any cable ties?"

"Yes, sir." The man's voice warbled as he rounded the cash register, sped to one of the aisles, and returned with the goods.

Stan used his teeth to open the bag, and cinched the plastic tether around the aggressor's wrists. "Call 911 and tell them two off-duty cops have a thief they need to pick up."

After he hung up, the shopkeeper said, "I thought he might kill me. I don't have money in the register at night."

"Glad we could help," Norris said.

"I thought you were deaf."

"I'm not deaf."

"But you two . . . those hand signals weren't normal. You looked like you were talking."

Ah, Hollister would love this one. The mandatory ASL

class for Officer Benton proved to be useful, although its goal of replacing Stan's antagonistic disposition with some semblance of sensitivity was still questionable.

"Funny, huh?" Norris replied.

After two on-the-clock officers arrived, took their report, and hauled the juvenile delinquent into the back of their cruiser, Stan turned to the cashier and asked, "So, where do you keep the gas cans?"

The man's face turned a deep shade of crimson. He sputtered when he said, "I already told you. We sold out yesterday."

Twenty-One

"I think you need to consider my suggestion before you disagree."

"No," Juanita signed. When Zach opened his mouth to protest, she repeated herself. "No."

"Then you need to bring your laptop to *The Basket Works.* I'll set up an office for you in the corner of the warehouse."

"No."

"Yes."

Juanita closed her eyes. They'd argued—no—they'd debated the subject for two days now. Neither budged; neither persuaded the other. Zach offered two choices: get a dog so she could continue working alone at home, or work at the basket supply shop.

"I want to work here. I don't want a dog."

"A dog will alert you to a prowler."

"I'll lock the doors."

"What if they glue the locks again and set the house on fire while you're in it?" Zach asked. "Huh?"

Juanita turned her face toward the stovetop and stirred the spaghetti sauce. If Zach saw her roll her eyes one more time, the debate might escalate into an argument. She'd try another tack.

"No one will come during the day. They come at night when they can hide. You are home at night."

"You don't know that. And besides, I'm not home every night." Zach leaned against the doorjamb, his hands shoved in his back pockets, a sure sign that he considered her response lame.

No one else in the immediate vicinity had reported similar vandalism. Was the incident isolated or did the instigator target the Hoyt family?

With determined speed and unnecessary flourish, Juanita signed, "Pastor Morrison has Mabel; I'll keep Chester loaded and within reach."

"Chester?" Zach asked.

"Chester," Juanita finger-spelled. "As in Winchester."

When Zach raised his eyes to the ceiling and frowned, Juanita realized she had miss-spelled. They didn't own a Winchester. "I meant Smitty. As in Smith and Wesson."

Zach's chest deflated. "If I were a caveman, I'd toss you over my shoulder . . ." In a dramatic sweep of his arm, he hefted a damp kitchen towel over his shoulder, ". . . and I'd drag you to the shop."

The prospect of winning the debate glimmered like the ray of sunshine that settled on the snowbank outside the kitchen window. How could she bear the idea of a cubbyhole in the warehouse when winter's pristine blanket covered the landscape beyond their house? She wanted freedom to wander from room to room, to wear her favorite slippers and well-worn sweater. More important, however, was the need for solitude. Editing wasn't a group effort. She'd face countless distractions at the shop.

Juanita slipped the towel off Zach's shoulder, leaned in, and kissed him. Although she hadn't intended to create a diversion, he abandoned his case. For now.

The aroma of garlic bread seemed to have drawn Izzy and Conner to the kitchen. While Izzy filled water glasses, Conner drained the pasta. Although he'd just watched Juanita toss the salad, Zach repeated the process before he took the bowl to the table. Juanita followed with a steaming bowl of sauce.

Conversation was nonexistent while two teenagers filled their bodies with carbs and calories. And lots of garlic. As the two slowed their eating, Conner put an elbow on the table and pointed to Zach. While he finished chewing, Juanita pointed to the elbow, which Conner slid off the table.

"Did you check with Pastor Morrison about the locks? Did anybody else get glued?"

"Just us," Zach replied.

"Do you think it was somebody who's mad about us living in the neighborhood, or somebody who's mad at the church?" Izzy asked.

"My guess is that it has to do with the warnings someone keeps sending to the pastor," Zach said.

"But how would anyone know we go to New Life Chapel? And how do they know where we live?" Izzy asked. "Is someone following us?"

All good questions. Juanita didn't want to agree with Zach's assessment, although she feared he was correct. If the vandal chose to damage their house because of their association with the church, the implication heightened her own sense of unease. It suggested the glued locks were a prelude for something more menacing.

"Nobody else found warnings plastered on their houses or in their mailboxes?" Conner asked.

Zach exchanged a knowing look with Juanita. Neither of them wanted to frighten their children, but they needed to be alert.

"It's impossible to tell if things are just breaking down because they're old, or if someone's tampered with them," Zach said.

"Like what?" Izzy asked as she grabbed another slice of garlic bread.

"One of the deacons had a flat tire. He pumped it back up and so far, so good. He might have a leaky valve—"

"Or someone let the air out," Conner said.

"Maybe," Zach replied.

"Anything else?" Izzy asked.

"Someone painted 'Bug off or I go berserk,' on the back door of the church."

Juanita put her fork on her plate. This was news to her. "No," she signed. "When?"

"Probably five seconds after they threw a brick at the security camera. The security company called pastor about ten last night. He filed another police report."

"What does that mean? 'Bug off or I go berserk'?" Izzy asked.

"They want the neighborhood block watch to disappear, turn out their lights, and ignore the clandestine activities going on between the houses and on the street corners," Zach said.

"Reminds me of the verse in John, 'The light shines in the darkness, and the darkness has not overcome it.' The thugs must think that if they extinguish the light, they can slink around in the gloom and make trouble." Conner leaned back against his chair and did a double take when he saw Juanita, stunned, staring at him. "What?"

Juanita pointed at Conner and tapped her palm against her breastbone twice. She knew her expression underlined her pleasure.

"I make you happy?" Conner asked.

Juanita signed, "Very happy. You are wise. I'm proud of you."

Conner's laid-back manner retreated at the compliment. Teenagers. Praise them but don't embarrass them. A fine line, and one Juanita didn't always walk with finesse. Though his cheeks colored, a measure of gratitude filled Conner's eyes.

"Do we need to get a guard dog?" Izzy asked.

Juanita flashed a disgruntled glare at Zach, who leaned back in his seat.

"I didn't say a word." His protest looked genuine, but the realization that Izzy expressed the same concern and solution as Zach sure didn't validate Juanita's fervent objection to owning a dog.

She pushed her chair away from the table and looked at Izzy. "Help with dishes?"

"Sure."

Juanita pointed to Conner and signed, "Take trash out?"

"I got it." Conner took his dinner plate to the sink, grabbed a large trash bag, and began his weekly rounds to empty the trashcans throughout the house.

As Juanita stood, Zach raised his hands and said, "I didn't say anything about a dog. Honest."

"Coincidence?"

"Izzy and I are wise," Zach replied. "You should listen to us."

Juanita watched Conner while he headed out the kitchen door and into the frosty night air. His movement at the corner of the house prompted the motion sensor to turn on a light. He wandered to the enormous trash can provided by the city, lifted the lid, and hung his heavy bag over the top of the receptacle. Instead of releasing the bag, he dropped it beside the container.

Zach joined Juanita at the sink and looked outside. Conner, who saw them watching from the window, lifted his hands, as if in surrender. He rubbed a hand against the side of his face.

Without bothering to grab his jacket, Zach raced outside. Juanita watched as the two looked into the trashcan, exchanged some dialogue, and then studied the area around the house. Zach inspected the yard, came alongside Conner again, and stared into the mammoth container one more time.

When they came back into the house, Juanita signed, "What?"

"Don't worry about it," Zach said as he grabbed his coat and his gloves. He went to the basement and came back upstairs with a bucket, which he filled with water and handed to Conner.

Conner took the bucket and dumped the water into the trashcan. The two repeated the process four more times, but neither provided an explanation. When they went back inside, stomped the snow off their shoes and took off their coats, Juanita saw Zach tell Conner that he would "take care of it in the morning."

While Juanita pressed them for an explanation, Conner wrapped his freezing fingers around both of her arms. "Not to worry," he said. "I need to study." He sped out of the kitchen, leaving Zach to answer. Or not.

"Just some junk in the bottom of the can."

"Why the water?"

"It will freeze by morning and then I can dump the mess into a trash bag and get rid of it without wallowing in the muck."

That made sense. Kind of. When Zach threatened to repeat Conner's antics and wrap his frostbitten fingers around her waist, Juanita bolted down the hallway. Although an impish grin accompanied Zach's teasing, she knew he also intended it to cover his worry over the trashcan. Whatever the "mess," Juanita knew it was something ominous.

~

Maybe he should write a letter of appreciation to the director of the city's refuse department. The only thing to appease the disgusting task that greeted Zach while dawn had yet to brighten the skyline, was the simple and oh-so-wise-design of the ninety-gallon container assigned to each household.

The monster receptacle, which was narrower at the bottom than the top, delivered its frozen contents after Zach turned it upside down and gave it a good whack. After he plopped the regular bag of trash into the bottom of the container, he double-bagged the doomed critters, ice and all, tossed the bag inside, and wheeled the household garbage to the curb.

It wasn't until Zach arrived at work that a second thought materialized. Perhaps his achievement wasn't an approved method for ridding the neighborhood of drowned varmints. In fact, a judge might find him guilty of an infraction of city code. Well, they weren't diseased—the pair of long-tailed rodents looked rather plump—so how much trouble could they render? It wasn't as if he could do anything about it now. The garbage truck showed up on his street as Zach pulled out of his driveway. He'd skip the letter to the city and utter a few words of apology to no one in particular.

After Zach powered up his computer and started brewing a pot of coffee, he wandered through the warehouse and turned on the lights. His mood lightened when he regarded the ample quantities of inventory that filled the shelves.

When he passed the area designated for reed dyeing, visions of dye-spattered Izzy and Paige came to mind. Their diligent efforts, evidenced by dozens of hanks of reed hanging from rows of heavy-duty clothesline, produced a rainbow of rich hues. In the end, the girls giggled about their stained footwear, and Zach ignored the blotches of dye that marked the cement floor beneath the mass of drying reed.

Zach stirred his one-half teaspoon sugar allotment into his coffee and tested the temperature with a tentative sip. He could walk outside and let the air cool his brew in about thirty seconds, or he could make a phone call while the stuff went from scalding to drinkable.

"Craig?"

"That you, Hoyt?" The voice on the other end of the call sounded as if he'd consumed a pot of coffee all by himself. The pastor, though, didn't drink caffeinated coffee or tea. His morning temperament was a natural byproduct of his zest for life, or so Zach surmised. He'd seen the man down before, but nothing buried Craig's joy. Nothing.

"Yep," Zach replied.

"Are you calling to tell me our banker found a way to lend us the funds we need to repair the roof?"

"I thought we decided not to borrow."

"We did. I'm just messing with you. What's up?"

"Wish I knew," Zach said. "Has anyone complained of vandalism lately?"

"Hmm. Not for a couple of weeks. Why?"

"Someone left a pair of rats in our trash receptacle."

"Dead?" Craig asked.

"They are now."

"I see."

"Why is my family a target? I don't get it." Zach gulped his drink, but his absentminded action brought tears to his eyes as the liquid scorched his throat.

"Well, you live in the neighborhood, you attend New Life Chapel, and . . . well . . . you're kind of pale-faced. Know what I mean?"

"I thought of that, but Juanita, even though she's American Indian, looks Hispanic. Lots of Hispanics attend New Life."

"Uh, when I said that before, I had you in mind." Craig punctuated his sentence with a chuckle.

"Okay, so maybe it's because *I'm* the pale face. What about the other white families at the church? No one has bothered them. It's not that I want someone else to be a victim, I just don't understand why we've been hit twice."

"I can't answer that."

"Don't say anything to Juanita about the rats. She knows someone put something in the trash. She doesn't need to know the details."

"Got it." A drawn-out sigh passed from Craig's phone to Zach's hearing. "Guess I should call Hollister."

Sumo? Zach's sweet coffee churned in his stomach. "What good will that do?"

"He stepped up patrols around the church after the spray paint incident. Maybe he needs to send a few cars through your end of the neighborhood as well."

"You think that will help?"

"Can't hurt. Serves as a deterrent, anyway."

"Okay. Thanks."

"Chin up, Zach. See you soon."

Zach lowered his phone to his desk, got up, and refilled his coffee cup. A knot gripped his shoulders and pinched his neck muscles. Something in the glued locks and the rats didn't fit the profile of random acts. They didn't just feel personal; they were personal.

A message with rats was easy to decipher, assuming the delivery person intended a message. Big mouth, tattletale, informer, snitch. Zach was unaware of having filled any of those roles.

What about the locks? What did that mean? His family was stuck on the outside, looking in? What? When his imagination reached a dead end, Zach rubbed his neck, winced at the discomfort, and turned back to his desk.

Shattering glass and a thud sounded near the front door. Zach's skin crawled as the hair on his arms and neck stiffened. His foot caught on the wheel of his chair as he leaped toward his office door. He managed to keep his balance, but only by slamming his upper body against the doorjamb. While his heart pounded, he turned the corner, examined the damage, and raced to the broken window.

No one. Nothing. Nada. Icy wind crept into the room like a sneaky infiltrator, absconding with the heat and stealing Zach's resolve.

He leaned over, picked up the rock, and hefted the projectile. When he turned it over, heavy black marker displayed the third message intended for Zachary Hoyt: *GO AWAY.*

Twenty-Two

Stan preferred the accolades to a dress-down, but if given his druthers, he'd stay out of Hollister's office altogether. Captain Snodgrass was by-the-book tough, but at least she didn't play games. Hollister took on the mantle of the acting chief with a sense of cloak and dagger, and Stan wasn't very fond of mysteries.

"I don't want to publicize your use of sign language in the gas station arrest. That would be the same as showing your hand in a high-stakes poker game."

Cloak and dagger. Poker. Same thing, as far as Stan could tell. Hollister wore a straight face, but was definitely sleight of hand.

"I wanted to congratulate you on your handling of the incident. Good work."

Norris didn't acknowledge the compliment, but stood at attention like the dutiful officer that she was. Stan tried to mimic her formal bearing, but his patience with Hollister thinned each time the man summoned him to his office.

"Thank you, sir," Norris said as she took a step backward, inching her way to the door.

"Dismissed."

As Stan reached for the doorknob, Hollister cleared his

throat. Stan steeled himself for another chummy chat.

"Norris, I need a minute with Benton."

Of course he did. Norris didn't pause as she wrenched Stan's hand from the doorknob and let herself out. Stan turned on his heels as a strand of heat wrapped around his neck.

"Sir?"

"Take a seat." Hollister pointed to the chair in front of his desk. While Stan sat, Hollister paced behind his desk. "You picking up any chatter from the folks at New Life Chapel?"

"Chatter?" Stan asked. Now Hollister thought himself a general during wartime, or an intelligence officer with Homeland Security? Stan squinted in order to refrain from rolling his eyes.

"What's the word at the church? Any more reports of vandalism or misbehavior?"

Misbehavior? The last Stan saw of that was at his ex-wife's house, or so he assumed, although her overnight guest seemed to have disappeared of late. The blue SUV was absent from the driveway every time Stan drove by during the last two weeks.

Come to think of it, Tina hadn't imposed on Stan to take Tyler and Lauren off her hands for unscheduled visitations either. DeWayne's absence didn't bode well for Tina's ongoing bout with what she described as stomach flu. Trouble was, any time Tina's life hit a bump, it always escalated into a body slam by the time its effects hit Stan.

"Anything?" Hollister asked again.

Dots of sweat assembled on Stan's neck and skull. This was not the time to second-guess Tina's circumstances. "Uh, not that I've heard. The last report was one Zach Hoyt made."

"Which one?"

"Uh, the one about the rock tossed into the window of his business."

"You didn't hear about the rats?" Hollister swung his head back and forth and said, "Wish I'd seen his face when he found those things racing around the bottom of his trashcan."

Every pocket of the city had its share of mice, rats, cockroaches, and other critters. Why would Hoyt think he was exempt? Stan responded to Hollister's amusement with a shrug. "Why would he report a problem with rats?"

"Because Hoyt thinks he's too good to live near vermin." Hollister's satisfaction only underscored Stan's assessment of the acting captain. Captain Snodgrass could return from maternity leave any day now. Stan banked his future on Hollister's misinformation about Snodgrass' wanting to retire. Working for the alternative—the arrogant pest sitting on the opposite side of the desk—was wholly unacceptable.

"Is Morrison pleased with the heavy police presence in the neighborhood?" Hollister asked.

"I haven't heard. Guess so." When Hollister's jowls drooped into a perturbed frown, Stan sought a more palatable answer. What did Hollister want? Credit. Hollister wanted credit for solving a problem. Credit and publicity. "Uh, people come up to me while I'm stationed at the door, before and after the church service, and tell me they're grateful I'm there."

Hollister flicked his head in Stan's direction, but instead of garnering appreciation for the comment, Stan encountered a face filled with disdain. Stan replayed his comment and attempted a swift recovery.

"Those folks know you arranged for security for all their meetings. Morrison's been pretty vocal, too. Says he can rest easy and focus on his flock."

"His flock?" Hollister asked. "He calls his congregation a flock?"

"He's protective. You know. Like a shepherd." Where had Stan grabbed that descriptive term? It wasn't in his vocabulary. At least it hadn't been. Must be the pastor's words did more than reach through the sound system to Stan's hearing. Was that a good thing or a bad thing?

"I want you to sign up for O.T. Thursday evening," Hollister said.

"This Thursday?"

"The church bulletin says Morrison has a meeting scheduled with the neighborhood watch members. I want you to be there."

"Why me?"

"You're my ears." Hollister raised his thick eyebrows, and when he drew them together, they formed the letter *M*—as in maniac. "Remember?"

Why did Hollister act as if he had the right to Stan's life? The man sounded and acted like a blackmailer. Stan signed up for the ASL course. Wasn't that penance for the act that got him into trouble with the acting captain in the first place?

Stan's brain screamed, "No," while his mouth uttered, "I can do Thursday."

"When they talk about security, I don't want you just standing at the back of the room. I want you to speak up."

"Speak up? Sir? I'm not a member of their neighborhood watch."

"Think of yourself as an accessory. A valuable accessory."

Wasn't that the term the law used to identify a co-

conspirator? A lawbreaker?

"What do you expect me to say?" Stan asked. The office was as hot as that fiery furnace Morrison talked about in his last sermon. The one where the three guys escaped untouched. Stan wasn't faring as well.

"Just make sure everyone in the room knows that Captain Hollister has their back."

"I can do that," Stan said. Although, his rendition would include the complete title of *Acting* Captain. Frederick Hollister wasn't Stan's captain any more than Morrison was his shepherd.

~

When Stan walked into the ASL classroom, he imitated Norris' unconcealed exasperation and returned a like greeting. Why was she ticked off? Hollister took the time to give her a compliment today, although he wasn't likely to enter the unofficial commendation into either of their personnel files. Stan had put up with ample police work for one day. Norris could stay on her side of the room; he'd stay on the other.

Before he had both arms out of his coat, someone tugged on the sleeve.

"Mr. Benton, where are Tyler and Lauren?" The tip of Izzy Hoyt's nose was still pink from the cold air that blanketed the Midwest. She wore a goofy looking hat and matching scarf, and a twinkle in her eyes that said she was still a kid. Lucky break.

"They're home with their mom tonight," Stan said.

Izzy's pleasure evaporated. She looked down at the packages she and Paige held in their arms. It looked as if they had gone to a lot of trouble to wrap some gifts in festive

Christmas paper and generous quantities of curling ribbon.

Stan followed the better part of Izzy's sign language to know that she informed Paige of his children's absence.

"We won't see them before Christmas, so can we give these to you?" Izzy asked.

"You bought Tyler and Lauren Christmas presents?" Stan experienced the same level of heat as he'd endured in Hollister's office. Why hadn't he envisioned this situation? Tyler and Lauren adored Izzy and Paige. Had Stan given them the opportunity, his children would have, at the very least, made something for the girls. Was he capable of pleasing anyone? Ever?

Izzy glossed over the question with a flick of her hand. "It's not much."

"C-H-A-L-K," Paige finger-spelled.

"And a couple of coloring books," Izzy added.

If he couldn't reciprocate, he could be gracious to a pair of teens who brought pleasure to his kids. "Thank you. You'll brighten their Christmas. A lot."

With the enthusiasm of two teenagers about to enjoy a long two-week break from school, Izzy and Paige raced to their self-assigned corner of the room. Stan watched the girls while they tugged off coats, scarves, hats, and gloves. They teased each other, mostly with exaggerated facial expressions. Once in a while, they reverted to sign language. Throughout the exchange, Izzy's laughter filled the room.

Their innocence and their sweet friendship brought a glimmer of peace to Stan's agitated and weary body. He'd do anything to fill his children's lives with joy—if only he knew how.

Suzanne and Juanita began the class right where they'd left off the week before. Stringing signs together to make something of a sentence wasn't too bad. Stan managed to keep up.

"Let's take a ten minute break," Suzanne said. "When we come back, we'll get started with what we call time indicators."

"Can you give us a hint?" Zoe asked. It wasn't as if the girl cared. She probably needed to know whether she should retrieve her pillow from the car so she could rest more comfortably.

"In a nutshell," Suzanne said, "ASL does not use tenses. In English we say, I eat, I ate, or I am eating. In ASL, eat is always eat."

"But what if I already ate?" Dottie asked.

"Then you wouldn't be hungry now," Zoe replied.

Suzanne forced a chuckle and answered, "We designate the timing by using words like yesterday." She lifted her right hand to her shoulder and lowered her fingers. "Or we sign *past*, then *night*, then *I*, and then *eat*."

"Like this?" Dottie asked as she made one motion and then several others. "Past night I eat?"

"Pretty much," Suzanne said.

Juanita finger-spelled, "G-O-O-D J-O-B."

Time indicators? Stan choked as he stuffed his little-boy tantrum back down his throat. He couldn't do this. Not tonight. He'd rather stand in the corner and bang his head against the wall.

"Hey, partner." Norris stood at arms length, a cup of coffee in each hand. She extended a hand. "You look like you could use a shot of something stronger than caffeine, but this is all I found."

"Yeah. Thanks." Stan took the cup and sipped.

"Why is Hollister messing with you?" Norris asked.

"Huh?" How would she know that?

"He keeps kicking me out of his office and making you stay behind. His 'thank you very much' for the gas station arrest was about as genuine as my vinyl alligator-skin wallet. Why's he looking for an excuse to talk to you in private?"

"If I told you our little secret, it wouldn't be private anymore, would it?" Stan scoffed and took another sip of coffee. "You don't want to know. Trust me."

"Trust you? Whatever he's doing sure sets you off."

"Are you a praying person?" Stan asked.

Norris pulled back, as if she needed to put more distance between the two of them in order to focus on Stan's face. "You're asking me about faith?"

"No, I just asked if you pray."

"They kind of go together, you know."

"If you say so," Stan said.

"Yeah, Benton, I pray. You have a request you'd like me to make for you?"

"Would you please pray that Captain Snodgrass comes back? Soon?"

"You're a little late with that one," Norris said.

Stan felt the color drain out of his face and melt into the floor tiles. "She's not coming back?"

"That's not what I meant. I've prayed for Snodgrass' return since the day you and I had our formal introduction to Sumo Hollister."

Stan's shoulders danced as Norris' earnest statement got the best of him. When he held his coffee cup out to her, she took pity on him and held it while he found the energy to lasso his frayed emotions.

"Thanks, partner. I needed that."

"You don't need more coffee." Norris tossed both cups

into the trash and led the way back to the classroom.

"Where is everybody tonight?" Stan asked. "Lots of empty seats."

"Probably the holidays. You know, people traveling and stuff. Well, except for Wellington."

"The Snake?" Stan asked.

Norris stopped in the hallway and turned to face Stan. "You don't know?"

"I don't know what?" Stan didn't care for the pinched features and the tension that pulled Norris' mouth into a narrow pink line.

"He's in the hospital."

"Somebody slice him up after he mouthed off to the wrong person?" Stan didn't mean to sound so glib, but the abrupt change in Norris' bearing caught him off guard. Whenever Tina switched gears like that, his only defense was a testy attitude.

"He's cut pretty bad."

"I was kidding," Stan said.

"I know you were."

"What did he do this time?"

"The responding officer took a report from Wellington's mom. The doctors checked her out in the ER, patched her up, and sent her home, but Wellington—"

"He beat his mother?" Stan didn't mean to raise his voice, but when several people turned around and stared, he tugged Norris' arm and walked away from the classroom.

"I'm telling you this all wrong. Let me start over. A neighbor called about a domestic dispute. When the patrol car pulled up, a man ran out of the building, covered with blood and holding a knife. Before he collapsed, the man ranted about some punk inside the building.

"The second officer on the scene checked out the apartment. He found Wellington and his mom, both beaten up. According to the report, the man kicked in the door, demanded money and booze, and when they didn't deliver, he started beating Wellington's mom. Wellington grabbed a knife and threatened him."

"If Wellington had the knife, how did he get cut up?"

"His mom told the officer that the man lunged at Wellington and wrestled for the knife. She couldn't see who had control of the knife, but in the end, both suffered severe cuts."

"How bad are they?"

"Wellington's going to be okay."

"The dude?"

"He didn't make it."

The story tumbled in Stan's head like a wet sack of marbles releasing its load. The facts smacked against each other, pitting his sense of justice against his distaste of the Snake. The noise and the clamor made him wince.

Wellington. The kid who hissed like a snake but lacked the bite to damage Stan's tire. He killed a guy? Would he fall into the abyss of the overtaxed juvenile court system? Would he get a fair hearing? A fair trial? A decent attorney? Stan stared, open-mouthed, at Norris.

"It gets worse."

"How?"

"The victim?"

"Yeah?"

"It was his dad."

Twenty-Three

Returning to Shelburg, Ohio conjured a multitude of "what if" visions, but nothing prepared Zach for the tug on the sleeve, the hushed conversation, and the subsequent ride to the hospital with Craig Morrison.

Zach was equally unprepared for the brisk walk across the treacherous parking lot. The wind howled and bit his ears as his nose progressed from sniffling to running to frozen. When they reached the entrance, Craig removed his fedora and ran his fingertips over his hair before he tugged his matching wool scarf away from his neck.

"Guess I should have let you retrieve your gloves and hat from your car," Craig said.

Zach's eye twitched as the cold induced a full-body shiver. "I didn't have time to grab them. When Juanita's battery died, I thought my assignment was limited to that of a chauffer. The winter-wear is in the closet at the house."

"I'm glad I caught you before you took off."

"I am too. I think," Zach replied. He wasn't sure about this, but after he dropped Juanita at the church entrance, his pastor leaned into the car and asked for backup. No matter the situation, it was Zach's intention to comply. "Any idea why he called you?"

"Not sure."

Zach took cautious steps toward the elevator as the ice-encrusted soles of his shoes met the glossy tile floor. He rubbed his hands together and waited for the ping of the elevator to announce its arrival. When they exited on the fourth floor, Craig went to the nurses' station and spoke with one of the women before gesturing for Zach to follow him.

What was it about a hospital that unnerved people? It was supposed to be a place of healing, of hope. No matter the occasion, even the birth of his two children, the sterile hallways and glaring ceiling lights left Zach with a queasy sense of unease. Tonight was no different. Well, that wasn't true. Tonight was probably worse than most other times.

He followed Craig into a dimly lit room with a curtain separating two patients. Craig greeted the man in the first bed. In return, he received a tight-lipped scowl and a grunt. The volume on the wall-mounted television inched up a few decibels.

Wellington lay on the second bed, his face turned toward the window. A sliver of light from the parking lot poked between the window frame and the closed blinds. Pretty poor entertainment for a teenager. Unlike the sassy persona he wore at the ASL classes, the boy looked small. Vulnerable. His left cheek bore a bruise, and heavy bandages covered wounds to his arms and hands.

Zach inspected the pair of chairs situated beside the bed, expecting to see a coat or scarf hanging over the back. Where was the boy's mom?

Craig cleared his throat, earning Wellington's attention. He groaned as he turned to face his visitors. A cut underlined his right eye. The skin around the wound bore sickly hues of black, blue, and yellow. A butterfly bandage protected a cut near his chin.

"Wellington," Craig said. "I'm sorry to hear what happened. Real sorry."

"I shouldn't have called you. Just go away." Wellington started to turn toward the window again, but not before a tear trickled down his face and marked his pillow. He flinched when he tried to lift his hand, so instead of hiding his pain, he gritted his teeth and repeated, "Go away."

"I know what happened. You can't blame yourself. Your dad . . . he made a choice that he couldn't undo."

"What do you know?" Wellington asked. As much as the kid wanted to sound tough, his weakness grabbed a piece of Zach's being. It hurt to breathe.

"I spoke to someone at the police station. An acquaintance," Craig said.

Zach appreciated that Craig did not call Frederick Hollister his friend. The story Hollister shared with the pastor, however, was one that no teen should have to suffer.

"You aren't responsible for anything. A couple of your neighbors witnessed the scuffle. Their accounts pretty much matched yours and your mother's."

"My mom?" Wellington wrenched his neck forward and spit. Zach recoiled and took a step backward, but when he tangled with the curtain separating the beds, the other patient responded by upping the volume on the television again.

"What about your mom?" Craig asked.

"She knows I didn't start it. Knows I tried to protect her."

"Where is she?" Zach asked.

"How should I know? She came in here after I got out of surgery, waited until I opened my eyes, and told me she never wanted to see me again."

Zach's lungs constricted a second time. When he gave Craig a dumbfounded look, Craig jutted his chin just enough for Zach to see that Craig understood. Zach, on the other hand, was baffled.

"Your dad abuse drugs? Alcohol?" Craig asked.

Wellington scoffed. "Since he lost his job. Used to work for the post office. Carried mail. Had income, insurance. All of it."

"What happened?" Craig asked.

"His cousin talked him into some easy money. They robbed a couple of places; both went down for seven years."

"How long had he been out?"

"Two years. He's been drinking and drugging for two long years."

"He beat you up before?" Craig asked.

"Nope. Just my mom."

"What changed?"

"He started doing meth."

"What about your mom? Is she clean?"

"As a whistle."

"What kind of work does she do?" Craig asked.

"Housekeeper. Her paycheck puts food on the table and pays the rent. That's all. My old man didn't care. He stole it anyway."

"Why did you call me?" Craig asked. "How can I help?"

"You can't. Go away."

"We're here to help," Zach said. "What do you need?"

"I thought you might know of some place I can stay when they let me out of here."

Zach managed to hold his ground and avoided grappling with the curtain divider again, but why wouldn't Wellington go home? His mom couldn't have meant her remark about never wanting to see her son again, could she?

"She blame you?" Craig asked.

Blame Wellington? Why would his mother blame the person who kept her from more harm? Why would Craig even consider such a scenario?

"Yep."

The comment knocked the rest of the air out of Zach's lungs. This didn't make sense. Craig didn't take his eyes off Wellington, but he splayed the fingers on the hand nearest Zach, inferring that the man had control of the conversation.

"She meant to take the beating just like all the other times," Craig said.

Wellington managed a miniscule nod. "Said I shouldn't have butted in."

"He was different this time, though."

"I'd never seen him so messed up before."

"Thought he was out to kill you both?" Craig asked.

First one tear spilled from his eye, and then a multitude fell in quick succession. "Was I wrong?" Wellington's voice was as tight and pinched as his face.

"You did what you believed you had to do. No one can know what might have happened if you hadn't stepped in." Craig's voice was smooth and soft, but the expression on his face was as pained as Wellington's was.

"I killed my dad," Wellington whispered. As the distraught teenager sobbed, his body started to shake.

"It wasn't your fault," Craig said as he put a quieting hand on Wellington's arm.

"She hates me. My mom hates me."

"She doesn't hate you, son. She's hurt and confused, just like you."

"Then why won't she let me come home? I'll die if I have

to go into foster care."

Craig exchanged a burdensome glance with Zach. "Let me see what I can do."

Do? Craig had no power over the courts and their assignment of children to foster care. Zach knew that much. Did Craig think he had someone in the congregation who might consider taking the boy into their home? Surely Craig didn't forget that Wellington attended the ASL class as an alternative to a juvie sentence for fighting. No way could Zach consider his own home. No parent of a teenage girl would dare invite the likes of Wellington into his house. No way.

"Whatever," Wellington said.

"You best give me more credit than that," Craig replied. "I intend to find a resolution for you."

Wellington stared at Craig, but his expression reverted to deadpan, the way Zach remembered it each time he saw the kid while he sat in the ASL class.

Craig touched Wellington lightly on the shoulder, offered a short prayer for healing—without Wellington's approval, of course—and said, "You rest and get well. Give all of this hurt to the Lord, son."

The empty stare took on a stubborn bent, but Craig chose to overlook the challenge. Zach, from his dumbfounded and feeble viewpoint, mumbled a lame, "Take care," as the two left the room and walked to the elevator.

Craig hit the button to call the elevator to their floor, buttoned his coat, and said, "Good thing we still believe in miracles."

~

The second half of the ASL class was nothing but a blur. Every time Suzanne and Juanita demonstrated the use of those time indicators, Stan's imagination went back to The Snake's first success with finger spelling: *O-I-N-K; D-I-E*. Did the kid's enrollment in the class make one dent of difference? Did it?

What about the others, like Suzanne Kirby and Juanita Hoyt? For all of their good efforts, community watch groups, and charity work, how did the members of a church like New Life Chapel think they might alter the lives of kids like Wellington?

If Norris got the details right, the kid never had a chance. It didn't sound as if he'd face any charges, but how would Wellington ever live with what he'd done? Even before the altercation, what chance did the sullen teenager have to make something of himself when his home life controlled his future? Were the do-gooders just fooling themselves—and the teens?

It wasn't just Wellington. One of the other teens assigned to the diversion program, the Goth girl who had more art inked on her arms than a museum had paintings, gave up her seat in the class. She elected to snub her nose at the Diversion Program's offer to keep her record clean of misdemeanors, and put a felony next to her name instead. Stupid kids.

The two remaining teenagers bolted at the sound of Suzanne's, "We're done. See you after the holidays. Merry Christmas, everyone."

Merry Christmas? A few of the others might pretend to have one, but for Stan, and probably most of his ASL classmates, the only thing he looked forward to was the passing of the money-grubbing holiday and the prospect of a couple of good football games on New Year's Day.

Hollister already assigned Stan overtime for New Life Chapel's Christmas Eve service, but, hey, who cared? As people emptied the classroom, Stan clenched his hand before he stretched his fingers and formed the question, W-H-O- C-A-R-E-S?

"Who cares about what?" Norris asked as she edged past Stan on her way to the door.

"Nothing." Stan glared at Norris with a look meant to suggest that he did not have to put up with his partner while he was off-duty.

"You can't fix everything, Benton," Norris said. "The best you can be is a good influence."

Why was Norris so slow to read Stan's mood? He grabbed her by the arm and caused her to stumble.

"What?" she asked as her tone grew impatient. No, Norris wasn't slow; ergo, the problem. She knew exactly which buttons she pushed.

"You think my lack of influence on The Snake led him to get violent with his father? Huh? You putting the blame on me?"

Norris tugged her arm free, but instead of exchanging another round of insults, she raised her hands and pointed her right index finger at the palm of her left hand in a perfect rendition of the ASL expression, "What?"

"We weren't sent here to save the world," Stan said between clenched teeth. When Norris blinked in a manner that looked a whole lot like confusion, Stan softened his tone. "Look, I'm sorry about Wellington. I am. But he's stuck with his puny life and all the ugliness his parents bestowed on him. I can't help. Neither can you."

Norris tugged her heavy knit scarf around her neck,

climbed the stairs to the main level, and held her bottom lip between her teeth while the two of them walked toward the door. At least the woman knew when to shut up.

Stan glanced at the closed doors that led to the sanctuary. No, he hadn't improved his small-minded self since Hollister forced the ASL classes on him. Yes, Stan was still a pig-headed and impatient person who didn't care for women. Nothing had changed. Another tug of his attention to the closed doors coincided with an increase in the temperature around his neck and ears. All he had to do was stand by this door during the Christmas Eve service and any other meetings at New Life to which Hollister assigned him security detail. Didn't mean Stan had to listen to the sermons. Nope. In fact, maybe he'd dig out some earplugs.

Stan had to sidestep Norris when they nearly tripped over Pastor Morrison and Zach Hoyt as they opened the front door. Before Stan could mumble an apology, he caught Zach's, "You didn't promise. You said you'd come up with something."

"Same thing," Morrison said as he regarded Stan and Norris. "I'm glad you're still here. Can we chat for a minute?"

Stan wanted to decline the invitation, but Norris answered for both of them with a polite, "Sure. What's up?"

For the next seven and one-half minutes, Stan's coat-covered torso picked up the same temperature as his hot neck. If he didn't leave soon, he'd pass out from heat exhaustion. He listened to Zach and the pastor relay the conversation they had at the hospital, all of which underscored Stan's opinion that Wellington was stuck. Foster care probably wasn't a lot different, or worse, than what the boy got from his mom and dad.

Stan zoned out for the rest of the exchange, but when an

abrupt silence fell over them, Stan lifted his face and examined each of the others' expressions. What had he missed? Whatever it was, it left Zach Hoyt wide-eyed and merited the pastor's blatant admiration of Norris.

"How?" Zach asked.

"The captain likes me," Norris said. "He'll let me work day shift, at least for the short term." She looked at Stan as if she wanted his affirmation. Affirmation of what?

Morrison eyed Zach and said, "What did I tell you about miracles?"

Zach started to reply, but closed his mouth.

"May I call Hollister in the morning?" the pastor asked Norris.

"Yes. Please."

"If you change your mind, you call me first thing, you hear?"

"I'm sure about this. No need." Norris bumped Stan's arm with her elbow and said, "Come on. We're outta here."

Stan, too reluctant to inquire as to the rather important turn in the conversation, dipped his chin in a farewell gesture to Zach and Morrison, and followed Norris outside like a dutiful puppy.

"Uh, what was that all about?" he asked as he unlocked his car door.

"No big deal. I'll take him."

"Take him? Take who?"

"Wellington. He can stay with me."

Twenty-Four

Juanita gasped as she caught sight of the clock. A quick peek at her watch confirmed her need to panic. Her current editing assignment was refreshingly delightful and free of errors. She delved into the engrossing story early in the morning, worked through lunch, and managed to forget about dinner plans. Her excuse would not impress her brood.

She tapped her fingernail against the tabletop while the restaurant's menu slowly filled her computer screen. After she ordered a huge quantity of pizzas using the online option, she powered off her laptop, picked up a stack of paper, and carried her ever-present dictionary, thesaurus, and *The Chicago Manual of Style* to the bookcase.

If she hurried, she could throw together a salad before the crew arrived, but instead of racing to the salad crisper, she grabbed the ready-to-bake chocolate chip cookie dough. How better to appease a hungry hoard than with the promising aroma of freshly baked sweets?

By the time the first blast of cold air filtered down the hallway and into the warm kitchen, Juanita had a pan of cookies cooling on a wire rack. Zach's greedy fingers reached the confections first, but when the hot chocolate burned his fingers, he dropped the cookie back onto the rack.

Multiple footsteps vibrated the floor and alerted Juanita to the arrival of the teenagers. She watched Conner as he tugged his arms out of his coat sleeves and reached for a cookie.

"Don't," Zach said as he put his hand between the cookies and Conner's grappling fingers. "They are hot, hot, hot." He blew on his fingers and licked the tips, just to make his point.

"Hungry?" Juanita signed. Silly question. She recognized that starving-teen look on all four faces. Zach's too.

Izzy, Paige, and Wellington pulled off their jackets and added them to the pile Zach and Conner started on one of the kitchen chairs. Wellington stayed in the background, and although he tried to look nonchalant, his serious expression suggested he was studying the animal life of a far-off planet. When his inspection landed on the cookies, he relaxed.

Juanita pointed to the heap in the chair and tipped her head toward the hallway.

"That's mom language for 'go hang those in the closet,' " Izzy said to Wellington.

"I'll help," he replied. He scooped several coats into his arms, favoring his right arm in the process, and waited while Izzy grabbed the rest. As he followed her down the hallway, Juanita rested her gaze on Zach.

Zach mouthed, "We're good."

While the pizza deliveryman took his time arriving with the main course, Juanita sat at one end of the table and watched her generous bowl of salad disappear. Zach pointed to the cookies, and as the famished teens and their starving employer gulped down the first round of sweets, Juanita signed, "Who dyed reed today?"

Wellington raised his left hand and turned his fingers until

Juanita could see his fingernails. "S-M-U-R-F," she signed.

Wellington looked at Conner and said, "Smurf? What's smurf?"

"Dunno," Conner replied. "What's smurf?"

Zach wagged his head back and forth before he passed the plate of cookies around the table again. "Old cartoon. Before your time. Smurfs were cartoon characters whose bodies were the same color aqua as your stained fingernails."

"Hard work?" Juanita asked.

"I'm T-I-R-E-D." Wellington looked exhausted, but the longer he sat at the table, the more color rose to his cheeks. For the first time since he trudged into the ASL class, Juanita saw a typical teenager instead of a youth who owned a toxic attitude and a burden to prove his place in the world.

"How many kits?" Juanita signed.

"We finished kits for three of Nancy's patterns," Izzy said while Paige counted on her fingers.

Paige looked up and signed the number thirty-six.

Juanita didn't need an announcement to know that the pizza had arrived. In a scene that suggested finely tuned choreography, four teenagers shoved their chairs away from the table and sped down the hallway. Juanita lifted her nose and sniffed, but the scent of melted cheese, warm crust, and spicy meats failed to materialize. The tromping footsteps made their way back to the kitchen.

"Am I late?" Holly Norris held her hat in her hand. Her heavy city-issued jacket appeared to add six inches to her girth. Still, the woman looked chilled to the bone. "I didn't mean to interrupt your dinner."

"Come in. Take a seat. Pizza is on the way," Zach said.

Norris looked at Wellington and asked, "You earned an invitation for pizza? I love you."

When Wellington's cheeks turned scarlet, Conner came to the boy's rescue with another offering of cookies. Holly grabbed two, but cookies were a poor substitute for dinner. Where were the pizzas?

Juanita surveyed the diminished contents of the salad bowl before she handed the remnants across the table to Holly.

With the same exodus the previous bell-ringer garnered, the teens sprang from their chairs and headed to the door. This time, the delectable aroma of pizza filled the house. Soon, one empty box after another ended up on the kitchen counter. Laughter and a few of Conner's burps, which he failed to cover with his hand, accompanied the feeding frenzy.

Zach sat back first, patted his belly, and watched Juanita from his seat at the opposite end of the table. "A good day," he signed.

The teenagers retreated to the basement to watch a movie while Juanita, Zach, and Holly stared at dinner's aftermath. Just like the cookies, half a dozen pizza slices remained. The rest? Gone. History.

"I didn't mean for you to feed us, you know," Holly said.

"Our pleasure," Zach replied.

"Thank you. Really. When I offered to take Wellington, I didn't think about school being out for Christmas break. Good thing I have some vacation accrued, but that didn't help today."

"Wellington seemed to enjoy working with us. He didn't complain about the reed dyeing process—something you don't want to know about, I'm sure—and I think he liked earning a few bucks."

"You paid him?" Norris clamped her teeth together. "I

didn't mean for you to do that."

"He earned it. Just like the others."

"How is he at your house?" Juanita signed.

"Pretty good. I mean, he's still a mess about what happened. The walls in my condo are pretty thin, and I've heard him sniffling and stuff at night, but once the snoring starts, he's out until the alarm sounds."

Holly shifted in her seat and looked at the disarray from the pizza feast. "He eats—well, you see he likes food as much as the others—and he's polite. He hasn't baited me like he did Benton, which is a relief. Wish I could do something about the sadness that weighs him down."

"I can't believe his mom won't let him go home," Zach said.

"I've met too many abused women on my watch to know that they don't always think clearly. Most blame the treatment on some shortcoming they have instead of laying the blame on the abuser. Even though she faults Wellington, I suspect his mom feels responsible."

"That's messed up," Zach said.

How different, their lives. Juanita watched Zach, the man who stood ready to defend her, protect her, and love her. What did Wellington know except mistreatment and cruelty? A lump caught in her throat. Juanita could not fathom the hurt, anger, resentment, and hunger for acceptance that defined Wellington's world.

Visions of the dwindling balance in Conner's college fund jabbed at Juanita's conscience. While she worried about her son's education, Wellington's mother sought to upend her child's existence. The boy had nothing on which to stake his future, and no one to love him through today's pain and tomorrow's uncertainty.

"My custody is temporary, you know." A pair of deep lines framed the edges of Holly's downturned lips. "I hope his mom has a change of heart."

"I hear Children Services has more children who need a place to live than they have families willing to take them in," Zach said.

"That's true, which is why the judge authorized me to foster Wellington for a while. Honestly? I can't do this forever. I think he knows it too."

"Now what?" Zach asked as his face took on an exasperated look.

"What?" Juanita signed.

"Someone's at the door."

"Maybe they ordered more pizza," Holly said in jest.

Juanita looked toward the hallway as she absorbed the suggestion. Izzy and Conner could have ordered more, but they couldn't eat any more. Could they?

As the conversation at the front door lingered, cold air skimmed into the kitchen and extracted a shiver from Holly. "I'm tired of winter."

"It just started," Juanita signed.

"I know."

Finally, the air current changed abruptly. Zach must have closed the door, but the vibration on the floor was more than Zach generated. More company?

"Norris? I thought that was your car. What are you doing here?"

"Benton?" Holly asked as she diverted her attention to the two children who bounded into the room after their father. "Hey, guys, what's up? You enjoying your break?"

"We get to make Christmas cookies tomorrow," Lauren said. "With frosting."

When Juanita signed, Tyler looked at his dad and said, "What did she say?"

"Uh, I think she said, 'that sounds like fun.' "

When Juanita confirmed his translation, Stan relaxed. "We didn't mean to interrupt, but Tyler and Lauren have something for your family."

"A Christmas present," Lauren said.

Zach looked at the pizza box Stan held in his hands. "Pizza?"

"Uh, no. We brought . . . Tyler, where's the bag?"

Tyler spun around, revealing a glossy bag with a snowman on the front. "Here."

"I'll go get the kids," Zach said.

Juanita leaned against the kitchen counter, put a finger to her lips, and then pointed to Lauren and Tyler. She picked up the box with the last pieces of pizza. "Hungry?" she signed.

Tyler's eyes lit up. "Can we have pizza, Dad?"

"Can we?" Lauren asked.

"Uh, no. Guys, we're just dropping off the gifts. We're not eating dinner."

"Y-E-S," Juanita finger-spelled. She made the signs for eat and sit. Without waiting for their response, she pulled a plate out of the cupboard, put the pizza slices on it, and pushed it into the microwave.

"Hey, Merry Christmas, you guys," Izzy said.

Paige waved to the children. Conner and Wellington stood near the doorway to the basement stairs, but when Wellington spied Stan, he slid behind Conner.

Stan crooked his neck so that he could see Wellington, and said, "You need anything?"

Wellington shook his head. "I'm good."

"She treating you okay?" Stan said as he gestured toward

Holly.

"Good. Yeah."

"If she gives you any grief, let me know. I haven't figured the woman out yet, but I might be able to lend a hand."

Holly slapped Stan and scoffed. "Don't listen to him."

Lauren and Tyler ignored the exchange and helped Izzy and Conner unwrap several rolled up drawings.

"We made these for you," Tyler said. "With the chalk and art paper you gave us."

"These are really good," Izzy said.

"That's my fish," Lauren said. "His name is Bubbles. Daddy got Bubbles 'cause Miss Fulgermuffin died."

"Your fish died?" Conner asked.

"Uh huh. Daddy buried her in the pond."

When Juanita put the warm pizza on the table, Lauren's fish tale was over. So, too, was the attention the teens had given their young guests. The four trampled down the basement steps while the young visitors plowed into the food. After some prodding, Stan ate half of a slice. The cookies didn't require any encouragement.

"So, what's with the pizza box?" Holly asked Stan. "Did you bring more?"

"Uh, no. The delivery guy ran up the sidewalk at the same time we rang the bell. He shoved the box into my hands and said, 'This is a special delivery. Guy paid me ten bucks to deliver this pronto.' Whatever you ordered sure doesn't weigh much."

"We didn't order anything else," Zach said.

When Zach's face contorted, it was the same expression Juanita saw on the night Zach and Conner took several buckets of water to their trashcan. Had someone targeted their house again? When a wave of lightheadedness clamped down on her, Juanita gripped the edge of the counter and kept her eyes glued to the floor. When the vertigo passed, she slid into the nearest chair.

Zach walked over to the table, picked up the box, and jiggled it. When he lifted the lid, Juanita squeezed her eyes shut.

"What is it, Daddy?" Lauren asked as she leaned over to see.

"Where's the pizza?" Tyler asked.

"Somebody messed up the order," Stan said. "Nothing here but trash."

The trash, which Juanita saw during the two seconds the contents were visible, was a piece of rope, tied like a noose. On the underside of the box lid, someone had scrawled, *Why are you still here?*

Twenty-Five

Stan stood with his feet apart and arms crossed over his chest, his best off-duty rendition of someone of authority. He'd dropped Lauren and Tyler off at Tina's place, then wound back around to the pizza shop located near the Hoyt's house. One Eugene Paar, the driver who agreed to talk with Stan after he finished his shift, seemed unimpressed with Stan's posture. The kid just looked tired.

"Let me rewind your comments. You tell me if I got the details right."

"Whatever," Eugene said as he looked at his watch. His eyelids looked as if they weighed ten pounds each.

"You deliver a stack of pizzas to the Hoyt house about seven o'clock. About a half-hour later, your boss sends you back to the same house with another pizza."

"Large pepperoni with extra cheese."

"The customer asked for an extra box. Isn't that odd?" Stan asked.

Eugene shrugged. "We get weird requests all the time. The guy asked for an empty box so he could split the pizza with someone who had to leave early."

"When you arrive, the customer intercepts you on the sidewalk in front of the house."

"Uh huh," Eugene said as his mouth stretched into a drawn-out yawn.

"What did he look like?"

"Huh? You think I pay attention to the customers? Who has time for that? People want their pizza. They want it hot. That means I have to move at warp speed."

"You don't think you could pick him out of a line-up?"

"A line-up? The guy ordered a pizza and two boxes. So what?"

"You didn't answer my question."

"Which was . . .?" Eugene rubbed his thumbs over his temples, maybe in an effort to keep his eyes open.

"Could you identify him?"

"He was white—maybe. He was stocky and had bad breath."

"So you don't think you could identify him," Stan said.

"Nope," Eugene answered.

"The man pays for the pizza, and then asks you to wait while he divides it between the two boxes. I take it you didn't watch the exchange."

"Had my eye on the ten-spot he gave me. First nice tip of the evening."

Stan's frustration mounted with every single comment. This delivery guy was the only person who'd seen the perp, and his eyewitness account was worthless.

"He hands back one of the boxes, tells you to take it to the house, and then what?"

"I don't know," Eugene replied. "He got into a car, I guess, while I went to the front door."

"You don't know if he drove away? Could he have walked away?"

"Like I said, I deliver hot pizza. I don't analyze the

customers." Eugene rubbed the back of his neck. "We done?"

"Yeah. Thanks for your time."

Stan watched Eugene slip out of the restaurant's side door. Just like the unidentified stalker, he disappeared into the darkness. Poof.

~

Stan tossed his keys onto the counter, hung up his coat, and turned on the television. He turned his back on the miniature screen and bumped the tip of the antennae as he headed into the kitchen. As the audio from the local news station sputtered into the room with the same intermittent transmission as the video, Stan struggled to decipher the words. Far has he could tell, the broadcaster had nothing to say about a mysterious delivery in a pizza box.

The bright light emitted from the open refrigerator glared against the glass shelves. Aside from a few bottles of salad dressing, ketchup, and mustard, all in various stages of emptiness, the shelves were bare. Traces of dried onionskin and a few rings from the bottom of slimy bottles accused Stan of neglect, as did the lingering odor of something he'd kept far longer than its shelf life.

Stan's stomach rumbled as he recalled the tantalizing aroma of leftover pizza that the Hoyts offered to their unexpected guests. He'd watched Lauren and Tyler consume the last of the slices with almost as much enthusiasm as they devoured the cookies. His children's bellies were full; Stan was grateful. Stan was hungry.

The offerings in the cupboard resembled the lack of abundance in the refrigerator. He grabbed the last envelope of popcorn from the box, stuffed it into the microwave, and poured himself a glass of tap water. When the kernels quit popping, Stan's fingers danced around the hot steam as he poured his dinner out of the bag. He plopped down on the couch and raised his water glass in a toast.

"Oh, that this were a cold beer." He extended his arm toward the television, "And that you, Miss Weathergirl, delivered your report on a high-density flat screen television that derived its programming from cable."

Stan stuffed a handful of popcorn into his mouth, tugged off his shoes, and lifted his feet to the top of the coffee table. How would he ever get out of this rut? He used his overtime pay to pick up a few Christmas gifts for Tyler and Lauren, but aside from a couple of inexpensive toys, the stuff was what they needed, not what they wanted.

Between the child support and the court's requirement that he provide all of their medical insurance, Stan was broke. Tina didn't make much at her job, but Stan wasn't convinced that her higher education would help her finances. By the time she graduated, she'd owe more in student loans than a poorly paid teacher could repay in a lifetime.

Where was that light? The one at the end of the tunnel? Obviously, Tina didn't see the glow either. Otherwise, she wouldn't have given him a heads-up about her plan to ask for an increase in child support. Where was he supposed to find more? And why now?

Dumb question. The answer sat squarely on Tina's expanding middle. The woman wasn't as sickly as she'd been, but she'd taken on the unmistakable attributes of a woman who was with child. Not his child. *De*Wayne's child. Tina hadn't filed a missing person's report on the man, but his absence probably had more to do with her sharp temper than what she perceived as Stan's bumbling efforts to parent Tyler and Lauren. Stan slammed the water glass onto the coffee table. No way was he paying for someone else's child. Wasn't going to happen. No way. No how.

~

Disarray and an unidentified stench greeted Stan as he entered Hollister's office. If it were summertime, a hoard of flies might descend on the room to feast on a month's worth of garbage. Stan took a step away from the desk.

What had he done to earn another punishing encounter with leftover pizza? Congealed oil left a scummy sheen on the pieces of pepperoni that dotted the half-eaten slice. The rank air made last night's popcorn a lot more appealing than the cheese-drenched blob that hovered at the corner of Hollister's desk. Couldn't the man slide the mess into the trashcan? What a pig. Stan's fingers twitched as he finger-spelled the three-letter word.

"Learn anything about Hoyt's latest threat?"

"Nothing useful."

"It was probably just some lowlife who lives in the neighborhood," Hollister said. "Hoyt's grating personality brings out the best in people." The acting captain gave Stan a know-what-I-mean kind of glance. Did he expect Stan to agree? Hollister continued his discourse while he paced behind his desk. "Maybe he's changed. What do you think?"

"Sir? I don't have a reference point like you do."

"No, you don't. Suffice it to say, Zachary Hoyt has the potential to annoy people. I don't see the stuff happening at his house and his business as having anything to do with the few things that occurred at the church."

"Are you backing off on the security detail at New Life?" Stan asked.

"Not yet. Morrison is pleased with my response."

Hollister didn't exaggerate the "my," but his choice of words was not lost on Stan.

Hollister cupped a hand to the side of his mouth and rubbed his jaw when he said, "Heard that from the president of the City Council." He finished his self-congratulatory remark with a wag of his bushy eyebrows.

Stan didn't stand at attention, but his muscles protested the prolonged exposure to Hollister's maniacal playtime. How this tiff between Hollister and Zach Hoyt became Stan's problem was beyond explanation. Its remedy was probably hiding out in the same place in the dark tunnel where Stan would find his financial freedom.

His paltry paycheck arrived in his bank account this morning. All he wanted was a trip through some fast-food drive-thru window, followed by a do-nothing evening at his apartment. Hollister, however, made no effort to release Stan from their little business meeting.

"How's Norris doing with the foster kid?"

"Wellington? Okay."

"He's behaving?"

"Seems to be."

"Yeah, until he gets restless. She better keep an eye on him."

"He's not a bad kid," Stan said.

Hollister did the eyebrow wave again and said, "Leopards don't change spots."

"You don't believe in second chances?" Stan asked. He needed one when he was Wellington's age.

Hollister's guffaw echoed throughout the room. "You're

funny. None of those kids ever turns his life around. The court system pretends they can rehabilitate the worst of them. They can't even redirect the ones who haven't committed anything worse than a misdemeanor."

The more time he spent in Hollister's presence, the more Stan prayed Captain Snodgrass would end her maternity leave and return a sense of justice, order, and cleanliness to this office. The more Stan prayed? Did he really believe that, or did the thought just slide into his subconscious as Sumo pounded his podium?

No matter. Hollister's parting comment was the one that hung over Stan as he trudged out the door and mentally derided the name and character of the man who just robbed him of the Christmas Eve he planned to spend with his children.

Twenty-Six

"Daddy?"

"Hmm?"

"Did you do something wrong?"

"I don't think so," Stan replied.

"Then how come we gotta go to the pastor's office?"

Zach, also summoned, dropped his chin, swallowed his grin, and studied his black dress shoes. They needed some polish. His eyes scanned the other pairs of shoes worn by the troops Craig had beckoned to the cramped room. Clearly, the man's request was impromptu; otherwise, he would have moved the group into one of the nearby classrooms.

Lauren persisted with her questioning, her troubled eyes glued to her father. Maybe if Stan wiped the worry off his face, he might convince his daughter that all was well. Just as it was on that Christmas night long ago. Did Stan forget the message already, or had he just tuned out the sermon while he stood guard in the vestibule?

While they waited for Craig, warm bodies pushed up the temperature in the room. Those who had already donned their winter coats before Craig summoned them, sloughed them off and draped them over their arms.

Holly Norris looked nice, decked out in a simple red

sweater and black skirt. Zach caught Juanita ogling the woman's black boots more than once. Boot envy. Probably similar to shoe envy. Zach didn't understand it, but it seemed that neither Juanita nor Izzy ever had all the footwear they needed.

Wellington's button-down shirt looked brand-new, probably a gift from his temporary guardian. Jeans and sneakers didn't look to have much wear either. Zach's opinion of Holly, which was already as high as the star that hung over Bethlehem, soared to a lofty realm. She had a good heart.

Wellington tugged at his shirt collar and cleared his throat. When he took a swipe at his damp forehead, Zach made an unauthorized suggestion, "Why don't we go next door? The room's a lot bigger."

Izzy put her hands on Lauren's shoulders, spun her around so that she faced the door, and whispered something in the little girl's ear before they crept out of the room. Why they were both on tiptoe was as mysterious as was the shoe thing. Lauren's giggles, Zach understood.

Juanita walked over, leaned her head against his arm, and released a hefty sigh.

"Tired?" he signed.

She answered with an up and down motion of her head against his arm. When she wrapped her arm around his waist, he leaned over and returned the sweet reminder that all was well in their world.

Yolanda Morrison, inherently flamboyant and owning more enthusiasm than any four walls could hold, whirled into the room with the intensity of a tornado.

"Merry Christmas, everyone. Wasn't the program wonderful?"

Of course it was wonderful. Yolanda oversaw every second of the production. Well, that wasn't fair. It really was an excellent production, regardless of Yolanda's need for affirmation.

"Loved it," Holly answered. "Thanks so much for inviting us."

"What did you think, Wellington? Was it everything you imagined?" Yolanda's soulful brown eyes rested on the teen's perplexed face.

Wellington's attention flitted from one person to another. Finally, his gaze landed on Zach's scuffed up shoes.

"Didn't know what to expect. Never been to church before."

Zach's shoulders pulled back and up, an involuntary response to something that shouldn't have surprised him.

"Never? Goodness, son, it's about time you joined us, then. This side of heaven, the church is the best place to be. Did you know Jesus said the people were His church? Not a building or a sanctuary, but the people. Imagine that."

Wellington's eyes almost bugged out of his head. Zach's chest expanded with pride when Conner—astute, just like his father—stepped in and lifted the weight of the conversation.

"Who decided to let Tim use a real drum this year? That was really cool."

Yolanda gushed at the praise. "My idea. He was good, wasn't he?"

"Well, now, let's gather 'round." Craig's frame filled the doorway. He clapped his hands together. "This is a mighty special night. Mighty special, indeed."

"Because it's Christmas Eve?" Tyler asked.

"That, too. Special in lots of ways." Craig looked at Yolanda and asked, "You know where I keep my camera?"

"In the file drawer?"

"Yes. Can you go get it for me?" After Yolanda left the room, Craig clapped his hands again. His zest was as acute as Yolanda's was enduring.

"Got it," Yolanda said as she walked back into the room and raised the hand that held the little instrument.

"Y'all follow me, please." Craig stepped into the hallway and led his band of wary followers back to the sanctuary. While the room was empty of worshipers, the crèche, with its babe wrapped in swaddling clothes, adorned the front of the chapel.

After they gathered at the foot of the raised platform, Craig climbed the steps so everyone could see him. Either that, or the devoted reverend was just more comfortable there.

"During our service I looked over the vast number of people who came to celebrate the birth of our Savior, and a sense of wonder filled my heart when I spied the people who comprise the haphazard group gathered before me now." Craig swept his arm from side to side, suggesting to the multitude that he meant every one of them.

He leaned forward, looked at Tyler, and asked, "This is a rather unusual looking family. Wouldn't you agree?"

"Huh?" Tyler asked. "Family?" He wrenched his neck until he could see Stan's face. Stan filled his fatherly role with his dazzling you-got-me look.

"Don't you love it when God's plan unfolds, especially in ways you couldn't have imagined?"

Zach's sideways inventory counted positive responses from Juanita, Izzy, and Holly. The number of deer-in-the-headlight expressions totaled four: Stan, Lauren, Tyler, and Wellington. Conner and Zach didn't count in the assessment, as they exchanged knowing glances with one another. Craig was fulfilling his most rewarding role.

"This isn't the first time y'all have gathered together as a group, is it?"

"We had pizza," Lauren said.

"At Izzy's house," Tyler added.

"That's what I heard," Craig said. "Also heard that Wellington has a safe place to stay." Craig inclined his head toward Wellington and said, "Also heard Zach Hoyt talked you into some manual labor that left you with turquoise thumbs. That true?"

Wellington ran his tongue along the inside of his mouth while he regarded his hands. He lifted them for Craig's inspection.

"I reckon it will wear off eventually," Craig said. "Listen, folks, my point is that our lives intersected for purposes we couldn't begin to comprehend. What's come out of it? Izzy shared her artistic talents with Lauren and Tyler, who gifted their artwork to the Hoyts. Officers Benton and Norris used what they learned in Juanita's ASL class to fend off a robber. Zach has reliable help at his shop. New Life has a reliable security presence, and more. What started as an antagonistic alterca—"

Lauren interrupted with, "What's a tag on a stick?"

Wrinkles outlined Craig's mouth and eyes when he looked at Lauren and said, "A disagreement."

"Oh."

"Something that started out poorly turned into relationships that made each of us better people. I like to think that the most important thing to come out of this is that some of you, for the first time in your lives, have heard about sin, judgment, God's grace, and salvation."

"Amen," Yolanda said.

"What you do with that is up to you, but God's invitation to join His family is the most important decision any of us will make in this life. Be wise. I'm here to lead all of you into the arms of Jesus. You just say when."

Craig gestured for Yolanda to join him. He took the camera, fidgeted with it for a minute, and squinted into the viewfinder until Yolanda pointed to the screen at the back of the camera.

"Just let me take the picture," Yolanda said as she retrieved the camera. "Go on. You get everyone in place."

When Lauren asked, "You want our picture?" Tyler groaned. So did Wellington.

"Come on," Craig said. "Look at this group. I love it. We've got the Caucasian, African American, Asian, American Indian—"

"American Indian?" Wellington asked.

Conner leaned over and fake-whispered, "My mom."

"I thought she was Mexican."

"Everybody thinks that," Izzy said.

Juanita put both hands on her hips, pulled them away, and delivered a string of signs.

"What did she say?" Tyler asked.

"She says we shouldn't talk about her as if she's not here," Izzy said. She turned to Wellington and added, "She wants to know where you're from. Korea? Japan? Taiwan?"

Wellington drew back and pointed to himself. "Me?"

Juanita nodded.

"Louisiana." When Wellington's response earned a smirk from Juanita, he conceded. "Point taken."

Craig spent the next two minutes assembling the group in a not-very-organized manner. When Yolanda announced that she had everyone within the picture frame, Craig stood beside her and examined his work.

"Not bad."

"Get up there."

"Me? No. This isn't about me."

Yolanda lowered her head and peered over the rims of her glasses when she asked, "Are these people part of this congregation?"

"I hope so."

"Then get up there."

"Yes ma'am."

Pastor Craig Morrison, friend, shepherd, encourager, and arbitrator, climbed the steps and made a space between Conner and Wellington before he turned his attention back to Yolanda.

"Say cheese." The camera's beam flickered several times before the strobe lit up the front of the sanctuary.

Some fifteen "cheeses" later, Yolanda had Craig inspect her work. When satisfied they'd collected an acceptable rendition of this mismatched entourage, they permitted the subjects to gather their coats and leave the building.

Zach zipped back into the chapel to grab the car keys he'd dropped on the front pew, and followed Stan and his children out of the building.

"Daddy?"

"What, Princess?"

"Can you and me and Tyler give our hearts to Jesus? Can we?"

"We can talk about it," Stan replied. He caught sight of Zach as he turned his head, and added, "We will."

"What about Mommy?" Tyler asked.

Stan held his head in a straightforward position while he

mulled over that request, but his "We'll see," earned a hearty dose of empathy from Zach. No way did he want to walk in Stan Benton's shoes.

~

Stan put the car into reverse and started to back out of the parking lot. He ought to let the engine warm up for more than half a second, but he needed to bolt.

"But, Daddy, I have to." Lauren's voice wavered. Stan heard her suck in a sob.

"Now? Right now?"

"Please?"

Stan didn't know which spoke louder: his sigh or Lauren's tears. He closed his eyes, shoved the transmission back into park, and climbed out of the car. The wind wrapped around his bare head as he opened the back door. Tyler let himself out, and when Lauren slipped on the ice, Stan scooped her into his arms and headed back toward the church.

Pastor Morrison and his wife stood on the landing in front of the door, both with their backs to the sidewalk.

"Can you wait a second before you lock up?" Stan called out.

"You forget something?" Pastor Craig asked.

"Uh, Lauren needs—"

"Come on inside," Yolanda said as Craig pushed open the door. "You need me to take you to the restroom?" Yolanda asked Lauren.

"No."

When Yolanda turned her inquisitive face on Tyler, he stepped back and said, "Not me."

"Well, then," Pastor Craig said, "how can we help you?"

"I wanna ask Jesus to live in my heart," Lauren said.

Stan squeezed his eyes and crimped his mouth. The emotion that accompanied Lauren's heartfelt plea rearranged every fragment of Stan's stubborn resolve. Tears—something as foreign to Stan as a woman's emotional makeup—clouded his eyes.

Pastor Craig seemed to wait for Stan to say something, but it was all Stan could do to swallow the lump in his throat and stiffen his spine. Anything else would take him to his knees.

Yolanda extended her hand to Lauren, "Let's go back into the sanctuary."

"Can we stand by the pretend baby Jesus?" Lauren asked.

"Do you know where the real Jesus lives?" Yolanda asked.

"Yeah. Two places."

That comment earned a double take from the pastor and his wife.

"Two places?" Pastor Craig asked.

"Yeah. He lives in heaven, and after I pray, He'll live in my heart. Right?"

Stan pulled in his lower lip and choked back the second round of unfathomable awareness that soaked his being. In this place, where a sense of God's majesty met damaged, sinful, human form, something deep within stirred Stan's spirit. Was it so simple? This grace thing?

While Pastor Craig and Yolanda reiterated the message of salvation using simple words that his children could understand, Stan looked at the crèche, the cross, and his hands. What he did with those hands, what he chose to do with his future, would define his eternity.

Pastor Craig looked at Stan and said, "You have any

objections to their desire to pray for salvation?"

"No." His voice, just a whisper, gained volume and strength as it joined in with the supplication that he and his children rendered to the God of the Universe. The God who saves.

Twenty-Seven

Life seemed to take on a different rhythm once Christmas, New Years Day, and the Winter Solstice faded into yesterday. Most days still wore a cloak of bitter cold, and the wind joined with the frigid temperatures to make any nighttime excursions downright painful, but spring and the promise of warmer weather loomed . . . somewhere on that still-distant horizon. Didn't it?

The old gas furnace worked overtime tonight, but with a tad more reluctance than Zach's underpaid laborers. He'd prayed over the tired unit more than once. The man who performed the annual maintenance on the machinery suggested that Zach put the mass of metal out of its misery. He offered to place a courtesy phone call in March to discuss the cost of a new unit. Zach could only hope he wouldn't find himself without heat in the interim.

The worst that could happen to undermine everyone's efforts to produce a high quality and financially successful weaving retreat was a late-season storm that might scare away the participants. The meteorologists who predicted the onslaught of wintry gloom with professional composure and unwarranted levels of cheer, transformed into frenetic doomsayers at the hint of foul weather and that ugliest of winter terms: blizzard. Last Zach heard, the storm stuck in the Plains had little hope of wreaking havoc on the Midwest. He held his breath.

He slit the tape that held the bottom of a packing box together, and added the cardboard to a nearby heap. The shipment that arrived earlier in the day marked the last of the inventory he wanted to have on hand when they welcomed the weavers, instructors, and other vendors to the retreat.

"You figure out where to put everybody?" Conner asked as he walked back into the warehouse. He wore a heavy sweatshirt, knee-frayed jeans, and unlaced high-top tennis shoes. He clasped his hands and blew on them.

"Cold?" Zack asked.

"It's as warm as Iceland in here. No problem."

"Furnace can't keep up."

Conner rubbed the tip of his red nose, and sniffled. "I'll survive."

"Let's just hope the pipes don't burst. Temperature's supposed to drop another twenty degrees before morning."

Conner picked up the drawing of the large room at the conference center where the vendors would set up their wares. "You have this many people selling supplies at the retreat?"

"Yeah. Why?"

"These designated spaces," Conner said as he tapped his finger on the pencil-marked diagram, "will house your competition."

"They're not my competition. None of the vendors sells basic basket supplies. Just us."

"Doesn't matter. They'll compete for the weavers' money."

"True," Zach said.

"You don't see that as a problem?"

"Have you listened to Nancy and Mae talk about what happens at a basket weavers' gathering?"

"Not really," Conner said. "Those two make me nervous. I try to keep some distance between us."

"Nervous?"

"They act like they want to pinch my cheeks and tell me what a good boy I am. I'm afraid that if they got mad at me, they'd take me by the ear and escort me to the woodshed."

"He's right," Wellington said as he walked into the room. "They're intimidating."

"I'll give you that," Zach said. "Especially Mae, except—"

"When she brings cookies." Conner finished the sentence for him.

"Any left?" Wellington asked.

"No," Zach replied.

"You ate them?" Conner's accusatory voice squeaked.

"No. *We* ate them. Remember?"

"Uh, are we almost done?" Wellington asked. "Holly said she'd pick me up at your house at nine."

"Yeah. You bet," Zach said. "Let me start the car while you check the doors and turn out the lights."

Wellington stuck out his hand. "I have a better idea. I'll start the car while you two close up shop."

He wanted the keys to Zach's car? What did the boy's rap sheet include? Fighting, not grand theft auto. Or so Zach recalled. This was one of those trust moments every parent dreaded, in spite of the fact that it was a friend of his child—and not his child—who posed the question.

Zach fumbled as he slid his keyring out of his pocket and watched the little security mechanisms as they thudded to the floor. Why not? If Holly Norris trusted the boy with everything she owned, what was a car? Zach picked up the keys and dangled them in front of Wellington.

"Do you have a license?"

"No."

"Then don't take the car out of 'park.' We'll be out in a minute."

Wellington and his victory swagger disappeared when the door slammed shut behind him. When Zach turned around, he encountered Conner's gaping mouth.

"What?"

"You trust him with your car?"

For the first time since they arrived earlier, Zach's neck and body gave off heat instead of hoarding it.

"Shouldn't I?" Zach asked.

"I'm not sure."

"Well, I guess we'll find out. You check the warehouse while I shut down the office?"

"Got it. Then I'll wait in the car," Conner said. He mumbled, "If it's still there," as he walked away.

It took longer than Zach anticipated to lock up. He forgot he had to save his spreadsheet. An unexpected and automatically installed software update added more minutes to the power-down process. With any luck, he'd find his car in the parking lot, two teens inside, and sufficient fuel in the tank to take them back to the house.

When Zach stepped outside, plumes of exhaust swirled into the atmosphere and rushed into his lungs. His body suffered a wholly different assault when he pried open the driver's door and found the vehicle empty.

"Conner?" he called out.

"Over here." Conner rounded the corner of the building and crossed the parking lot. Wellington, who followed, held something in his hands. When they neared Zach, he heard both of them panting.

"What's going on?" Zach asked.

"I saw someone," Wellington said.

"Where?"

"At the corner of the building." Wellington pointed. "Over there. I chased him."

"You what?"

"I chased him. Knocked him down, but he got away."

"You confronted—what? A thief, homeless guy, murderer? What were you thinking?"

"I just did it. Didn't think about it." Wellington leaned forward and put a hand on his knee. He choked in air and said, "He was just a vandal. He didn't murder me."

"Did you go after him too?" Zach asked Conner.

"I heard them scuffling. The guy was gone before I got there."

Wellington held up his other hand. "Here."

"Spray paint?" The waves of fear that seized Zach's body suddenly flat lined. In the same instant, his anger monitor bleeped to its highest point. "Somebody painted the building?"

"They didn't get very far," Conner said as he cupped his hands over his ears.

"Get in the car," Zach said. "I'll be back."

"It's just a couple of letters. Worry about it tomorrow," Conner said before he shut the door.

Since the vandal conveniently popped the lightbulb that was supposed to illuminate the back door, it wasn't easy to make out the damage. Conner was right. It wasn't bad. The artist relegated his graffiti—if that's all it was—to the door and not the brick walls. It was the second scenario, that of a vandal intent upon encouraging Zach and his family to get out of Dodge, that commenced a dull throbbing in his head.

Zach climbed into the car, checked the time on the dashboard, and rummaged in his pocket. He pulled out his phone and handed it to Wellington. "Better call Holly and tell her we're late."

"You want me to mention the spray paint?"

"We'll worry about that in person." Zach pulled onto the roadway and ran a tumble of words through his brain. He came up empty. "What words use 'B-E-S' as the first three letters? Is that a gang thing?"

"You're asking me?" Wellington said.

"I'm talking out loud. That's all."

"I've never seen that before, not that I'm privy to gang artwork," Wellington said.

"Me either," Conner said. Then he and Wellington began what sounded like a contest.

"Best."

"Bespectacled," Conner replied.

"Besiege."

"I've run out already."

"Me too," Wellington said. "No wait. Be smart."

Conner took up the challenge and replied, "Be stupid."

"Be scum."

"Be silent," Zach said. "You're making my headache worse."

"Be shushed," Wellington said.

"I think he meant it," Conner said. "No more."

"What did he look like?" Zach asked.

"The paint can guy?" Wellington asked.

"Yeah. Kid? Teenager?"

"Nope. The guy was old. Heavy, too."

"Did you see his face?"

"Kind of. It was dark back there."

"Think you might recognize him if you saw him again?"

"No. Well, maybe." Wellington scoffed when he said, "I could probably identify him by his breath. Man, the guy stank."

Zach crossed the unlikely graffiti prank off his list of possible motives. As with the previous incidents, the perpetrator intended harm to a specific target. Just as before, Zach's sense of fair play cried out, "Why me?"

Twenty-Eight

Norris hollered past the open window and waved Stan back to the cruiser. "Lunch has to wait. We have a call."

When he stepped back and let the front door of the deli close, the action cut off the fragrance of freshly baked bread and his hope for a full belly. He'd eaten a paltry dinner the night before and didn't bother with breakfast.

Stan took the passenger seat, slammed the door, and repositioned his hat as Norris pulled away from the curb.

"What've we got?"

"Domestic dispute."

Another one? The number of houses in an uproar rose during the holidays in spite of the songs that encouraged peace and goodwill toward men. This year the calls for assistance didn't decline as people got back into their everyday routines. The lousy weather didn't help.

"What do we know?"

"Neighbor called about an altercation that went from screaming inside the house to pushing and shoving outside."

"Where?"

"Meadowlark Drive."

Stan clutched his chest as his heart missed a beat. "Number?" he asked.

"519."

His indecent response slipped out of his mouth before he could catch it. He'd apologize later, assuming he survived the present.

"What's the matter with you?" Norris asked.

"That's Tina's place."

Norris's glance was quick, but her wild eyes and panicky expression mirrored Stan's dread. "You want me to call for backup?" she asked. "Keep you out of it?"

"We're here. Let's go."

The dispatcher called it right. Tina and DeWayne weren't duking it out in the driveway. No, their audience watched them as they yelled at each other over the muddy mess that might be a yard if the weather weren't still pretending it was winter.

They stood about four feet apart, their faces leaning toward each other and their mouths shouting what had to be insults. They looked like a couple of professional wrestlers trying to take each other down with words instead of tangling in the ring.

Well, no, that wasn't exactly right. Tina, clearly the aggressor, had mud on her hands and forearms, and a streak smeared her cheek and ventured into her hair. Except for her shoes and the hem of her jeans, her clothes were clean. DeWayne, who continued to wag his finger in Tina's face even as the squad car pulled up, had muddy handprints on his white shirt, and his pants looked as if he'd found himself on his knees in the mud for more than one of Tina's takedowns.

Tina's reaction to her ex-husband stepping onto the sidewalk filled all of Stan's expectations. Maybe more.

"Don't you dare interfere, *Officer* Benton. Get off my property." Tina glared once more at DeWayne before she turned on Stan and marched in his direction. "I mean it. Get out. Now."

"We can't do that," Norris said. Her voice was as smooth as butter. "We're responding to a complaint."

Tina turned on her heels and shouted at DeWayne, "You called the cops?"

"I did not," he screamed back.

The nosy neighbors earned the next of Tina's tirade, "Who? Who called? You all go back into your ugly little houses and mind your business. You hear?"

A couple of the neighbors followed Tina's suggestion. Most of them waited for more drama.

"Ma'am," Norris said, "You need to calm down. We don't want to take you to the station, but if you don't calm down, you leave us no choice."

Tina's eyes narrowed into accusatory slits. When Norris didn't flinch, Stan decided to award his partner with some assistance, although she didn't need any.

"Why don't we all go inside?" Stan asked. "Hmm?"

DeWayne, who inched toward them with an abundance of caution, said, "Yeah. We need to go inside. You don't belong out here. Not in your condition."

Stan grabbed Tina's fist before it made contact. If he'd missed, the wallop would have knocked out DeWayne's front teeth. Yep, she had a temper. It'd been more than a while since he'd seen it in such fine form.

"Inside," Stan said. "Now."

Tina started to say something, but Norris lifted her finger, pointed it toward the front door, and said, "Start walking. You choose which direction." She illustrated Tina's choices when she lifted her handcuffs. "Well?"

Tina lit into DeWayne the second Norris shut the door.

"What part of 'I don't want you here' don't you understand?" She turned, not to Stan, but to Norris, and said "Can you get him off my property?"

"If that's what you want."

"Good." Tina turned to Stan and said, "Why don't you do your job and escort DeWayne to his car?" She notched up her chin and spit her tirade while she folded her arms across her chest, which drew Stan's attention to her midsection.

Tina took on her don't-even-go-there glare, the one she delivered every time Stan picked up his children. When would she address the unfolding event? She looked as if she were five or six months along already. Did she think her pretending would make it go away?

Stan lifted his eyes and turned toward DeWayne. "Let's go," Stan said as he opened the door.

When they stepped onto the porch, he surveyed the neighborhood. Where did Tina get off telling people they had ugly little houses? He'd trade his apartment for a place on this street in a heartbeat.

Most of the crowd had dispersed, but when Stan and DeWayne walked down the steps, a few of the stragglers tsk'd their disapproval while wearing their holier-than-thou façades.

The elderly woman who lived next door started up the walkway leading to her door, but turned to Stan and said, "I seen you. Aren't you their daddy?"

"Lauren and Tyler?"

"Aren't you?"

"Yes, ma'am."

The woman pulled her lips together and emitted an unflattering, "Pfft. You best keep an eye on their mama. She and that one," the woman said as she pointed to DeWayne, "they be setting a pretty poor example for those young'uns. Seems to me you ought to do something about it."

Stan glanced at DeWayne and said, "Yes, ma'am. Go on inside."

When Stan started to grab DeWayne's arm, the man retreated. "I'm going, but I need to ask you something."

"What?"

"How can I get Tina to listen to me?"

"That's your question? You want me to tell you how to communicate with Tina?" Stan couldn't help himself. The chortle escaped before he could reel it in.

"I'm not trying to be funny."

"What then?" Stan pointed to the SUV's door.

DeWayne unlocked the vehicle and opened the door, but didn't take his seat. "I'm dead serious."

"You keep trying to communicate with Tina and you might be more dead than serious," Stan said. The remark may have sounded glib, but it wasn't too far from the truth.

"You know how she is. Always has to have her way," DeWayne said.

"Looks to me like you managed to have your way with her. What's your beef now?"

DeWayne held his position during the verbal assault when he answered, "It wasn't like that."

"I'll bet."

Norris came out the front door and did a double take when she saw Stan speaking to DeWayne.

"Listen, I need to talk to you," DeWayne said.

"We got nothing to talk about," Stan said.

"You care about your kids. Right?"

"You threatening my kids?" The hair on Stan's neck stood on end.

"No. That's not what I meant. You care about Lauren and Tyler. I care about the child that's coming."

That remark stymied Stan more than DeWayne's ludicrous need for this little powwow. "That's news to me. Where you been?"

Norris walked up to the pair and said, "Mr. Davis, you need to leave. Now. Benton, let's roll."

"I'm leaving." When DeWayne's hand moved toward his coat pocket, Norris reached for her gun. DeWayne's wan complexion lost its color. He raised both hands and said, "Whoa. My card. I'm just getting my card."

Norris took a step back, but didn't move her hand from above her holster.

DeWayne reached into his coat, used two fingers to pull out a business card, and handed it to Stan. "Please call me."

Stan didn't answer when he took the card. After DeWayne took his seat, Stan closed the door, patted the roof of the SUV, and waited until DeWayne pulled out of the driveway before he started walking back to the cruiser.

"Call me?" Norris echoed.

"Whatever."

Before Norris pulled away, Stan looked at the house. Tina stood in the living room, looking out the window. Stan's heart may have softened a lot since he gave his life to the Lord. He thought he'd worked through forgiving Tina, and maybe he had, but that didn't mean he'd learned how to relate to her. Not even. DeWayne Davis was on his own.

~

If he had an appetite, this was the place to appease it, but the strawberry and whipped cream-topped pancakes the children at the next booth devoured didn't hold their typical appeal. Instead, a whiff of the coffee the waitress lowered to the table attacked Stan's queasy stomach as if he'd just bottomed out on a roller coaster. "Come hungry," DeWayne had said. "I'm buying."

Well, DeWayne wasn't here yet, and neither was Stan's desire to sit in the booth and pretend he cared about the little chat DeWayne begged to have with him. If Stan had just kept his mouth shut instead of sharing the domestic quarrel incident with Pastor Morrison, he'd be at home, sleeping in on his one day off work.

When the waitress made another round with the coffee pot, her generous refill sloshed down the side of his cup and puddled the tabletop. The mess resembled the scene outside.

The blue SUV pulled up to the front of the restaurant, and when DeWayne climbed out of the vehicle he had to sidestep a channel of murky, half-thawed slime that defied nature's attempt at evaporation. He wore his signature button-down shirt tucked into a pair of gray slacks. When he entered the building, he took care to scuff the wet debris clinging to his polished black leather shoes. Is that what caught Tina's eye? His clothes? Or was it his SUV, or maybe his office job, the one that promised a promotion into management?

DeWayne walked to Stan's booth and took his seat. "Sorry I'm late. Got a call from my mum."

His mum? Who talked like that?

"What'll it be?" the waitress asked. She pointed to DeWayne's empty coffee mug. "Want some?"

"Please."

"Ready to order?"

"I'll have a veggie omelet, egg whites only, and hold the

onions."

The waitress paused at DeWayne's request, shrugged, and started scribbling on her note pad.

"Hash browns?"

"No. Just wheat toast. No butter."

DeWayne's bland choices served to whet Stan's appetite. As long as "mummy's boy" was buying . . .

"You?" the waitress asked.

"Farmer's platter. Turkey sausage, eggs scrambled, home fries. Uh, no whipped cream on the pancakes, but extra syrup."

"Got it."

"You hungry?" DeWayne asked as the waitress walked away.

"Not really." Stan sat back in his seat.

"Listen, I know you think I'm out of line about meeting you, but I need your help with Tina."

"I doubt I can be helpful, but I'm all ears."

"I don't understand why she won't marry me."

The guy could have made that comment when Stan wasn't in the middle of sipping his coffee. He choked down the hot liquid and wiped his mouth with his napkin. "Excuse me?"

"Not only has she declined my requests to marry, she's asked me to walk out of her life altogether. I don't think I can do that."

"Might be to your advantage," Stan muttered. He flicked his hand at DeWayne. "Sorry, I shouldn't have said that."

"I understand."

"You understand what?" Stan asked.

A perplexed expression fell over DeWayne's face, as if he wasn't following his own conversation. "Never mind. What I thought you might explain is why Tina is adverse to marriage."

Stan's response tarried while he tried to choose his point of reference, uncertain whether to voice disbelief in Tina's attitude or his apparent misunderstanding of DeWayne's comment. In the subsequent silence, Stan studied DeWayne. The man's question was genuine. Maybe Stan needed to formulate a truthful answer. Did he have one?

"Uh, as you know, things didn't end well for the two of us," Stan said. They hadn't started well either, but DeWayne didn't need to know the details.

"She told me you two married because she got pregnant."

"Yeah," Stan said.

"She said she wouldn't get married a second time just because she's pregnant."

"No?"

"Why are you surprised?"

"You don't think she planned this pregnancy?"

"Of course not. Why would I think that?" DeWayne asked.

Stan started to deliver a rude retort, but clamped his mouth shut.

"I asked her to marry me months ago. Before she even knew she was pregnant. Her answer then, as now, was 'no.' "

"But, the two of you . . ." Stan waved his finger back and forth. Where was he supposed to take this conversation?

"We agreed to live together instead of making things official. Things went well for a time, but when she got pregnant, everything changed. I don't know why."

When the waitress placed the breakfast platter on the table, Stan dug in. He came up for air after he'd decimated his scrambled eggs and half of the stack of pancakes. DeWayne's plate looked untouched except for a corner missing from one of the unbuttered pieces of wheat toast.

"Look," Stan said, "I didn't understand Tina when we were in high school. I didn't know how to make her happy when we got married. Having two kids didn't bring her the joy she wanted. You think I have a clue as to what you need to do to woo my ex-wife? Really?"

DeWayne dropped his napkin on the table and said, "That's just it."

"What's 'just it'?" Stan asked.

"What you said. About being happy. I don't think Tina believes she has the right to be happy. She's got the notion that she's been a horrible person and that her life stinks."

Stan looked at the man who walked into the restaurant's door, and gestured for him to join them. Stan had done one thing right. Knew he was in over his head where Tina's heart and soul were involved.

Stan stood, let the newcomer slide into the booth, and said, "DeWayne Davis, I'd like you to meet Pastor Craig Morrison."

Twenty-Nine

"Tell me what I need to know about Frederick Hollister," Craig said.

"What do you mean?" Zach asked.

"He called me this morning and asked if I'd put in a good word for him."

"With whom?"

"The mayor."

"What does Hollister have to do with the mayor?"

"His predecessor isn't returning to the precinct."

"He wants you to recommend him for the job?"

"He does. He asked if I thought the actions he took regarding the incidents at the church and those reported by members of my congregation were handled professionally."

Zach rubbed the back of his neck and said, "It's not as if he prevented anything."

"We don't know that," Craig said. "Stepped up patrols might have lessened the number of incidents."

"Didn't seem to help me at my house or at the shop. It still bothers me that Juanita and I got hit three different times."

"You think it was something personal and unrelated to your membership in this church?"

"You got me. Why are you asking my opinion of Hollister?"

"Aside from being privy to the incident with your sister back in high school, I don't appreciate his methods for getting recognition."

Zach ignored the pang that the past rekindled and asked, "Why? He's just asking for a personal reference, more or less. Right?"

"Maybe, but he sent Stan Benton on the same errand a couple of days ago."

"You lost me," Zach said.

"Last time I had a casual encounter with Stan, he brought up Hollister's name. Said he thought the acting captain had done a fine job of protecting the members of my flock."

"That doesn't sound like Stan's verbiage."

Craig chuckled. "More like mine. I know. Or maybe words Hollister heard me use. What got my attention was Stan's behavior. Man was uncomfortable, tripping over himself."

"You think Hollister put him up to it?"

"Hmm. We may be on the same wavelength, Zach."

"Do you have second thoughts about recommending him?"

"Can't put my finger on it, but something doesn't feel right to me. Know what I mean?" Craig asked.

"You're asking someone who has little regard for the man."

"I trust you to be objective," Craig said.

"It may not be fair of me to say this," Zach said, "but I don't trust Hollister today any more than I did back in high school."

"You think he's self-serving?"

"He got a lot of attention every time he responded to things that happened in this neighborhood. Most police captains don't find the need to soak up the limelight whenever they answer the call of a citizen in need."

"Maybe that's the part that doesn't sit well with me," Craig replied.

"He was a grandstander way back when. As far as I've seen, he doesn't act much different now."

"I'll have to give some more consideration to Hollister's request. My friendship with the mayor is important to me, and I don't want to put my two cents into the pot if I don't know what that donation might cost me."

"Wise words," Zach said.

"Yolanda wanted me to ask you if you need any help with that basket thing you got going on next week."

"The weaving retreat? How does she even know about it?"

Craig sat back in his seat and rocked back and forth a couple of times. He looked content, in his comfort zone.

"Not much gets past my wife. She's the eyes and ears of this place—next to the Good Lord, who knows everything."

"Did Juanita talk to her about it?"

"Must have. Yolanda wanted to know if you need help serving meals."

"That's a kind offer, but we're good. Participants are on their own for breakfast and dinner. We only have to worry about lunch, and the conference hall amenities include catering. They'll put up a buffet line and staff it with a couple of people. Izzy and Paige are in charge of setting up snacks, brewing coffee and tea, and keeping coolers filled with bottles of water."

Craig's forehead furrowed as he asked, "You're pulling

the girls out of school?"

"We got lucky with our timing. School's out for a couple of days for teacher conferences."

"Ah, that luck thing. I see. You need help registering folks? Stuff like that?"

"Conner and Wellington are in charge of registration."

"I like the sound of that. Does my heart good to hear Wellington's finding his way around his circumstances. What about passing out supplies and such?"

"Is Yolanda *looking* for something to do?"

"I don't think so."

"Maybe she'd like to sign up to take a class," Zach suggested.

"Basket weaving? Yolanda?"

"Why not?" Zach asked.

"Because she's already involved in ninety-five things. She doesn't need lessons on how to be a basket case on top of all that."

"You've been waiting for a way to interject that term into this conversation, haven't you?" Zach asked.

"Couldn't help myself," Craig said as he slapped his hand against his knee. "Do you know how many times I've wanted to call you that during the Finance Committee meetings?"

"That would notch up my credibility with the others, for sure."

"Yes, sir. Next time we take a vote on the budget, I'll introduce you as the congregation's only bona fide basket case." Craig shoved his chair back and stretched his arms as he stood. When he walked Zach to the door, he clapped him on the back. "You just give me a call if Yolanda can help you from becoming that basket case, you hear?"

~

If Juanita had to rate this day on a scale of one to ten stars, she'd have to give it more than the number of twinkling lights she might count on a clear night. If a Best Mothering Award were in the offing, Izzy might challenge her more experienced resume and steal the accolades.

Juanita hadn't had this much fun with children running through the house since her own were little. Today brought sweet reminders of Izzy and Conner, when innocence and wonder filled their days. It wasn't so long ago that simple things like coloring books, Kool-Aid, and peanut butter and jelly sandwiches lit up their worlds.

Conner and Izzy's normal routines now included frequent visits by Wellington and Paige, and an untold number of sleepovers, but their most recent request to include Tyler and Lauren caught Juanita by surprise. Izzy and Conner swore they needed the children's assistance on a secretive undertaking that began mid-morning and extended throughout the afternoon and evening.

Just to be certain they had ample time to complete their task, they talked Juanita and Zach into letting their guests stay overnight. When Zach promised he could wrangle a full night's sleep while taking charge of three boys, Juanita decided she would step up to chaperone the three girls. Unlike Zach, Juanita did not expect to sleep.

Over the course of the day, the artwork Izzy, Paige, Tyler and Lauren created for their project cluttered every inch of the dining room table. After they put their paints, paper, chalk, pens, and pencils away, they gathered their goods and pounded down the stairs to join Conner and Wellington, who claimed they were wrestling with a complicated computer programming assignment. All of them made it clear to Juanita that neither she nor Zach were to descend the steps to the basement for any reason.

A gust of fresh air and a whiff of take-out dinner preceded Zach's kitchen entrance. While holding four boxes in one arm, he inched open the basement door, yelled, "Dinner," and then backed away when feet reverberated up the stairs.

Two children and four teenagers washed hands, poured drinks, and assembled around the table at warp speed.

"You brought pizza?" Juanita signed.

Zach clenched his teeth in an "I'm guilty" pose and said, "It was either pizza or Brussel sprouts and pickled eggs. The pickled eggs sounded messy."

"Ew. Gross," Tyler said.

"What are brushed sprouts?" Lauren asked.

"They're double gross," Wellington said.

"Good choice, Dad," Izzy said. She lifted the lid to the nearest box, held it out to Juanita, and said, "Here, Mom. Help yourself."

Juanita pulled out a piece with a thick covering of melted cheese, inhaled the enticing aroma, and took a bite. "Good," she signed. "Anyone want salad?"

With no responses in the affirmative, Juanita picked up her pizza and took another bite. She could skip the salad too.

"Hey, Mr. Hoyt," Wellington said. "Did you get that spray paint off the door?"

"Nope. I just bought a can of paint and put a fresh coat on the mess. Two coats, actually."

"You could have just finished writing out the word."

"Which word?" Conner asked with his mouth still full of

pizza. When he caught Juanita looking at him with disapproval, he covered his hand with his mouth. When he finished chewing, he looked at her and said, "Sorry."

"I think my favorite word was bespectacled," Wellington said.

"What are you talking about?" Izzy asked. She finger-spelled while she spoke so Paige could keep up with the dialogue.

"We made up words that the vandal was trying to write," Conner said.

"Well, you both got them wrong," Zach said. "In daylight, the letters turned out to be *B E R* not *B E S*."

"Berry," Wellington said. He, too, finger-spelled for the benefit of Paige and Juanita. Not only did Juanita appreciate the consideration, she patted herself on the back for her part in teaching the teenager how to sign.

Conner pointed at Wellington and said, "Beryllium."

"Burlesque."

Izzy pulled her lips together and did something that looked like "pfft," to Juanita. "That's *BUR*, not *BER*," Izzy said.

"Bermuda," Conner added without giving Wellington a chance to redeem himself.

Wellington worked his lips, pulling them together several times to make the letter *B*, yet coming up empty. "Bermuda shorts," he said as a smug air wandered across his face.

"Berlin," Conner said.

All eyes turned on Wellington, who said, "Ah . . . I like this one. Berserk."

"Ooh," Conner said. He lifted the top of his nose with the next challenge. "Beriberi."

"Wait." Zach said.

"But, we're not done," Conner said.

Zach put down his pizza, turned a befuddled face on Wellington, and said, "What did you say?"

"Bermuda shorts."

"After that."

"Uh . . . berserk."

Zach's jaw hung so low that Juanita could have counted his molars and his wisdom teeth. He stared at the table before he wiped his hand over his mouth and stood.

Juanita reached for his arm. "What?" she signed.

"I'll be right back."

All eyes followed Zach as he went down the hall. Juanita felt the pulse of his steps on the stairs as he went to the second floor of the house. The smack of the closet door against its frame alerted Juanita to Zach's place in their bedroom, but his reason for abandoning his dinner, his family, and his guests, was beyond her imagination.

She motioned for everyone to grab more pizza and eat, and while the children exchanged silly chatter, Juanita nibbled on a chewy piece of dough. With some effort, she kept at bay the apprehension that tarried after Zach exited the room.

When Zach returned, he held a piece of paper and a book in his hand. First, he unfolded the paper and handed it to Juanita. "See anything odd?"

She'd seen this before. Zach kept notes about the vandalism reported by the church. Zach pointed to one of the items. Juanita didn't know what to make of the incident then, and didn't know why it was a matter of interest now.

"I don't understand," she signed.

"This is what someone painted on the back door of the church."

"What?" Izzy asked. "I can't see from here."

"Bug off or I go berserk," Zach said.

"What's bee's work?" Lauren asked Tyler.

"I dunno," Tyler said.

Zach lowered the book to the top of the table, turned to the back pages, and ran his finger down one of the index pages before he flipped open to another page that revealed dozens of portraits, the smiling faces of his high school classmates.

Juanita's confusion seemed to drive up Zach's angst. What did his yearbook have to do with the vandalism at the church and *The Basket Works*?

He pointed to a photo. With Conner peering over his shoulder, Zach asked, "What does that say?"

"Most likely to go berserk. Huh? What does that mean?"

"You're a senior. Don't people put things like *Most likely to become President of the United States*, and stuff like that in your yearbook?"

"Yearbook? Dad? Nobody buys yearbooks anymore. I don't think they bother to compile them. Everything's online."

"That's not my point. Don't you give each other nicknames and make pronouncements about your peers and how they will change the future?"

Conner, Wellington, Izzy, and Paige all looked at Zach as if he were from another planet—or, more correctly, another era. Juanita wanted to come to Zach's defense, but she didn't get his point either.

"Doesn't matter," Zach said. His pinched mouth exposed his irritation. He stuck his finger on one of the photographs, turned to Wellington, and asked, "Does this guy look familiar to you?"

"Huh?" Wellington glanced at Conner, searching for an

explanation that Conner wasn't able to provide. Wellington leaned forward and studied the photo. "Nope."

Zach now looked more bewildered than irritated. "Never mind."

"What, Dad? What's going on?" Izzy asked.

"Nothing. Don't worry about it." Zach closed the yearbook and shoved it out of the way. He picked up his cold slice of pizza, stuffed it into the microwave, and waited for his dinner to warm.

Although the others returned to their food fest, Juanita couldn't help but notice that Zach's toes tapped impatiently while he waited. Something was amiss.

Just as he lifted his pizza to his mouth, he put it down again. He pulled his cell phone out of his pocket. If Juanita had thought Zach upset before, the caller's message drew a reaction that rested somewhere between confused and horrified. His side of the conversation gave no clues.

"All of it?"

"When?"

"That's not acceptable."

"No. Two days. Not four."

"Absolutely not."

"That's ridiculous."

"Of course I have a copy."

"Fine."

Zach ended the call and stared at Conner. Zack closed his eyes for a moment before he lifted his gaze to Juanita.

"You're scaring me," Izzy said.

"Me too," Lauren said.

"I'm sorry. Everything's fine. We just have a last-minute adjustment to make for the retreat. We'll figure it out."

"Who was that?" Conner asked.

"The manager of the conference center."

"And?" Juanita signed.

"Their fire suppression system malfunctioned."

"What does that mean?" Izzy asked.

"They have a sprinkler system in the building. One of the sensors failed and set off the system."

"You mean it flooded?" Izzy asked.

Zach's voice faltered when he answered. "He said if I wanted to see the damage in person that I needed to bring my hip waders."

Thirty

Zach fumbled with his keys until he found the one that opened the side door to the church. Once he closed the door behind him, he shoved the keys into his pocket. As he followed the lighted hallway to the church secretary's desk, the rich alto voice of the pastor's office assistant, who also served as the choir director, accompanied him.

Although Angelene's choice of songs wasn't of the ilk that trilled off his own tongue, Zach appreciated the gospel tunes, the ones where the promises of God prevailed over the trials of life. Indeed, as he neared the doorway, Angelene's lilt transcended from woeful blues to the realms of faith triumphant. He could use some of that today.

When Angelene looked up and caught Zach watching her, her cheeks colored. "You sneaking up on me, Zach Hoyt?"

"No, ma'am. I just came to add my 'amen' to your worship song. Amen, amen."

"Your voice says, 'amen, amen,' Zach Hoyt, but your face tells me you got a world o' trouble. That what brings you here this morning?"

"I'm here to collect some paperwork."

"Oh, I forgot. Hold on a minute while I find that

envelope." Angelene lifted several piles of paper, rearranged a stack of unfolded bulletins, and stopped her hunt only after her gaze landed on the top of the credenza. She handed the envelope to Zach. "Here it is."

"Thanks." Zach started to turn away, but Angelene caught him before he could edge his way out of the door.

"You can't leave while you carry such a heavy load. You gots to give it to the Lord. Easy to tell you haven't done that, Zach Hoyt."

Why the woman always included his surname when she addressed him was unclear. Zach's own mother used to call him Zach Hoyt whenever she needed to communicate his need to pay close attention to her. Regardless of Angelene's objective, she held his attention now, and her statement levied a direct hit. No, he hadn't prayed about the convention center disaster. He just panicked and entered his find-a-way-to-fix-it mode.

Angelene tilted her chin toward the envelope in Zach's hands and said, "I know those documents don't have anything to do with your trouble. Those things are just legal lingo formalities. What do we need to ask our good Father before you go on your way? Hmm?"

"You probably know *The Basket Works* is sponsoring a big workshop."

"Sister Yolanda said something about it."

"We ran into a problem with the venue."

"Did you rent out that convention center?"

"Yeah. You heard about it already?" Zach asked.

"Not from anyone here. I drove by the place on my way to work this morning. I don't know what happened, but they were pumping a river out of that building. I had to drive through the mess. Splattered dirty water all over my clean car."

"It was that bad?"

"Looked like they were hauling ceiling tiles, wet wallboard, and flooring out of the place. The parking lot was packed with as many dumpsters as repair trucks."

"You know of a place I might be able to rent on a two-day notice?" Zach asked.

"Honey, let's give up a prayer and seek an answer from the One who knows best."

"You're right."

Zach took the chair that sat next to Angelene's desk, but when she put a tablet of paper and pencil into his hand, he balked. He did not have time for whatever the woman had planned.

"Angelene . . ."

"You need to be specific. How many people you sign up for this workshop?"

"One hundred forty-four weavers."

She pointed to the paper. "Write that down. Anybody else?"

"Eight vendors need a place to set up displays, and so do four of the instructors."

"Write that down. What about food? Sister Yolanda wondered how you planned to feed everyone."

"I already told her," Zach said. Told her what? That the conference center's own catering company would handle lunch? How? They didn't have a kitchen any more than they had a usable room for weaving. "Lunch. We're supposed to provide lunch."

"Write that down. Lunch for 144 weavers, 8 vendors, plus—how many teachers?"

"Eleven. Plus my crew: Mae, Nancy, Wellington, Conner,

Izzy, Paige, Juanita."

"And you. You'll probably get hungry some time over three days." She pointed to the numbers and said, "Add 'em up."

"One hundred seventy-one."

"Whew, that's a big number, Zach Hoyt." Without waiting for Zach to bow his head, Angelene commenced a short and direct request for divine assistance. She patted his hand as she said, "Amen," and as he stood to leave, she yanked on the same hand and said, "You need to sit back down while we wait on the Lord."

"I need to run," Zach said.

"No you don't. You got to sit here and listen to God's answer."

"Angelene . . ."

"Zach Hoyt, would you slow down? Sit down. Now."

Zach sat.

"What about work tables? Those weavers need tables, right?"

"Yeah. The conference center—"

"Do you have a diagram with your setup?"

"I don't see how sharing these details will help me find a new venue."

"Zach Hoyt, I didn't expect to see you this morning." Craig stepped into the office. He extended a warm handshake and a more pleasant smile before gesturing to the envelope resting on Zach's lap. "I see you got your papers. Good. Are you helping Angelene with her filing or have you given her a new assignment?"

"Uh, I was just about to leave." Zach made an attempt to stand, but Angelene tugged on his arm and with nothing more overt than the suggestion she wore on her face, she directed him to his seat. Again.

"Zach's just itemizing his prayer request," Angelene said.

"You have a need this morning?" Craig asked.

"Yes, he does, and the Good Lord has answered him already."

He had?

"I just need your go ahead so's I can tell Zach it's all under control."

She wanted the pastor's approval? For what? Zach scratched his head while Angelene got up, opened Craig's office door, and directed the men to follow her inside. Once she and Zach sat in the chairs opposite the pastor's desk, she took the notebook from Zach.

"He has to find a place for his basket weavers to make some baskets."

"What happened to the conference center?"

"Flooded," Angelene replied. "Might as well be destroyed, for all its worth right now. Seems to me, Pastor Morrison, that our spacious fellowship hall can accommodate a handful of teachers, their students, and some worktables."

"What?" Zach asked.

"I see. Anything else?" Craig's tone was calm and matter of fact. Wait until he got the details.

"Looks as if Sister Yolanda might want to call in her kitchen crew, too. Those weavers will want nice homemade lunches to sustain them for three days of strenuous basket weaving. Uh huh."

"Wait," Zach said. "I appreciate your train of thought, but the church doesn't have thirty-six folding tables or the number of chairs needed for so many people."

"You can rent them. Can't cost nearly as much as renting the conference center, can it?" Angelene looked at Craig and asked, "Am I right?"

"You ought to pay her some heed," Craig said.

"You're serious?" Zach asked.

"Of course I'm serious. You don't have time to play games, mister."

Some forty-five minutes later, Angelene hung up the phone and beamed.

"Tables will be here the night before you need them. Plenty of time for you all to set up. Yolanda's working on the menu and the kitchen volunteers. All you need to do is get your deposit back from that conference center, cut a check to the rental company, and give Sister Yolanda the cash she needs to buy some food. Oh, and you better advise all your students, teachers, and vendors that they have a new destination. When you tell them that," Angelene said with a wink, "you make sure they know this alternative site is a heap better than the one you originally found. Yes, Zach Hoyt, you tell them that."

As Zach's blues gave way to the realms of faith triumphant, he rendered his own "Hallelujahs" down the hallway and out the door, where he encountered deep azure skies and brilliant sunshine—the most hopeful and gratifying display he'd seen since some sprinkler system went awry.

Thirty-One

"Hey, Conner, come on in." Stan opened the door to his apartment but wanted to close his eyes to Conner's reaction to what was Stan's pathetic version of Home Sweet Home. The teen hadn't experienced dorm or college apartment life yet, so maybe this was something to which he could aspire.

If the content and condition of the amenities caught Conner by surprise, he either didn't care or was too considerate to mention it. He took a seat on the sofa as if he'd visited the apartment a hundred times before and the middle cushion had his name on it. He handed Stan one of the two bags he held in his hand.

"Picked up take-out for everybody tonight. Thought you might like a bite."

"You can't bring me dinner. No, no, no."

"But, it's a Tommy Boy sub."

"A Tommy Boy sub?" Stan could feel drool sliding down his chin. "Well, maybe just this once." He unfolded the top of the bag and took a whiff. Heaven in a white carryout bag. "Thanks."

"You're welcome. Just don't touch the contents of the other bag until you've wiped the grease off your fingers."

"Yeah. About that. What, exactly, have you and the

others been up to? I heard what you said when you called about authorizations and minors, and all that, but I didn't get it. Not really."

Conner's eyes danced with pleasure—a rather uncommon sight in a teenage boy. Then again, Stan found nothing common about the Hoyt children.

"Ready to see?" Conner asked. He didn't wait for a response, but pulled out three copies of a paperback book, the cover of which looked somewhat familiar. "Hot off the press."

"What is it?" Stan accepted one of the copies, studied the child-like rendition of a goldfish that swam in a bright blue watercolor ocean, and took in the title, *Fish Tales, Some with Words*.

He opened the front cover and read, *contributions by Conner Hoyt, Izzy Hoyt, W.E. Holly, Lauren Stanley, Tyler Stanley, and Paige Dott.*

"Izzy and I wanted to use our real names, but do you like the others? The pen names?"

"Huh?" What word might Stan use to describe his present state? Flummoxed?

"Wellington didn't want to use his real name because he didn't know if his mom would blow a gasket, especially when he wrote about personal stuff. So he—"

"Borrowed Holly's name," Stan interrupted. "Does she know?"

"I don't think so."

"She'll be pleased." Stan's fingertip rested on the Lauren Stanley and Tyler Stanley names. "Who picked Stanley? Was that your idea?"

"Nope. Lauren and Tyler picked it after Paige decided she wanted to use her Grandma Dottie's name somehow."

"Well, I'm touched. No, more than that. I don't know what to say." Stan flipped through the pages, some filled with colorful artwork, some with words. "That's kind of you to use some of their pictures."

"They wrote stories too."

"Stories?"

"Sure. Like kids' bedtime stories. You'll love them."

"What prompted you to do this?" Stan asked.

"Izzy started it. She asked Mom to help her write and illustrate a children's book. She wanted to record the stories Mom used to share when we were kids, before either of us knew how to sign." Conner shrugged when he said, "I think the story time meant more to us than the stories did to Mom. Izzy asked for help with the book when Mom was buried with work, and Mom said she didn't have anything to contribute."

"So Izzy decided to write her own stories?" Stan asked.

"Yeah, but it was at the same time Lauren and Tyler started coming to the ASL class. They kind of inspired the rest of this." Conner held up another copy of the book. "Pretty cool, eh?"

"More than cool. If I need more of these, where can I get them?"

Conner wiggled his eyebrows and said, "I am your discount source, although you can find the title at your favorite mega-online store."

"You're joking."

"Check it out, man." Conner stood. "Hey, I gotta deliver the rest of those Tommy Boy subs before they get cold. See ya."

Stan closed the door after Conner left, and pushed the mouthwatering Tommy Boy sub aside. As he turned the first page, he held the same level of gratitude as an honored guest at the king's table. Which he was.

~

Stan turned to the page that held Lauren's story. A lump rose in his throat as he read *Who's Counting?* aloud:

> "But, Daddy," the little girl fish cried, "we don't have room for more fish. We're enough already."
>
> "Little girl, how big is your heart?"
>
> "Big as the ocean."
>
> "What happens when a new fish is born? Does the ocean get bigger or does it just make room for one more?"
>
> "If it got bigger, it would flood the land, wouldn't it?"
>
> "Yes it would," the wise daddy fish said.
>
> "Then the ocean makes room for one more."
>
> "Do you think the ocean is a happier place when another fish gets to play in the water?"
>
> "Yes."
>
> "How much love does your heart hold?" the daddy fish asked.
>
> "As much as the ocean."
>
> "Can your heart make room for one more fish, my princess?"
>
> "I think so. Yes."
>
> "What if the fish turns out to be twins? Can you make that much room?"
>
> The little girl fish giggled when she said, "Yes, Daddy."
>
> "What if they were triplets?"

"Yes, I have room."

"Quadruplets?"

"How many is that?" the little girl fish asked.

"Four—I think."

"Four? Yes, I can make room for four."

"What if—"

"Yes, I can make room in my heart for more."

"Do you have a limit?"

"Yes. A gazillion."

"How many is a gazillion, my girl?"

"I don't know, but if it's more than I can count, my heart will lose count too. Then it'll just make room for the rest."

THE END

Stan wiped his eyes as he lowered the book to his lap. The little girl who penned the fish story might be more sensible and wise than her father. Did Lauren wish to reverse the dialogue and ask her daddy to accept the new child?

Stan may not have acknowledged it, but the birth of a new baby, although not his own, would change his children's lives and, therefore, his own. Did his heart measure up to that ocean? Good question. In an effort to defer the mental tussle, he turned back to the Table of Contents.

Stan directed his attention to Tyler's contributions and turned to the first of his son's pages, which were entitled, *Haiku*. Tyler? A poet? When did that happen?

One fish, two fish, gold
Overfed in small glass bowl
Both went belly-up

Stan winced at Tyler's first entry. He put that in print? For all time? Surely, Lauren was unaware.

Good and round on top
Sadly flat on the bottom
Oh dear where's that spare?

Good grief. Another clever but telling insight into their personal lives. If Lauren might tear up at the first Haiku, Stan might have to consider a move out of town after reading the second one. He braced himself for the third.

Holstered gun at waist
Tells bad guys to straighten up
Peacekeeper father

Stan read the third one again . . . and again. He tried not to talk about his job around his children, yet in these simple words, Tyler's praise rendered Stan speechless. In those three lines, Tyler wrote of restraint and negotiation skills. The third line recognized what Tyler perceived as the outcome.

A mixed blanket of humility and conviction pressed against Stan. In reality, did Stan employ those attributes? Did he earn that auspicious title? Once in a while? Often? Ever?

He needed to step away from his children's writing for a moment. This was too much to absorb. Maybe Wellington's story would lift Stan's troubled spirit.

Wellington's contribution, which looked to be a lot longer than an essay, bore the title, *Beyond the Shallows*. The drawing beneath the title, obviously created by someone with more art experience than either of Stan's children, depicted a fish at the ocean's floor, hiding between two rocks.

The blue fish, with its exaggerated almond-shaped eyes, provided a pretty good caricature of Wellington, although when Stan considered that Wellington called himself The Snake, wouldn't an eel be more appropriate than a blue fish?

This is where my life started. Well, not "started," exactly, but where I first learned to make my own decisions. So this is where my self-directed life began. That's a better introduction.

In the beginning this place was my hideout. Somewhere along the line, after I got sick and tired of hiding, it became my hangout. This is where I learned to peel tobacco out of a discarded cigarette, and where I got high on the burnt remnants of some human's joint. This is where I learned that the truth was costly and going with the flow was the cheap and easy way.

My mom and dad didn't care much if I went to school or not. Neither of them had an education. They thumbed their nostrils at the fish who swam with thousands of other fish. They preferred being outcasts.

Usually they were too busy fighting to care where I went. Dad used to guzzle vast amounts of ocean moonshine and couldn't find work. Mom worked her job, and another one for him, and fed on bitterness.

One day, when I was what fish genealogists call a teenager, I went to my rock hideout and fell asleep. During what must have been a horrible storm above the water, everything down below started to churn.

The picture that accompanied the text resembled a dust storm, but an underwater variety. Sand and seaweed whirled around the wide-eyed blue fish, a starfish, shells, and several shrimp.

When everything settled back to the bottom of the ocean, my rocks weren't in sight. Just as I panicked, a small group of fish swam by. They stared as they passed, traded jokes I couldn't hear, and then turned around to greet me.

I couldn't believe my good fortune. I figured the mighty current tossed me to a new place with new opportunities. My new fish pals, although I didn't know it at the time, used the occasion to add a clueless, shy, and lonely fish to their hard knocks school. I had a sense of belonging, something I didn't know I lacked.

The page opposite this part of the story showed a group of fish with sunglasses, snide smirks, and droopy pants. Instead of earlobe expanders, the fish had expanders in their pectoral fins. Not something Stan could have imagined . . . ever.

I found my old hideout while I swam with my new friends a few days later, and since they liked the place, they hung out with me there.

Even though I'd only show up at home when I felt like it—usually when I needed a rest from carousing with the gang—my parents didn't care about my whereabouts.

It wasn't until much later that I realized my absence opened the door to my dad's angry disposition. Where physical altercations had been rare, my mom's bruised scales and puffy eyes became commonplace. She didn't complain, but blamed herself. It wasn't my place to disagree . . . until . . .

The next picture was a view from the bottom of the ocean, looking up. A red and white bobber rested on the surface of the water. Beneath a boat, a fishhook dangled from a fishing line.

People say that elephants never forget. I wish fish didn't have any memory at all. One scene, etched in my miniscule mass of gray matter, won't fade, much less disappear.

I woke up to my mom and dad exchanging an endless string of hateful words that were so hot they could melt a coral reef. Mom screamed about her tedious life while Dad blamed her for everything he never achieved in his sorry existence. At this inopportune time, some hapless fisherman dropped his line. The hook fell squarely between my parents.

At first I thought Dad meant to skewer himself, maybe in an act of defiance. Instead, he caught the line just above the hook and dragged it toward my mom. He meant to hook *her*.

I interfered. I mean, I had no choice. I couldn't let him do that. In the tussle that followed, I dislodged the line from between his clenched teeth at the same time the fisherman yanked on his fishing pole. The hook caught Dad's mouth as it pulled taut. His eyes went wild, and then rage consumed his face. He fought all the way to the surface, but when the net hit the water and scooped him out, all that remained was a glimmer of sunshine dancing on the water.

Above the water, on the human side of existence, the fisherman probably gloated and slapped himself silly for pulling in such a prize. Down below, in my world, I encountered the unforgiving face of my mom.

Every now and then I swim by the old place, not where the rocks form a hangout for a group of petty juvenile delinquent fish, but that place I used to call home. Sometimes I see her cleaning the habitat or preparing a meal. More often than not, she's just resting on the ocean floor, her fins and gills moving just enough to keep her in place. She doesn't have bruises anymore. Or a mean mate. She doesn't want her son anymore. Forgiveness isn't in her makeup.

I hang with a new school of fish now. A kindhearted fish took me into her home. Her heart, too. Before she could teach me how to care about someone else, she showed me how to care for myself. To forgive myself. Wasn't easy, but she did.

Maybe one day I can pass that caring, and love, and forgiveness on to my mom—if she'll let me. She needs it as much as I did.

The final drawing was that of a school of fish, with the blue fish at the center. One, with a dorsal fin that resembled Holly Norris' auburn hair more than it did a fin, wore an easy grin. The other fish, each in an understated way, resembled Izzy, Conner, Lauren, Tyler, and Paige, and others. Stan wasn't certain, but he thought the likenesses included Pastor Morrison, Juanita and Zach Hoyt, and maybe the artist intended for that goofy looking bald fish in the background—the one with the police badge on his chest—to conjure the image of Officer Stan Benton. A sense of humility spilled over Stan. In this artist's rendering, he was in good company.

Thirty-Two

Zach was beat. Spent. Exhausted. After he oversaw the assemblage of tables, chairs, and vendor spaces in New Life Chapel's fellowship hall, he directed another group of volunteers in the placement of signs meant to help each participant navigate the building.

Indoor signs pointed to the registration table, restrooms, classroom, vendor area, and the kitchen. More signs designated the location of snacks, water, coffee, and tea. Earlier in the evening, activity in the kitchen rivaled that of the fellowship hall as Sister Yolanda and her host of volunteers packed the refrigerator and pantry with foodstuffs, and completed as much as they could in advance of tomorrow's lunch.

For her part, Sister Yolanda beamed at the progress made by her enthusiastic crew—almost as much as she had when she coerced Zach into letting her have full responsibility for the menu and all things related to food. She promised the meals prepared in the church kitchen would rival the city's most highly acclaimed caterer.

Conner and Wellington offered to set up the outdoor signs first thing in the morning, but when they learned "first thing" meant they had to lower the signs into the ground at six o'clock, they negotiated Wellington's need to spend the night at the Hoyt house. Which, of course, initiated Izzy's request to have Paige spend the night too. Juanita had a handle on that part, or so Zach hoped.

If he'd known the extent of the set-up routine—much less the unknowns that would reveal themselves tomorrow and the two following days—might he have had second thoughts about hosting this crazy event?

Of immediate concern was the prospect that the arrival of around 200 participants, workers, and volunteers might turn the house of worship into a place of chaos. Zach swallowed hard. He knew two things: when he delegated a task, he had to trust the person who took the assignment; it was too late for second-guessing a basket weaving retreat.

With the preliminary set-up at the church completed, Zach drove to the shop and gave his attention to the vast quantities of basket kits that they assembled for some of the instructors. Beyond those boxes were the ninety-six kits to be included in the merchandise *The Basket Works* hoped to sell. He'd already loaded into the trailer the various boxes of raw inventory, pieces, and parts that Nancy and Mae suggested they have on hand for the ardent weavers.

Tired was an understated description of Zach's physical condition. Why he assured everyone that he could load the trailer without assistance was beyond him. It sounded like something a good boss would say, but the speaking was a lot easier than the solo doing.

After he rearranged the stack of boxes toward the back of the trailer, he stepped out in time to see a pickup truck pulling away from the back of the building. This was not the place for a convenient turn-around. The front parking lot served that purpose. If not for the incidents with the broken window and the spray paint, Zach might not have cared. Too late, he thought to read the truck's license plate.

He went back into the building for another load, but paused while he contemplated his circumstances. He redirected his steps to the front entrance, noted the locked door, and jiggled the handle for good measure. A glance at the parking lot revealed nary a soul.

Zach dragged the last of the inventory to the trailer and stood back while he surveyed the quantity therein. The instructors' kits were already sold, but the greater part of the supplies, those he hoped he wouldn't have to pack back into the trailer at the end of the retreat, were available for purchase by the students.

It looked as if they'd break even on the event, so sales of their own kits and inventory would add to a thin bottom line. They'd measure the success of the retreat, however, when they earned the repeat patronage of the folks who participated in the event.

As Zach started to go back inside to set the alarm and lock up, the pickup truck appeared again. This time, the driver leaned out of the open window and yelled, "Where is everybody?" He delivered his question with the inflection of an accusation.

Zach walked toward the truck and said, "What do you mean?"

"Where are all the basket weavers?"

"Are you asking about the retreat?"

"I don't care what you call it. Where are they?" Talk about terse. What was this guy's problem?

"We had to move it. The conference center—"

"Yeah, I saw the mess at the conference center. Some guy told me to come here. So, where are they?"

"We moved the venue to New Life Chapel. It doesn't start until tomorrow, so how can I help you?"

"Tomorrow? I heard it started today and ran for four days." The man's ruddy complexion grew a few shades darker. So did his tone.

"It runs three days." Who was this guy? One of the vendors, maybe, or one of their employees who got the details wrong? Seemed a stretch, in spite of Zach's lack of experience in basket retreating.

"That's not what I was told."

"Are you with one of the vendors?"

"No."

"You a weaver?" Zach sucked in his skepticism with that one. This guy didn't look as if he knew how to play nicely with others.

"No. When's the thing start tomorrow?"

"Look, if you're not a vendor or a weaver, you won't get access to the building."

"You can't turn people away. That's discrimination."

"No, that's how private events work. Now, if you'll excuse me, I have work to finish here."

The balled-up fist didn't leave the top of the man's steering wheel, but he unclenched and clenched it a few times. He seemed to be searching for the words he needed to verbalize his annoyance. His choice of expletives, and their prolonged duration, echoed off the back of the building before bouncing into the stratosphere.

Only after the truck pulled away from the building and headed down the street did Zach take his fingers off his cell phone. While the device might pave a way to call the cops, it was no match for any immediate danger the man might impose. Maybe Zach needed something a little more daunting in his pocket.

He checked the lock on the trailer again and returned to the building. Zach made a not-very-professional sign that Conner and Wellington would need to place in front of the damaged conference center. Although Mae and Nancy personally contacted at least ninety percent of those who signed up for the retreat, those few who might arrive at the conference center needed to know where to find the new venue. Besides this sign, what else had he forgotten?

Zach waited for the call to connect, all the while he watched the sun make haste toward the horizon. So much for unloading the trailer while it was light. So much for sharing a warm dinner with his family.

"Craig?"

"Zach Hoyt, how you doing?"

"I'm doing. Hey, please thank Yolanda for me. The work she and the other volunteers accomplished today was outstanding. They've been a godsend."

"Right you are on that account. He sends just who and what we need at the perfect time. Are you calling to add to your need list?" Craig let out a chuckle. Was he jesting or did he know that Zach needed something more?

"You give any consideration to security detail at the church?"

"For a bunch of basket weavers?"

"Uh, maybe not so much for them as for those who seek them."

The pause on the line supplanted every remnant of humor. "I'm listening."

~

Stan decided not to question his new assignment, much less complain. Easy peasy. Hollister's desire to ingratiate himself with Pastor Morrison and his influential community-minded friends dribbled down to Stan's level in the form of regular daytime work hours playing security at New Life Chapel. An unexpected perk was Yolanda Morrison's insistence that he plan on working his way through the buffet line each of the three days.

The culinary perfume wandering out of the kitchen and resting in the area near the registration table had Stan's mouth watering. Until noontime, or until two teenage males devoured the supply, he had an option to help himself to any of the dozen pastries Conner and Wellington snagged from the snack table. The way those two ate, he put better odds on lunch than brunch.

Stan picked up a cinnamon muffin and stuffed half of it into his mouth. He brushed the dusting of sugar off the front of his uniform and then consumed the other half. He reached for his coffee cup, which one of the kitchen workers refilled more than once already, when the shrill clang of metal hitting metal sounded from the fellowship hall.

As he reached for his holster and started toward the source of the bedlam, the hair on Stan's neck and arms stood on end. Mae and Nancy walked out of the room, nearly tripping Stan.

"Let me through," he said as he tried to sidestep them.

"Why?" Mae formed her mouth into the letter *O*. "That's just the scissor sharpener." She patted his arm. "Everything's fine in there."

Stan let his trigger finger relax as he lowered his hand. "I think I need to stick my head in there anyway."

"While you do that, we need to find Zach. Any idea

where he went?"

"No," Stan replied.

"I think he went to get something out of the trailer," Conner said. "Can I help with something?"

"No," Mae said. "I just thought he might want to find a better place to put the scissor sharpener. The weavers will riot if they have to listen to that for three days."

"If they don't, we'll mutiny," Nancy said.

Conner jumped to his feet. "I'm on it."

Stan looked at his coffee and pushed it aside. Between the caffeine and the heavy jolt inspired by the sharpening tool, it might take all day for his heart to regain a normal rhythm. He'd better cool it with the sugar too.

When Conner returned a minute later, he said, "He wondered how he got such a nice spot to run his equipment."

"What do you mean?" Wellington asked.

"He says most people who let him attend a weaving workshop put him by an exit, and if the weather's nice, they ask him to go outside."

Stan looked out the window and said, "It's supposed to be nice all day."

"Yeah. I told him I'd help him move his stuff. Wellington, are you good with the registration table for a few?"

"Take your time, bro. Everybody's already here. Well, except for these few." Wellington pointed to a small pile of nametags before he turned his attention to a chocolate-glazed donut.

The man who walked into the registration area didn't look much like those already assembled in the fellowship hall. Looked more like an outdoorsman than someone who might sit at a table and make baskets. His hat suggested he enjoyed deer hunting.

When the man walked past the table, Wellington waved his arm at him and, with his mouth full of donut, emitted a muffled "Wait. You have to sign in."

The deer slayer ignored him and started toward the weaving room. Stan blocked his path.

"You have to sign in."

"No I don't."

When he tried to duck past him, Stan raised his arm in front of the man's chest.

"If you aren't registered, you can't go in."

"Who's gonna stop me? You?" The guy was big. Not just tall big, but muscle big. His face got red as he contracted his eyes. .

"Sir, I'm asking you to leave."

"I'll leave when I'm done with my business here."

"No, you'll leave now."

"Listen," the menace said as he leaned his face toward Stan, "I think your little security detail is scheduled to go on a break. Beat it."

"What part of a police uniform don't you understand? You think this is a costume party?" Stan asked. He wouldn't mind smacking this guy in the chops. Wouldn't take much to rile him up a few notches, something bound to warrant a punch or two, but the thought of another charge of overreach might not look good on his professional resume. When Stan's imagination flew to Tyler's portrayal of his father as a peacekeeper, he quelled the urge to add to the bait he'd already launched.

"What? You some off-duty cop, or something?"

Wellington, who somehow managed to swallow his donut without choking, said, "He's not off duty, dude."

Mr. Outdoorsman took a step backwards and ran his gaze up and down Stan's person. "Where's your patrol car?"

"I don't need a car to make me official, sir. I am, in my official capacity, asking you to leave. If you don't turn around now and walk out that door, I will invite one of my similarly-uniformed peers to come pick you up and give you a ride in their patrol car."

Stan's offer earned a genuine look of contempt. The man turned around, grabbed one of the pamphlets sitting in front of Wellington, and strode out of the building.

"Piece of work," Wellington said.

"Motive."

"Huh?"

"What's the guy's motive? Was he staking out the place? Looking for someone? What?"

"Maybe he heard this place was full of basket cases and he had to come see the spectacle for himself." Wellington crinkled his nose at his sarcastic remark, and reached for another donut.

"I heard that," Mae said as she rounded the corner. She pointed her finger at Wellington. "I think you're cute, but some of those weavers might not appreciate your sense of humor. You keep in mind that those weavers pack some pretty hurtful weapons in their toolkits: awls, scissors, weaving shears, pocketknives. You name it."

Wellington wiped his mouth with his hand, which removed only a portion of the powered sugar and none of the glee that clung to his upper lip. "Yes, ma'am."

Stan stood up straighter. Good to know. The question in Stan's mind was what the hunter might be packing.

Thirty-Three

After Juanita watched the delivery truck pull out of *The Basket Works'* parking lot, she set the alarm and locked the front door. They'd closed the showroom for the duration of the weaving retreat so she didn't have to worry with walk-in customers, but someone had to fill the online orders as soon as they posted.

She wouldn't complain about the quantity and dollar volume of today's sales. Both were good things, but preparing each of the orders for shipping consumed more energy than she'd stored up for one day.

On the way home she calculated the time she had versus the time she needed to prepare dinner for her family. The former fell short of the latter. She could only hope they'd filled up at lunchtime with generous portions of Sister Yolanda's buffet.

Zach's occasional text messages spoke of a good first day for the weaving retreat. The participants seemed to enjoy themselves, and sales at the mini retail shop *The Basket Works* set up at the church were brisk. Brisk was good. Very good.

Had she been wrong to voice her negative opinion of the retreat? In her mind, she was the good steward where Conner's college funds were concerned. In reality, was she the "oh ye of little faith" member of the family? Regardless of her misgivings, gratitude and relief accompanied Juanita as she pulled into the driveway, stepped into her kitchen, and began another task.

Spaghetti was an easy fix, especially since she had a bag of ready-made meatballs in the freezer. While she boiled water and heated sauce, she prepared a tossed salad. When all was ready, she remained the sole occupant of the house. Where was everyone? She turned the burners to their lowest setting and fitted each of the pans with a lid.

The garlic scent seeping from the oven caught the attention of Juanita's empty stomach. Unlike today, she'd prepare for her assignment with the online sales tomorrow by remembering to pack a lunch.

When the oven timer announced its completion of the bread-warming process, she peeked inside to confirm the edges of the bread were crusty and the cheese melted. A glance at the clock said her dinner companions were thirty minutes behind schedule already. Except for the telltale sign of garlic, no one would notice if she helped herself to a piece.

It took three minutes of deliberately prolonged nibbling to consume the bread. The action served to whet her appetite. The second piece lasted less than two minutes. How could she still be famished? Surely, no one would care if she had a tiny bit of salad while she waited. By the time her family joined her at the table, she'd emptied her salad bowl twice.

"Sorry we're late," Zach said. "Dottie was late picking up Paige."

"A good day?" Juanita signed.

"It was a blast," Izzy said as she dove into her dinner.

The girl's assignment appeared not to have taken the same toll as the tasks fulfilled by Zach and Conner. They both looked cross-eyed with fatigue and seemed to have trouble holding up their forks.

"Paige and I had so much fun. I mean, it was pretty easy for the two of us to keep the drinks and snacks ready. Boy, those women like sugar. You should have seen all the sweets they put away."

"I was whooped by the time we opened the front door," Conner said.

"Why?" Juanita signed.

"We had to set up the stuff we wanted to sell in our vendor booth."

"I thought you did that last night."

Zach said, "I hauled everything out of the trailer last night, but didn't set up the space until this morning. I didn't think it would take as long as it did."

"Good thing we had Wellington's help," Conner said.

"What about tomorrow?"

"We won't need Wellington and Paige until the last day. They have tomorrow off," Zach said. "How did things go at the shop?"

"I'm exhausted," Juanita signed. "We did well today."

"Good to hear," Zach said.

"Do you want to swap places tomorrow?" Conner asked. "I can work at the shop if you want to help at the retreat."

"How can I help? I can't register people or answer questions."

"I can," Izzy said. "If you want to handle the drinks and the snacks, I can work the registration desk."

Hmm. Which task would better suit the worn out mother? Another day of pulling inventory and packing boxes didn't sound fun, but running between the kitchen and the snack area didn't sound much better. "I want to see the weavers," Juanita signed.

"Then we'll switch," Conner said. "The three of us."

Zach's face lit up at the decision. Although he wore his fatigue as overtly as Juanita did, he seemed pleased. Happy.

"Guess what else we sold today?" Izzy asked. When she stole a look at Conner, Juanita wished she could have heard the laugh that accompanied Izzy's apparent pleasure.

Conner gave his father a sideways glance and said, "I added something to our inventory. Copies of *Fish Tales*."

"You tried to sell your fish stories to basket weavers?" Juanita signed.

"When I told him we didn't have any place to display the book in our vendor space—" Zach started to say.

Conner finished his dad's sentence with, "I set a stack of them on the corner of the registration desk." His enjoyment worked its way through his tired bones and landed on his face when he said, "Nobody bought one when they first signed in, but Wellington and I promised to get a couple of the authors to sign copies if they bought one."

"You had a book signing for a collection of fish stories at a basket weaving retreat." Juanita signed. An unusual marketing ploy.

"We did. Sold eleven copies," Conner said.

"So far. Wait until I man the desk tomorrow," Izzy said.

Zach didn't say a word. He didn't have to. The crinkled lines around his mouth spoke for him.

When Juanita signed, "I'm proud of them too," Zach winked at her.

"I'm ready to call it a night," Zach said.

"Dad, it's eight-thirty," Izzy replied.

"Yep. The Hoyt bus leaves for the church at seven tomorrow. Make sure you get up in time to eat."

"No problem. If I oversleep I can have a donut or two," Izzy said.

Judging from her exuberant, bouncing-off-the-walls condition, Juanita didn't care to ask how many of the little pastries Izzy consumed on Retreat Day One. It was better not to know.

~

Juanita replenished the coffee carafe and ventured to one of the doors leading to the fellowship hall. It was eleven o'clock already, and this moment marked the first time she could stop and take a break. This drink and coffee thing was not a one-person assignment. Either that, or Juanita needed to consume the same level of sugar as Izzy had yesterday.

Juanita pushed her sweaty hair away from her neck. She couldn't hear the chatter or the noise issued by the crowd gathered in the room, but the activity generated within looked like a well-organized and well-received weaving frenzy.

She had a hand in preparing basket kits, signs, and nametags. When their venue changed at the last minute, she helped allocate and assign the space within the room for the various vendors and classes. None of that prep work evoked the scene that caught her attention now. Who knew?

Slinking between the aisles that separated one class from another, Juanita studied the weavers and their baskets. Each class had three long tables arranged in a U-shape. Attentive instructors wandered from one weaver to another, probably answering questions or advising them of the next step in the process.

Depending on the class, some weavers looked unhurried and satisfied, and gabbed with one another. Other groups, with projects that appeared to require more attention to detail—especially those who worked on a basket that wasn't much larger than a thimble—paid no heed to their peers. No chitchat, no banter. Just studious attention to their miniature pieces of art.

Juanita counted a few men among the weavers and instructors, but for the most part, the participants were women. Many wore evidence of their obsession with all things baskets: embroidered aprons, T-shirts, or basket charms dangling from necklaces. Most of the students had toolkits sitting within reach, all generously stocked with a myriad of tools and supplies.

Cable ties, clothespins, screwdrivers, water spray bottles, spoke weights, shears, and more littered the tables. At one of the classes, each individual worked under a contraption that was both a light and a magnifier. At first glance, the place looked as if it were in total disarray, but . . . the baskets. Some were cute; others were pretty, shapely, or whimsical. Some were absolutely magnificent.

The vendors, whose spaces lined the perimeter of the room, were as varied as the class projects. The weaver could purchase hardwood bases, pottery sleeves and embellishments, patterns, or kits. One seller offered basket-themed stationary and note cards. Another peddled a large assortment of leather handles and straps.

When Juanita reached *The Basket Works'* booth, Mae greeted her with outstretched hands and a platter of snickerdoodle cookies. More sugar? Good heavens.

Juanita picked up a basket kit, one of the ninety-six she and the others painstakingly prepared for sale at this shindig. About twenty kits sat on the shelf. She pointed to the kit in her hand, the bags on the shelf, and lifted her open hands, palms up.

"You're looking for the rest?" Mae asked.

Juanita nodded.

"Gone. Sold."

Juanita raised her eyebrows and pointed to the shelf again.

"Really," Mae said. "Gone."

Juanita put the kit back on the shelf and clapped her hands together. If Mae could interpret sign language, Juanita would tell her how much she loved her, and Nancy too, for suggesting this retreat and doing so much to make it a success. Instead, she mouthed, "Thank you," pressed her hands to her heart, and returned to her snack and beverage duties.

Thirty-Four

Basket Retreat Day Three. Stan sat in the parking lot at New Life Chapel, seeking motivation to get out of his car and play the part of the noble sentry one more day. He'd had more than his share of donuts, coffee, and shrill women's voices to last until the turn of the next century. It wasn't that this assignment was wearisome. He was bored stiff.

Lunch was the highlight of the past two days, although he wasn't certain whether the greater appeal came in the form of excellent food or from the shy but pretty kitchen helper who flirted with him. Maybe she was flirting. It'd been so long since Stan cared whether a member of the opposite sex took an interest in him, he didn't have instincts to trust any longer.

Not that it mattered. His life was already complicated. He had to learn to deal with DeWayne and Tina's upcoming nuptials, soon to be followed by a new baby. Stan would do whatever he could to help Lauren and Tyler with that adjustment. He didn't need to add another person to the mix, although she was rather cute. And her smile? Hypnotic.

Stan pulled his hat off the seat and stepped into the gray mist that didn't quite live up to rainfall. Although the weather cast a pallor over the day, the women walking toward the building didn't seem to care. How did these folks keep up this level of cheer? Did basket weaving attract inherently happy people, or was the mood of the participants a product of a three-day escape from their real lives? Regardless, the level of expectation and bliss didn't seem to falter, not even on a dismal spring morning.

The first round of the scissor sharpening equipment sounded about two minutes after Stan entered the building. No way could Zach let that guy work in the fellowship hall. A glance toward Wellington, who manned the registration table again this morning, earned a grimace.

Wellington clapped his hands over his ears and said, "Can you go find Zach? I think he's in the kitchen. Somebody needs to tell him to move that dude somewhere far away."

"Yeah, like the farthest corner of the basement. I'll be right back."

"Good morning, weavers." Zach's voice boomed over the sound system.

"Never mind," Wellington said.

"Welcome back. We have a couple of housekeeping items to share with you before you delve into your weaving. First, we have a nice variety of pastries this morning, but we also have a healthy supply of yogurt and fresh fruit, so please help yourselves.

"Next, we know the sharpening machine wears on everybody's nerves, but the service is indispensable, and we know some of you haven't had a chance to get your shears sharpened yet. We will relocate the equipment to the far end of the hallway." Zach pointed with his left hand. "Go out these doors and take the first left.

"Lunch will be at 11:30 today, instead of noon. Since we finish at three o'clock instead of six, we want to step up our schedule a little bit as well. If you finish early and have time, or if you have to wait for your travelling companions, we'd love it if you'd pitch in with some of the cleanup. Ask a teacher or a vendor if you can lend a hand, or find one of the retreat crew and we might be able to find something to keep you busy. It has been an absolute pleasure to host all of you. We hope you'll join us when we do this again. Enjoy the day. Happy weaving everyone."

Volume picked up as soon as Zach signed off. Fortunately, the screech of the scissor-sharpening tool was no longer in the mix.

"Good morning, Officer Benton, Wellington." The voice was melodious. He hadn't noticed that before. A rich voice. Kind of sultry. Stan rubbed the tips of his ears, certain they were scorched red, just like his neck and face.

"Morning," he mumbled. "Excuse me. Gotta help move the scissors guy."

When he returned to the registration area, Wellington sat back in his metal folding chair, folded his arms behind his head, and emitted a long, long hiss. "Your macho image withered like a tire loosing air. What's wrong with you, man?"

Stan chomped on the accusation, cleared his throat, and attempted to deflect the jibe with, "You finally admitting to your deeds of darkness?"

"Don't change the subject. You a dweeb or something?"

Dweeb? Isn't that the term Stan applied to DeWayne the first time he met the man? Stan's free cup of coffee, chocolate éclair, and strawberry yogurt chose this moment to mingle one with another. The churned result wasn't pretty. Or comfortable.

"Huh?" Wellington had more opinion to spew. "Must be something wrong with her. You know? Why's she interested in you?"

The Snake was back, circling Stan like a menacing viper. As with Stan's first encounter with the teen, Wellington used words instead of venom. This time, he spoke instead of spelling with his fingers. The little twerp spoke the truth—about Stan; not the girl.

"She's just polite. Give it a rest."

"You blind, man?"

"Realistic, not blind."

"You know she's good looking, don't you?"

"Put a sock in it, Wellington."

"But she *likes* you. That's like . . . a miracle. You gotta grab holda opportunities when you get them. Could be a decade before another one gives you the time of day."

"Excuse me." One of the weavers walked up to the registration table. She wore a colorful pair of robin's egg blue pants. A tan apron protected her tie-dyed T-shirt, although its purpose wasn't clear. She toted half a dozen clothespins along the top edge of the apron.

"Can I help you?" Wellington asked.

The kid sounded pleasant, polite, and almost cultured. Beneath the veneer, however, lurked a reptile. Granted, Wellington seemed a lot more civilized since Norris took him into her home. Stan would give her credit for that.

What would happen, though, when Children's Services had to find him a permanent home? Was there such a thing for a fifteen-year-old kid? Would any sane adult take him into his home if they knew about the incident between Wellington and his father?

"I promised that young girl who was here yesterday that I'd buy one of those *Fish Tale* books." She turned to Stan and said, "She got me with the poem about a peacekeeper father. My husband's a sheriff. You ought to buy a copy. See for yourself."

"Yes, ma'am," Stan replied.

Instead of mocking Stan, and probably losing the sale, Wellington sucked in his bottom lip and coughed. His customer pointed to the stack of books lying on the table and pulled some greenbacks out of her apron pocket. "Can I have two, please?"

"Sure can. You want signed copies?"

"Signed? Who's here to sign them?"

Wellington pointed both thumbs in his direction. "Uh, me."

"You're one of the authors?"

"Yes, ma'am. I'm Wel—W.E. Holly." Wellington opened the cover on one of the books and pointed. "See? That's me."

"I'd love for you to sign this. Can you make one of them out to Dorothy, and the other one to Daphne?"

"Uh, only if you spell them for me," Wellington said. "And if you want Izzy and Paige to sign, too, you'll find them at the snack table today."

"Hey, Stan." Zach walked up, tipped his head toward the source of a succulent aroma, and said, "Why don't you and I grab lunch before they open the buffet line?"

Go downstairs? To the buffet line? Stan felt his neck warming at the thought of another encounter with that fetching smile and those captivating topaz eyes.

"Uh, I'm supposed to stay here. Sister Yolanda will bring something up later. But, thanks."

"Officer Benton, I believe you are entitled to a fifteen minute break. Conner will join Wellington at the registration table, so you have no need to worry. Nothing will get by those two," Zach said.

Wellington passed the signed books to his satisfied

customer as Conner appeared in the doorway. "Yep. We got this covered. Get going. Take your time, now. You hear?"

~

Her momma named her Pearl, after her great-grandmother. The name was fitting. Pearl. Luminous, radiant, one-of-a-kind. And interested in Stan Benton enough to slip him her phone number.

After finishing another mouthwatering lunch prepared by Sister Yolanda and her workers, Stan's plan was to wipe the incriminating elation off his face. As he climbed the steps—two at a time—he knew that wasn't going to happen. Stan donned his best intimidating glare and walked to his assigned position near the front door.

"You dog," Wellington said. "Look at you. Mr. Hoyt lend you some of his courage?"

"What are you talking about?" Conner asked.

"Look at 'im. Doesn't he look different to you?"

"Different how?"

Wellington let his shoulders droop halfway to his waist when he said, "All lovey-dovey. Can't you see it, man? He's got it bad."

"Aren't you hungry?" Stan asked. "Why don't you two go get some food? I can cover for you. It's not as if new people will come in to register, and nobody's asked a question in at least two hours. If somebody wants to buy a book, I can help with that too. Get outta here. Go on."

Wellington scooted his chair away from the table and headed toward the stairs. "Come on, Conner. We gotta check out the source of Officer Benton's sunny disposition. Maybe we can find some good vibes down in the chow line too."

Conner gave Stan a head-to-toe exam as he followed the little smart aleck down the hallway. Stan's mature response was to lift his eyes and inspect the ceiling. Sunny disposition? He did feel lighter, expectant. Did he have the nerve to call her? Ask her out?

The hollow reality of his circumstances slammed the door shut on the sunlight. How could he ask her out? Yeah, he could take a little of his overtime pay and maybe treat her to a movie, but what about after that? How long would she settle for walks in the park or free concerts in the square downtown? Who was he kidding?

Wellington's laughter filtered up the steps and down the hallway. Who would have thought that Wellington could laugh? Be happy? Be as close to normal as a teen might get? His circumstances changed when Norris opened the door to a better world. Who was Stan to close the door on circumstances that could change his own world? He wanted happiness too. To move forward instead of treading in place.

Stan fingered the little piece of paper resting in his shirt pocket. He could do this. It was time.

Later in the afternoon, when she walked out of the church with several of the other women who helped prepare lunch, Pearl stopped for a moment, put her hand on Stan's arm, and told him what a pleasure it was to meet him. She batted her eyelashes like a flirty thirteen-year-old. Stan spluttered like a backwards sixteen-year-old.

While the world disassembled around him, Stan's mind raced with possibilities. Weavers packed up their baskets, purchases, and tools, and vacated the premises in droves. Vendors scurried to their cars and vans, loaded up their unsold wares, and packed up their shelving. Where would he take her? It would have to be some place casual; otherwise, he'd have to spend his entertainment funds—the budget item he just concocted in his head—on new clothes.

"Stan?" Zach stuck his head around the corner and asked. "Can you give a hand over here?"

"Sure. What do you need?"

Zach led Stan into the fellowship hall where only a handful of weavers remained. Five ladies sat in a cluster, all working on the same basket, and all with intense and not very happy expressions on their faces.

When Zach saw him looking at the students and their instructor, he said, "I need to nudge them out of here, but that's not why I asked for your help. See that door back there?"

"Yeah."

"Do you know how to back a trailer?"

"I do."

"Conner can't back up a cart hitched to a riding mower. Could you hop in the SUV and back up the trailer to that door? If you'd do that, Conner and Wellington can start loading up inventory and I can use my charm to invite the stragglers to finish their baskets at home."

"Maybe you need to suggest the teacher finish her class using facetime on her computer."

"Not a bad idea," Zach said.

"You know I'm supposed to man the front door."

"You're already thirty minutes past your clock-out time. Here."

Stan caught the key ring, walked out the back door, and mulled over Zach's request. The space was narrow and probably not intended to accommodate a trailer, but Zach must have unloaded the trailer here, so it was doable. It might take a minute or two. Maybe three.

After seven minutes, Stan tried to open the back door, but found it locked. He walked around the building, but stopped mid-step as he entered the vestibule. The eerie silence and the absence of any other person put his nervous system on high alert. The wind crept in behind him, tussled several pieces of paper off the top of the table, and urged them into the hallway. The only sound he detected was his heart pounding in his chest.

Whimpering. Coming from the fellowship hall. Stan reached for his gun as he stepped forward. He scanned the hallway. Empty. Both direction.

"Take it easy." Zach's voice. "Nobody needs to get hurt."

"Shut up." The deep voice held an angry, sinister edge.

When Stan glanced into the fellowship hall, he glimpsed the face of the deer slayer, the furious man who tried to crash the retreat on the first day. Before he could blink, the man leveled his sights on Stan. The gunshot reverberated throughout the large room as the bullet embedded itself in the door's metal frame. At the sound of metal slamming metal, Stan's reflexes drove him to the floor, far too late to save himself had the shooter taken better aim.

When the screams from within the room subsided, the shooter yelled, "Close the door. The next one won't miss. My other targets are a lot closer."

Motive. What was the guy's motive? Couldn't be robbery; had to be personal. Something between him and one of the weaver's? An instructor? Who?

"You need to put down the gun and come out," Stan yelled. He wiped the side of his mouth and gulped air. Someone—probably one of the people in the building who ran to safety—must have called 911. Sirens approached the building. Lots of them. They were too far away to matter right now.

The perp answered with another round to the door, which induced another series of screams and crying.

When Zach called out, "Stan, close the door," Stan had no choice but to comply.

Thirty-Five

Zach's heart thumped at the same time the door slammed shut. The situation was out of control the moment the deranged man stormed into the fellowship hall. How it escalated to gunfire in less than five minutes was incomprehensible.

Three days. The man spent the past three days creating a plan that would give him access to this retreat. No matter the motive, the fact that he nursed his grudge during the time since he confronted Zach in the parking lot at *The Basket Works* sent a chill through Zach's being.

How did he get in? He didn't come in the front door. When Zach went outside to help one of the vendors put a box in her car, no one entered the building. During the retreat, they kept the doors locked. People could exit; they could not re-enter. But when Zach walked back into the fellowship hall, there he was, pointing a gun at two women and Nathan, the scissors sharpener.

"What do you want?" Zach asked.

"What's your name?" the intruder asked.

"Zach. Zach Hoyt."

"You think that because this is your party, Zach Hoyt, you have a right to know? Huh?"

"I think we all want to know why you're keeping us here."

"Ask her," the gunman said as he waved his gun toward the woman with shoulder-length brown hair, the weaver who lingered long after all the others left the retreat. She looked to be about thirty and although she had pretty features, her appearance was unkempt and mousy. Her demeanor was that of a wounded fawn.

"Howard, please don't do this." She didn't look at him when she spoke, but she knew him. She feared him. For what the connection might be worth, Zach now knew the thug's name.

"Don't do what? Give you what you deserve?" The veins on the gunman's neck stood out, signaling his rage.

"I didn't do anything," the woman whined.

"No? When did this retreat start? Huh? Why did you have to come a day early? Who is he?"

Zach pressed his back against the folding chair. The woman had to be the wife. The wife who lied to her husband. Zach swallowed hard. This might not end well.

"Who is he, Stacey?"

"There isn't any 'he.' "

"You're not going to lie to me anymore. Understand?" Howard lifted the barrel of his handgun and aimed it at Stacey.

"I went to my sister's before I came here."

"Sure you did."

"I did. Call her. She'll tell you."

"She'll tell me what you want me to hear. *You* tell me why you lied." Howard lowered the gun, but his finger still tap-danced on the trigger.

"Would you have let me visit her if I'd asked? Huh?"

Howard's face, already red, took on a darker hue, as did his expression.

Was this the way most abused spouses reacted? After they cowered, they tried to defend their actions, and when the abuser tossed out the excuses as immaterial, the victims spewed what they'd held back since the last altercation? Zach steadied himself for the onslaught that was sure to follow. What he needed to do was diffuse this. Somehow.

"Your trouble shouldn't spill over to these other people. Why don't you let them go?"

"The host wants to be a hero?" Howard scoffed. "I don't think so." He turned to the other woman. "Who are you?"

Zach liked Hattie Matrice. She grew up in the south, a descendent of slaves. The elderly woman shared her history and exposed her sweet spirit when Zach asked her to give him a five-minute lesson on the use of sweet grass. She laughed, even after he told her he was serious. They enjoyed the brief conversations they managed during the course of the retreat, but she never agreed to teach him her art. Told him he needed to sign up for one of her eight-hour classes.

"My name's Hattie."

"How old are you, Hattie?" Howard asked.

"Seventy-six."

"How's your heart? Is this little episode too taxing for you?" As if Howard cared. He spoke in a menacing, condescending tone.

"My heart's just fine, thank you. It's my sugar level I got to watch. If you keep me too long, I'm likely to run out of my insulin. I only brought what I need to get me through today."

Zach wanted her statement to be a lie. Somehow, he knew she spoke the truth. How could he end this quickly and without anyone suffering harm?

Howard turned on Nathan next.

"Who are you?"

"Nathan."

"Cute apron."

Nathan looked at his shop apron before he turned a bewildered face toward the intruder.

"Well, Nathan, you don't look like a basket weaver to me. Why are you here?"

"I had a vendor spot. I sharpen weaving shears and scissors."

"An honorable profession. Can't make a whole lot of money doing something so lame."

"No, sir. I don't."

"Why'd you come then? You like being around all the womenfolk?"

Nathan cowered at Howard's insinuation. When Stacey clutched her throat, Hattie put her hand on the younger woman's arm. Zach couldn't breathe.

"M-m-my wife was a weaver. I started the business when she was alive. After she passed, I kept it going for something to do, I guess."

"Uh huh. Sure. How you holding up, Nathan? You have any medical emergencies planned?"

"I could use a smoke." No wonder Nathan didn't mind the event coordinators shoving his sharpening business outdoors. Zach hadn't put the two pieces of the puzzle together before, but Nathan's willingness to relocate had surprised Zach. Now, taking in the strong scent of smoke, mingled with the odor emitted by his profuse sweating, it made more sense.

"Bad habit," Howard said. "But thanks for propping the door open for me while you enjoyed your last one."

Nathan ventured a glance at Zach and muttered, "I'm sorry. This is my fault."

Howard lifted his head at the sound of sirens. Too many for Zach to count, but their number was sufficient to inspire Howard to end his little chitchat.

"All of you. Get up. Line up against that wall."

Zach followed the two women. Stacey clung to Hattie and kept her eyes on the floor. Although the elderly woman wore tears in her own eyes, she whispered, "Shh, you're all right," as the two took unsteady steps toward the wall.

As Zach pressed his back against the cement block and turned to face his captor, he gauged Nathan's ashen complexion and rapid breathing. The man looked as if he might collapse from hyperventilation.

"Look at me," Howard said. When Stacey didn't respond to her husband's command, he bellowed, "Look at me."

"Take it easy." Zach voiced his words with clarity and at a volume that belied his fear. "She's scared."

"Be brave, girl," Hattie whispered to Stacey. "You're not alone."

"I said . . . look at me." Howard's menacing timbre equaled the terror he incited as he raised his gun and pointed it at each of his hostages.

If Zach were outside, looking into the room, he'd see a scene that resembled a firing squad. It occurred to him that a blindfold would be an act of charity. He'd never considered that before, but as he contemplated the execution of the three people who stood with him, he knew he didn't want to witness their deaths. No, better to be the first one shot.

~

Stan heard movement within the fellowship hall, followed by steps on the stairwell. Maybe the gunman wanted to improve his odds by eliminating the number of entrances to his command center. Taking his hostages downstairs represented a smart move on his part, and suggested the perp wasn't a dummy. It also presented a more daunting and dangerous situation for his hostages.

The slam of the door to the basement echoed like the heavy metal doors that divided prisoners from their keepers. In this case, the action drew another barrier between the victims and their worthless security officer. Nevertheless, until it was deemed safe to open the door to the fellowship hall, this was nothing but speculation on Stan's part.

With his gun in one hand, Stan bypassed the locked chapel and started down the hallway to his right. He opened doors and scoured the interiors. The first two rooms were empty, the third locked. He tapped on the door.

"It's Officer Benton. Anyone in there?" He heard a chair scrape against the floor, but no one answered. "It's me. The guy who likes chocolate eclairs and Sister Yolanda's cooking." Every participant knew Sister Yolanda. If that particular comment didn't give the occupants a reason to trust the man who knocked, nothing would.

The door inched open and a pair of fearful eyes peered through the crack. "It's him," the woman whispered. Stan recognized her as one of the vendors. The second person to slip out of the room was her helper, maybe her daughter.

"Anyone else in there?"

The older one shook her head.

"Follow me," Stan said as he led them toward the front door. "Hug the front of the building. Stay away from the basement windows. When reinforcements come, stay put, and raise your hands. Follow their instructions."

Stan returned to the hallway. The next door didn't have a lock. "It's Officer Benton. Anyone here?"

"Can we come out?" The voice belonged to Conner.

"Yes. Hurry up. Take the front door, then hug the front of the building. Join the others."

Conner stuck his head out of the door but hesitated before he stepped into the hallway. Wellington emerged next.

"Anyone else in there?"

"No."

"Go."

The next rooms were empty. When Stan started back toward the door, he met two uniformed officers, both with guns drawn and wearing expressions reserved for those times when every law enforcement officer fought to remember each lesson learned from his training classes and exercises, his rookie year, and every ugly incident thereafter.

"Sounded like the gunman took the hostages to the lower level." Stan gestured to the area behind him. "Rooms along that hallway are empty. Chapel was already locked, so no one's there."

When the three officers inspected rooms along the hallway opposite the side Stan had already checked, they found three more people, Izzy among them.

"Where's my dad? Where's Conner?" She grabbed Stan's arm as he led her toward the front doors.

"Conner's outside. Go on."

"What about my dad?"

"Go stay with Conner. We'll see to your dad."

Izzy missed a step and stumbled. The officer on the other side of her, a woman not much bigger than the teenaged girl, grabbed Izzy's arm and kept her from hitting the floor.

"I'll go with her," the policewoman said.

Izzy looked at Stan, eyes filled with tears, and her chin quivering.

The scene outside stalled Stan's heart. He counted at least ten cruisers, each delivering one or two occupants willing to put their own lives on the line in order to restore law and order. Behind the official vehicles, which included the SWAT van, were several large vans with transmission dishes attached to their roofs. The media had arrived too.

Among the first responders was his immediate supervisor, Sergeant Mike Graham. He stood in the parking lot where some of the officers had gathered. Four uniformed men and women huddled with Conner, Wellington, and the two vendors.

Stan held no complaints against Graham, although it might have been nice if the man hadn't acquiesced to the countless incidents in which Hollister singled Stan out for special assignments. The sergeant's only comment was, "I follow my superior's directives, no matter how questionable their wisdom or their motive."

Benton approached Graham's group.

"How many suspects?" Graham asked.

"Just one. Armed, dangerous. Already fired off two warning shots when I arrived on the scene."

"I thought you were already on scene."

"Yes, sir. I was outside when the suspect entered the building."

Graham didn't reply to Stan's confession, but the dark flash that passed over his superior's features told Stan more than he wanted to know. Zach's off-the-cuff comment about Stan's time card didn't hold a drop of water. The decision to move the trailer would draw discussion some other day.

"How many hostages?"

"At last count there were five weavers and one teacher in the fellowship hall. The two vendors are over there." Stan pointed to the woman and her helper. "That leaves Zach Hoyt and the scissor sharpener guy. Some people might have been cleaning up the kitchen. I don't recall seeing Yolanda Morrison leave. Izzy Hoyt got out. She's over there, but I don't see her friend Paige."

"At least eight hostages, then. Maybe more." Graham put his hands on his hips and studied the front of the church.

The female officer who helped Izzy out of the building said, "According to a couple of the witnesses, four of the weavers left before the gunman entered the building."

"Four hostages then. Or more."

"Excuse me," another officer said. "The kid over there says he needs to talk to Officer Benton. In private."

Stan scowled when he saw Wellington's animated face. Didn't Stan look busy?

"Come here," Wellington said. He waved his hand. If his intent was to end up on television, his gestures might put both of them in the middle of the "Breaking News" screen.

"Calm down. What's the matter?"

"It's him. Over there." Wellington gestured toward the crowd standing near the media vans.

"Who?"

"The guy who spray-painted the Hoyt's warehouse."

"He's here? Where?"

"I can't point to him. He might recognize me."

"Which one? What's he wearing?"

"The big dude with the suit and tie."

Stan struggled to dislodge the lump that obstructed his throat, and nearly gagged on the bile that accompanied the lump. He turned away from the sight and looked Wellington in the eye. "The man with the pale blue shirt? The one talking to the African American reporter?"

"Yeah. Him."

"You're sure."

"No doubt," Wellington said. "Who is he? Looks important."

Dread, heat, and astonishment crawled up Stan's spine. If the spray paint vandal was involved in all the other incidents related to New Life Chapel, did his need for public acclaim lead him to stage something as ominous as a hostage situation? With gunfire?

Stan lowered his voice to a whisper when he said, "You can't say a word. Not to anyone. Do you hear me?"

"But—"

"You have to trust me on this. I mean it. Not a word. Promise?"

Wellington's brow crumpled into fine lines. "Yeah. Sure. Promise."

"Thanks for the heads-up. Go back to the others, but not a word."

"Wellington?" Norris ran up and grabbed the boy by his upper arms. "Are you hurt?"

"I'm good." Wellington looked at Stan and said, "I'll be over there. I need to let you do your job."

"You okay, partner?" Norris asked. When Stan didn't answer she said, "This isn't your fault. Don't even go there."

"We might have more problems than those that lie inside the building."

Thirty-Six

Juanita ran her hand through her hair and inspected the sheen that her freshly shampooed and cut locks cast in the mirror. The occasion left her feeling pampered, relaxed. After the busy week preparing for the retreat and lending a hand during the first and second days, this reprieve was more than welcome. It was heavenly.

She pressed her tip into her hairdresser's hand as she stood and made her way to the front desk. While she waited for the receptionist to present the credit card slip for her signature, Juanita watched the television in the reception area.

The interruption of the scheduled program by an urgent news report caught the attention of everyone in the room. A sense of horror enveloped Juanita when the video panned a scene with innumerable policemen and emergency vehicles, and ended with the camera focusing on New Life Chapel.

She grabbed a copy of the advertisement sitting on the desk, scribbled, *turn on closed captioning,* and shoved the paper in the face of the astonished receptionist. The woman knew Juanita couldn't hear, and so she scrambled to find the key on her television remote, all the while Juanita's brain screamed, "Hurry, hurry."

Her phone. Juanita had turned off her phone. She dug

into her handbag and fumbled to grab the little device while she glued her eyes to the broadcast.

The closed captioning finally trailed across the bottom of the screen:

> We repeat: witnesses here at New Life Chapel report that after a man entered the premises and took several people hostage, they heard at least two gunshots. Police confirmed that no one sustained injury as a result of that gunfire.

Gunfire? At New Life? Juanita grabbed the edge of the receptionist's desk as her legs wobbled. While keeping her eye on the captioning, she strained to see the faces of the individuals gathered in front of the building.

> At last report, the number of hostages is unknown. Although unconfirmed, authorities believe this is the act of one individual.

Juanita pulled in air. There. Conner stood near a group of police officers. She recognized Wellington, although he faced away from the camera. But where were Izzy and Zach? She had to go. Now.

She scribbled a haphazard signature on the receipt the receptionist presented to her, gave up on the search for her phone, and raced to her car.

Calm down. She needed to calm down. With her heart in her throat and tears in her eyes, she backed Zach's car out of the parking spot, gritted her teeth while she waited for a break in traffic, and pulled onto the street. When she reached the first stop light, she tightened her grip on the steering wheel to keep her hands from shaking.

I'm coming. I'm coming. Please, Lord, protect my family and the others.

The drive shouldn't have taken more than ten minutes, but several blocks away from the church, an officer stood at the intersection, diverting traffic to a side street. If she had a voice, she'd call out and demand that he let her through. Instead, she pulled over to the first empty curb, parked the car, and started running.

The officer who prevented her from driving to the church may have called out to her. Juanita didn't care. She didn't stop. As the church came into view, the scene looked more severe than what the television camera portrayed, if that were possible.

The policeman who blocked her progress held up his hand and said, "You can't go there."

Juanita waved her hand at him, but he didn't—couldn't—understand her plea. She held up a finger and reached into her handbag, which made the officer stand up taller and raise the hand nearest his holstered gun.

She opened the top of her handbag, held it out so he could inspect the contents, and signed, "Wait. Help me," as if he might have some experience with the deaf. Fat chance, but at least he might understand Juanita's lack of speech.

When he relaxed his defensive posture, she pulled out her driver's license. Maybe the Hoyt name would tell the officer all he needed to know to let her pass. He looked at it without producing any hint of recognition, and handed it back. Again, he pointed to the direction from which she'd come.

How to explain? She opened her left hand, palm up, and poised her right hand as if she held a pen.

"You need paper?" he asked. Without waiting for a

response, he handed her the small tablet he kept in his shirt pocket, and also gave her a pen.

Using the microphone he wore above his breast pocket, the officer called someone. In the slow-motion minutes it took to gain access to the property, Juanita thought she'd crumple.

As another officer escorted Juanita toward the building, she spied Izzy. Her daughter, her child—alive, safe, and whole—came running. When Izzy buried her face in Juanita's bosom and wrapped her arms around her, hot tears dampened the front of Juanita's blouse.

As Conner's arms encircled her, Juanita couldn't hold back her own tears. When the three released their embrace, she pulled back so she could sign. "Where's your father?"

Izzy turned her stricken face toward Conner, who cast a sideways glance at the building. Before he could answer, Juanita signed, "He's inside? A hostage?"

Conner bit his lower lip and winced as he nodded his head.

"Who else?"

"We don't know for sure. At least one teacher, one student, and the man who had the scissors booth," Conner said.

"Are others missing?" Juanita signed.

"Maybe. They think some people were in the kitchen when the guy got inside. No one has seen Sister Morrison or Paige."

Zach? Yolanda? Paige? This was too much. Juanita's balance faltered and she stumbled backwards. The policeman who accompanied her to the scene grabbed her arms and held her upright until her world quit swirling. He guided her to the back of one of the ambulances. Ambulances? But, no one was hurt. She teetered again when she considered the obvious. No one was hurt. Yet.

"Mom, you need to sit down," Conner signed.

"I don't want to sit. I want to find your father," she signed.

Conner pointed to the back of the emergency vehicle. "Just climb on the back and sit for a minute."

With the help of the attendant, Juanita hoisted herself to the space between the open rear doors, and let her legs dangle over the back of the vehicle. When the attendant tried to put a blood pressure cuff on her, Juanita signed, "Tell her I'm fine. Just worried."

She held her fingers over her mouth while she studied the activities of the various groups congregated in front of the church. How foolish she'd been to worry about money, about Conner's college funds. How everything paled—their home, their cars, their educations, their stuff . . . all of it—in light of a life without her beloved. Juanita's eyes brimmed with tears. If she could, she'd change places with Zach right now. Her life for his. Lacking that option, she reached out her hands to her children. Their circle formed, she lifted her eyes toward the heavens and offered her silent petition.

Please, Lord, don't let the gunman hurt anyone. Hold Zach and the others in your protective embrace. Shield the innocent, give wisdom to the mediators, and guard the officers who stand in harm's way.

~

As the single-file line made its way down the first set of stairs, Zach paused at the landing. Was anyone still downstairs? If so, how could he alert them? How would they know where to hide?

Who might be hiding down there? Conner and Wellington were upstairs when this catastrophe unfolded. If they couldn't run out the front door, they would have taken cover somewhere on the main level.

Zach's stomach reeled as he recalled the assignments. After Izzy and Paige boxed up the leftover snacks, they offered to help clean the kitchen. And what about Yolanda and her crew? How many more people could Howard grab and take hostage?

"Who told you to stop?" Howard asked.

Zach turned around and asked in a loud voice, "Where are we going?"

"I'm famished. Thought we'd get a bite to eat." Howard directed his hostages toward the second set of stairs.

"The kitchen?" Zach asked. His voice gained volume as he asked, "You think we still have food in the kitchen?"

"Just go," Howard replied.

Zach needed to stall. "Seriously? You're hungry?"

"What part of 'go' don't you understand?" This time, Howard pointed his gun at Zach, who responded by continuing his descent to the lower level.

The kitchen. It figured. How did Howard know it was the only room in the basement, besides the janitor's closet and utility room, without windows? He acted as if he knew the footprint of the building. How? Did someone slip him a copy of the layout they passed out to the participants, the one-page map that directed the weavers to their class assignments, the restrooms, the area designated for snacks, and the kitchen?

As Zach stepped into the hallway, he examined his surroundings. No escape plan emerged. Nothing. When he detected muffled noise coming from a classroom on the far side of the kitchen, Zach raised his fist to his mouth and started coughing. He coughed and hacked all the way to the kitchen and after Howard closed the door behind them.

Zach pointed to the sink and emitted a raspy, "Water," as he pointed to the sink.

"Whatever," Howard said.

Zach continued to cough while he took a glass out of the cupboard and filled it halfway. As he gulped the liquid, he could only hope that the sound of the cupboard slamming and running water covered the escape of the people who hid in the classroom.

"Now what?" Zach asked. His hand swept the empty room. A few pots and pans sat in the drain rack next to the sink where someone abandoned several damp towels. Work, interrupted. Except for a box filled with snacks, the countertops were devoid of food.

Howard pointed his gun at Hattie. "Go get me a chair. If you don't come back, I'll shoot Stacey."

Hattie walked back toward the door, and when Howard held it open, she stepped into the hallway. Zach heard her footsteps over the linoleum floor, but they faded as she reached one of the classrooms. As she returned to the kitchen, the scuff of a chair against the floor accompanied her.

Howard closed the door, locked it, and took a seat.

"What about the others? Don't you think we need a few more chairs?" Zach asked.

"Looks like the ladies keep this place clean. Take a seat on the floor."

"You can't ask Hattie to sit on the floor," Zach said.

"I'm not asking. I'm telling."

When Zach started to step toward Howard, Hattie put her hand on his arm. "I can sit on the floor."

Zach waited until the others lowered themselves to the floor, and then selected the empty space closest to Howard.

"What do you want?" Zach asked.

"What do you mean?" Howard replied.

"You're here and you have hostages. Why? What do you want?"

"I want the name of Stacey's boyfriend."

"I told you. I don't have a boyfriend," Stacey said.

"Liar. You expect me to believe you were at your sister's the other night? You can do better than that. Who is he?"

"You're confusing me with your ex-wife. She's the one who had a boyfriend. Remember?"

"Hard to forget. You sound just like her when you lie."

"I'm not your ex-wife," Stacey said, and then she muttered, "Not yet."

"Not yet?" Howard asked.

"Listen, Howard. Just shut up and listen."

Zach's spine stiffened as Stacey's replies veered from passive to aggressive. Hattie, whose gentle hand had calmed Zach just moments earlier, failed to gain the same response from Stacey.

Howard rubbed his jaw with his free hand. "What's his name?"

Stacey's shrill voice quavered when she said, "I do not have a boyfriend."

"Maybe not today. But you did, didn't you?"

Howard's question extinguished Stacey's fiery temper as fast as a fire hose might douse a match. Her retort sputtered and her face took on an ashen hue as she let long stringy locks hide her unspoken reply: guilty.

Howard reached into his pocket and pulled out a cell phone. He kicked at Stacey with the toe of his boot. When she looked up, he handed her the phone and said, "Call him. Now. This isn't Zach Hoyt's party anymore. I want to invite him to my party."

Thirty-Seven

Norris, the officer of the law who never flinched in the face of danger, recoiled as Stan relayed the accusation Wellington made against Acting Captain Frederick Hollister.

"Hollister? No way." Norris said. "Why would he do that?"

"Listen, Norris. Remember the kid who delivered the pizza to the Hoyt house? He said the man who ordered the pizza and an extra box was white and thickset. Wellington described the man who spray-painted Zach's building as stocky. Both of them said the perpetrator had bad breath. You ever get a whiff of Hollister?"

"Not really."

"He stinks."

"I thought it was just his filthy office."

Stan's mouth dropped open.

"What?" Norris asked.

"I remember. The day after the pizza and noose delivery, Hollister called me into his office. He had half a pizza sitting on the edge of his desk. Pepperoni. Lots of cheese. Same thing the customer ordered along with the extra pizza box. It's him. I know it."

"You can't 'know it.' No way," Norris said. "It doesn't

make sense."

"Do you know how much Hollister's pushed me to say good things about him to Pastor Morrison? Hollister thinks Morrison will tell the mayor how wonderful he is. Do you have any idea how much he wants to replace Captain Snodgrass? Huh?"

Norris' eyes narrowed. "You never said Hollister tried to get you to talk him up."

"How could I?" Stan asked. "The man has kept me on a leash since I messed up and pulled Juanita Hoyt's car over for that broken taillight."

"Fine. Let's say he's responsible for spray-painting and for depositing rats in trash bins. He thinks it makes him look good when we respond to the incidents. Do you honestly believe he might be so rash as to hire someone to take people hostage? To encourage them to fire a couple of rounds?"

"I don't know." Stan tapped his foot at the speed of sound as he ran his gaze over the front of the church. He looked at Norris when he repeated, "I don't know."

"Whether he's involved or not, we have a job to do. A man inside that building is holding hostages. We're here to get people out."

Sergeant Graham motioned for Stan and Norris to join him.

"We identified the owners of the vehicles still parked in the church parking lot."

Stan leaned forward and looked at the list. Two last names matched.

Graham pointed to one of the names and said, "Looks as if Stacey West's husband followed her here. Her car's still here, and his pickup is over there."

Graham produced two photos. "Recognize her?"

"Yeah. One of the weavers. She was still here when I went to move Zach's trailer."

Norris' head snapped when Stan answered. Yeah, she got it right. Stan abandoned his post at the front door.

"Anything unusual about her?"

"Quiet. Kind of clingy."

"What do you mean?" Graham asked.

"She seemed to hang around every day until everyone else left. If she found someone to talk to, she latched onto them until they could find an excuse to leave." Stan recalled the annoyed faces on several of the weavers who sat near her.

"Why did she stand out to you?" asked Graham.

"Dunno. I felt sorry for her. She seemed lonely. You know. Kind of lost."

"What about him?" Graham pointed to a photo of the deer hunter gatecrasher.

"Who is he?" Norris asked.

"Howard West."

"Husband?"

"Yes," Graham replied. "He was the subject of about a dozen domestic disturbance calls, but all were more than three years ago. This is the new wife."

"He tried to gain entry the first day of the retreat," Stan said. "I sent him on his way."

"Did he ask for his wife?"

"No."

"Did he threaten anyone?"

"No."

"Demeanor?" Graham asked.

"Pretty nasty."

"You think he has the potential to do harm?"

Stan looked up at his sergeant and said, "Aside from the

warning shots? He could get ugly."

Commotion at the front of the church drew Stan's attention. Two of the women who served lunch today ran down the steps, surrounded by four uniformed officers. As they escorted the women to Graham's command center, Stan said, "That's Maxine Stillwell on the left. The younger woman is Nadine Blount."

"Where's my wife?" Pastor Morrison, panting and overtly distressed, pressed through the mass of uniforms and directed his question to Stan.

Graham stepped forward before Stan could reply. "Craig Morrison?"

"Yes, sir."

"Sergeant Graham."

"You're in charge?" Morrison asked.

"Yes."

"Why isn't Hollister heading up this situation?"

Graham ventured a glance at the distant gathering. "He's dealing with the media."

Anger flashed over the pastor's face. He looked over his shoulder where he could see the media, the vans, the cameras, and Hollister's blathering mouth. The top cop was using a life and death situation to further his career. Wellington got it right. No question about it. Stan turned back toward Morrison.

"Where's my wife? Is Yolanda one of the hostages?"

"She's hiding," Maxine said.

When Morrison started to speak again, Graham raised his hand and said, "Let me get this first."

"Where were you?" Graham asked.

"We were in the kitchen," Maxine replied.

"Who?"

"Me, Nadine, Yolanda, Paige, and Ruthanne."

"Ruthanne?"

"Ruthanne Moore," Morrison said.

"You've been hiding in the kitchen?" Graham asked.

"At first. We split up when we heard them coming downstairs."

"Do you know where the gunman took them?" Graham asked. "Which room?"

"The kitchen. Zach Hoyt talked really loud when he asked the gunman why he wanted to take his hostages into the kitchen. I think he knew people were still downstairs, and it was his way of warning us."

"Are they in the kitchen now?"

"Yes."

Graham turned to his crew and asked, "Why the kitchen?"

"It's on the interior of the building," Stan said. "No windows. One door."

Graham looked at his notes. "Where are Yolanda, Paige, and Ruthanne?"

"They must still be in one of the classrooms," Maxine said."

"How did you get outside?"

"We didn't hear anything for a long time, so we snuck down the hallway. Then we took the stairs to the fellowship hall and made a run for it," Maxine said.

"You were in the fellowship hall?"

"Yes, sir."

"It's empty?"

"Yes, sir."

"Excuse me." Graham stepped away from the group, motioned for the four officers who listened to Maxine's report, and said, "Scour the main room, and then take positions in the stairwell."

Stan and Norris strode to the building with the other two officers. Stan didn't know either of them, but the clammy skin and nervous twitch on the face of the younger one didn't do a lot to boost Stan's confidence.

~

"H-h-he's not answering," Stacey said. Her hands shook as she returned the phone to Howard.

"What's his name?"

"Let it go. It was a long time ago. He doesn't mean anything to me anymore." Stacey scooted back against the wall. She flinched when Howard kicked his chair. He stood over her and pointed the gun to her head.

"Just like I don't mean anything to you anymore?"

Stacey cowered as tears spilled over her cheeks. Nathan, quiet until now, scooted toward a corner and braced himself against the cabinets. He wrapped his arms around his middle, leaned forward, and gagged.

"It's time to stop this, Howard" Zach said.

"Says who? Are you more than just the basket-weaving host? You her new beau?" Howard turned the gun on Zach.

"No, I'm not." Zach breathed in through his nose and pushed the air out through his mouth, deliberately matching the length of the intake and the expulsion of air. He couldn't do anything to calm his heart rate. "Look, before this goes any further, why don't you let Hattie and Nathan go?"

"Why would I do that?" Finally, Howard pointed the barrel of his weapon toward the floor.

"I don't think you want to be responsible for Hattie's

blood sugar pushing her into a coma. Come on. She needs her meds."

Howard's beady eyes delivered countless rounds of bullets to his wife, and then to Zach. "You're right. Get up, Hattie." Once Hattie was on her feet, Howard released the cylinder on his revolver and spun the mechanism. All of the chambers held ammo; their caliber—probably .357; maybe .38 special—intended to inflict maximum harm.

When Zach started to rise, Howard flicked the cylinder back into place and aimed his gun at Zach's chest.

"Sit down."

How could Zach sit? Hattie stood stock still in front of a disturbed and angry gun-toting heathen. When Zach hesitated, Howard pulled back the hammer.

"Sit."

Hattie looked at Zach, raised her eyes toward the heavens, and put a hand on her heart. Zach clenched his teeth as he lowered himself to the floor. Hattie might be prepared to die. So was Zach. That didn't mean this was her time. Or his. Maybe it was in God's plan for Zach to put an end to this. Zach closed his eyes. *How, Lord?*

Howard walked to the door, unlocked it, and held it open. "Have a nice life, Hattie."

When Hattie looked back at the others, her eyes brimmed with tears.

"Go," Zach mouthed.

After Howard secured the door, he hung his head and mocked when he said, "I kind of liked Hattie. Hate to see her leave."

When he turned back to his hostages, his nostrils flared and a fierce wave of rancor darted over his eyes. His chest heaved as he gauged the unexpected.

"Easy," Zach whispered. "Take it easy, Howard." Zach raised both of his hands—as if that might help diffuse Nathan's unpredictable and incredibly dangerous attempt to outmaneuver Howard.

The pasty-faced and unassuming scissors sharpener held the blade of a finely tuned set of shears against Stacey's throat.

"Put down the gun." If Nathan's hand wavered with the same intensity as his voice, Stacey was history. Nathan and Zach would join her in the two seconds it would take Howard to unload two bullets.

Thirty-Eight

Stan motioned to the three officers stationed above the landing in the stairwell. Footsteps, faint but swift, made their way toward the stairs.

"Halt," Norris bellowed. "Raise your hands."

"It's me. Hattie Matrice." The voice of the soft-spoken sweet grass basket instructor was little more than a whisper.

Stan rounded the landing and studied Hattie. She was alone, and silence loomed in the hallway behind her. He reached out his hand.

"Come on up. Hurry."

Hattie's slender fingers grasped Stan's hand with unexpected strength. He led her up the second set of stairs.

"You all right?"

"I am . . . but the others . . ."

"Let's get you out of here," Stan said as he led her toward the door that opened to the fellowship hall. "I'll be right back," he said to Norris.

"Are you hurt?"

"No, but I need my medicine. My bag's still at the table over there." Hattie's fingers trembled as she pointed.

"This one?" Stan asked as he reached under a chair.

"Yes. I need to check my blood sugar."

"We'll get some help with that. Talk to me while we go outside."

"That man? He's got a gun and he keeps pointing it at everybody. He's mean. Awful mean."

"We think he's Howard West. Stacey West's husband."

"That's him. He's mad as a hornet about her being with some other man."

"Who's he holding hostage?"

"Now? Just Nathan, Zach, and Stacey."

"Did he say what he wanted?"

"The name of her boyfriend. He made Stacey call him. Told her to 'invite him to the party.' You ask me, I think he means to kill both of them."

"Is the boyfriend on his way?" Stan asked—as if that might happen.

"He didn't answer the phone. That just made the husband madder than he already was."

"Where are the others?"

"What others?"

"You didn't see anyone else when the suspect took you to the kitchen?"

"No. Not a soul."

Stan took Hattie to an ambulance and conferred with the attendant before he briefed Sergeant Graham. When he finished his report, he ran past the officers posed at the front door and took his place with the other three who waited in the stairwell.

"What's the status?" Stan did a double take as he studied the face of the sweaty officer who asked the question. This guy made him nervous. The nano-second glance Norris delivered to Stan suggested that she shared his concern.

"Three hostages: Zach Hoyt, Nathan Greenfield, and the

perp's wife, Stacey West. Hattie described Howard West as volatile, and his anger escalating."

Norris turned to the soaked phenomenon dressed in a blue uniform and said, "You need a break?"

"Aw, don't worry about Prentice," the other officer responded. "He drips puddles every time he hears a siren wail. He's cool. Right kid?"

Prentice flashed an annoyed scowl at his partner and replied, "I love you too, Garcia."

"Shh," Stan said. "Listen."

A man's infuriated yelling filtered down the hallway and into the stairwell.

~

"What do you think you're doing?" Howard screamed at Nathan, and while rage filled his eyes, bewilderment fell over the rest of his face. "Get away from her."

"No."

"Nathan? Let her go," Zach said as he reached toward Stacey.

"Stay back, Zach. I mean it." Nathan held Stacey by the hair. Her eyes bugged as they darted from Howard to Zach. How could she breathe? She didn't dare move.

"Get away from her," Howard roared again. He pulled back on the revolver's hammer and pointed it at Nathan.

"Wait. Stop. Hold on." Zach pointed to Howard. "Just hold on." When Howard narrowed his eyes at Zach, he pressed his lips together. Waiting. "Let's talk this out." Zach turned to Nathan and asked, "What are you doing?"

"He won't hurt her. He's only doing this because he loves her. He wants to scare her so she won't cheat on him again."

Howard snorted.

"See?" Nathan asked. "He loves her. He won't hurt her."

"You think Stacey's your ticket out of here?" Howard added clarity to his question when he cackled. "You're an idiot."

"Nathan, you have to put the scissors down," Zach said.

"I can't. It's too late. The second I let go, he'll shoot me."

"No he won't. Right, Howard?"

"You two tripping?" Howard asked. "You want to know how much I love my wife? Let her go."

"No. You put down the gun." Nathan's voice held a surprising degree of authority. He meant it. "Stacey, you and I are going to stand up now. Real slow. Come on."

Howard's respirations lengthened and deepened, as if he were preparing to launch himself at his unexpected opponent—or maybe he intended the action to gather the courage he needed to pull the trigger.

Zach's heart raced as he assessed his distance from Howard and his closer proximity to Nathan. He couldn't touch Nathan. One slip of his fingers, and he'd slice Stacey's throat, whether he intended to or not. Howard was too far away for Zach to tackle him.

"Let her go," Zach repeated. "This is too dangerous. She'll get hurt. That's not what you want. Come on, Nathan. Let go."

"No way." Nathan, now standing, used Stacey as a human shield. The man looked a lot more like a coward than he did a hero. What did that make Zach?

"You're not leaving this room," Howard said.

"Put your gun down," Nathan replied.

The pain in Zach's chest was as fierce as that jarring moment when an engine running full throttle seizes. The sensation multiplied when Nathan eased the edge of the blade into Stacey's skin. A dribble of blood trickled down her neck.

"Howard." Stacey's plea was as noiseless as a lazy waft of air slipping over a flower petal.

"You're crazy," Howard said.

"Yes, I am," Nathan said. "Put the gun on the floor."

To Zach's amazement, Howard complied. He leaned over and placed the revolver in front of his feet.

Nathan peered from behind Stacey and said, "Shove the gun over here with your foot."

Howard sneered at Nathan before he raised his foot just far enough to push the gun forward. At the same time, he looked at Stacey and said, "It wasn't supposed to end this w—"

Howard froze at the sound of someone running past the room and toward the stairwell.

~

As when Hattie made her escape, footsteps sounded down the hallway. This time the tread was heavier and the runner made no attempt to be quiet.

"Halt. Police," Prentice yelled.

The steps pounded on the first set of steps.

"Halt," Prentice screamed.

The runner, still out of view, continued his ascent, and was mere seconds from reaching the landing.

Prentice tried again. "Halt!"

Garcia pushed Stan aside and moved toward the landing. He held his arms out, his trigger finger prepared to discharge his weapon. A sickly wave of heat engulfed Stan as an image of Paige darted into his mind. "No," he yelled. "She can't hear."

When Garcia didn't respond, Stan leaped over the railing and threw himself in front of Garcia.

As Stan landed on the stairs, the thrust of the bullet seared his body with unforgiving heat. During what had to be a warped sense of time, his senses misfired and his legs gave way. Stan thrashed his arms as he sought to right himself, but he was no match for the stairs that rushed up to meet his plummeting head.

~

As a deafening gunshot resounded throughout the hallway, and as the boom echoed against the walls, the angry sheen in Howard's eyes darkened. His ruddy face turned scarlet. "All those cops outside? They'll think I killed somebody."

He scrambled for the gun on the floor at the same time Zach lunged toward it. An earsplitting boom filled the room as the gun discharged. As pain wracked Zach's head, his body flailed on the linoleum floor. He gasped, seeking air. When he found none, he squeezed his eyes shut and blinked several times, but darkness descended like a thief.

~

Juanita panicked at the rush of personnel toward the building. Horror rested on Izzy's face. Conner followed the activity and gaped.

"What?" Juanita grabbed Izzy's arm.

Izzy turned, but she failed to reply. Juanita turned to Conner.

"Tell me."

"I don't know. It sounded like a gunshot."

Juanita's knees buckled, but Conner managed to grab her and hold her weight until she regained her senses. Seconds later, Izzy flinched.

"What?"

Conner grimaced when he said, "Another gunshot."

Juanita covered her quivering mouth with her hand. It couldn't be. No. This wasn't possible. She managed to stay on her feet when a line of police officers pushed everyone farther away from the building, but finding herself in the midst of the media only increased her disorientation and her dread.

Cameramen hoisted their equipment and panned the church, the police activity, and the crowd. Reporters planted their bodies with a full view of the church behind them and competed with one another to gain attention over the airwaves.

When one of the news crew stuck a microphone in her face and asked for Juanita to confirm her identity as the wife of one of the hostages, Conner stepped between the two and led his mother away. As he sheltered her with his arm around her shoulders, and Izzy hovered beside her, Juanita sensed the presence of an untold number of pursuers, fast on their heels.

She turned, ready to air her anger in the form of waving hands and accusations, but instead, came face-to-face with Wellington. The teenager looked more childlike and vulnerable than Juanita thought possible. Of course he did. Norris was in harm's way too.

Juanita opened her arms, swept Wellington into a hug, and motioned to Izzy and Conner to join her embrace. Through the silence, sobs racked their bodies and tears marked the grass at their feet. Juanita didn't need to look at Conner to know that his slight movements accompanied a prayer.

God had to protect Zach. He had to. How could she live without him? Juanita considered Job, the godly man who, in the midst of suffering and loss, cried out, "Though he slay me, I will hope in him." Was her faith that strong? Her hope that boundless? She increased her hold on Izzy and Conner as the answer quieted her fears. *He's in your hands, Father God, and I trust you.*

Thirty-Nine

"Why did he have to die?" As Lauren stood over the burial plot, her tears stained the overturned soil. She turned toward Tyler, her bottom lip trembling. "Was God too busy to save him?"

Tyler took her by the hand. "God can do everything at once. Pastor Morrison says God has a time for everyone to die."

"But I wasn't ready to say goodbye." Lauren wiped her nose with the back of her hand and sniffled. "Can we get another one? Can we, Daddy?"

With his immobilized left arm tucked against his chest, Stan used his functional appendage to put a mound of dirt on the makeshift coffin. He handed the little spade to Tyler.

"Want to help?"

"Sure."

"Another one?" Stan asked. "What if it dies too?"

"He'll be my friend until it's his time to die."

"I don't know if that's a very good idea."

Lauren rocked back and forth on the soles of her feet. "It'll be different next time. Please?"

"Guys, how many fish have you lost since you brought the first one home?" He lifted his index finger. "First, it was the little black and white angel fish."

"Steinway," Lauren said as she lowered her face toward the ground.

"Then the two I won for you at the fair." Stan raised two more fingers.

Tyler pulled his lips into a rounded pout that resembled the action of a sucking goldfish. "Fennington and Mr. Riches."

"And what about Miss Fulger . . ."

"Miss Fulgermuffin," Lauren said. She hung her head.

"I don't think I want to risk any more fish," Stan said.

"But, Daddy . . ." Lauren's eyes brimmed again.

"Let me think about it," Stan said as he led the way back into his apartment.

Another fish would lead to another funeral. How many did Lauren think she could take? When she found Bubbles floating belly-up in the tank, the poor kid was so distraught that she hadn't touched her breakfast.

Stan looked at the clock and asked, "You guys hungry?"

"Starved."

"According to Sister Yolanda, lunch will be here in about five minutes." When Tyler frowned, Stan said, "Don't tell me you're tired of her cooking. I'm not."

"That's not it," Tyler replied.

"I know," Lauren said.

"You know what?"

"Tyler wanted someone else to bring lunch today."

Stan couldn't hide his pleasure after that remark. If he had his druthers, the delivery gal would be the second-best cook in the county. And that would make him very, very happy.

Tyler ran to the door as soon as he heard someone

knock. "Dad, you need to come here."

Stan walked to the door and stopped. "It's you. Uh, I thought Sister Yolanda—"

"Cooked for you today?" The smile Pearl awarded Stan fetched a neck-warming flush. "Don't you worry about that. She did. When I heard the sad news about Bubbles, I offered to deliver her meal so that I could offer my condolences."

"What's a condolence?" Lauren asked.

"I want to tell you how sorry I am to hear about your goldfish."

"Oh. It's okay. He's out back by the bushes. Wanna see?"

"Uh, maybe later, Lauren." Stan stammered when he said, "Come on in. Please."

Pearl carried Yolanda's heavy warming tote to Stan's miniscule kitchenette, and made her way back to the door. "I have another load. Be right back." She looked at Tyler and asked, "Can you get that dish out of there and serve up some of those fixings while I go back to my car?"

"Sure."

Stan watched his children follow the routine they established after the doctor released him from the hospital. They both took on their new helper roles with more enthusiasm than a new goldfish ever elicited from the pair. The fact that Tina allowed—and encouraged—the children to spend more time with their father, taught Stan a lesson in humility.

His gratitude extended to his ex-wife and her new husband. Nothing could have prepared Stan for that achievement. He wasn't privy to DeWayne's conversation with Pastor Morrison, and he didn't claim to know the condition of Tina's heart. Whatever transpired after Stan introduced the two men during that breakfast meeting at the restaurant, led Tina to soften her heart enough to let DeWayne back into her life and to let him be the father of their child. It called to mind Stan's wish for a miracle.

Lauren put plates, silverware, and napkins on the table while Tyler filled up glasses with ice water. The glimmer in Stan's eyes deepened when he counted place settings for four. No question, they liked her too.

When Pearl knocked again, he opened the door and gaped. "Um . . ."

"Lemme see." Lauren stepped around Stan and guided Pearl and her unexpected companion to the sofa. "Can I hold him? Can I?"

"That's a . . ." Stan let his remark trail off. He couldn't sound more awkward and goofy if he tried.

"It's called a kitten," Pearl said as she handed the little calico bundle to Lauren and lowered a small pet carrier to the floor.

Tyler climbed onto the sofa and scooted next to Lauren. He ran his fingertip over the animal's tiny ears. "Is this a boy or a girl?"

"Girl," Pearl replied.

"What's her name?" Lauren asked.

"She doesn't have one yet. Do you think you could help me pick one?"

"We get to name her?" Tyler asked.

"Before you answer, you need to know that these two have vivid imaginations when it comes to naming pets." Stan kept his distance. He'd never owned a cat. Didn't know what to do with one.

"Do they?" Pearl asked. "Well, let's hear some suggestions."

"Spot," Tyler said.

"She doesn't have spots. Those are patches," Lauren said. "Ooh, I like that. Patches."

"Cinder," Tyler replied.

"Princess."

"Tiger."

"Lulu."

"Pajama."

"Huh?" Lauren asked. "Why would you call a kitty Pajama?"

"Look at her. All those colors look like my pajamas. You know, the ones I had on this morning."

Stan gave Pearl a sideways glance and said, "I tried to warn you."

"How about PJ instead of Pajama?" Pearl asked.

Tyler shrugged. "I like Lulu better than PJ."

"I got it. Petunia," Lauren said.

"I like that one," Pearl replied. "What do you think, Tyler?"

"Petunia? Like a flower? I guess that's okay for a girl cat."

"Stan?" Pearl asked.

"You want my opinion?"

"Of course."

"Petunia's a great name. Love it."

"Done." Pearl stood and asked, "Why don't you put little Petunia in her carrier while we have some of Sister Yolanda's famous food?"

Once they gathered around the table, Pearl lowered her head and offered a prayer, making sure she mentioned—as she did every time she stopped by with a dinner and her captivating presence—how grateful they all were for Stan's safekeeping.

Later, she shooed the children into the living room while

she cleaned up the kitchen. After they chatted over a cup of coffee, Pearl tapped the tabletop and stood.

"Walk me to the door?"

"Sure."

"Before you send me on my way, Mister Lawman, you have to make a decision."

Stan twisted his neck so he could see Pearl's expression. His dumbfounded and hasty reaction sent a spasm over his shoulder and arm. He gasped in the eye-watering aftermath, and when Pearl attempted to soothe him by running her hand along the collar of his shirt, heat crawled up his neck. If she touched his ears, she'd scorch her fingers. "I do?"

"You have to decide whether you want me to leave this little darling at your apartment, or whether you want me to take her home. Of course, if you keep her, I'll have to visit—frequently—so I won't miss the sweet thing."

A cat? Pearl thought Stan capable of caring for a cat? "You mind if I put that to a vote?"

"Not at all."

Stan and Pearl walked into the living room where two young children sat in awe of their tiny feline guest.

"Guys, instead of a fish, would you consider taking care of Petunia?"

"You mean it?" Tyler asked Pearl.

"If you promise you'll take good care of her for me," Pearl said. "That includes feeding her when you're here, and cleaning out the litter box, especially now, when your dad can't do it. Oh, and I'd have to visit a lot, too."

"I promise," Lauren said.

"Me too." Tyler leaned down until he was eye level to the kitten and said, "What do you think, little one? You'll get a lot of love here."

Stan swallowed the lump that rose in his throat. He could have lost this time, this life with his children. God saved him, a fact that stuck with Stan from the moment he opened his eyes in the morning until he fell asleep each night.

"Stan?" Pearl asked. "Are we in agreement?"

Stan tapped his finger to his lips and gave Lauren and Tyler the once-over. Stan paused when his eyes caught Pearl's lovely eyes resting on him. As a grin plastered itself on his face, the action teased the muscles in his neck and sent a pang toward his shoulder. He gulped a ragged breath, but at the same time, he inhaled the sweet aroma of life.

"I'm game. Welcome home, Miss Petunia."

Forty

Conner sat in Zach's well-worn chair and gawked at the pile of mail Mae dumped on top of the desk.

"More letters?"

"If you don't quit scowling, one of these days you won't be able to erase those tiny lines you keep wearing on your forehead. You're too young to be so serious."

Conner tapped the stack of letters addressed to *The Basket Works*. "It was 'serious' that prompted people to write all of these."

"Maybe so, but those folks just mean to encourage you and help you through the aftermath."

"A lot of these say the same thing: 'Loved the retreat, can't wait until next year.' "

"We asked for feedback. Why are you surprised?" Mae asked.

"Maybe it's the repetitive requests to hold the retreat at New Life Chapel again so that Sister Yolanda can feed them." Conner looked up at Mae and pointed a finger at her. "The content of these letters is so similar that it seems as if someone organized a letter drive. You know anything about that?"

"I had nothing to do with that . . . that stack of mail. Just enjoy the compliments and the well wishes, and take note of their requests. It sounds like all those weavers already moved past the Howard and Stacey tragedy. You need to do likewise."

"I'm trying."

"What would your dad say about your attitude? Eh?"

Conner ran his tongue along the inside of his mouth and took in Mae's practiced brashness with a sidelong glance. His muscles tugged up the edges of his lips when he answered. "He'd tell me to answer these letters, help you and Nancy unload the shipment that came in this morning, and then to hightail it home to study."

"He'd have more than that to say. Trust me." Mae crossed her arms and said, "He'd tell you that he expected you to come home from college next year and handle all of the registration duties for the second annual basket weaving retreat."

"He'd probably make me come home every weekend for a month to dye reed and cut basket weaving kits for the instructors."

"You bet he would."

"Guys? I'm right here." Zach's eyes might still protest the strain it took to focus on written material, but he was present in body, whether he contributed to the workload or not.

Mae jerked back her head and gave Conner a knowing look. "What did I tell you? He shouldn't be back to work yet."

"I'm fine," Zach said. "Mostly."

"You still have symptoms, boss. Bad ones." Mae turned back to Conner and added, "Oh, I hate to see him suffer."

"Mae?" Zach asked. He loved the woman, but the drama drained him faster than Conner and Wellington could demolish an extra large pizza.

Mae ignored Zach. "He never listens to me. He tunes me out the minute he walks into this place. The fact that he wants in on our conversation proves his brain is still too big for his skull. Maybe you'd better take him home."

Hmm. An interesting description of a concussion. At least she hadn't accused him of being too big for his britches.

"I appreciate your offer, son."

"My offer?"

"To come back every weekend to prepare kits for the next retreat. Can I get that in writing?"

"Uh, I have work to do," Mae said as she scurried out of the office.

"I'm in trouble now," Conner mumbled. "You think we can hire Wellington again? He liked making a few bucks."

"I think he liked your friendship more than the money," Zach said. Talk about a transformed life. God was generous with second chances where Wellington was concerned.

"He'll be back in town this weekend. Can we invite them for dinner?"

"Them?"

"Yeah, his mom reserved a trailer so they could haul the stuff she put into storage."

"His mom's pulling a trailer all the way to Pittsburg?"

"Wellington's uncle will drive."

"You could have offered," Zach said.

"You're not funny," Conner said.

"Am too."

"Can we get back to the dinner question?"

"You need to check with your mother, but you have my okay."

"Thanks." Conner started to open one of the letters, but

put it back down. "Can I ask you something?"

"Listening."

"I never understood why his mom reacted like she did, first when Wellington defended her, and then when she threw him out. Why would she do those things?"

"We can only guess. Let's do what we can to help them heal instead of passing judgment."

"I hear you." Conner picked up the letter and ran the letter opener under the flap on the envelope. Before he opened it, he put it back on the pile.

"It'll take you a month to read today's mail at that rate," Zach said.

"Probably. Did you know that it was Wellington's story in the *Fish Tales* book that prompted his mom to call her sister?"

"How'd she hear about the book?"

"Gotta love the media for that one."

"The media? What did they do?"

Conner's worry lines reappeared. "You don't remember a lot of the details, do you?"

"You're looking at me like I'm a dufus, so I guess I missed something. What?"

"After the shootings, reporters kept doing follow up stories."

"Why?" Zach's attention span was pretty short these days, and he was about to lose his end of this conversation.

"They all wanted a tidbit of news that their competitors hadn't already reported. When they interviewed one of the basket weavers, she mentioned that she loved the contributions Izzy and I made to the anthology she bought while she was at the retreat."

"You got free press for your publication?" Zach asked.

"Don't laugh. We sold hundreds of copies that week."

"Nice. You put your share of the profits into your college fund?"

"Of course."

"Wait a minute. Wellington used a pen name," Zach said.

"One of his mom's friends bought a copy and she figured out that W.E. Holly was Wellington. When his mom read Wellington's short story, she called her sister, got in touch with Holly Norris, and then had a long heart-to-heart with Wellington."

"How's Wellington doing?"

"He sounds good. Really. His mom got a job already, and his aunt and uncle have treated both of them like, well, like family."

"I'm happy to hear that."

"Yeah. And get this. He's writing a novel."

"No way."

"Way. He says writing takes his mind to far-off places where his characters can do incredible things. He describes the effort as a weird form of freedom."

"Huh?" Zach rubbed the side of his head. He needed Conner to take him home. Juanita would fix him a nice lunch and tuck him into bed for a comfy afternoon nap. The image produced a drawn-out yawn.

"Doesn't matter," Conner said. "Funny thing, though. Some literary agent contacted Wellington a couple of days ago. Must be some of the professionals saw some promise in his writing."

"Not yours?" Zach asked.

"The woman asked him about the people who contributed the artwork."

"Izzy had to like that. Anybody offer you a contract yet?"

"I think my technical and computer expertise rated higher

than my story contribution. I'm counting on a college education to help me make my footprint in the working world."

"That's pretty funny," Zach said.

"What?"

"Your choice of words sounded so . . . literary."

~

Warm air skimmed Juanita's face as she emerged from the woods. She squinted in the bright sunlight while she peddled. She kept one hand on the handlebar while the other grappled for the sunglasses she'd stashed in her pocket. Once she clutched the eyewear and lifted it to the bridge of her nose, she put her hand back on the handlebar and picked up speed.

The long bike path that circled the park's perimeter tempted her today—that and the sweet perfume that lingered beneath the lush green canopy. She was tired but didn't want to stop. Everything that surrounded her testified to God's glory, His goodness, and His promises.

What word might describe the contentment that accompanied her on this impromptu excursion? Satisfaction tangled with gratification as the answer materialized. Delight. If she had a twelve-hundred-page thesaurus on hand, she wouldn't find a more appropriate choice. Delight.

The word *thirst* imposed itself on her reverie and directed her to a park bench. Juanita gulped some of the water from her bottle, leaned her head against the back of the bench, and gazed into an endless expanse of blue. A jet's fading vapor trail wove its way through a patch of slow-moving clouds that dotted the sky. Bliss. Not a bad second choice for her current condition.

Blessed. Another appropriate term. How close they'd come to finding themselves victims of other people's recklessness. Juanita looked at her wrists. She could still feel the weight and the cold steel of the handcuffs. That broken taillight and all the angst and mandatory ASL lessons, and every little thing that followed paled in comparison to the events that played out at the basket weaving retreat.

All the fallout from the taillight, though, played a part in so much of what happened when that crazed Howard West slipped into New Life Chapel. God had a plan. Even back then when none of them knew it.

Stan. Juanita took another drink and chuckled. Poor Stan. He'd apologized to Juanita and Zach so many times that she'd lost count. He roared into their lives with a chip on his shoulder, an ex-wife at his throat, a hole in his wallet, and two precious children. Since their first meeting, Stan took a bullet to that shoulder, forgave the ex-wife, and filled those empty pockets with love. God's love. Pearl's interest in the lawman was just icing. Stan's transformation filled Juanita with awe.

As did Wellington's new life. He suffered unspeakable circumstances and grief, and yet God put Holly Norris in Wellington's path. Another inexplicable and unforeseeable situation that arose from that faulty taillight. What a wise God. When the crisis at the retreat threatened Wellington's well-being, his mother's heart softened—an answer to prayer.

Juanita tugged the elastic band out of her hair, gathered the stray hairs that blew across her cheeks, and twisted the mass of long locks back into a ponytail. She watched a young mother who ran behind a baby stroller at the same time she talked to someone via the Bluetooth she wore over her ear. The young woman's efforts looked like too much work, but too soon Juanita would cede her own day-to-day parenting responsibilities.

A flicker of sorrow poked at Juanita's good mood. How troubling it would be when it was time to drive Conner to a dorm and watch him walk into his new life. She would be thrilled for her boy, yet mournful of her emptying nest. Izzy would follow too soon after. Wherever their futures led, Juanita would be their fervent cheerleader. That would never change.

Juanita relished this gorgeous day in spite of those recent things that didn't end well. How does one reconcile something as senseless as the tragedy that played out after the retreat? How reckless Howard West had been. His anger blinded him to consequences—life-changing, irreversible consequences.

Zach's recovery from his concussion would take time, but he could have been victim to one of the bullets in Howard's gun rather than the recipient of a harsh kick to his head by Howard's steel-toed boot. Instead, when Howard heard the gunfire in the stairwell, he lunged for his gun and fired off the shot that hit his wife.

Consequences. Howard sat in a jail cell awaiting trial. Stacey found herself committed to a wheelchair. Whether Howard intended to scare Stacey, rather than harm her, did nothing to heal her damaged spine. Nathan insisted on playing the "what if" game despite the police department's conclusion that he may have saved three lives with the unorthodox threat he made toward Stacey. Nathan's actions forced Howard to put down his weapon, which was no small feat. Nathan blamed himself, although it was Howard's finger on the trigger that paralyzed Stacey's legs.

And Hollister? What a foolish man. No one pressed charges against him for the antics he hoped would earn him the title of captain, but he ruined his career. Last Juanita heard, the man voted by his high school classmates as the student Most Likely to go Berserk found himself demoted to patrolman and reassigned to a precinct far, far away from the one he hoped to command. Why he employed the word *berserk* to hint at his identity was another mystery. Perhaps, like the graffiti artist who signed his work, Hollister, with his inflated ego, thought himself more ingenious than his victims.

It seemed to Juanita that the self-induced losses and sorrows, those consequences that arose from bad judgment, were the most difficult to reconcile. In the aftermath, God stood ready to forgive—the offender need only ask.

Juanita stowed her water bottle, climbed on her bike, and headed toward home. She mouthed, "Hello," to the pair of cyclists who passed by as they headed in the opposite direction, and when her cell phone vibrated against her hip, she stopped and pulled to the side of the path.

Conner's text message read, *Dad's done in for the day. We'll be at the house in about ten minutes.*

Ten minutes? She was a good fifteen minutes from home. Maybe twelve if she pumped her legs faster. When she joined traffic stopped at a light, she tried to catch her breath, but her heart rate didn't relax to any measureable degree. She resumed her hasty pace when the light turned green, and just before she reached the corner where she had to turn right, she caught sight of a police cruiser headed toward her.

Juanita raised her left arm, turned down her street, and giggled. She might not have taillights, but if she'd learned just one thing about the law, it was to signal her intent to turn. That, she would never forget.

ACKNOWLEDGMENTS

I offer a world of thanks to my early readers: Fran Naumann, Brian Krause, and Sue Copeland. Their time, feedback, and cheer are precious to me, as are their friendships. To my mother, who devours my stories chapter by chapter, and then cover to cover, I give an abundant measure of gratitude. Her tireless encouragement and exceptional editing skills make me a better writer and remind me of the wealth of blessings I haven't earned, but that have been granted to me.

Thank you, readers, for traveling to Shelburg, Ohio with me, a fictional town full of imperfect people who faced real-life tragedies, circumstances, and challenges. Just as the Zachs, Juanitas, and Stans we meet in our imperfect world, we have hope when we encounter the love, forgiveness, and grace of our perfect Savior, Jesus, Yeshua. If you don't know Him yet, be assured He's looking for you. He wants all of you. It starts when you give Him your heart. Go ahead . . . you have everything to gain.

If you enjoyed this story, please consider writing a book review. Every author appreciates and needs those priceless gold stars and reader comments. I look forward to sharing another adventure with you soon.

ABOUT THE AUTHOR

VALERIE BANFIELD, a long-time resident of Central Ohio, headed south and planted her toes into the sandy soil near Florida's Gulf Coast. She is a basket weaver, an avid reader, and a passionate supporter of microfinance. She counts her participation in international short-term missionary campaigns among her life's most blessed and humbling journeys, and firmly believes that when we give God control, He rocks our world.

Valerie shares some of her lighthearted insights—those things learned from the human end of the leash—within the *Walking the Dog Blog* tab on her website. Visit her online at www.valeriebanfield.com.

Don't miss these riveting tales

by Valerie Banfield:

Deluge: When Yesterdays Collide

Checkered: A Story of Triumph and Redemption

Deceived: A Case of Mistaken Identity

Gifted: A Basket Weaver's Tale

Anchored: A Lamp in the Storm

Sidetracked: If Yesterday Steals Tomorrow

While I Count the Stars: A Novel

Made in the USA
Lexington, KY
21 June 2019